DEDICATION

For Lucy, a special courageous little dog who taught me the meaning of unconditional love. Not a day will go by that I won't miss her sweet, smiling face.

HAUNTED BY THE KERES

LAUREN JANKOWSKI

Crimson Fox
PUBLISHING

TURNER, OREGON

HAUNTED BY THE KERES: Book Four of the Shape Shifter Chronicles
Copyright © 2014-2017 by Lauren Jankowski.

Published by Crimson Fox Publishing
www.crimsonfoxpublishing.com

Cover art by Najla Qamber Designs.

ISBN: 978-1-946202-47-5

Second Edition.

CHAPTER ONE

She could see their shadows pass by the tree she
perched in, their quiet footsteps as loud as shotgun blasts
to her heightened hearing. A breeze rustled through the
branches that hid her slender form. It was spring, but the
icy tendrils of winter still hung in the air. Her nostrils
twitched as she took in the scent of the two men below.
The woman crouched down on the thick branch, her
fingers spreading over the rough bark, and watched as they
stepped into view. Her unnaturally luminous green eyes
remained fixed on the ground below while her sharpened
hearing took in the sounds around her. The footsteps of
the two men, an insect crawling on a nearby branch, the
rustling of the leaves, and in the distance she heard what
sounded like a fox.

"I'm telling you, she went the other way," the first man
— the shorter of the two — insisted. He wore practical
clothing: a dark jacket, plain T-shirt, and jeans above his
sneakers, stepping lightly as he moved. The woman in the
tree was impressed with how quietly he walked and the
neutral colors he wore helped him blend in better with the
surroundings. He bent down and picked up a stick,
spinning it around between his hands.

The taller man, dressed nicely in tailored clothes, shook his head. The woman stared at him, curious about his insistence on wearing such impractical clothing. It was such a hindrance. The wind swept through the trees again, rustling through the two men's apparel, bringing the scent of the koi pond, located toward the south end of the property.

"The trail was too obvious," the well-dressed man remarked, taking another step forward.

"Too obvious? A couple broken branches and some bent grass were *too obvious*?" the first man asked incredulously, following his companion. He tossed the stick away.

"She wanted us to find that trail. I'm telling you, she left it to throw us off," the other man responded with a hint of irritation. "Now be quiet for a second. I'm listening."

A chill that had nothing to do with the breeze traveled over her flesh. Out of the corner of her eye, she thought she glimpsed something in the next tree. Her body went rigid as she turned her attention toward the tree, but saw nothing. The woman blinked a few times and turned her attention back to the ground where the two men were searching. Spreading her arms, she stepped off the branch and dropped to the ground. The wind howled through her ears as she sped toward the earth.

Once she was on the ground, the woman executed a fast reverse spin kick, sending the first man sailing backward. Before the second man could react, she dropped into sweeping kick and knocked him to the ground. Lunging over to him, she knelt on one knee. In a split second, she had her sais out, silver glistening in the sunlight and the sharp points gleaming. She pressed one against the second man's throat. The other she pointed at the first man as a warning. He had climbed to his feet, jolted a little, and held his hands up in surrender.

"Dammit, Isis. That really hurt," Nero groused as he

rubbed his aching chest. She turned her attention to Jensen, who raised his hands and grinned mischievously.

"I surrender," he said. "Unless, of course, you want to punish me."

She stared at him, puzzled. "I don't believe disciplinary action is needed, so I assume you are making a sexual innuendo."

Nero chuckled. "We usually refer to it as flirting."

Isis glanced between both of them, before spinning her sais and sliding them back into her belt. She smoothly rose to her feet and offered her hand to Jensen. He accepted it and she pulled him up.

"You sure you don't feel cold?" Nero asked, zipping up his jacket even more. He looked pointedly at the black catsuit she wore. Jensen's expression reflected disbelief, while Isis merely looked over at him. It had been a few months but Nero still forgot she wasn't a typical shape shifter.

"I only feel the extremes in temperature," she reminded him as they started to make their way back to the mansion. She glanced over her shoulder. Remington was testing her, Jack, and Coop to get an idea of just what the protectors were going to be up against. Orion had suggested Nero and Jensen take Isis outside to observe her abilities outdoors. She knew he was concerned about the amount of time she spent inside. Even Jack walked the property regularly. Isis didn't enjoy wasting time outside. She felt her time was better spent researching what little information they had on Grenich. Still, now that she was outdoors, she found the air was quite pleasant.

"Is there anyone else out here?" she asked no one in particular.

"Sly might be around, but she would probably be on the other side of the property," Jensen responded. "Why do you ask?"

"I thought I saw something in the trees, but it could have been a trick of the light," Isis answered, cracking her neck.

"Or a bird," Nero offered. She looked up at the clear blue sky.

"I would have known if it were a bird."

"Oh right. The heightened senses," Nero said, stopping suddenly. Jensen and Isis paused, looking back to him. He nodded up at the balconies outside the room doors.

"Say, Isis," he began, a small smile dancing across his features. "How would you get up onto one of those balconies?"

She followed his gaze, studying the mansion. "Do you want me to climb up to the balcony again, Nero?"

"Only if you want to," Nero replied, sticking his hands in his pockets. Jensen gave him a sideways look and chuckled. Isis glanced back to them, shrugged, and then ran toward the mansion.

"You're a child, Nero," Jensen said as they watched Isis push off the wall with her foot. She sprang up and grabbed onto one of the stone balusters.

"Come on. You can't tell me that isn't fucking cool," Nero protested, watching as she pulled herself up and stood on the coping. Isis dropped onto the balcony and tested the door, opening it and disappearing inside.

"Okay, I admit, it is pretty incredible," Jensen agreed, humoring his friend, as they continued walking toward the mansion. He paused and looked back to where Isis had ambushed them.

"That's what I'm talking about," Nero said as he stepped up on the back porch and opened the door.

~~*~*~*

Jade looked up, startled, when the door to her balcony opened. Sunlight streamed into the dimly lit room and the curtains fluttered as the door swung open. Sly's back muscles tensed up. Both women watched as Isis moved across the room, exiting to the more brightly lit hall. She moved without sound and practically glided through the space, not acknowledging either of the two women. Sly pressed herself up on her elbows, arching her back slightly. She was topless, allowing Jade to better massage her muscles.

"Okay," Jade muttered with a shake of her head. Since her return to the mansion, Isis often seemed to be in her own world. When she wasn't burying herself in research, she remained in the shadows, observing the occupants of the mansion going about their daily routines. Jade found she no longer recognized the woman she had once known — a naïve young protector with a mischievous glint in her eyes. Isis was now cold and distant, unreadable, and even alien at times.

"She's gotten *a lot* more interesting," Sly mentioned, sounding mildly amused.

"It's been a strange winter," Jade replied, returning her attention to Sly's back. Sly tilted her head down, glancing back at Jade.

"I'm assuming you're referring to more than your young teammate's disregard for closed doors."

Jade furrowed her brow as she continued to rub Sly's smooth warm flesh. "Isis is ... different. Her mannerisms, the way she thinks, the way she fights. It's not like typical shape shifters. It's the same with Coop and Jack."

"I believe that's what Set was aiming for, darling," Sly pointed out, smiling wickedly. "Speaking of fighting, how many bruises is old Remington sporting these days?"

Jade grinned, focusing on massaging the few knots out of Sly's muscles. "More than he would admit. I doubt he's any closer to figuring out their strategies."

"You protectors and your need to analyze everything to death," Sly teased as she folded her arms in front of her again, resting her chin on them. She groaned in pleasure as Jade worked a particularly difficult knot out.

"And what would you suggest we do?"

"Uh, they're living weapons. Take off the leash, let

them loose at whatever Grenich target you can find," Sly answered easily.

"They're not animals, Sly."

"Not ordinary shape shifters either," Sly countered, turning her face to the side. "They're not meant to be sedentary. From what Orion has told us, they get bored easily and when they're bored, they're more dangerous. You've got this amazing advantage now and you're letting it go to waste."

Jade continued massaging Sly's back, becoming lost in her own thoughts. Sly knew her lover was concerned about the experiments and how sheltered they seemed to be. In the months since they had returned to the mansion, neither Jack nor Isis had ventured off the property. Coop came and went as he pleased, but the other two didn't seem interested in the outside world. Shae offered to take Isis out almost every day, but she continually turned her down.

Sly rolled onto her back and folded her hands behind her head. "Things have been much too quiet around here. I don't understand how protectors can stand it year round."

"If you want something to do, I'm sure Steve or Loman could dig up some cold case files for you," Jade teased. Sly arched an eyebrow at her lover.

"Me caring about humans. That'll be the day."

Jade leaned over and kissed her passionately, exploring her mouth. Sly sat up and pulled her closer, wrapping her strong arm around Jade's waist. Her lips travelled down Jade's long neck, feeling the tension gradually leave her lover's body. Jade pulled off her shirt and tossed it aside, placing her hands on the sides of Sly's face and capturing her lips again. Jade had been much too tightly wound the past few months, stressing out about everything. The return of Isis and Orion had meant many sleepless nights as Jet and Lilly tried to figure out the best way to deal with the Grenich threat.

Sly had begun kissing Jade's breasts when the protector's phone buzzed on the nightstand. Both women groaned and Sly dropped to her side on the bed as Jade leaned over to grab the phone. She let out a huff of irritation and grabbed her shirt, pulling it back over her head.

"It's from Alex. Remington wants to see what Jack and Isis can do with wooden training weapons," Jade explained, pulling her hair out of the back of her shirt. "Alex wants Shae and I there, probably to make sure he doesn't get killed."

"Remington's old as time, I'm sure he can manage," Sly said. "Let's call Alpha and spend the night in."

"Alpha doesn't like coming to the mansion and I'm not up for a trip to the Lair. Remington will need a hand with the experiments," Jade responded. "They're getting better at training with normals, but they still have the occasional slip-up. Jack broke Malone's rib last week during a relatively easy sparring session."

"Jade, your being a protector can be a real damper on the love life sometimes."

Jade smiled. "As you are so fond of reminding me and yet you love me anyway. My evening is pretty open. We can spend the night together if you like or you can head out to the Lair. I'm sure Alpha would welcome your company."

Sly pursed her lips, considering what to do. She had been dividing her time between the mansion and the Lair during the unusually cold winter and she missed her forest. The protectors were incredibly boring, being almost all work and no play. The rebels were more fun, but the noise in the Lair often became intolerable and their openness to all species — including humans — was not something Sly was fond of. She reached for her shirt and pulled it on over her head, attaching the collar about her throat. Glancing over her shoulder, Sly watched as Jade left.

"Another day, more of the same," she said to herself as

she crossed the room and pulled open the curtains. The afternoon light filled the room, chasing away any lingering shadows. Jade had decorated her room in shades of green, her favorite color. There were a number of well-cared for plants located throughout the room. Jade had always had a green thumb and enjoyed gardening. It was a hobby Sly found extremely dull.

Briefly, Sly considered looking for Jet and Orion but decided against it. The two men, whom she had taken to calling Gloom and Doom, had been poring over what little information they had on Grenich for the past few months, along with Lilly and usually Remington. The winter had been an uneasy one and Sly was wondering why the Corporation hadn't struck. *You have two of their most valuable assets. They should have done something by now,* she often told Jet and Lilly.

Striding across the room, Sly opened the door and almost walked into Coop. He dipped his head in greeting and continued down the hall. Sly closed the door and followed him, noticing how he glanced sideways to track her nearness to him. The sconces in the hall were not lit but would be in the next couple of hours, as soon as the sun began to set.

"Any news from the warfront?" she asked, trying to match his stride. Sly couldn't match the smoothness of his gait or the unnatural silence of his footsteps, but she could keep up with him. Sly knew he probably checked his speed so she could. In the past few months, she had discovered how slippery experiments could be.

"I am not aware of any fronts to this war, if you're referring to Grenich. To the best of my knowledge, things are still quiet," Coop answered, puzzled. His glowing blue eyes remained straight ahead.

"Still getting the hang of figurative language, I see," Sly observed with a small smile. Though Coop was much better at recognizing common phrases and metaphors, he still had difficulty with it.

"I have been out for longer than Isis and Jack, but that doesn't mean I have had extended contact with normals," Coop answered, pausing when they reached the second floor landing that overlooked the main hall below. He leaned on the railing, looking at nothing in particular. Somewhere below, Sly could hear the click of nice shoes on tile. She assumed it was Jensen.

"I wish the Monroes would act already. Protectors are so stuck in their ways. They always need to analyze every single detail no matter how insignificant," Sly said, thinking aloud. "It's a defect of the group and a huge part of what makes them so boring."

"They wish to think up a foolproof strategy," Coop replied, his voice flat. "At least, that's my understanding of it."

Sly looked over at him, observing the experiment for a moment. "What's going on in that mysterious mind of yours, Coop?"

Coop glanced at her and then looked back down the hall. "I often find myself wondering what a world without Grenich would look like. I do not think it is possible, not with the deep cover operatives in the governments around the world. Wherever there is power, Set and Pyra have some hand in it. There is a possibility that without the Grenich Corporation the world would descend into chaos and anarchy. There is also the danger resulting from liberating experiments."

Sly leaned against the railing and crossed her arms over her chest. "What do you plan to do if we do manage to destroy the Grenich Corporation?"

"It is very unlikely I will survive to see the end of this war," Coop responded, looking up to the windows high above them.

"Ever the optimist, I see," Sly remarked. Coop gave a small shrug as he turned his gaze back to the black and white tiles below them.

"Simple logic. I will be on the front lines against an

enemy who has taught me everything I know. The enemy continues to evolve, much faster than I do. The more recent experiments have more knowledge and skills than I possess. I was barely able to best Isis in the Meadows and she wasn't at full-strength," Coop explained his reasoning. "When I turned against the Corporation, I knew the price would probably be my life. As long as Grenich falls, it is a price worth paying."

"Out of curiosity, do all experiments go into battle assuming they won't survive?"

"We don't even think about it. We are only concerned with completing our mission."

He straightened up when Brindy and Hunter, Jet and Lilly's daughters, stepped into the main hall. They were laughing and leaning against each other, sharing in a joke or story. Sly followed Coop's gaze down to the women below, a knowing smile dancing across her lips. Over the winter, she had noticed Brindy spent a lot of time with Coop and the experiment seemed to relax in her presence. They had become an odd pair of friends and their interactions were quite entertaining to watch.

"If you're going to die, might as well live first, right?" Sly observed with a suggestive grin.

Coop looked over at her, his brow furrowing. "Am I not living now?"

Sly rolled her eyes up at the ceiling. "You need to spend some time with Nero. It would help you get the hang of our pesky linguistics."

Coop still looked mildly confused, as his attention traveled back to the sisters below. Brindy looked up to the second floor, smiling at the two shape shifters. Coop raised one hand in greeting.

"I wish Orion and the Monroes would figure out a target to attack," he mentioned, looking down at the red carpeting they stood on. "Waiting makes me uneasy."

"*That* is something we agree on," Sly said.

~~*~*~*

In the meeting room of the mansion, Jet studied a dossier. Lilly, his wife, sat to his left. She smoothed the sleeve of her green dress and brushed some long golden hair behind one ear, her attention fixed on some papers in front of her. Orion sat across the table, paging through a book he had borrowed from the Meadows. The curtains were drawn away from the windows and the sun lighted the plain room.

"This lull is bothering me, Orion," Jet said as he closed the dossier, running his hand over the smooth cherry wood of the long table. Orion nodded, distracted. He turned another page in the book, glancing at the small black writing.

"I know. The Corporation should have made some attempt to retrieve Isis and Jack by now," he agreed, closing the book and looking over to Jet and Lilly. "Set is patient and likely biding his time. When he strikes, you can assume it will be violent. Knowing him, there will also be a certain amount of chaos involved."

"Do you have any suggestions for how to prepare for that?" Lilly asked, interlacing her fingers in front of her. Orion turned his head to the side, biting the inside of his cheek.

"We need to remain vigilant, but our focus should be on liberating the main facility in this state. Our best chance at achieving that would be to gather as many allies as possible and then launch a surprise attack," the eldest Deverell began. "The truce between rebels and protectors is a start, but it won't be enough. Not even close."

"We had already planned to make contact with the other shape shifter groups. I don't think the vigilantes will respond, but the seducers and thieves might," Jet stated. Orion sat back, pressing the thick spine of the book against his hand.

"Even if they all responded favorably, which is unlikely,

it would not be enough to bring down the Grenich Corporation. Shape shifters alone cannot defeat Set."

Jet looked at him as he sat back in his chair. "Whom does that leave? Humans? Guardians?"

"You're suggesting contacting the other supernatural races," Lilly observed. Jet glanced over at her and then looked at Orion, incredulously.

"You must be joking."

"Earth is the crossroads to a number of worlds," Orion explained, opening the book he held. "Admittedly, I'm not as well-versed in them as I wish I were. However, I've spent most of the winter reading up on them. There were five races who allied with the guardians during the War of the Meadows: the shape shifters, the Seelie Court, the lycanthropes, the vampires, and the Magic Orders. As a reward for their loyalty and bravery, four of the races were given their own realms, or worlds — whatever you want to call them. The shape shifters remained on Earth to protect the crossroads between these worlds and also to aid the guardians in keeping the balance."

Jet dragged his hands down his face. "Orion, that was millennia ago. The races went to their worlds and they remained there."

"They have occasionally stepped through their gates to Earth," Lilly pointed out. "Humans haven't seen them because they exist on a different wavelength, one most mortals cannot see."

"Some members of the Seelie Court have been known to change their form so humans can see them, which is probably where a lot of paranormal stories and beliefs come from," Orion added. "Well that and shape shifters occasionally fucking up and shifting in front of humans."

"Yes, yes, yes, this is all very interesting," Jet stated. "There are a couple problems with your suggestion. First, it would take months to set up meetings with the heads of these lands, which would require the aid of the guardians. We can't Appear in those worlds. Second, the gateways to those universes are hidden and I'm not sure I'd know how to find them."

"Hecate and Cliodhna would know," Lilly said. "They are in charge of magic and they also keep watch over the other worlds. They would be able to get in touch with the ambassadors."

Jet massaged the knuckles of one hand with the other. Like all protector leaders, he had learned the lore of the supernatural races when he was younger. He had no real firsthand experience with them aside from when he was named leader of the protectors — the day he and Lilly had wed. Even then, they had not interacted much with the other species. He glanced over at Lilly and she smiled supportively.

"The old alliances are still in place," she reminded him. "If you call upon them, they need to at least listen to your request."

"The other supernatural races have always been very cloistered and unconcerned with matters on Earth," Jet responded as he leaned back in his chair. He could feel the warmth of the sun on his back. Summer could not arrive soon enough for him. Jet looked across the table when he heard pages rustling. Orion had opened the large brown book again and was flipping through the thin tan pages.

"They might not be as dismissive as you expect," he said, pushing the book across the table and pointing at the left page. "According to this record, some of their lands still bear scars from the War of the Meadows. If Earth falls, the Meadows will be vulnerable. If that happens, all their worlds are at risk."

Jet pulled the book closer, skimming the passage Orion indicated. *Wherever Chaos set foot, the land died and nothing would grow there again. He was unnatural death and that was what he brought,* the protector read. Jet sat back, wondering how he would go about convincing the supernatural races to face that kind of evil again. Though Orion and Lilly seemed optimistic about the other races, Jet was much more pessimistic about the situation. From what he had read, they remained in their lands and were uninterested in taking part in the skirmishes of others.

"It can't hurt to try," Lilly stated softly.

"All right. I'll contact Adonia tomorrow and set up a meeting with Hecate," Jet relented, sliding the book back to Orion.

~~*~*~*

Isis and Jack watched as Remington adjusted the gauntlets on his wrists. He was wearing a pristine fencing uniform. About a month after Jack and Isis had returned to the mansion, Remington had requested a demonstration of their skills. He wanted to get an idea of how they would fight against a regular shape shifter. They had been puzzled when he didn't wear any armor or other protective clothing, but he insisted it was unnecessary. In a matter of minutes, Remington suffered a sprained wrist, fractured ankle, cracked ribs, and countless contusions and abrasions. Though he was an experienced warrior, Remington was no match for the experiments. The guardians healed him, but the trainer was still sore for a week after the session. That was the last time he attempted to measure their skills without some kind of protective clothing.

Both Jack and Isis stood silently at attention, waiting for instruction. Shae, Alex, and Jade sat on the edge of the boxing ring. The experiments turned their necks and looked toward the stairs. A moment later, Jensen and Nero came into the training room. Nero had a bag of pretzels, which he was crunching loudly as they moved across the room to where the folding chairs were. Remington glanced up at them, his brow furrowing.

"Don't mind us," Nero called over to the group, dropping down into one of the chairs. "We're just here to watch."

He put the bag of pretzels on the ground and brushed the salt off his hands. Jensen sat down in the chair next to Nero with an amused smile on his face. Isis turned her attention back to Remington, glancing over at Jack, who was studying her. His glowing brown eyes reflected something akin to curiosity.

"Jade, Alex, Shae, would the three of you mind suiting up?" Remington requested as he retrieved his helmet. "There are a couple maneuvers I would like to try tonight."

"Remington, I'm still aching after last week's sparring matches," Alex protested even as she hopped off the ring. Jade was already moving toward the closet at the back of the room. Shae hung back with Alex, obviously not eager to repeat last week's training session. She was still sporting a couple good-sized bruises. Even when they held back, the experiments landed quite a few blows.

"I wouldn't ask if it wasn't necessary," Remington responded, turning his gaze back to the experiments. "I'm sure I don't need to remind you both that you're dealing with normals. If you could slow down just a bit so I can see what you're doing."

Jack and Isis exchanged another look, still puzzled. The normals at the mansion were so peculiar to them. They didn't know how to do some of the things they asked, which were often nonsensical. Even Coop had difficulty accommodating them and he had been on the outside for decades.

"Isis, could you step forward?" Remington asked, pulling the helmet over his face. He walked over to the wall and retrieved a finely made wooden sword. Isis stepped forward, her attention fixing on the wooden weapon. The light from overhead gleamed on the bamboo-colored sword.

"Now, if you were going to disarm—"

Before Remington could finish, he was on the ground with Isis standing over him, holding the wooden weapon.

Her boot was on his neck. Nero's laughter broke the stunned silence in the training room. Isis stepped back and reached down, offering her hand. Remington grabbed it and she helped him back to his feet. He pulled off his mask.

"If you could let me finish, that would be helpful," Remington said, mildly irritated. Isis looked up at him and handed back the wooden sword.

"This exercise is pointless. You will not get an accurate measurement of our abilities and strategies if you hinder us," she pointed out. Jack remained still, his glowing brown eyes watching the two shape shifters in front of him.

"If I can't see what you're doing, I won't know how to train with you or how to prepare the other three," Remington explained. She still looked skeptical, but backed up a couple steps and got into the ready position. The trainer pulled his mask back on and held the wooden sword so it was vertical in front of him. Isis watched him as he advanced, her gaze never moving from the approaching trainer. Even when Remington was within striking distance, Isis remained still as stone. Remington feinted to the side and brought the sword up for a powerful overhead strike. Faster than the naked eye could see, Isis had her arms crossed over her head, blocking the sword, and lashed out with a powerful front kick that sent the trainer sprawling.

Remington pushed himself up with his hands and pulled the helmet off again, coughing violently as he tried to get his breath back.

"Well, at least I was able to see what you were doing," he said, winded. "Mostly."

"I would never move that slow in an actual combat situation," Isis stated. Remington coughed again and glanced over his shoulder to where the other three stood, suited up and waiting. He got back to his feet and smoothed his fencing clothes.

"I want to see how the two of you work in tandem," Remington explained to the two experiments. They exchanged another look, one of hesitation.

"I would advise against that," Jack warned as they looked back to the four protectors in front of them. "One-on-one is difficult enough for normals."

"It's all right, Jack," Remington reassured him. "Just remember to take it easy and don't go at warp speed. This isn't a battle. It is practice and we need to be prepared for whatever Grenich throws at us."

Jack glanced over at Isis. She looked at him and then at Remington, nodding once. She turned and walked a couple feet behind Jack. Remington approached the three, who still stood off to the side. Alex was shaking her head, not wild about the idea.

"Remy, maybe we should listen to him," Shae suggested.

"This is the only way we'll be able to get some idea about Grenich strategy, Shae," Remington explained. "We can't expect the experiments to constantly be saving us. If we're to help them, we need to understand our enemy."

Shae let out a breath, looking very unsure as she moved over to where Alex was standing a few feet away.

"If you could all grab a wooden sword," Remington instructed, placing a hand on Jade's shoulder as she moved toward the wall.

"Fight as dirty as you can. Use whatever underhanded tactics you can think of," he spoke under his breath, not turning around. "We need to find their limits."

Jade stared at him. "You want me to grab a knife off the wall? Maybe a sword with an actual blade?"

Remington gave her a dry look. "Obviously not. Chances are it would just get turned on us."

"Guardians have mercy, Remington," Jade shook her head and dragged her hands down her face. "Fine, we'll fight dirty. But I'm telling you, I don't think they have limits. At least not any we can push them to."

Remington pulled his helmet on and retrieved his wooden sword where it still lay on the ground. He glanced over at the experiments. Jack stood a little closer than Isis, who was looking off toward the boxing ring.

"Okay, same rules as all our other practice sessions. Don't forget tap outs, no grabbing weapons off the wall, no breaking bones, and I would prefer you stick to using hand-to-hand combat," Remington reminded the experiments, neither of whom moved. Jack was paying close attention, but Isis seemed uninterested in the session or Remington's instructions.

"Begin," Remington ordered.

He and Alex advanced on Jack while Jade and Shae went for Isis, their steps muffled on the dull green mats. Jack started to circle around the shape shifters. Alex lunged at him and he jumped to the side, lashing out with a kick that hit her in the ribs and another that struck her in the temple, knocking her down. As she was recovering, Remington swung at the experiment's head with the sword and he dropped down into a sweeping kick. Once Remington was down, Jack leapt up in the air into a reverse kick that caught Alex in the back and sent her crashing to the ground again.

Shae leapt at Isis and the experiment grabbed her sword, pulling the other shape shifter off balance. She punched the helmet with a strong cross. Jade lunged at her from behind, thrusting her sword forward. Isis leapt up and seemed to disappear briefly, until Jade was suddenly forced to her knees when Isis landed on her shoulders.

"Whoa!"

"Fucking hell!"

Isis ignored Nero's and Jensen's exclamations of shock and awe as she executed a front flip, throwing Jade onto her back. Isis turned and backed up until she felt Jack's back against hers. Shae, Alex, and Remington had all gotten back to their feet and Jade was using her sword to push herself up again, grumbling something under her breath.

"They are persistent," Isis observed.

"I'm having trouble fighting at such a reduced speed," Jack admitted.

"Don't reduce your efficiency too much. They want to know what they're up against," Isis responded. "The other experiments won't accommodate them. They will not be shown mercy. If they are to survive, they need to be properly prepared."

Jack was quiet for a moment. "Don't do them any lasting harm."

Isis stepped away and approached Jade and Shae again. They both swung at her and she threw herself backward, flipping back to her feet immediately as if she had springs on her back. She punched Shae in the stomach and landed a vicious back kick to Jade's sternum, knocking her to the floor again. Isis straightened up and brought her knee up into Shae's face. The blow knocked her backward as Jade flipped back to her feet. Isis leapt at her, striking at her with a roundhouse kick. Jade narrowly avoided being kicked in the face. She backed up a couple steps and Isis advanced, but then turned and ran back at Shae, who had just gotten up. The experiment leapt into the air, locked her legs around the other shape shifter's neck, and swung her body around, forcing the shape shifter back to the ground. Shae gagged and tapped her leg twice. Isis released her and looked over to Jack as he threw Alex into Remington, knocking them both back to the mats.

Isis rolled out of the way when Jade brought her sword down where her head had been. The experiment scurried to her feet, grabbed Shae's abandoned sword, spun around, and pressed it against the back of Jade's neck.

"I can take you down if you wish, but at this point in the fight, you would be dead," Isis stated. "If this had been a real fight, the four of you would have been incapacitated long ago."

Jade pulled off her helmet, her face bathed in sweat.

She was panting as she looked at Isis with something resembling apprehension. The woman before her had no qualms taking life, as she had proven a couple months ago when she went on a bloody rampage.

"Remington, I can taste my spleen," Shae groaned from the floor. Both Jack and Isis looked at her, confused.

"Not literally," she mumbled when she noticed Isis' gaze. Shae grimaced as she pushed herself into a sitting position. Neither experiment was panting, sweating, or even slightly winded. Isis could see the normals were feeling unsettled. For them, fighting an experiment was like fighting a phantom.

Remington and Alex had both removed their helmets and they looked just as worn out.

"You know, Remington, you could have avoided a lot of pain and embarrassment," Nero mentioned as he got to his feet, clearing his throat. "Isis, what's the highest number of opponents you've taken on at one time?"

"Ninety-seven," she answered without hesitation. Nero's eyes widened significantly and his mouth dropped open. The rest of the protectors had similar shocked expressions.

"Um, okay. That's — that's a lot," he said when he managed to find his voice again. He scratched the back of his head, looking over at her. "Why exactly did you have to take on that many people?"

"I had to retrieve some sensitive information for Grenich from a highly-guarded facility. There were hostiles I had to get through. I got through them," she answered. Nero stared at her, glancing back at Jensen. The well-dressed man simply shrugged.

Nero blinked a few times and looked over at Jack. The lights in the training room seemed a little brighter due to the setting sun and their buzz was clearly audible in the quiet room.

"Seventy-two," Jack answered before Nero had a chance to ask. "Similar circumstances."

"That's impossible," Remington finally spoke up as he helped Alex to her feet. Jade had already pulled Shae back to her feet.

"Your eyes are very wide and you're not blinking as much as you should be," Isis observed. Shae snorted at that and then grimaced at the ache that flared up in her body.

"You were armed, correct?" Remington asked, blinking a few times. Aside from shock, there was the faintest hint of fear in his expression. Jack and Isis had become accustomed to that look in normals. Jack was more concerned with it than Isis. She knew she was dangerous and didn't see the point in trying to hide or deny it.

"Yes," Isis answered the trainer.

"There were very few times when we weren't," Jack added. Remington stroked the back of his head. Isis watched him closely. He seemed to be baffled by the numbers, which were probably higher than normals were used to.

"It is unlikely we killed all of them. Odds are a few were just permanently maimed," Isis continued, watching the shape shifters in front of her. "We didn't aim to kill unless that was the specific mission. Our orders were often to complete the mission and neutralize any threats that were in our way."

There was another moment where no one in the training room knew quite what to say. Shae coughed quietly and Alex cleared her throat. It was so quiet that even the softest sounds seemed to be amplified.

"Isn't neutralize just a nice way of saying kill?" Alex asked, pulling off one of her gloves. She hissed when she saw the skin on one of her knuckles had split. Bright red blood was smeared across her hand. A couple drops dripped from her hand and splattered on the thin, dull green mats that covered the floor of the training room.

"Not necessarily, but killing is the most effective way to neutralize a threat so it was often what we did," Isis responded. Jack held his head up as he stood at attention.

"I know you've told us before, but could you refresh my memory about an experiment's weaknesses?" Remington requested as he massaged his forehead. He leaned against his wooden sword. The trainer was favoring one leg and it was likely he was going to have more than a few bruises and contusions.

Isis hesitated, glancing over at Jack as she assumed a similar stance. Remington looked between the two of them, waiting patiently. All three experiments were very hesitant when it came to revealing weaknesses. It was another result of the intense battle conditioning they had undergone while in the Corporation.

"All experiments have different weaknesses, but there are a few we have in common," Jack began. "Alcohol and most other narcotics will cause organ failure. Destroying the brain or the heart will result in instant death."

"Our other organs will regenerate, but it will take longer than most superficial wounds. A vital organ will take between a half-hour and an hour to heal," Isis added. "Blood loss isn't really a concern, unless the experiment is ill or a limb is severed. Severed limbs will not regrow. If you encounter a hostile experiment, always aim for the head first. It's your best chance."

Remington turned his attention to the three women, unable to mask his concern. It didn't take an experienced trainer to see the odds were against them. They hadn't landed a single blow on either experiment, both of whom had purposely slowed down as instructed.

"I think we can call it a day," Remington said softly. Both Isis and Jack relaxed their stances slightly.

"Thank the guardians," Jade grumbled, wincing as she rotated her shoulder. She was obviously hurting.

"We'll pick this up tomorrow, right?" Alex asked, rolling her neck.

"As long as it's not at night," Shae chimed in. "The Monroe children are throwing that bash at the Lair for

Devlin. Isis, you're not getting out of it."

"I do not think that is a wise idea," Isis responded, watching as the protectors put away their training weapons.

"I disagree," Remington stated, to the shock of almost everyone in the training room. "It is the perfect opportunity for you to reacquaint yourself with your protector heritage. Jet and Lilly would rest easy knowing two experiments were watching over their children."

"It would offer us an opportunity to practice acclimating to the world of normals," Jack suggested. Isis looked over at him, skeptically.

"So it's settled. We train in the afternoon, party at night," Shae declared happily, almost bouncing with excitement. "This is going to be fun. I can't wait."

She practically bounded up the stairs. Jade and Alex followed shortly after, their gaits noticeably stiffer than they had been. Remington moved over to where Nero and Jensen were still sitting, retrieving his water bottle from the bench behind them. Jack moved toward the stairs and Isis turned her attention to the weapons wall, studying it. Her ears were sharp as she listened to the conversation behind her.

"I assume you'll both be at the Lair tomorrow," Remington mentioned, looking over to where Isis was standing.

"When have I ever passed up a chance to hang with rebels?" Nero said, looking up when Jensen got to his feet and crossed the training room to where Isis was. He made sure he stayed out of striking distance as he stood nearby. She turned her head a little and he did the same. She looked back at the wall, as did he. Over the winter, Isis and Jensen had developed their own method of communication. It was a language of subtle gestures — almost a dance — that required no words.

"If you wouldn't mind doing me a favor," Remington's stern Irish brogue continued. "I want to know how experiments act in an environment like the Lair, one they can't completely control."

"Seeing as how I'm going to have my hands full, I would suggest asking the Four to do the covert spying," Nero responded as he got to his feet, slapping the back of Remington's shoulder. "Glad to see you're learning how to trust them though and not infantilizing them at all."

Isis glanced back at the two men, noticing Remington look up to the ceiling and shake his head. The trainer often seemed exasperated with the youngest Deverell. Nero's personality was very different from most of the other protectors she met. Remington grabbed his towel and water, following Nero out of the training room.

Isis watched as the tall trainer disappeared around the bend in the stairway. She turned her glowing gaze back to the wall of weapons, studying her reflection in a sword.

"You will also be at the Lair tomorrow," she stated. Jensen smiled as he looked over at her.

"Why? Did you want to reserve a room?"

"I want to get an idea of how many mansion residents will be there," Isis responded. "It will help me assess the probability of an attack."

Jensen chuckled, turning his attention back to the wall. He stared at a silver spear with runes carved in the staff.

"You might want to check with Hunter. She's the—"

He was cut off when Isis grabbed him and yanked him toward her, kissing him passionately. His shock quickly melted as he returned her ardor, his hand gently resting on the small of her back. The lights in the training room brightened briefly and both their temperatures rose a few degrees. After a moment, she stepped away and Jensen opened his eyes, staring at her.

"Not that I mind, but what in the name of the guardians was that?" he asked, wiping his mouth.

"I was testing a hypothesis," she answered, her brow creasing as she looked up at the lights. Isis stepped back and moved to the stairway. Jensen straightened his already straight suit, letting out a breath before jogging after her.

"May I ask your hypothesis?" he said when he caught up with her.

"Still formulating it," Isis responded. "I do not have enough data to properly explain it yet. I will tell you about it when I have what I need, if you wish."

They exited the training room and she turned toward him, her glowing green eyes fixing on him.

"I do not believe you should go to the Lair tomorrow. You are the last Aldridge and a good fighter," Isis stated in her typical blunt way. "Grenich wants you dead and the bounty on your head is high enough for assassins to take risks."

Jensen grinned. "Why Isis, I do believe you are concerned for my well-being."

She stared at him, her brow furrowing a little. "You are a valuable ally. Why would I not be concerned for your well-being?"

Jensen's grin fell. "If I spent my life avoiding risks, I would never leave the safety of the mansion. Besides, you'll be watching my back. There's no safer place in the world."

Her attention remained fixed on him as she tried to figure out how to respond. Jensen was a mystery to her and his actions made little to no sense. She opened her mouth as if to argue and then closed it again. Jensen winked at her.

"I'll see you at dinner."

Isis watched his retreating back as he headed in the direction of the library. He was an unusual normal. Jensen was one of the very few who had never been afraid of her and he spoke to her as though she were just another normal. He should be afraid of her, but he was not. It was an anomaly she hadn't yet figured out.

Isis continued toward the main stairwell, ascending it swiftly and moving through the halls to her room. When she reached her door, Isis opened it and stepped inside.

She rarely turned on the lights and the drapes were always drawn. Grenich had taught her to view darkness as an ally. It offered cover from snipers and hostiles, giving her an advantage over those who would do her harm.

Once she was inside, Isis closed the door behind her, locked it, and walked through the entire room, her gaze sharp for anything out of place. She checked every corner, ran her hand behind every piece of furniture, and examined every surface no matter how small or narrow. It was a routine Isis performed every time she entered the space. Once she was satisfied she was alone and her room was free of any kind of surveillance, Isis stripped off her catsuit and laid it on the bed. The shadows were growing as night approached. Walking toward the bathroom, she moved to the shower and turned it on. The hot water streamed down in a powerful jet. After a moment, steam began to cloud the glass. Isis stepped cautiously inside, looking around the bathroom one last time before shutting the smoky glass door behind her. She closed her eyes and turned her face up toward the water.

"Seven series."

The whisper was so soft Isis almost brushed it off as an auditory hallucination. She turned her face out of the stream and blinked a few times, scrubbing some of the water off her face. The bathroom was obscured through the foggy glass walls. The feeling of soft fingers trailing across her shoulders, barely even touching her flesh, caused her to spin back toward the water, lashing out with the edge of her hand. There was nothing there. Isis swallowed and squeezed some of the water out of her short hair. Her sharp senses continued to analyze the bathroom. It was empty. She was still alone.

The revolting feeling of a smooth wet tongue dragging up her back caused Isis to spin around again, her right fist coming up in a hook punch. Again there was nothing. The water temperature seemed to drop a few degrees.

"I can taste you, seven series," the raspy whisper was

right next to her. Isis turned off the shower and opened the door, stepping out into the bathroom. Her eyes traveled around the empty space, searching for anything. They fixed on an unusual shadow against the wall to her right. It was formless and had a smoky appearance. She moved to the towel rack and the shadow remained in place. Grabbing a towel, Isis wrapped it about her slender form. Her attention never moved from the shadow. It began to move to the side, a mouth full of perfect teeth slowly appearing as it grinned. Isis felt the temperature drop even lower and her breath fogged in front of her.

"You may be hidden from me in this space, this protector haven, but do not think for a second that I don't know exactly where you are," the mouth spoke.

"Who are you?" she asked and it clicked its tongue at her. Placing a hand on the countertop behind her, she found it was so cold it stung her sensitive palm. Isis calmly removed her hand from the frigid surface.

"The dog does not need to know its master's name. It only needs to obey," the shadow chided as it continued moving around the bathroom. "Seven series, do not become a thorn in my side. This is a warning and from me you will only get one."

"Set," Isis said and the shadow rushed at her, stopping mere inches from her face. She leaned back a little but continued looking to where the eyes of the shadow would be. If it had them.

"You can astral project, but your ability to do so is hampered by the guardian magic protecting this place. You are no threat to me," Isis stated. "Go away. You are a nuisance."

A deep chuckling seemed to echo in her mind. "Your arrogance will be your undoing, seven series. Make no mistake, I'm still holding your leash and if I desire, I will use it to choke the life out of you."

Isis watched as the shadow dissipated. She turned and left the bathroom.

CHAPTER TWO

In the Meadows, Electra sat in the crowded library. Her bright blue eyes were intently watching the numerous guardians and messengers rushing about. A few guardians sat at the large tables, which were scattered about the open area. Electra craned her neck, attempting to better see around the towering bookshelves. She sat with her fingers interlaced, one foot resting on the edge of the table and the other flat on the ground. The afternoon sun beamed in through the stained glass windows, each depicting scenes from the legends and history of the guardians. Out of the corner of her eye, Electra noticed a messenger in a pastel blue dress looking at her foot on the table disapprovingly. Electra ignored her, her mind racing with a thousand thoughts.

In the months since Isis' return, a strange quiet had fallen over the Meadows. Things went on as they always did, but it troubled Electra. She wanted to know why the history books had been censored, and when. Passion was also bothered by the censorship but she was more concerned with Isis' readjustment with the protectors. Electra hadn't seen much of her twin over the winter months. Isis had only visited the Meadows once since her release, which Electra could understand. Still, it was difficult spending time with her sister. She was so different, so distant. Electra would never admit it outright, but she didn't recognize Isis anymore. She did her best to act normal around her, but Electra got the distinct impression that Isis noticed her discomfort.

A large book dropping in front of her with a loud bang interrupted Electra's thoughts. The noise echoed through the quiet library, drawing the attention of most of the guardians and messengers. Electra looked up at Phoenix and spread her hands out to the side.

"What the hell, Phoenix?"

The redheaded fire guardian stood across from her friend, smiling from ear-to-ear. The sunlight caught the sparkling gold designs sewn into her scarlet dress, making it glimmer.

"You looked as though you were a million miles away," Phoenix stated as she dropped down in the seat across from Electra. "So what is it? A lover or sister troubles?"

Electra shrugged, glimpsing Athena behind the enormous wrap-around desk. There was a stairway behind the desk, which led down to the room where the ancient tomes were kept. Athena was sitting at the desk, reading a small book with a purple cover. She wore armor similar to the guards in the Meadows. Her hair was held back with strategic braids that went around her head.

Phoenix glanced over her shoulder, following her friend's gaze. "Surprised Athena hasn't come over to swat at your foot. I know how fond the two of you are of each other."

"Phoenix, I need to know who the last person was to have that tome I told you about," Electra whispered, glancing around to make sure no one was eavesdropping on their conversation. "But there's no way she's going to tell me. Athena has always hated me."

"Hate to break it to you, Electra, but Athena hates pretty much all the women in the Meadows. Though she does seem to have a specific grudge against Passion," Phoenix responded, looking over her shoulder once more at the stern-looking woman. Her eyes roamed around the rest of the library, a half-smile creeping across her face. "But we might be in luck."

Electra looked behind her when Phoenix gestured in that direction. A few feet away, a younger guardian man was standing beside a bookshelf. The sun caught his curly black hair and highlighted the shimmer in his skin. He was very attractive and most of the younger guardians were looking at him, including a small group from the lands of dawn off to the side. The man didn't seem to notice as he reached up for a book on a shelf above his head. He gripped the one he wanted, but brought down a couple extra. The group of girls giggled as he jumped away from the falling books, scrambling to pick them up and put them back on the shelf. He was obviously embarrassed and it made him clumsier. Electra noticed Athena look over at him, shake her head, and turn back to the book she was reading.

"This might be the first time he has lived up to his name," Electra stated as she swung her leg off the table. She and Phoenix crossed over to the guardian. Though he was a little older than they were, he didn't have their confidence, which made him seem much younger. He wore the indigo robes of the night realm. The trim around the sleeves and neck was maroon to show he was an emotion guardian, or would be after his apprenticeship.

"Lucky," Electra greeted warmly, causing Lucky to jump and look up from his book. He had piercing turquoise-colored eyes, darker skin, and classic good looks. *That man could have been carved from stone,* Passion had once observed. Phoenix draped her arms over his shoulders and leaned her head against his.

"Oh no," he said, shaking his head and closing the history book he was looking at. "Whatever you're planning, I want no part of it."

Phoenix stuck out her lower lip, pouting, while Electra looked at him innocently. A few of the messengers looked over at the three younger guardians before turning their attention back to whatever task they were doing.

"I just wanted to come over and say hello," Electra protested, acting as though she were hurt. Lucky looked at her suspiciously.

"The last time you just wanted to say hello, Donovan yelled at me for almost an hour about my not being a messenger or your errand boy."

"And if Donovan didn't ignore messengers, my mother wouldn't have to resort to underhanded tactics to send him a message," Electra protested, a hint of ice sneaking into her voice. "And I'm fairly certain he didn't mind getting that message. He's just busting your balls because he's an ass."

Lucky placed the book back on the shelf, fumbling as he tried not to displace the other books. He became very fidgety, obviously uncomfortable. *Guardians, I wonder if he has ever even had sex,* Electra thought, struggling not to roll her eyes.

"Come on, guys, we're all friends here," Phoenix interjected, turning her attention to Lucky. "Look, we just need a little help getting some information from Athena. Donovan won't throw a fit over that, will he?"

Lucky scoffed. "You think Athena's going to tell me anything?"

"You'd have a better chance than either of us," Electra pointed out as she leaned against the bookcase. The bumpy bindings pressed against her toned arm. She adjusted the sleeves of the crimson shirt she was wearing.

"True," Lucky conceded reluctantly.

"That's the spirit," Phoenix said happily, patting his shoulder. "And if you like, Electra and I will put in a good word to any guardian who has caught your eye. So, are you interested in anyone? Man, woman, neutral?"

"I'll ask Athena whatever you want, but only if you

stop prying into my personal life," Lucky replied as he crossed his arms over his chest. Phoenix raised her hands in surrender, still smiling. She gestured for Electra to ask what she needed.

"I want to know the last guardian to look at the first tome concerning the War of the Meadows," Electra explained, quickly clarifying, "The last one before me."

Lucky sighed and stepped away from them, crossing the library to the desk where Athena was sitting. Phoenix turned her attention back to her friend.

"We should probably act like we're talking about something," Electra mentioned. "In case she looks over here."

"Agreed," Phoenix replied. "What's new with you? I haven't seen much of you the past couple months."

"We saw each other at the Changing of Seasons ceremony a few weeks ago," Electra pointed out. She looked over her shoulder when she noticed Silver out of the corner of her eye. The guardian metalsmith was wearing her usual work clothes and soot decorated her in random patches. The goggles on her head caught the sunlight. Her fingertips trailed over the bindings until she found the one she wanted. She plucked it off the shelf and then disappeared somewhere among the rows.

"You were a million miles away then too," Phoenix mentioned, brushing some hair behind her ear. "You've been lost in your head for a while now, Electra. What's going on?"

Electra fingered the binding of one of the books, her eyes wandering over the titles. "This whole Grenich thing is just really unsettling."

"Tell me about it," Phoenix agreed. "Everyone seems to be on edge, especially with Isis being back and all. Resurrection — talk about upsetting the natural order."

Electra was quiet, preferring not to talk about her sister. There were several guardians on the High Council who thought they made the wrong decision letting her go free. The experiments made the guardians nervous, especially the older ones. Donovan had told Passion there were a few older guardian men who weren't opposed to sealing up Jack and Isis for eternity, a punishment reserved only for the most heinous prisoners. The guardians would never take life, but there were some punishments that many considered worse than death. Being locked away in the oldest section of the dungeons indefinitely was one such punishment. Both Passion and Electra had been extremely upset by the callousness of those guardians who wanted to inflict that punishment on the two experiments.

"Heads up, Lucky's coming back," Phoenix's voice brought Electra out of her ruminations. She looked over to where Lucky was making his way back to them, squinting against the bright afternoon sun.

"That was quick," Electra mentioned, brushing a lock of hair behind her ear. Now that the weather was getting warmer, she planned to shorten her hair a few inches.

Lucky shrugged. "According to her records, the last guardian who looked at that particular tome was Aneurin."

Phoenix looked over at Electra, who scratched the back of her head. To go look at the ancient tomes, guardians had to be accompanied by one of the Keepers. They also had to sign in with their sigil, which was unique to each guardian. Aneurin had his carved into a ring, which he never took off.

"Aneurin's a pain and has a *massive* superiority complex," Phoenix said. "But would he really censor tomes without the express permission of the High Council or the Muses? I mean, Clio alone would have a conniption fit if anyone touched those volumes without permission."

"I don't know, Phoenix," Electra said, hooking her thumbs in her pants. "After all that's happened, is anything outside the realm of possibility?"

~~*~*~*

Shae watched her cousin as Isis confidently walked into the rebel Lair, unbothered by the blasting music or numerous dancing rebels and patrons. Isis paused just before a doorway, remaining in sight of her three teammates as per the rules of her release from the Meadows. Her eyes were never still, darting over the entire club as she observed all the activity surrounding her. She was wearing her catsuit, but Shae had managed to talk her out of wearing the sunglasses and driving gloves. Earlier in the afternoon, Shae had tried to explain what people normally wore to clubs but Isis didn't understand the point of restrictive flashy clothing. It was difficult enough explaining why she couldn't bring her guns. They called Alpha ahead of time to let her know about the experiments and the likelihood of them bringing weapons. Surprisingly, Alpha hadn't objected so long as they didn't bring firearms. *You better keep an eye on them, because the first sign of trouble and you'll all be banned for eternity, truce or not,* the rebel leader had growled.

"Think she's going to be okay?" Hunter yelled over the throbbing dubstep music. Shae shrugged and spread her hands. She honestly didn't know how Isis would react to the new chaotic environment. She seemed to be doing all right. Both protectors watched as Isis and Jack made their way over to what had once been the check in desk. The twins behind the desk beamed and waved at them. Isis turned and moved away, pausing at the doorway to the main dance floor, her body still noticeably rigid. Brindy came up next to her younger sister, wrapping an arm around her shoulders.

"Less talking, more shots," she said. "Come on, Hunter. The night is young and we're not the designated drivers. First round's on me. Devlin and Declan are already at the bar."

Hunter laughed and let her older sister lead her away and they disappeared in the darkness, punctured only by the occasional dim blue glow of a laser light. Shae glanced behind her, noticing Jack hanging back by the entrance. His glowing brown eyes were darting all over the place. *Guardians, I really hope their heads don't explode,* Shae thought as she bit her bottom lip. She was starting to question whether bringing the two experiments was such a good idea. Jade clapped a hand down on her shoulder, interrupting her thoughts.

"I'm going to catch up with Alpha. Can you and Alex handle these two?" she asked, glancing over her shoulder to where Nero was already grinding with a few neon-haired rebels. He noticed her looking in his direction and gave her the thumbs up before a rebel with neon-yellow hair grabbed his face and pulled him into a deep kiss. The music continued to thunder throughout the club. The rebels writhed and swayed with the rhythm.

"I'll help out," Jensen came up beside Shae, looking over to Jade. "We'll be fine. Catch up with your partner."

"Sly's partner," Jade corrected with a smile and a raised eyebrow before she turned and moved in the direction of the stairs. She soon disappeared within the crowd. The club was even busier than it typically was. The rebel Lair was often packed, but it was usually much easier to move through the space. Alex came up beside them, her black hair shining even in the dim blue lights. The club lit up with different primary colors as the strobe lights started blinking.

"I'm going to go up to the library room for a little bit," Alex said. "This music is going right through my skull."

"All right. Want me to bring you a drink?" Shae yelled over the music, looking over her shoulder when Jack approached. His eyes were still wandering around, a remarkably smooth motion. A rebel with neon purple hair, complete with matching lips and eye shadow, came up alongside him and he watched her curiously.

"No. Just text if you need anything," Alex replied as she moved off in the same direction Jade had gone. Isis approached them, her gait smooth, almost gliding. She moved aside whenever a dancing rebel came close to touching her.

"I would like to go to the upper floors," she stated, her glowing green gaze wandering around the club. "I cannot get an accurate reading of this location and the possible weak spots without seeing it from different vantages."

Shae resisted the urge to roll her eyes. She knew Isis was naturally on edge all the time, but it was tiring after a while. The flashing lights glimmered on the catsuit and more than a few rebels looked her up and down. At her throat, her silver charm gleamed, standing out even in the low lighting.

"Come on, ice queen, relax and let loose a little," Shae urged. "We're perfectly safe. There are no threats in the immediate area that require our attention."

"You have used that term on multiple occasions. What is an ice queen?" Isis asked, her brow furrowing a little. "Or is that based on my given name? Nicknames are supposed to be shorter than given names."

Shae looked over to where Jack was still watching the dancing patrons, ignoring Jensen's snickering at Isis' question. Jack looked enthralled, as if he had never seen dancing before. He took a large step back when a rebel came close to him, obviously hesitant to allow invasion into his personal space. Shae continued looking around at the rebels. Many had painted their lips with a neon glow, which made it look as though there were different colored disembodied mouths floating in the club.

"How high up would you like to go?" Jensen asked and Isis looked over at him.

"It would be wise to do a sweep of each floor," she responded. "The Lair is five stories. We can start on the third floor. The middle floor will give me an idea of where to concentrate our sweep as well as ideal ambush sites."

Jensen turned to Shae, smiling. "We'll be on the third floor looking for possible ambush sites if you need us. Think you can handle Jack on your own?"

Shae grinned as she looked over at the experiment when he approached them. "I'll manage. If not, all of you are just a text away."

Jensen turned his attention to Isis, who was talking to Jack.

"I'll go high, you stay low," she instructed him and he nodded his understanding. Isis turned back to Jensen, who swept his arm in the direction of the staircase. The two moved around the numerous rebels and other patrons. Shae let out a breath of relief and turned her attention back to Jack, who was watching her.

"We should go to the main dance area," Jack suggested. "It will give us a better view of the crowd and the bar."

"Do you dance, Jack?" Shae asked, smiling at a nearby rebel. The woman turned toward her and matched her movement so their bodies moved in rhythm together.

"I know of the basic concept, but no, I have never needed to dance before," he replied, approaching when she beckoned him. Shae held out her hand, which Jack took very hesitantly. She pulled him toward her.

"Dancing isn't something you need to do, unless you are born a dancer," she said. "Sometimes we do it to unwind. Sometimes we do it because we want to."

Jack watched her, amazed by how she managed to match her movements to the strange music. She spun into him, pressing her back against his chest.

"It's all about feeling the music in your very core and the pleasure at the sensation. It's a language we speak with our bodies," she continued to explain. Jack closed his eyes, his heightened sense of smell absorbing her scent. There was a subtle hint of peaches and dew. He opened his eyes again and looked at her.

"Just follow me," Shae said, leading him to the main dance floor. Jack blocked out all the other information flooding his senses, focusing on Shae. They moved to where the music was louder and the crowd larger. Jack took a step back, unsure. Shae reached forward and took his hand again, her green gaze capturing his. Jack glanced to the side and then allowed her to lead him forward.

~~*~*~*

Jensen leaned against the railing next to Isis. They were on the third floor and Isis was surprisingly mellow. She wasn't visibly tense and she seemed to be as relaxed as she got. Her glowing eyes wandered around the Lair, never stopping. Jensen watched as Nero brought out a couple beers to the rebels he was chatting up. He beamed at something one of them said, his attention travelling up to the third floor. Spotting Jensen, he raised his beer bottle and gestured toward the women. He leaned over to them, saying something, and they both snickered as they looked up to Jensen.

"I don't suppose there's any chance you picked up any of that," he mentioned, still needing to yell to be heard over the thundering music. The primary color strobe lights began flashing again, bathing the club in reds and yellows and greens.

"Nero told them of your heritage and their less known legacy of being highly adept at sexual intercourse," Isis responded without missing a beat, looking up when different colored lasers started flashing. "He says your sexual prowess is second only to the Deverells and now he wishes to know if they would be interested in group intercourse. They seem intrigued."

When Isis turned toward him, only her glowing eyes were clearly visible. "I do not understand your insistence on living under your own name. A new identity would increase your chances of survival."

She leaned to the side, looking past him. Jensen turned his head so he could follow her gaze down the hall. The strobe lights came on again, a gold hue flooding the space, illuminating the hallway. There was a short figure standing near the doorway, wearing a strange cloak. The hood was up so Jensen couldn't make out his features. The man, Jensen assumed, resembled a little monk in his nondescript robe. *Probably stepped out of one of the fetish rooms for a bit of air,* Jensen thought as he turned his attention back to the floor below. The smell of smoke and plastic hung in the air with just the faintest hint of sweat. Out of the corner of his eye, he noticed Isis straighten again as her gaze returned to him.

"I do not want to live under an assumed identity because I have no desire to hide," Jensen answered her question. "Shape shifters already know what I look like so it would be rather pointless anyway."

Isis watched him for a moment before looking down to the dance floor. The yellow strobe lights began blinking, bathing her in the primary color. It flashed red, then blue, then green. Each time her skin took the hue of whatever color was lighting up the Lair.

"Nero is imbibing alcohol," she observed, her eyes still roaming over the crowd.

"It's what one tends to do at a club. The rebel Lair is known for their fine assortment of alcohol, most of it quality stuff," Jensen said. "I've never been a fan of public drinking."

"You'd be foolish to do so, with the amount of people trying to kill you," Isis remarked, her attention never moving from the first floor. Jensen couldn't help but chuckle at the blunt statement.

"Well, there's that too."

The strobe lights started blinking again, illuminating the dancers with various colors. Isis moved around Jensen so she was positioned on his other side. Her attention had shifted and was now fixed over her shoulder.

"What's wrong?" Jensen asked. Isis glanced at him, turning so her back was against the railing. She leaned back, resting her elbows on the wooden ledge beneath the thick golden rail.

"It might be nothing," she answered, withdrawing a

long knife in one smooth motion. "Would you mind holding onto this for me? I don't want to lose it."

Jensen stiffened and swiftly opened his jacket, attempting to hide the blade from passersby. "Bloody hell, Isis! You can't just wave a weapon around in public."

"I'm not waving it around, I'm handing it to you," Isis replied, still holding the grip out. He took it from her, making sure he didn't slice her palm open in his haste. Looking around to make sure no one had seen the weapon, Jensen tucked the large battle knife in his belt, hiding it with his jacket. No one in the hall appeared to notice the weapon, which allowed him to breathe a sigh of relief.

"If there's a threat—" Jensen began, but Isis raised a hand to his lips.

"I need you to be quiet for a moment. I'm assessing our surroundings," she explained, looking down to the dance floor again. Jack and Shae were toward the center of the floor. Jack was just as alert as she was, looking around at everything. Their eyes met and Isis lifted her chin up. Jack glanced to where she was indicating, looked back up at her and nodded once.

Jensen looked around, trying to find what the experiments had noticed. The club was a few degrees cooler than normal, especially with the size of the crowd. His eyes traveled across the open space above the dance floor and he noticed another shorter man, identical to the one near the doorway on their side. He was dressed in the same plain brown robe with a hood obscuring his features. Jensen squinted as he tried to get a glimpse of the man's face. The lights began flashing, illuminating the space in golden light again. The strange colors highlighted the man's unnaturally pale flesh, which looked ... scaly. Jensen turned and noticed another shape in the entrance of the nearest hall. Looking down, he noticed more shapes lingering in the doorways and entrances on the first floor.

They're everywhere, Jensen realized as the lasers came on

again, plunging the Lair into shadows.

~~*~*~*

Declan stood up, raising his shot glass. "To my twin brother. May the guardians watch over him as he travels the world."

"Salute."

Brindy and Hunter both raised their shot glasses in the air, toasting their older brother. The rebels sitting with them smiled and downed their shots. Devlin wrapped his arm around the waist of an orange-haired rebel. Hunter looked around, wondering where her own twin had gone. Cassidy always managed to disappear when they were at the Lair.

"I am going to miss this place," Devlin said, drawing Hunter's attention back to the table. "Declan, you should come with me."

"And leave all this behind? Not a chance," Declan replied. "All that diplomacy and leadership stuff is boring. You're the one being groomed for an advisor role and it's definitely one I don't envy."

Hunter smiled as she looked at her brothers. Though they were twins, their personalities were quite different. Declan had always been carefree and free-spirited, much like her and Cassidy. Devlin took more after their parents: responsible, serious, and concerned with the affairs of shape shifters — protectors in particular. It was no surprise when the Monroes had chosen him to train for an advisor role. Both twins had inherited their mother's light-colored hair and sapphire eyes, as had Brindy. Hunter looked much more like her father with her dark hair and blue-green eyes.

The music continued thundering, making conversation almost impossible. The twins soon left with the rebels they were drinking with, heading toward the dance floor. Hunter watched them leave. They passed Jack, who stepped into the bar area. The experiment was barely illuminated by the lights behind the bar but his glowing brown eyes stood out in the dimness. Hunter frowned when he leaned over the bar, speaking to Wylie. *Experiments can't have alcohol,* Hunter remembered as she watched the short interaction. Wylie looked concerned as she reached under the counter and Jack moved back out into the main dance area.

"Jack and Isis seem to be doing okay, at least better than when they first came to the mansion," Brindy mentioned, her gaze wandering to where Jack had been before turning back to her sister. Hunter drank from her beer bottle, enjoying the sensation of the cool liquid sliding down her throat. Though it wasn't as sweltering as it usually was in the Lair, it was still very warm.

"I've noticed the looks you and Coop have been exchanging," Hunter replied. Brindy gave a half-smile, crossing her arms on the table.

"Have you *seen* him? The man is insanely built. And those abs? Damn, talk about engineered perfection," Brindy responded, looking up when a man passed by their table.

"You always did have a thing for the brooding types," Hunter commented with a wicked smile. "Why haven't you fucked his brains out yet?"

Brindy chuckled as she picked up her margarita. "Because I don't want a broken arm. I mean, how do you even go about flirting with an experiment?"

"Ah see that's the benefit of their straight-forwardness," Hunter replied, pointing the neck of her bottle at Brindy. "You just go up to him and say, 'I want to fuck you.'"

Brindy laughed and shook her head. The music changed. A strange short whistle sounded, stopping almost as soon as it started. Hunter looked around for the source of the noise, but couldn't find it. She looked back to her sister.

"So where is Coop? I thought for sure he would come along."

"He said he'll be along later. He wanted to—"

Brindy was cut off when a strong arm suddenly wrapped around her throat and dragged her off the chair. Hunter swiftly jumped off her chair, moving to help her sister, when she felt a blade slice the air where her back had been. She grabbed her bottle and swung, smashing it against the face of her would-be attacker. Hunter froze in shock and horror at what she saw.

The attacker was a shorter creature dressed in a plain brown robe, which was now partially soaked with beer. The lacerations on its face were dripping a thick yellow substance, which had a consistency similar to blood. He held a nasty looking crudely made blunt weapon. Whatever he was, he wasn't human or shape shifter. The face was pointed and triangular like a lizard's, with no visible nose or eyes. What little flesh Hunter could see on his face was chalky white except for the thick charcoal-colored lines that went directly across and down the face, forming a cross. A long gray tongue slid out of his lips, running around the pointed face and cleaning the blood from the lacerations. The creature opened his mouth revealing hundreds of curved pointed teeth. The kind used for ripping flesh apart.

The music was drowned out by screaming and animalistic shrieking. The creature in front of Hunter pounced, leaping forward with his weapon. Instinctively, Hunter grabbed the nearest chair and held it in front of her like a shield. She inhaled sharply when the sharp tip of the weapon stopped inches from her face. Hunter threw the chair as hard as she could and the creature lost its grip on the weapon. It let out a hissing screech and lunged at her, tackling her to the ground. The back of her head connected with the floor, dazing her. Hunter fought and struggled with the creature on top of her. It buried its hooked teeth in her shoulder and shook her viciously, causing her to scream. There was the blast of a shotgun and the creature let her go with a snarl, darting off. Hunter turned on her side, watching as the creature launched itself at a rebel.

"Hunter, you okay?"

Hunter barely heard Wylie's voice or the second shotgun blast. Her eyes fell on where her sister lay a few feet away in a pool of her own blood. A pool that was rapidly growing. Brindy was struggling for breath, blood creeping out of the corner of her mouth. Hunter scrambled to her feet, ignoring the chaos around her. She was almost to her sister's side when one of the large windows exploded inward. Hunter covered her face against the shower of glass. When she looked up, terror immobilized her.

Standing in the middle of the room across from the entrance hall was an enormous gray monstrosity. It vaguely resembled a lion, except the creature was double the size of an adult male. Instead of tawny fur, it was dark gray. Muscles rippled underneath the tough skin and its glowing yellow eyes fixed on Hunter. She could see the enormous fangs poking out from under its lips. They looked to be about the size of her hand. The creature began to advance on the terrified shape shifter. Behind it, more of the lizard-like men clambered through the broken window.

~~*~*~*

Jade and Alpha were in the middle of a pleasant conversation in her office when the screaming and crashing started. It sounded as though a war had spontaneously begun. Alpha, sitting behind her desk, swung her legs off the desktop while Jade stood from her chair and looked toward the black door.

"What the fu—"

A bullet pierced the large window in Alpha's office and

both women threw themselves to the floor. Jade motioned for Alpha to put her desk chair in front of her, which Alpha quickly did. Cold air whistled through the large hole in the pane of glass. Jade crawled over to the side of the desk, pressing her back against it.

"Don't suppose you have a remote for the lights in here?" she whispered over to Alpha. The rebel leader smiled thinly and reached up to the top drawer of her desk, pulling it open and removing a small black switch. Another shot sounded and more glass broke, causing both women to flinch. Alpha pressed a button and the lights dimmed until only a couple lamps lighted the office.

"Can you draw the curtains?"

Alpha pressed another button and the drapes slid shut with a soft whooshing sound, concealing the enormous glass window. Jade peered over the desk, making sure the sniper couldn't see them. She looked back to Alpha, questioningly. The rebel leader wiggled the remote.

"It pays to have a couple techies on hand," she explained, pressing the first button again so the lights came on and illuminated the large office again. "We've got some girls who just love engineering and gadgets. Such talents come in handy."

"Are you hit?" Jade asked. Alpha glanced over her shoulder, harrumphing when she saw the large holes in the red wall.

"Fucking protectors. Every time you come around, you bring destruction with you," she grumbled as she adjusted one of the thick cuffs on her wrist. Jade reached up to the desk, feeling around until she found the phone. The door burst open and three strange-looking creatures charged into the office. Two ran up the walls while the third launched itself straight at Jade, knocking her backward. Alpha reached under her desk, pulling out the sawed off shotgun she kept there, and fired at the creature on top of Jade. The shot hit him directly in the temple, destroying his skull and showering Jade with yellow blood and bits of brain.

"Well, there's a new kind of golden shower," Alpha mentioned offhandedly. Jade glared at the rebel as she pushed the bulky carcass off her.

"Really?" she asked as Alpha tapped the middle drawer in her desk with the muzzle of her gun. The rebel's attention never moved from the walls in her office.

"I can't help it. Sometimes life just hands you one," Alpha responded as Jade pulled open the drawer she had indicated. She grabbed the silver handgun inside, quickly slid out the magazine and checked it before sliding it back into place. Jade moved so she was standing back-to-back with Alpha, her gun pointed at the opposite wall.

"Let's kill these things and then go help the others," Jade whispered, her eyes sharp for any kind of movement.

"I'm more interested in saving my club and the rebels who live here, but that seems to line up with your plan," Alpha mentioned. "So we'll do it your way."

The creatures came into view again, launching themselves at the women. Both fired and the creatures fell to the ground, dead. Alpha put the sawed off shotgun back on the desk, opened another drawer, and pulled out a black Beretta.

"After you," she said to Jade, gesturing toward the office door. The force had splintered the doorframe and damaged the top hinges, which Jade was sure Alpha would complain about later. Jade moved to the door, Alpha following on her heels.

~~*~*~*

Jensen leapt back when another of the strange short men swung at him with a sickle. The sharp curved blade sliced through his jacket, but missed his flesh. Sweat was dripping down his brow.

"Hey! This is a nice suit," Jensen snapped as he thrust

forward with his long knife. The creature blocked and kicked out at him, snarling. Jensen feinted right and when the creature went to block, the protector buried his knife in its throat. It took a bit of effort and Jensen had to put his weight into it, but he managed to pierce the flesh. When the creature fell, Jensen put a foot on his chest and jerked the blade free. Foul-smelling yellow blood streamed out of the wound.

Jensen wiped his brow with the back of his hand, looking over to where Isis fought. She put one foot on a creature's chest and pushed off, using her other foot to strike him under the chin so he fell backward. When she landed, she immediately dropped down to avoid the blade of another creature. Coming up, she slammed her elbow into the attacker's face. She spun around and cut open the creature's throat before turning her attention back to the one she had knocked down. Before he could climb back to his feet, she had buried the longest prong of her sai in his skull. Isis kicked the carcass off her weapon, turning her attention back to Jensen. Yellow blood had sprayed up in her face at some point. By Jensen's count, she had already killed several of the creatures but he was certain she had killed even more. Whereas he was struggling to fight two at a time, Isis was cutting through them as if they weren't even there.

Hearing a hiss nearby, Jensen leaned over the railing and stabbed one in the head with the knife Isis had handed him. The creatures were crawling up the wall as though gravity didn't affect them. The one Jensen stabbed plummeted to the ground, landing on two other creatures. Their animalistic hissing was heard all over the Lair and the stench of blood was heavy in the air.

"What are these things?" Jensen yelled over to Isis as she leapt up and skewered one on the ceiling, who had been trying to get the drop on her from above. She yanked her sai free as the body dropped to the ground and withdrew a throwing knife from her boot.

"Followers of Set, low-level demons," she answered, hurling the knife with impressive ease. Jensen leaned back as the knife sailed past him, sinking deeply into the skull of another creature that had been advancing on him. Jensen thrust forward when one creature attempted to pounce on him. Using his attacker's forward momentum, Jensen tossed him over the railing.

"How many do you think there are?"

"Depends on why they've been sent, but I've never seen a pack smaller than a hundred," Isis answered as she ran to the wall, pushed off it with her foot, and punched another creature in the face. She stomped on its throat, grinding her heel until the creature choked up blood. She approached the creature she had killed earlier and retrieved her throwing knife, wiping off the blade on the creature's robes. The sound of a loud growl, similar to a big cat, drew their attention to the first floor. Both Isis and Jensen returned to the railing, peering over it. They both ducked back behind the cover of the wall when a wave of crossbow bolts rained on them. There was a series of loud thunks as the bolts embedded in the opposite wall.

"They brought a werelion," Isis observed as she stood back up, thrusting her sai back and through another follower. She yanked her weapon free and the creature fell.

"Wereanimals are extinct. The last of them were destroyed in the early 1900s," Jensen said as he looked down to the main dance area, wincing when he saw Nero sail backward and crash into a section of tables and chairs. The dance floor was already littered with dead and wounded rebels, but many more were still fighting fiercely. They used whatever they could grab to fight against the followers. One rebel woman with bright pink hair had grabbed the leg of a broken chair and was using it to bash in the skull of a creature with a crossbow. As he searched the crowd, Jensen couldn't find the Monroes, Shae, or Jack. The sound of a crash brought his attention back to the left, where Isis had thrown one of the creatures into the wall. She deflected a couple strikes of his crude weapon, her sais flashing as she stabbed the creature repeatedly in the chest. Pinning him against the wall, she drove the longest prong of the weapon straight up through the creature's chin and into its brain. Yellow fluid streamed down her arm as she yanked her weapon free, allowing the body to drop.

"Don't get distracted," Isis warned as she snap kicked another attacking creature. "Make sure you destroy the brain. You don't want these things coming back."

Jensen lashed out at another creature. He was a little unnerved by how unbothered Isis was about the chaos surrounding them. Violence didn't faze her in the slightest.

"Jensen, Isis, what the hell is going on?"

Jensen turned when he heard Alex's shout. She was standing in the entrance of one of the halls, holding a fire axe dripping with yellow blood. There was a nasty-looking scratch on her cheek, which bled lazily.

"I was in the library room when a shelf fell over. The next thing I knew, there were about ten of these weird reptile-looking creatures crawling on the walls and trying to attack everyone in the room."

"They're followers of Set," Isis answered, holding her sais at her side. "Is that weapon adequate? I could lend you one of mine."

Jensen turned to look at Isis, wondering just how many weapons she had managed to sneak into the rebel Lair. She had no pockets. Most of the weapons were tucked in the belt she wore around her waist or in her boots. What he found most remarkable was there were no bulges to indicate she had weapons on her. She seemed to pull them out of thin air. *Definitely need to find out where she gets her gear,* he thought. The nauseating stench of the creatures' blood turned Jensen's stomach. It was a different smell than normal blood; one that had a distinct scent of rot. It was similar to the smell of necrotic tissue.

Alex turned and buried the pointed edge of her axe in a

creature's skull. She yanked it free and the body crumpled. Swinging the axe again at a creature running toward them, Alex buried it in his head, knocking him flat on his back. The creature twitched and shook before going still.

"Seems adequate enough," Alex said as she pulled the axe free. "Do we know where Shae and Jade are?"

A shotgun blast sounded from somewhere below them. Isis turned and buried the prong of her sai in the chest of a follower trying to creep up behind her, pulling it free again. He swung at her with a curved blade and she easily ducked under it, moving behind him and stabbing the back of his neck. The creature fell and she kicked the body out of her way.

"This would be much easier with my guns," Isis mentioned. She moved over to the railing and looked down to the dance floor when the music cut out. A creature's hand shot up, grabbing for her throat. She leaned back and plunged her sai straight through the wrist, pinning it to the ledge. Yellow blood dribbled up around the wound. The creature howled and shrieked in agony, thrashing about and trying to pull its hand free. Isis was unbothered as she turned back to the two protectors.

"One of you, call the mansion. We need back up and I want my guns," Isis instructed, ignoring the agonized howls and struggling of the creature as she yanked her sai free, letting him fall. "I'll watch your backs and keep them from swarming you."

Isis turned her attention back to the attacking creatures, slashing the face of one. Jensen exchanged a concerned look with Alex before pulling out his cell phone.

Alex blocked a blow from a follower who attacked her from the right. She deflected the crude sword with the axe. The creature feinted and thrust forward, nearly impaling the protector. Alex spun away from the thrust, ending up behind the creature. She swung the axe, burying the head in the back of the creature's neck and he crumpled. A forked slimy tongue caressed her cheek and she pulled away from the revolting sensation. The creature on the ceiling lunged at her, only to be brought down by Isis' sais.

"Coop should be here in a few minutes," Jensen reported as he returned to them, stabbing an advancing creature.

"Not sure the normals have that long," Isis said, lifting her leg and kicking back, knocking down the creature behind her.

~~*~*~*

Jack stabbed and sliced at a follower, eviscerating the creature. Yellow blood sprayed up in his face. Shae was nearby, fighting back the swarm of creatures. There was a nasty gash on her arm, but she seemed to still have use of it. Jack spun into a reverse kick, knocking another creature away.

He saw a follower tackle a rebel and snap at the young man, attempting to bite his face. Jack moved to the man's aid. He yanked the follower off the rebel and threw the creature. The creature yowled as he slid across the floor, crashing into another follower. The regular lights came on, flooding the hotel with brightness. A few of the followers let out angry hisses, but continued their brutal attack. The stench of rot and blood was beginning to get overpowering. The ground was slippery with the amount of blood being spilled. Pools of yellow and red mingled on the ground.

Jack and Shae both turned at the sound of another roar. Shae lunged forward, stabbing a follower who had been advancing on Jack. No matter how many they killed, more of the weird creatures kept coming. They were everywhere. On the walls, on the floor, on the ceiling, in the halls. Shae paused to wipe some sweat from her brow. Jack ran toward her and leapt up into the air. Shae lunged out of the way, watching as his knife sunk deep into the skull of another creature that had been behind her.

"Nice jump," she complimented as Jack pulled his knife free. He glanced over at her before lunging at another attacker, quickly dispatching the creature.

"We need back up," Jack mentioned. "These things travel in large packs and they don't stop until they're dead or their quarry is."

Shae let out a yelp when another creature got in a lucky strike and sliced the back of her shoulder. She kicked backward and spun around, thrusting forward with the battle knife Jack had given her. The blade went through the creature's throat, yellow blood flowing down her hand. As she pulled the blade free again, Shae noticed Wylie and Amber run out from the bar area. Wylie was reloading her shotgun. The ground seemed to shake and Shae looked over to Jack, who was watching the bar area with wide glowing eyes.

A huge lion-type creature emerged from the bar, its glowing yellow eyes fixed on the two rebel bartenders. Shae moved across the floor to help when the creature turned on her, causing her to stop mid-step. The animal bared its enormous fangs and roared as it started advancing, glass and wood crunching under its enormous paws. Shae held her battle knife, which looked ridiculously small compared to the animal in front of her. She started backing up.

"Jack, what the hell is this thing?" Shae called over to the experiment without taking her attention off the advancing animal. Out of the corner of her eye, Shae could see Jack circling around the creature, attempting to stick to whatever shadows remained. The melee around him and bright lights made it difficult, but he managed somehow. The animal's attention remained fixed on Shae as she continued backing up while Jack's eyes were fixed on the monster. Right as Jack began to raise his knife, the large animal turned on him and swatted with one of its enormous paws. Jack managed to roll under it, but the creature caught him with a back swing. The blow sent Jack flying and Shae winced when he slammed into a wall. Jack fell to the floor, some plaster sprinkling down on his head. He looked a little dazed and there was a large gash on his head, which was already sealing up. The creature began stalking toward him.

There was a barely audible metallic whisper and the creature's skull seemed to cave in. The enormous monster crumpled in a heap and Shae looked up to where the noise had come from.

Isis was standing on the railing up on the third floor. She lowered the guns she held, glancing at Shae. Then, the experiment turned and hopped off the railing, disappearing.

~~*~*~*

Hunter fought back against the five creatures grabbing at her. She screamed when one grasped her short hair and dragged her backward. They were trying to pull her outside and Hunter decided she would rather die than be taken hostage. She kicked out at one reptile-like man, catching him in the gut. He stumbled back a couple steps, but otherwise seemed unaffected. Hunter glanced over her shoulder, feeling a twinge of panic when she saw one creature reaching for the door, which was closer than she had thought.

"No! No!" she yelled, scratching at the face of one of the reptilian creatures who held her. The sound of metallic shots caused the small group to scatter, all hissing angrily. Hunter was dropped to the ground. She winced as glass shards cut into her palms. The young protector looked in the direction of the shots.

Coop stood in the middle of the staircase, holding a gun similar to the ones Isis had. His firearms were silver, instead of black like hers. He smoothly moved to the handrail and leapt over it, dropping to the ground. The experiment landed with unnatural ease and grace, moving forward as soon as his feet touched the ground. He was at Hunter's side in a matter of seconds, firing a few more shots to scatter the strange creatures even more. Grabbing ahold of Hunter's arm, Coop pulled her to her feet and pushed her behind him. His glowing eyes never moved from the creatures in front of them. Their heads moved side to side like snakes and they made strange hissing noises. The creatures were never still and never quiet.

"Where are your brothers and sister?" Coop asked, his eyes sharp as they scanned the area for enemies. Most of the reptilian men had fallen back, growling and hissing at the experiment. Hunter was clutching Coop's arm, her nails digging into his flesh. For one of the first times in her life, she was scared. She had been around rowdy drunks and pervs who got a little too handsy before, but these creatures were a new danger. Hunter heard flesh tearing and looked over to the bar area, feeling vomit rise in her throat when she saw two reptilian men tearing apart the body of a rebel. They snapped at each other, fighting for meat from the corpse.

"Hunter, focus!" Coop ordered. "Where are your siblings?"

"Brindy!" Hunter remembered her sister, running away from Coop. She heard him yell for her to wait, but ignored him as she sprinted to the staircase. Brindy was still lying beside the staircase in a pool of her own blood. Hunter reached her side and felt nauseous all over again. Her sister's eyes were glassy and her entire body was trembling. Hunter ignored the warm feeling on her knees as she knelt in blood.

"Brindy, the cavalry has arrived," Hunter attempted to reassure her sister, taking one of her cold clammy hands. Brindy seemed unable to focus on anything, but winced when she heard another gunshot.

"Coop, help!"

Coop moved over to where the two sisters were,

glancing down at the wounded protector and assessing the situation as fast as he could.

"She's lost a lot of blood," he observed, glancing over at the creatures. "She's going into shock."

Coop looked around, spotting a rebel with neon yellow hair nearby. The scent was masculine, but all outward indicators suggested a woman. Coop swiftly moved over to her and ducked when she swung the chair leg she was holding.

"Are you a good shot?" he asked, pressing his gun into her hands when she nodded. "There's a severely wounded shape shifter over by the stairs. I need you to cover me so I can help her. Can you do that?"

The woman was wide-eyed with fear and her heart hammered in her chest, but she followed Coop as he returned to the side of the stairs. He stripped off his jacket and withdrew a long knife from his belt. He knelt down beside the two sisters, unaffected by the sound of gunfire. Trusting a stranger to watch his back was a risk, but one he had to take if he wanted to do any good.

"Coop?" Brindy's voice was faint and shaky. Hunter looked at him, her wide blue-green eyes pleading. Coop handed the youngest Monroe his knife, which she took without question or protest.

"It's me," Coop assured her as he set about assessing her wounds. They were too clean to have been made by one of the crude weapons carried by the followers, yet there was a slight raggedness to the wounds that suggested a sharp serrated blade. *Only the higher ups and their personal cleaners carry weapons like that,* Coop remembered, looking around again. Balling up his jacket, he pressed it against the deep wounds in her stomach. She cried out and squirmed, blood creeping out from the corners of her mouth.

"You have to try to remain still. I need to staunch the blood flow," Coop said, glancing around. The followers seemed to focus their numbers in the main areas, which told Coop something else was coming. Whatever it was, it was probably a lot nastier than followers and a werelion.

"You're so tense."

Coop looked at Brindy, ignoring the warmth of her blood beneath his hands. It was already soaking through the jacket. She needed guardian healing, desperately. If she didn't receive it in the next few minutes, she wasn't going to make it.

"Experiments often tense up in the midst of a battle. It keeps us ready for an attack," Coop explained. Brindy smiled faintly at him, coughing. She grimaced in pain.

"Brindy, I'm going to need you to stay awake," Coop stated when she started to close her eyes. "You need to stay awake for a little while longer."

"Easy for you to say. You don't sleep," she protested. She shuddered again. Coop looked over at her, noticing she was beginning to have difficulty breathing and her skin had an unnatural pallor.

"I used to, ages ago," he replied, his gaze darting around as he remained alert for an attack.

"I wish I could have shown you Rome, like we talked about in January," Brindy said quietly, letting out a shaky breath. "I'm scared, Coop."

"Don't be. I won't let anything further happen to you."

He could see tears welling up in her glassy eyes and, unsure of what else to do, reached out and gently brushed some hair away from her face.

"You need to Appear with her in the Meadows," Hunter said insistently, but Coop shook his head.

"I can't. See how the creatures are hanging around, just out of range? They're waiting to catch a ride," he explained. "If even one got into the Meadows, it would be very bad."

Hunter looked around and saw the creatures on the ceiling and peeking around the walls. The rebel turned and shot at one who was crawling across the wall over the staircase.

"If I start to disappear, they'll rush you and chances are at least two will manage to get to the Meadows. We can't risk that," he finished as he turned his attention back to Brindy. He frowned, noticing her eyes were closed.

"Brindy? Brindy, wake up," Coop commanded, pressing two fingers on the side of her throat. He felt around for her pulse, ignoring Hunter's questions. Unable to find the young protector's pulse, Coop started doing chest compressions. Next to him, he heard the rebel fire another few rounds.

~~*~*~*

Alex and Jensen stood in the midst of numerous bodies of the reptilian followers. The creatures' yellow blood oozed out from the wounds they had received. Both protectors were tired and sweaty. They were covered in grime and blood. The smell in the Lair was awful, a combination of blood and rot. Isis was also covered in grime and blood, but she hadn't broken a sweat and continued to move with ease. Nothing was slowing her down. She was using everything around her to fight. Pushing off walls, leaping onto the railing, gliding across the floor, and darting straight at any hostiles. They had seen her swing her body around a pillar to knock down two creatures.

Jensen glanced to the side when he heard another round of bullets being fired somewhere across the open area. Isis soon emerged out of one of the hallways, holstering her gun as she moved toward them. She drew her sais from the sheaths she wore on her belt, not slowing her pace. A follower sprang up from behind the railing overlooking the main dance floor. Without even looking, Isis thrust out her sai, burying the longest prong deep within the center of the creature's face and yanking it out again.

"This floor is clear," she reported as the creature plummeted. "We should move down to the second."

Jensen glanced over at Alex, wondering how much longer they could keep fighting. The lights went out, plunging the Lair into darkness. The club became unnaturally quiet the instant the lights went out, as if a mute button had been pressed. Jensen and Alex felt a hand on their shoulders shortly before Isis pulled them down, next to the wall.

"You two need a moment to regain your energy," she whispered. "Followers can't see in dim lighting, not as well as shape shifters can. Stay against the wall and you will be safe."

There was a strange brief whistling and then a spotlight came on with a loud snap. Jensen rested his head against the wall behind him, taking a moment. The followers were quick and brutal. He found he had to think two moves ahead of them to avoid getting eviscerated. Even then, Isis had to watch his back. Jensen was a skilled fighter, but he had his limits. He could hear Alex panting next to him. Both of them looked to the large white beam, which was aimed at the bottom floor.

"Hello? Is the owner of this establishment still alive? Or anyone else for that matter?"

The jaunty masculine voice echoed throughout the Lair and the change in Isis' posture was instantaneous. She went rigid and Jensen noticed a tremor travel down her arm. Her glowing green eyes widened and it was as close to scared as he had seen her since her return.

"Isis, what is it?" Alex asked. Isis didn't answer as she crawled on all fours to the railing, straightening up just enough so she could peer over the ledge. Jensen glanced over at Alex, but his attention was drawn to something over her shoulder. There was a small group of followers who appeared to be frozen in mid-step a short way down the hall. A few had their mouths open, all had their weapons drawn, but it looked as though they had been petrified in amber. Alex followed his gaze and stared at the strange scene. Jensen swallowed and moved over to where Isis was near the ledge, peering down at the dance floor.

Standing atop the DJ table was a man dressed in a cream-colored suit with a matching bowler hat. He was holding a fancy cane and his hands were folded over the silver knob on the top. Jensen squinted when he noticed the dark circles around the stranger's eyes — the symbol of Ares. His pale blue eyes roamed about the club, searching for someone or something.

"I'm the club owner," Alpha's strong voice came from the second floor. Jensen looked down to where she stood with Jade. "Who the hell are you?"

"Ah. Good evening, my lady," the man said as he removed his bowler hat, revealing a full head of sandy brown hair, and bowed low in Alpha's direction. "Allow me to introduce myself. My name is Nick Chance and I am the local Grenich liaison."

Isis sank down, hiding from view. Jensen glanced over at her, noticing she had closed her eyes. Jensen looked back to Nick, who put his hat back on and crossed his hands on his cane again. His fingers were long and it looked as though he had recently had a manicure.

"I come to extend an olive branch," Nick continued, to which Alpha laughed loudly.

"Well Nick, you sure have a funny way of doing so," she said. Nick's sharp features clouded briefly, but his smile remained in place.

"It was rather impolite to barge in unannounced, I admit. Very bad manners on our part, but a necessary demonstration. You see, a war is coming. I assume all of you feel it, that tension in the air. It sends chills down the spine — it's almost orgasmic." He shivered and let out a breath, smiling even wider. "Now, Jet and Lilly have made a very foolish decision to keep two very dangerous weapons under their roof."

Nick paused, sniffing the air. "Oh, so there are three

here tonight then?" He sniffed again. "And the last Aldridge too. My, what interesting patrons the rebels have."

Alex looked over to Jensen and he leaned down to Isis.

"Now might be a good time to shoot him," he suggested. She looked up at him.

"That is not a wise strategy," she whispered. Jensen looked back over the ledge at the strange man. He noticed movement in the shadows behind Nick and felt his heart skip a couple beats when he spotted Cassidy sneaking up on the strange man.

"Don't know what you're talking about, Nick, but I would suggest speaking quickly and clearly. Rebels aren't known for our forgiving nature," Alpha warned coolly. The smile seemed to widen on Nick's face. He twisted and clobbered Cassidy with the head of his cane, dropping the young protector quickly and efficiently. Turning back to an infuriated Alpha, Nick spun the cane around once and held the bloodied knob close to his face. He ran his tongue over the silver knob, licking the blood off, smirking.

"I come here on behalf of Set. He wishes to extend a hand of friendship to all non-protectors. They have chosen their side and it will be their downfall. If you ally with Grenich, you will be under our protection and you will be spared any further ugliness. As you are undoubtedly aware, we are *very* good at war."

Nick raised his hand and snapped his fingers. Jensen looked to the side when he saw a glint of light. The followers melted away into a pile of ash, disintegrating within a matter of seconds.

"Our friendship would be very beneficial to the rebels, as local assassins will attest," Nick mentioned. "And should you offer information that leads to the Corporation reacquiring its stolen goods, the rewards shall be far beyond your wildest dreams."

Nick tapped his cane three times on the DJ table. Smoke began to rise around him and the sigils carved in the wood of the cane started to glow.

"I will leave you to bury your dead and consider this most generous offer. I trust you will choose wisely."

His pale blue gaze turned to where Jensen was on the third floor. The glowing sigils brightened even more and the smoke thickened.

"See you around," Nick said, already sounding far away. There was an enormous flash of light and a puff of white smoke. When it cleared, the table was empty and the representative had vanished.

CHAPTER THREE

The Lair was in shambles. Broken glasses and bottles, shattered windows, tables and chairs scattered in complete disarray, makeshift weapons abandoned wherever they had been dropped, holes and tears in the wall. There was blood everywhere — sprayed across the walls and the floor.

Jet stepped into the rebel Lair and was surrounded by the moans of the wounded and dying. He heard his adopted son, Jay, enter after him. The protector leader moved through the club in a daze. Everywhere he looked, there were wounded shape shifters. Or dead ones. There was also a strange amount of ash scattered across the floor.

A shimmering light appeared to his left and within seconds, Amethyst and four other healers stood there. Jet could hear Amethyst give orders to the healers and the glass crunched under their feet as they hurried off to help the wounded. Steve stood next to him, not saying a word. He had arrived first and made sure there were no more enemies lurking about before giving Jet the all-clear signal.

"Jet?"

It was the first time Alpha had ever spoken to him with anything resembling compassion. There was no bite to her words and if it had been any other time, Jet would have been shocked and probably a little uneasy. As it was, he could barely turn his head to look at her. She had a large cut going down her cheek and another across her chest, likely made from some kind of crude blade. Bruises decorated her arms and he was sure her sleeveless shirt concealed even more. Her tight jeans were ripped above the knees, but Jet couldn't tell if that was purposeful or the result of the fight. Her dark eyes regarded him and she lifted her chin in greeting to Jay.

"They're in a room on the second floor. This way."

She began to walk toward the stairway. Jet hesitated, unsure if he wanted to follow her. Alpha reached the bottom step and waited for him. He turned to Steve, trying to think of what to say. Out of the corner of his eye, Jet could see twin women in red uniforms sweeping up the shattered glass. Both women looked exhausted, but continued sweeping.

"Stay here. Keep an eye out for any trouble. See how everyone else is. And give Isis and Jack the thing Orion sent," Jet requested, his voice shaking a little. Steve nodded, understanding what Jet wanted. He moved toward the dance area and Jet turned back to Alpha, Jay following close behind. Every step seemed to take effort and everything sounded distant, like they were walking through a tunnel. As they started to climb the stairs, Jet noticed the shape shifters on the stairs would shrink away. Most still looked terrified.

"Are they okay?" Jet wasn't sure if he asked the question out loud. Alpha looked at him and then the shape shifters on the stairs. She reached down and smoothed one's hair.

"Hallucinogens and an ambush by reptile men aren't the best mix," she answered as she continued leading him up the stairs. "The drugs will wear off by morning. After that, it's anyone's guess."

Jet cleared his throat. "Sly said she would stop by later."

Alpha nodded, the only indication that she had heard him.

When they reached the second floor, Alpha stopped Jet and turned to face him. "This is supposed to be a safe haven, Jet. Grenich came onto my turf and killed a lot of my people."

Jet was still unable to process everything and didn't know how to respond. When Jade called to tell him what happened, he couldn't believe it. Malone, Devin, and Ajax had all wanted to come, but Jet didn't want too many people on the scene. Knowing them, they had probably followed anyway. Lilly had gone to the Meadows to get the healers and was waiting for him there. *I'm glad she doesn't have to see this,* he thought as a burning sensation developed in his eyes. Jet was doing his best to remain stoic, but it was increasingly difficult.

"This will not go unpunished," he swore to Alpha. "I give you my word."

"No, Jet. None of this diplomacy, fair trial by guardian bullshit," Alpha responded sharply. "You've got three living weapons. I want you to point them at that fucking place and pull the trigger. I want every last one of the scumbags responsible for this slaughter to be hunted down and obliterated."

Jet inhaled shakily, closing his eyes for a moment. "I cannot promise you that. I can only give you my word that justice will be done."

Alpha grumbled something under her breath and continued down the hall. Jet followed her until she stopped at a door and knocked once. Upon receiving no answer, she opened it and stood aside, gesturing for the protector to enter. His breath caught in his throat as he walked into the well-lit room. The curtains were drawn over the windows, blocking out the night.

The first one he saw was Coop. The tall man was standing against the wall, his stormy glowing blue gaze fixed on the door. When he saw Jet, he silently stepped past him and left the room. *He was standing watch,* Jet realized as he looked over his shoulder, watching the experiment disappear somewhere outside. Coop's blood encrusted hands had not escaped his notice. Stepping further into the room, he could hear soft sobs and prepared himself.

"Dad!"

Hunter's shaky voice almost broke his heart as his youngest ran over to him, wrapping her arms around him like she had when she was much younger. He wrapped his arms around her, hugging her tightly, and gently kissed the top of her head. When she winced, Jet looked down and noticed her wounded shoulder. It was wrapped with a makeshift bandage that was already soaked in bright red blood. He glanced up when her twin brother, Cassidy, stepped around the corner, holding a towel to his head. There was a nasty-looking gash on his forehead, which was bleeding heavily. Only the towel prevented blood from getting into his eye. Cassidy looked shell-shocked and swayed a little on his feet. Jet wondered if he had a concussion.

"You're hurt," he observed, trying to get a better look at Hunter's wound. "You both need to get to the Meadows right now. Jay, please go with them."

Hunter sniffled, unable to stop crying. The last time Jet had heard his youngest cry, she had been a toddler. Though they were emotional creatures, shape shifters didn't cry as often as humans did. Jet watched as Jay led Hunter and Cassidy out of the room before turning back, steeling himself for what he knew he would find.

Jet stepped further into the room and he soon saw the bodies. Declan was hunched over the body of his twin brother, oblivious to the rest of the world. Brindy's body was closer to him. She had been covered in a bloody coat, likely one that had been used to try and stem the bleeding. Jet stepped toward the bodies, stopping when he was standing in front of them. Devlin had been stabbed in the chest and it looked as though his throat had been slit. Declan was bleeding from more than a few wounds himself, but his attention remained fixed on his fallen brother. He didn't even acknowledge his father and Jet wondered if he even knew he was there. Jet sank to his knees, his eyes never moving from the bodies of his children. *I shouldn't have let them go out,* he thought. *We knew Grenich was overdue to attack. They should have stayed home, where they were safe.*

Though Jet knew he never would have been able to keep them locked up in the mansion, he still felt the heavy weight of self-recrimination. He heard Alpha step back out into the hall, closing the door behind her. Once the door closed, Jet felt the tears flowing down his face and he let out a wail of grief.

~~*~*~*

Jensen looked up when Isis dropped from the fifth floor. She landed in a crouching position and straightened up almost immediately, moving over to where Jensen and Nero were sitting on one of the benches. A number of rebels were staring at her and a few leaned forward to look upward, marveling at the height. Isis was alert as she always was, her eyes wandering all about the club. Jensen was also on edge, adrenaline still coursing through his body. He looked around at the destruction. It looked even worse in the regular light.

"Am I supposed to be able to taste my internal organs?" Nero moaned. He was lying on the bench, one arm draped over his face. Jensen looked across the way to where one of the healers was fixing a rebel's broken arm. She was a younger black woman, dressed in the soft pink shades many healers wore. Jensen watched as she gently took the rebel's arm and held her hand over it, purple light emanating from her palm. Within moments, the bone snapped back into place and the large gash on the shape shifter's arm vanished. The rebel stared at his repaired limb, wonderment reflecting on his face. He flexed his fingers a few times and looked up at the healer, who stood up again and moved over to the next wounded rebel.

"It is not possible to taste your own organs. It is likely you have internal damage and what you taste is blood," Isis stated, bringing Jensen's attention back to them.

Nero lifted his arm and looked at her. "Has anyone told you that your bedside manner needs *a lot* of work?"

Isis looked puzzled. "I am not modified for such work."

Jensen noticed Steve standing near Amethyst, who pointed over to them and gestured to the young healer. The woman moved over the destruction and approached them. Jensen was happy to see she had at least worn sandals. In the Meadows, guardians often went barefoot. With the amount of glass and debris covering the floor, Jensen didn't even want to think about how torn up her feet would have gotten.

"Hello, I don't believe we've met before," Nero said when the young healer knelt in front of them, his fake brogue slipping into place. "I'm Nero Deverell, youngest son of Dayton."

Jensen grinned and shook his head, wondering if there was anyone his friend wouldn't flirt with. Nero was known for his flirtatious nature and his reputation wouldn't change anytime soon. The young guardian smiled shyly as her hands hovered just over his body, purple light emanating from beneath her palms.

"My name is Eir," she said politely as she continued to examine him, her brow furrowing. "My goodness, every one of your ribs has been broken or cracked."

"A giant werelion batting you about like a cat toy will do that to a shape shifter," Jensen mentioned. Eir looked over at him, shocked. Wereanimals had been extinct for so long, they'd been reduced to a scary monster only found in stories and old texts. Jensen turned his attention to the tear in his jacket and shirt. *No saving this,* he thought, irritated, as he examined the ragged slit the follower's weapon had left. The clothing was filthy with the rancid-smelling blood. He rubbed his forehead, trying to wrap his mind around what happened. An old memory of fire and screaming came unbidden to him. Jensen cleared his throat and straightened his already straight sleeves, banishing the images from his mind.

As Eir began to care for Nero — who kept insisting he was fine and didn't feel a thing — Jensen turned his attention to where Isis was. She crouched next to a body, lifting up a corner of the sheet covering it. The three experiments had been the only ones who emerged unscathed from the attack. Jack approached her and Isis glanced up when his shadow fell over her.

"Eir, I don't think I've seen you around the Meadows before," Nero's voice was a little stronger. Jensen looked back to him and noticed he had been healed. The youngest Deverell now sat up and was laying the charm on thick.

"Oh, I just started my apprenticeship not that long ago," Eir replied, still shyly. Jensen looked around to the other healers, not recognizing any of them. *Must be the newest apprentices,* he thought as he watched one of the two men step over a broken chair and approach an unconscious rebel man. Though young, they moved with the distinctive guardian grace and their skin shimmered faintly.

"First time on Earth?" Jensen asked, to which she nodded.

"It's rarely ever like this. You should let me—" Nero began.

"Eir!" Amethyst's stern voice sounded over all the other noise. "There are numerous wounded shape shifters who need attention. Quit dawdling and get to work. This isn't a vacation."

Eir bowed her head and stood up, hurrying off to care

for a wounded rebel who lay nearby. Nero flopped back against the platform behind them, observing the mess that surrounded them.

"Alpha must be so pissed," he said, looking over at Jensen. "How many casualties?"

Jensen cleared his throat and pressed his palms together. Nero had been unconscious when they found him and remained so while the bodies were covered up. He didn't know about the losses they had suffered, having only come to a few minutes before the healers arrived. Jensen could see his friend looking over at him expectantly and heard Nero's cell phone buzz in his pocket, as it had been doing for the past half-hour. Jensen's own phone had been going off regularly. He assumed it was the Deverells wanting to know if everything was all right.

"Jensen? What is it? What happened?"

"Hey," Jade stepped in front of them, saving Jensen from having to answer. "Orion wants us to collect some samples to bring back to the mansion. Can you two help Steve protect the guardians?"

"Can I watch over young Eir?" Nero asked suggestively.

"Guardians have mercy, Nero, can you not think about sex for one damn minute?" Jade snapped as she turned and moved off to where Isis was still examining a chewed up body. Jack was using tweezers to pull something out of the gory mess that had once been a shape shifter. Nero and Jensen's attention was drawn to Coop as he entered the dance area. One of the healers, the younger of the two men, scurried away when Coop passed by him. The experiment didn't pay him any heed. Of the three experiments, Coop was by far the most accustomed to the outside world. He was able to move differently, more like a regular shape shifter, than either Jack or Isis, and the nervousness of others didn't put him on edge quite as much.

"Coop," Jensen called his name and the experiment

paused, looking over to him. "I think Orion wants you to help collect samples. Jade knows more than I do."

Coop turned his gaze to the DJ table, moving toward it and hopping up on the step behind the table, standing where the DJ normally would. His stormy blue eyes traveled over the area where Nick Chance had stood only a couple hours earlier. He tapped the table with a blood-stained finger.

"Someone should swab this table. There is some kind of residue and a scent that's unfamiliar to me," he mentioned, hopping down from the DJ area. "I will return shortly."

Nero and Jensen both watched him as he disappeared around a corner, likely heading for the bathrooms. Nero looked back at Jensen, expectantly. Jensen leaned back, turning his eyes up to the domed ceiling.

"Fifteen rebels were killed, another twenty wounded," Jensen began. "We lost a few protectors as well."

~~*~*~*

Isis looked over her shoulder to Nero and Jensen, noticing the change in Nero's posture. He slumped over his knees, dragging a hand down his face. Gone was the flirtatious lothario and in his place was a grieving man. Isis turned her gaze back to her three teammates as Jack stood up, screwing the top back on the vial he held.

"Jet's going to Appear back in the Meadows with the bodies," Jade mentioned as she rubbed the back of her neck. "Lilly's waiting for him there. They'll need to make arrangements."

Jack glanced over at her before removing another vial from the case Steve had brought them. He went over to the DJ table, where Coop indicated there was residue. Shae watched him go, waiting until he was out of hearing range before turning back to the three women and leaning forward.

"Jack got really weird when that guy appeared," she mentioned. "He went rigid and hid behind the stoop. If I didn't know better, I would have sworn he was afraid."

Alex glanced over at Isis. "You had a similar reaction."

Isis turned her attention upward, examining the walls and windows. She wasn't interested in discussing Alex's observation. Alex exchanged a concerned look with Jade and Shae. Around them, the moans of pain had lessened as the guardians continued healing the wounded.

"Isis, who is he?" Jade asked, her tone gentle but urgent. Ignoring her, Isis walked away. She jogged up the steps and headed for the stairway, disappearing around a bend. She made her way up to the third floor, moving for one of the unlit empty hallways. Most of the bodies had been taken downstairs and there were only a few patches of blood on the floor. Looking over her shoulder to make sure she was alone, Isis leaned back against the wall and ran a hand over her face. She closed her eyes and tried to will the unease from her mind. Memories of being hung on a rack by her wrists, a knife carving into her flesh went through her mind. She cleared her throat and focused on the information her senses were taking in. If she was to be any use, she had to remain in the present. Isis let out her breath again and resumed her search for any evidence that might be useful to Orion.

~~*~*~*

Orion paced up and down the main hall of the mansion, wringing his hands neurotically. Remington and Sly watched him from the stairway. Remington was sitting on the bottom steps, hands clasped in front of him. He looked as though he had been punched in the chest with a sledgehammer. Sly, who sat much higher up, felt similar to how he looked, though she hid it under her normal nonchalance. Grenich had attacked the protector leaders, murdered a couple of their children and tried to take another hostage. If it wasn't a war before, the Corporation was making sure it was where they were headed.

All three shape shifters turned when they heard the door in the garage open. A few moments later, Isis crossed the main hallway, heading for the library.

"Isis?" Orion called, but she ignored him as she continued down the hall. Jack stepped into the hallway next, carrying the case Orion had sent. He handed it to the older shape shifter.

"You need to contact your brother now," he stated, glancing behind him when Coop stepped into view. The other experiment passed by them and moved smoothly up the stairs. He didn't acknowledge anyone in the hall. Remington stood up as the others gradually filtered in, all looking nothing short of exhausted.

"Roan?" Orion asked as he took the case from Jack.

"Nick Chance showed up tonight," Jack said and Orion blanched at the name. "Roan knows more about him than any of us, so it is in our best interest to utilize his knowledge."

Jack turned and walked to the stairs, quickly ascending them. Orion looked up and saw his youngest brother standing a few feet away with Jensen. He looked down at his case, a tremor going through his hand. The clock in the hall alerted the occupants of the time with a series of loud chimes. Sly descended the stairs, nodding to Jade.

"Who is Nick Chance?" Alex asked, sounding worn out. Her face was filthy and her dark hair was slick with sweat. Jade and Shae didn't look any better. Just by looking at them, it was obvious it had been a hell of a fight.

"He's a Grenich enforcer, similar to Tracy," Orion began. "They are quite different in their approach to their job. It's difficult to explain, but the best way I could put it into words is Tracy's more akin to a surgeon whereas Nick is a butcher. Roan will be able to explain it better than I, so

I suggest contacting him as soon as possible. I'll analyze these samples and report my findings."

He hurried off, climbing up the stairs and disappearing down a hall. After a moment, Remington stepped forward. He laid a hand on Alex's shoulder, giving her a small half-hearted smile, before turning his attention to the whole group.

"You've all had a long night. Get some rest. I will meet with Roan and speak with all of you in the morning," he said. They dispersed until only Remington, Jensen, Alex, and Sly remained. The four shape shifters looked to the side when Isis re-entered the hall. Her glowing green eyes showed no trace of weariness.

"I wish to accompany you to speak with Roan," she stated. Her back was ramrod straight and she held her head high. "I must know of the enemy and it would be useful to have someone with Grenich experience there."

Remington looked at her, considering the offer. There was a possible conflict of interest, but Isis didn't sentimentalize familial bonds the way others did. She approached every situation with her mind on strategy and based her decisions purely on logic. Roan being her biological father was just a fact and probably not an important one in her mind. Even if she hadn't been an experiment, Isis was an adoptee. She didn't see Roan as family, except in a strictly genetic sense, and therefore would have no connection to him.

"Very well, if you think it would be beneficial," Remington consented.

"I would like to accompany both of you," Alex said, stepping forward. Remington looked over at her. Of her three teammates, Alex was probably the one Isis was most comfortable with. Being openly aromantic-asexual, Alex experienced no desire for romantic attachments and found fulfillment in platonic relationships. Since the majority of shape shifters were non-monogamous with high sex drives, Alex had always been a bit of an outsider. Strangely, it was this experience that made her more comfortable with the experiments. She understood what it was like to not only be different, but also to be thought of as something that needed to be fixed. Alex treated the experiments like shape shifters, while also respecting their needs in regards to personal space, which they seemed to appreciate in their own way.

"Isis, do you have any objections to Alex accompanying us?" Remington asked, glancing at his watch. It was well after midnight.

"None. It would be beneficial to have another member of the Four there," Isis responded. Remington turned his attention to Jensen and Sly, who stood off to the side. Jensen looked like hell. His nice jacket and shirt had been torn and his face was smeared with sweat and a yellowish substance. He was leaning back against a pillar, one foot resting against it. Judging from his expression, the protector was only half-awake.

"Don't worry, old boy," Sly said, a smile subtly curling her lips. "We'll hold down the fort until the Monroes get back."

Remington raised an eyebrow, skeptically, but nodded once. Isis approached Jensen, standing a few feet from him. He leaned forward, just enough to rest his forehead against hers. She didn't flinch at the contact.

"Running off again, are we?" Jensen whispered, looking into her glowing green eyes. "Don't you ever rest?"

"I do not sleep and I was modified for long drawn-out battles, so I can go much longer without meditation," Isis responded matter-of-factly. "I will return. You will see me in the morning."

Jensen leaned back. "Well, I'm going to drop if I don't get some sleep. I will see you lot tomorrow at some point. Best of luck."

Isis watched him ascend the stairs and disappear down one of the halls. She turned her attention to Remington and Alex, moving back toward them. In a matter of seconds, they disappeared from the main hallway in a bright flash of light.

~~*~*~*

In his cell in the dungeons, Roan slept on a soft bed. He was on his side with one arm curled under the pillow upon which his head rested and he had pulled the blanket up to his shoulder. The assassin's sleep was usually troubled, but on this particular evening, nightmarish images didn't haunt his rest. The temperature was perfect in the dungeons in the Meadows and it was silent.

The lights in the block brightened, piercing the darkness and stirring Roan from his rest. He didn't open his eyes but let out an irritated groan, turning away from the glass wall and yanking the blanket over his head. The faint sound of footsteps came down the hall, becoming more pronounced the closer they got. It sounded like more than one shape shifter, but Roan didn't know or care exactly how many there were.

"Whatever it is, it can wait until tomorrow," Roan grumbled when the steps stopped in front of his cell. "Ignore my brother's melodrama and fuck off so I can get back to sleep."

"It cannot wait."

Roan's eyes snapped open when he heard the quiet voice. He hadn't heard it many times, but he would recognize it anywhere. Tossing the blanket off his head and rolling over again, Roan blinked a few times against the onslaught of light. Raising a hand to shield his eyes, he stared at the figure in black who stood before the glass wall.

Isis, one of his daughters.

She wore a catsuit, her Blitz regalia, and stood in a confident stance. The light reflected on the shiny black material, glistening on the silver charm she wore at her throat. She was willowy, modified for maximum speed and agility, though she had always been on the thinner side, even before Grenich got ahold of her. Her dark hair was still cropped extremely short. She had her mother's features and took more after Passion than him, but Roan recognized a shadow in her that he knew all too well.

Beside her stood Remington and his adopted daughter, Alex. Neither one had aged a day. With all the trainer did, Roan expected him to be sporting a couple gray hairs, but it was as dark as ever. Alex looked as though she had been in a nasty brawl and Roan felt his heart speed up when he noticed the yellow blood on her clothing. He could smell the fetid stench even through the guardian glass. *It's going to take her weeks to scrub that smell out of her clothing. If she can,* Roan thought, remembering his few encounters with Set's followers, none of which were pleasant.

Roan craned his neck, looking over Alex's shoulder for their guardian accompaniment. They needed to have at least one to see a prisoner. He could just see the top of Electra's head behind the shape shifters. He clutched the blanket around his waist and cleared his throat.

"If you could all turn around for just a moment," he requested. Remington and Alex looked confused until Roan gestured over to the chair where he had hung his clothes. Electra shook her head and turned around, as did the other three. Roan got out of bed, clutching the blanket around himself, retrieved his clothes, and moved behind the privacy screen.

"Judging by Alex's clothing and overall appearance, I'd say Grenich attacked tonight," Roan mentioned as he pulled his clothes on. "Must have been quite some fight if you're here to see me at this ungodly hour."

Roan stepped out from behind the privacy screen as he pulled his shirt over his head, moving back toward the glass and tapping it twice with his knuckle. The shape shifters turned back around and Roan stopped in front of Isis, studying her. She met his gaze, her face betraying no emotion. *Probably still doesn't fully understand the concept,* Roan thought. Looking at her, he was reminded again of how much he despised Grenich. There was nothing he wanted more than to take an active part in bringing down the Corporation. There were a number of creative tortures he dreamed of inflicting on Set.

"My question is what couldn't Orion answer that I can?" Roan continued easily, leaning with his shoulder against the glass.

"We need you to tell us what you know about Nick Chance," Isis answered. Roan gave a small half-smile, which he was sure more resembled a grimace.

"Well that explains it. Nick Chance — there's a name I haven't heard in quite some time. Tell me, does he still paint the masculine symbol around his eyes? Guardians, he always looked absolutely ridiculous," he said, moving over to the chair. "If he was off Corporation grounds, I must admit my surprise. Chance was never what you would call ... oh, what's the term? Emotionally stable? Mentally sound?"

The assassin laughed nostalgically, as he grabbed the back of the chair in his cell and dragged it over to the glass, folding his tall body down into it. Isis looked off to the side and the other two protectors looked at Roan expectantly. Interlacing his fingers behind his head, Roan tipped the chair back so it was on two legs.

"How do you mean?" Remington asked and Roan chuckled at the question.

"The man is a sadist and he is quite proud of it," Roan stated, his piercing green eyes travelling past them as if he were looking back in time. "Most Grenich employees do their job for the money and have no feelings about what they do. They're completely numb to it. Old Nick? Well, Chance does what he does for fun. He was an enforcer and also a pusher. It was his job to test the experiments' limits, but he tended to be a little too good at his job. If memory serves, he was particularly fond of the skinning test."

"The skinning test?" Alex asked. She looked as though she didn't want to hear the answer.

"Experiments have regenerative abilities," Isis explained, her voice flat. "Approximately a year after these abilities are activated, experiments are flayed to make sure these abilities work properly. It also tests how resistant to bacterial infection we are."

"In the other laboratories, experiments are usually anesthetized during the procedure," Roan continued as he dropped his arms, wishing he had some good whiskey. "When Chance would do it, the experiment would be wide awake. He claimed it was to test their pain threshold, but everyone knew it was because he liked to hear them scream. Sick fuck he is, he probably got off on it. He decorates the walls of his offices and home with skins he has collected over the years, nasty business. So he's back in town? That *is* surprising."

"Why?" Remington asked.

Roan lifted his shoulders, interlacing his fingers across his stomach. "He didn't exactly part on good terms with Set. Experiments are worth millions; all the research and work that goes into them isn't cheap. Chance tended to get carried away with his work."

Alex shifted her weight. "He killed shape shifters."

"Quite a few. Set got fed up with his investments winding up in the crematorium and so he sent Chance away somewhere. I always hoped he was toiling away in some factory, supervising gadget construction or some other inane shit," Roan stated with an amused grin. Remington studied him for a moment, puzzled.

"Your brother blanched at the man's name and Alex mentioned that even the experiments were unnerved by him. You are completely unbothered and I can't help but wonder why," the trainer observed. Roan smiled, looking up at the old protector.

"Chance is a monster. He terrified almost everyone at the Corporation. Being a sadist, he has very little fear and no empathy. There were only three people who ever scared him and therefore could control him. Set, Pyra, and myself."

Roan rose to his full height, studying the four people on the other side of the glass wall. He was surprised to see Electra's eyes were red-rimmed. Chance had almost certainly killed someone she knew, someone she was close to. The question was who. There was a sudden and uncomfortable feeling of unease that crept through Roan's mind as he wondered where Passion was. He didn't see her regularly, but knew she frequently visited Jet and Lilly on Earth.

"Why would he be scared of a mere shape shifter?" Isis asked. "If not even experiments scare him, why would a normal?"

Roan looked back to her. "That is a question with a complicated answer."

"We've got time," Alex said. Roan looked over at her, then at Remington, studying the trainer. He looked weary and Roan could read the grief in his expression. *Must have been one hell of an attack,* the former assassin thought.

"Nick Chance holds some rank in the Corporation. When Orion and I were there, he held a lot of favor with Set, though not so much with Pyra," Roan began. "Nobody dared even look him in the eye for fear of disrespecting Set. Even the scariest monsters in the Corporation would walk the other way when Chance was coming toward them. He's used to people being afraid of him and it made him an arrogant entitled shit.

"One day, Orion screwed something up. Some blood test or procedure, a minor mistake that was easily fixed, no harm done. It was shortly after he had begun to form the Resistance in the Corporation, so it might have been done on purpose. He never told me and I never asked. Somehow, Chance got wind of the mistake and he decided to punish Orion. He grabbed my brother in the middle of the night, dragged him into one of the inquisition rooms and proceeded to torture him for a week. Now, I may not be Orion's biggest fan, but I don't take very kindly to people torturing my kin. It could damage my reputation."

"How did you respond?" Isis asked and Roan chuckled, looking off to the side. It was one of the few pleasant Grenich memories he had. Running a hand through his sleep-mussed hair, he looked back to them.

"I found a two-by-four and beat Chance within an inch of his life," he replied. "The man's a decent fighter, but he's overconfident. I just walked into his office and whack!"

Roan punctuated the end of the sentence by smacking his palm against the glass. Both Remington and Alex flinched, almost imperceptibly. Electra did too and then muttered something Roan couldn't hear. Isis just stared at him, unaffected by the loud noise.

"There was no reprisal for your actions?" she asked.

"Quite the opposite. I got a raise. Set appreciated when his enforcers took initiative and weren't intimidated. Even then, Chance was becoming a problem. He had his uses, but more often than not he was a headache," Roan answered. "If they are letting some slack in his leash, I would advise you to proceed with caution. Make no mistake, Chance is a very dangerous enemy. He fights dirty and he enjoys killing, the bloodier the better. He's an animal, one that needs to be put down and I recommend you do it quickly."

"Are there any strengths or special abilities I need be aware of?" Isis asked. Though it repulsed him how Grenich had experimented on her like a common lab rat, Roan did like her no-nonsense way of operating. It would keep her safe and therefore alive.

"To the best of my knowledge, Chance is not a revenant. So he does have the ability to feel pain, but I don't know for certain what he is. A two-by-four did a pretty decent job of messing him up, so I imagine guardian silver would be effective as well," Roan explained. "Orion knows where to get it, if the guardians are still dragging their feet with their whole pacifism no-interference song-and-dance."

Remington, Alex, and Electra looked over at Isis. The question of her weapons, as well as Jack's, had been hanging over their heads for a while. Orion was very tight-lipped about where the weapons had come from, often deflecting when the question was posed. *We have more important matters to discuss,* was his go-to answer. The experiments weren't forthcoming either and they were quite protective of their weapons, almost aggressively so.

"I already know your answer, but your best course of action would be to give me temporary leave," Roan began, drawing attention back to him. "You could put a tracking device on me or some other locating beacon. I'd be more than happy to kill Chance and come right back to serve out eternity."

Remington crossed his arms and studied Roan. There was a dangerous gleam in the assassin's eye, so subtle most would not see it. Roan was a killer, one who enjoyed his job. He was an addict looking for a fix and now that the opportunity had presented itself, the man was eager to take advantage of the situation. Roan held Remington's gaze, watching him expectantly.

"You know that's not going to happen. The guardians and protectors are not in the habit of employing assassins," Remington responded. "No matter how despicable the individual, we do not murder."

Roan looked at him. "Remington, this is war. You and I both have enough experience to know that no one is going to walk away without blood on their hands. Even your respected leaders will need to get their hands a little dirty."

The trainer turned away from the cell, walking down the hall. Electra went next, followed by Alex. Isis turned to leave but paused when Roan tapped the glass. She looked over at him again.

"You have to embrace both parts of your personality, Isis and Blitz, if you're going to win this fight," Roan said softly, so as not to be overheard. "No matter what the protectors and guardians tell you, in war you have to do morally questionable things for the greater good. The trick is finding a balance between the two. I was never able to, but perhaps you will succeed where I failed."

She studied him and Roan couldn't tell if she was considering his words. Isis turned and left, vanishing down the hall. Roan looked after them, watching the empty space until the lights went out again. He yawned and turned away from the glass. Flopping back down on the bed, he closed his eyes and waited for sleep to come.

~~*~*~*

In a Grenich laboratory, two employees were unpacking boxes of framed skins and hanging them on an empty wall. The entire office was painted in cold shades of gray and white. There was a steel coat rack near the door and a long desk at the far side of the office. One wall had already been covered in frames with different hues flesh, all of them perfectly preserved. A small gold plate with four numbers was at the base of each frame, identifying the owner of the flesh. The employees were hurrying, knowing the office occupant would be back soon. They still had a few more boxes to unpack. He would not be pleased if they weren't finished when he returned.

The door swung open and a man in a cream-colored suit entered the office. He took off his bowler hat, which matched his suit, and tossed it onto the coatrack.

"Can't you dumb cows go any faster?" he sneered, undoing a button on his suit. "Your presence depresses me. And you're boring."

They didn't respond, but moved faster. The man crossed the office to his desk, grabbing a round glass paperweight. He hurled it and it shattered against the wall near the woman's head. They both let out a yelp of fear and cowered, turning back to look at him.

"I am your superior! When I enter the room, you better fucking acknowledge me," he snapped. They mumbled shaky apologies, bowing low, before turning back to their work.

"Tired of torturing small animals and children, love?"

Nick smirked as he sat behind the desk, resting his feet on top and folding his hands over his stomach. "Well, if it isn't the ancient cunt. How is your life of servitude? Wait, don't bother. I don't care."

Tracy smiled as she stepped into the office. "Charming as ever, I see."

"Is there any particular reason you're here? Shouldn't you be on your knees somewhere, sucking an investor's cock?" Nick continued, smiling tauntingly as he tapped his thumbs together. Tracy laughed quietly and crossed the room so she stood on the other side of the desk.

"Oh Nick, Nick, Nick. You've been back for a week and already you're a nuisance," Tracy chastised with a condescending shake of her head. Nick made a talking motion with his hand.

"Since you're here, make yourself useful and fix me a drink. Scotch, the good stuff," he said as he pulled open a drawer. He grabbed the long wooden box inside and put it on the desk, flipping open the top. He pulled out a long cigar and held it under his nose, inhaling the strong scent while watching Tracy. She simply smiled, not moving.

"Need I remind you, yet again, that we are the same rank in this Corporation? I know how difficult it is for you to retain knowledge, but if you could at least make an effort, Lord Set and Lady Pyra would be very impressed," she cooed. Nick's eyes narrowed at her and he chopped the end off of his cigar.

"We are not of the same rank, not even close. You're a servant and I am the son of a necromancer," he growled, reaching for a lighter on the desk. Tracy leaned forward and delicately snatched it away.

"Oh love, you are the illegitimate offspring of a necromancer. A bastard, a mistake, a failed abortion," Tracy replied, tapping the edge of the lighter against her cheek. "Therefore, you *are* of the same rank as revenants. Be thankful Lord Set has some use for you, otherwise you'd be subject to experimentation. Though I daresay you'd fail at that like you have everything else in your life."

Nick pulled out a switchblade and got to his feet, fury flashing in his eyes. Tracy looked up at him, unbothered, and then glanced over to the petrified workers behind her. Both were shaking uncontrollably and looked about ready to piss themselves.

"You are dismissed," Tracy called over her shoulder, waving them away. "Mr. Chance and I have matters to discuss. Be gone."

They all but ran out of the office, the door swinging shut behind them. Tracy looked back to the enraged man in front of her.

"Temper, temper, love," she warned coolly. "Unless you want to go back to the hellhole you were imported from."

Nick closed the switchblade with a snarl and sat back down. His body was still rigid and his expression reflected the hatred he felt for Tracy. He put the unlit cigar in his mouth, resting his feet on the desk again.

"You carried out an unauthorized attack on the rebel club, killed two of the protector leaders' children," she began, tucking the lighter into the breast pocket of her business suit. "You used followers and a couple of our products without permission. It was messy and unprofessional. Set appreciates bold moves, but he doesn't appreciate when they're done behind his back. It reflects poorly on the Grenich Corporation."

Nick took the cigar out of his mouth and laid it on the desk. He stood from his chair and made his way over to the mini bar.

"No, what reflects poorly on the Corporation, is sitting around idly when someone steals your products," Nick argued as he dropped some perfectly square ice cubes into a stout glass. "The mission was a success. Jet and Lilly stole two top products so I responded in kind. It gave the shape shifters a taste of what they're up against."

"It also lost us a lot of potential allies. Shape shifters don't take kindly to being slaughtered, love," Tracy pointed out. Nick poured scotch into the glass and turned around, putting the cap back in the bottle.

"But it does send a message about who is in charge," Nick replied, swirling the liquor in the glass. "Shape shifters are a weak species, especially the protectors. And it was a hell of a lot of fun."

"What of the followers? The ones who weren't killed?" Tracy asked.

"Deathfire," Nick answered, sipping his scotch and grinning triumphantly. "They're little piles of ash now."

Tracy closed her eyes and massaged her forehead, frustrated. Whatever Grenich achieved, Chance could easily destroy with his impulsiveness.

"So you went to the rebel club, killed a bunch of shape shifters, name-dropped the Corporation, proceeded to incinerate our own allies, and you succeeded in doing what exactly?" she asked. Nick shrugged and continued drinking his scotch. He moved across the room to where the frames of flesh hung on the wall, looking at the numbers on the plaques at the bottom of each frame.

"He was there," he pointed with his glass at one case toward the middle of the wall. Tracy stood from the chair and crossed the room, looking at the number. The flesh in the frame had been treated before being put under glass. It looked as fresh as it had the day it was peeled from the body. She pulled out her smartphone and selected the database app the Corporation had designed ages ago.

"The Lock series, unimportant," she said when the file

came up on the small screen. "He's a nuisance. Granted not as much as you, but an outdated malfunctioning weapon is no concern of Set's. It would be helpful if you had killed him."

"I didn't," Nick muttered as he moved over to the unopened boxes. He handed Tracy his drink, which she reluctantly took. Moving one box off another, he opened the bottom box and sorted through the frames. Finding the one he was looking for, he pulled it out and placed it to the side. Digging down further, he removed another frame and held it up to the light, looking at it almost reverently.

"These two were also there. I believe they are of more value," Chance said, trading the frames for his drink. Tracy looked at both of them, her eyes lighting up at the numbers on the golden plaques.

"How can you be certain?" she asked as she put one on top of the other.

"Before I gave the signal to attack, I looked through the eyes of a couple followers," Chance answered, sipping his scotch. "I'd recognize 7-299 anywhere. Crazy bitch almost took out one of my eyes. 7-295, unremarkable as always, but I remembered him being one of Set's Key possibilities."

"How did you remember the Lock series?" Tracy asked, watching as Nick flopped down on the couch in the office. He smiled widely before finishing his scotch.

"When I skinned him, I collected what I could of his blood in a bucket. After I finished, I threw it in his face," Nick paused, sticking out his lip as though pouting. "Nothing happened, but it was funny so it wasn't a complete loss."

Tracy was unbothered by his sadism. All of the higher ups in Grenich knew of the childish glee he derived from torturing the experiments. It made them tougher and so Set tolerated the bastard's disturbing proclivities. Then Nick had become a little too bold for his own good and got carried away with his fun. Tracy put the frames off to the side, moved to the far side of the couch, and sat down at the edge. Her guns were in their holsters and she was ready to draw should Nick be tempted to try anything.

"Set wishes to offer you an official position," she began. "But it comes with some conditions, all of which are non-negotiable."

"Color me intrigued," Nick said, tossing the glass over his shoulder. It shattered on the ground somewhere behind them. "Go on."

Tracy smirked and rested her arm on the back of the couch. "The necromancers were impressed with the display of strength, rash though it was. Set believes you could be a useful asset, hence his summoning you. He believes you would be well-suited to be the head commander of the Grenich army. You would be in charge of releasing the experiments into battle. When we take prisoners, whichever ones are unsuitable for experimentation would be yours to do with as you please."

"What's the catch?" Nick asked, his expression resembling a hungry dog's.

"First, you will only attack when and what Set commands. No more sloppy random assaults like the Lair," Tracy said. "Don't worry about getting bored. He will utilize you frequently now that Grenich is taking a more active role in this war."

Nick rolled his eyes. "Fine. Next."

"I am to accompany you at all times. I am to be Set's liaison with his troops, so when I speak it is in his voice. Part of my job now is to make sure you don't get out of line," Tracy paused, noticing the look of irritation on Nick's face. "It's not a cake-walk for me either, love. For however long this war lasts, I am basically a glorified babysitter to a grownup child. A babysitter you wouldn't need if you had even a modicum of impulse control."

She stood from the couch, looking up at the wall of skins. The bright lights in the office glinted on the clean glass.

"Fine, we'll be boring and do it your way," Nick acquiesced, sullenly. "As long as I don't have to do paperwork."

"Splendid," Tracy said, turning so she was facing him again. "He's got a mission for you, one I think you will enjoy. Tell me, Nick, how would you like to wipe out a species?"

CHAPTER FOUR

There was a somber mood in the Meadows as preparations were made for the funeral of Brindy and Devlin. All the guardians wore darker shades, their clothing dull to reflect the state of mourning they would observe for the next month. A few messengers were preparing the mausoleum for the interment ceremony scheduled to take place at dusk. Chairs had already been arranged. The room was mostly empty but for the messengers and one shape shifter.

Hunter watched as the messengers hung gauzy gray curtains, which almost looked like delicate mists, from the ceiling. They were arranged so they formed an opaque screen between the area where the service would take place and the rows of tombs behind them. Not very many guardians or protectors were interred in the guardian mausoleum, though it was a grand structure. Guardians rarely died — only a few had fallen in the War of the Meadows. Protectors died more frequently, usually in the line of duty, but they were often buried or cremated on Earth alongside humans.

Hunter sat back, numb to everything. She was barely even aware of the dull throbbing in her shoulder where that creature had bitten her. The young shape shifter had been to her fair share of funerals before. Being the daughter of the leaders of the protectors, she and her siblings were expected to make appearances at certain events. But never in her life had Hunter lost so close a family member. Tears burned in her eyes and she covered them with her hand.

"Do you want some company, kid?"

Hunter took a deep shuddering breath and looked over toward the familiar voice. Nero gave her a sympathetic smile. She scooted over a seat, allowing him to sit in her vacated chair. He looked up at the messenger who was fastening the gray curtain. Hunter sniffled and wiped away a few stray tears.

"Thought you'd be with your family, in the healing wing," Nero mentioned as he leaned back in his chair. He was wearing a suit, which was odd for him. She had only ever seen Nero in a suit once before: at Orion's funeral. She looked down at her own funerary clothes: gray dress pants, a similarly colored shirt, and a nice jacket to go over it. Most of the women in her family would be wearing long-sleeved dresses, but Hunter had never looked good in a dress. She was too petite and flat. *I have the body of a teenage boy*, she once complained to her mother.

"I can't be there," Hunter said. "I can't handle this. How do humans do this? Everything is so gray and hideous. Brindy hated this color. She hated it."

Nero wrapped an arm around the younger protector's shoulders, comforting her as she broke down sobbing again. He rested his head against hers, sympathizing with her grief. In his many years, Nero had been to more funerals than he could count. It was hardest when there was a personal connection to the one who had died. The majority of shape shifters didn't believe in an afterlife. For them, death was final, the end of everything. It made it a more profound happening and a more painful experience.

"My brothers and I, before we came back to the

mansion when Isis first arrived, spent about twenty or so years in Greece," Nero began. "We had a lot of friends there, some of whom were protectors who had been living there since the First World War. Hell, even Jensen seemed to enjoy the time we spent there and he's usually a complete emo. We were bunking with a friend of ours, Raj, and his family. Raj was a great guy, one of the best poker players I've ever encountered. Lost quite a bit of money to him."

Nero smiled as his mind drifted back to better times. Hunter had stopped crying and was now wiping away her tears, waiting for him to continue.

"Anyway, a few years before we came back, about late December, we got into a skirmish with a group of separatists, larger than anyone anticipated. Things happened so fast, we were lucky to get out alive. None of us got away unscathed. We lost a lot of good people, including Raj."

Hunter frowned when she noticed something odd about the mausoleum. Nero's voice began to fade away and the marble walls became hazy, slowly morphing into a black and white hallway. Hunter straightened up, looking down the hall. Her vision had suddenly become colorless. Two people were coming toward her, a man and a woman. They were conversing quietly, but their voices had a strange echoing quality.

"The gateway will be guarded, but we can create a back way into the world," the woman said. As she got closer, Hunter could see she was light-haired, likely a blonde. She looked so familiar but Hunter couldn't place where she had seen her before. She couldn't see the man's face.

"Hunter?"

Hunter blinked and the mausoleum was back in place. The messengers had hung the curtain and left. Nero was staring at her, obviously concerned.

"You okay, kid? You kind of zoned out there for a bit," he explained. Hunter rubbed her eyes again, nodding. She felt a little nauseous and light-headed.

"Yeah, I just . . ." she hesitated. "Have you ever felt like you were seeing through someone else's eyes? Not in a metaphorical sense?"

Nero looked bewildered. "Can't say as I have."

Hunter grimaced and rotated her aching shoulder. She didn't understand why it still bothered her. The guardians had healed her without any sort of complication. Out of the corner of her eye, she could see Nero watching her.

"Maybe you should see my brother, just to make sure everything is all right," he suggested. Hunter ran her hands over her face. Something was wrong, but she doubted if Orion would be able to figure out what was afflicting her.

"I'll talk to him after the service," she mumbled behind her hands. After a moment, Hunter dropped her hands from her face and got to her feet. Nero did the same, gesturing with his arm. Hunter moved past him and started down the aisle with Nero following beside her.

~~*~*~*

Isis stood with the other members of the Four and Jensen in front of the Healing Wing. They were standing watch while the bodies of Devlin and Brindy were prepared for the ceremony. As was tradition, Jet and Lilly were inside the room with the healers and their other children. Their eldest daughters, Jetta and Robin, had both Appeared the previous morning so they could take part in the ceremony. Passion and Electra were also with them in the healing wing, lending their support to the protector leaders, who had always been family to them.

Artemis stood nearby with the Deverells, Steve, and Remington. The guardian women were dressed in plain long-sleeved black dresses and wore black netting over their faces, a guardian tradition. There was no shimmer to their clothing, as there usually was. The entire Pearl Castle had been transformed to reflect the somber mood. Veils were draped over all the beautiful statues as well as the faces carved in some of the benches and chairs. Curtains were draped over all the portraits and the guardians not wearing the clothes of mourning wore black and white braided ribbons as a sign of respect.

Isis looked off to the side when a shimmering light appeared in the center of the castle. Seconds later, three women and a man stood there. Two of the women had jet-black hair while the other woman was a redhead and the man had reddish blond hair. They were all wearing similar clothing to everyone already in the hall.

"Is that Velvet?" Isis overheard Shae whisper to Jade. She sounded awestruck.

"The one and only," Jade answered. "I wonder where Darton is."

Isis watched the woman cross the hall to where the other shape shifters were standing and greet them solemnly. Though it had been more than a century since she had been co-leader of the protectors, Velvet still carried herself like royalty. Isis hadn't met her before, but had studied the lineage of all the mansion's occupants months ago. Her eyes traveled over to where Jack and Coop were standing, separate from the other mourners.

"Grandmother."

Isis looked back when she heard Hunter's soft voice, watching as the young shape shifter ran over to her grandmother. The two embraced and while they did, Velvet's gaze landed on Isis. The experiment averted her eyes, glancing back in the direction Hunter had come from when she heard footsteps. There was something different about the youngest Monroe and Isis intended to figure out exactly what after the mourning period. She watched Nero saunter over to Jensen and whisper something to him. Jensen nodded and Nero moved across the hall to stand with his brothers.

The sound of quiet steps drew Isis' attention up to the

main stairway of the castle. Adonia was descending with Aneurin. Judging from the stiffness of her gait, the queen of the guardian women was displeased about something. Isis imagined it had something to do with Aneurin, who had been a regular nuisance since the experiments' release. It seemed like he sent a messenger every other day with addendums about how to deal with experiments. Isis still didn't understand why he didn't confine them if he were so concerned about their being free.

Both Aneurin and Adonia approached the Four. Aneurin gestured for Jack and Coop to join them, which they did.

"I'm afraid we have a bit of a situation," the guardian king began, pressing his hands together as he looked at each of the experiments. "You see, services such as this one are held in the mausoleum, which is sacred space to the guardians. Only shape shifters who are recognized as protectors and guardians are allowed to enter."

"You have *got* to be kidding me," Shae said under her breath, shaking her head as she looked over at Alex. "Is he really going to do this now? Of all times."

"Isn't the Meadows as a whole sacred to the guardians?" Jack asked and Shae struggled not to laugh at the innocent question. Isis noticed Jade elbow her and shake her head in warning. Aneurin seemed annoyed at the interruption, but maintained his relaxed demeanor.

"Anyway, I'm going to have to ask the three of you to wait out here during the interment ceremony," he finished. The three experiments were not offended at the request. They rarely ever were. They nodded and Aneurin smiled.

"Your acquiescence is most appreciated," he stated before moving away to stand near Artemis. Isis glanced over at Shae, noticing her furious expression.

"You are displeased," she observed. Shae looked over at her cousin.

"Damn right I am. Why didn't the three of you protest?"

The three experiments were quiet for a moment, obviously not understanding Shae's anger. Isis looked to the side when she heard someone approaching them.

"We are not protectors," she answered. "Guardian custom dictates that certain areas are reserved for protectors and guardians. I do not understand the motivation behind such rules, but many of your customs elude my understanding. Your practice of grieving is also strange and not something we experience, but it does not offend us. Why should we intrude on your rituals if it doesn't negatively affect us?"

"You are a protector, descended from a long line of them," Jensen put in. "Coop and Jack might be too. You should not be punished for something that was done to you."

Isis studied him, once again mystified by their logic. She didn't understand why they got so worked up over so trivial a matter. While it seemed as though she had been considered a protector in her former life, it was impossible that she would be considered one anymore. All the blood on her hands and the things she had done for the Grenich Corporation, as well as the threats she had neutralized once she was out.

"Isis, is it?"

Isis turned to her right, noticing Velvet standing a few feet away from her. Isis turned to face her, standing at attention.

"I was wondering if I could speak with you for a moment?" Velvet asked, gesturing toward the front entrance of the castle. Isis moved to where she gestured, allowing the woman to guide her outside. The sun was beginning to set already. The service would start in another hour. The diplomats from other universes would be arriving any minute. In the distance, Isis could already see shapes of guardians who would attend the interment.

"So, you're one of the daughters of Passion?" Velvet began once they were outside the castle, leading Isis off to the side.

"That is my biological heritage, yes," Isis confirmed.

"My son has written much about you in his letters to me," Velvet continued, adjusting the shawl she had wrapped about her elbows. "I was at your mourning service back when you were believed dead."

"I was dead briefly," Isis mentioned, crossing her hands behind her as they walked. Her catsuit shimmered in the fading light as did the charm at her throat. She had been allowed to wear her weapons, so long as they were only blades. Deciding to show restraint and not expecting to encounter any enemies, Isis had brought her sais and a couple throwing knives.

"So direct," Velvet observed with a smile. "I like that. Tell me, do you know who I am?"

"I know you are Jet's mother," Isis began. "Your husband was Caedmon. He was leader of the protectors for just over a hundred years, one of the shortest reigns of a leader. You are a former seductress, from a long lineage of seductresses and seducers, which caused some debates among protectors. You had two children by Caedmon and three by other lovers. After Caedmon's death, Jet and Lilly were named leader of the protectors and you retired to Tuscany, where you reside to this day."

"You are a studious one. Controversy always seems to follow the protector leaders, doesn't it?"

"Your son faced scandal of a different sort when he came out as monogamous," Isis stated, her gaze remaining fixed in front of them. She was paying attention to everything around her, as she always did. She could hear the pumas in the tall grasses in the distance. The air smelled fresh and felt cool against her face.

"Yes, well, marrying a guardian didn't exactly quell the concerns of our people. Still they managed to persevere, they always do," Velvet remarked. Isis hesitated, glancing over at Velvet. The former seductress was looking off into the distance.

"You obviously wish to ask me something you don't want anyone to overhear," Isis pointed out. "What is it?"

Velvet turned toward Isis, her light blue eyes shimmering. "The protectors are a noble faction of shape shifters. They have always fought for truth and justice in an unjust world. The morality is admirable, but impractical. It is a messy world we live in and sometimes we have to get our hands dirty to do the right thing.

"I understand you know who murdered my grandchildren. You know the men responsible. Jet and Lilly are excellent leaders and will want them brought to justice. However, you and I both know that places like Grenich are above laws. Be they shape shifter, man, or guardian, a place like Grenich will never be held accountable or face consequences for their actions."

Isis studied the woman in front of her. "If I understand you, you are asking me to kill the parties responsible for the Lair massacre."

Velvet looked up the walls of the Pearl Castle. "I know you are under intense scrutiny, but from what I've been told about Grenich, you were modified specifically to operate in that moral gray area."

"You are grieving and may regret what you are requesting," Isis said. "I will try to get justice and if it requires my killing those responsible, I will do so. However, I cannot promise that will be what happens."

Velvet looked at her for a moment. "Perhaps you are more protector than you think."

With that, the former seductress turned and started making her way back to the castle. Isis looked up at the night sky. It was already dusk and she thought about the moon. Her glowing green gaze traveled down to the forest. It was a new moon, which jogged her memory. The new moon was important, a special day for the followers of Set. She rested her hand on the pommel of one of her sais, tapping it with her finger. The shape shifters would be in the mausoleum for most of the night, as would many of the High Council. Afterwards, they would return to the mansion. She could slip out and be back at the mansion before anyone noticed her absence. *You need to find the balance between the two sides of your personality, Isis and Blitz,* Roan had told her.

Isis turned and sprinted back to the castle, dancing around a guardian from the dawn lands on her way inside. The guardian gasped and took a step back, but the experiment ignored her.

~~*~*~*

"Roan? Oh Roan? Come out, come out, wherever you are."

Roan pressed his back against a rough wooden crate, holding his breath and willing himself to wake up. He could hear the sharp click of the woman's heels on the stone floor. They stopped a few feet away from the boxes he hid behind.

"Come on, love, I only want to have a chat. Just a nice little tête-à-tête between old friends," her words echoed throughout the empty space. Roan could feel sweat start to drip down his temple. He stayed low to the ground as he shuffled back a row of crates, which towered over him. For the first time in his life, Roan wished he was an experiment. What he wouldn't have given for the ability to scale the crates.

"You can't hide forever, assassin," the voice became colder. "I might be tempted to visit your whore in the Meadows. What was her name again?"

Roan bit his tongue, knowing she was trying to provoke him into making a mistake. He darted toward another row of boxes, glimpsing the back of her blonde head for the briefest of seconds.

Roan was woken up by a stinging slap across the face. He raised a hand to his cheek, struggling not to punch whomever was next to him. The assassin couldn't hide his shock when he saw Orion sitting at the edge of his bed.

"Awake?" his older brother asked and Roan nodded, unable to speak. He could feel tremors wracking his body as he struggled to hide how much the nightmare affected him. Orion glanced up at Astrea, who was watching the two of them. She stood with her arms crossed, her face unreadable.

"Thank you, Astrea. I can handle it from here," Orion said as he set his bag on the desk. The dungeon-keeper turned and left, her steps fading down the hall.

"You should know that if you try anything, Astrea will be here in a heartbeat. She's connected to this dungeon and she knows whenever something is out of sorts, such as an assassin acting like an idiot and making a run for it," Orion continued as he opened the bag. Roan noticed how red and raw Orion's hands were. His older brother had been obsessively cleaning again and then scrubbing his hands afterwards. The bright light in the dungeons enhanced the angry shade of red. Roan could smell a faint hint of the strong chemicals Orion cleaned with.

"*Former* assassin," Roan corrected him, flopping back.

"We'll see," Orion replied as he pulled an ampoule of cloudy liquid out of the bag. Roan looked over at him, studying his older brother as he shook the ampoule. The cloudiness disappeared and sparkling flecks of silver were visible in the now clear liquid.

"You're wearing funeral clothes," he observed. "So Nick Chance did kill someone?"

"He did," Orion confirmed, a small tremor going through his hand. He pulled a syringe from the bag, removing the plastic cap. *That explains the cleaning,* Roan thought. Orion's most severe obsessive-compulsive tendencies manifested when reminded of Chance. Roan always theorized it was a form of PTSD.

"Time for an inoculation," Orion explained, tapping the edge of the syringe on the desktop. Roan swung his legs off the bed, gripping the sheets around his waist. Numerous scars decorated his torso, the most noticeable being the jagged one near his abdomen where Draco had impaled him with a large knife all those years ago.

"Whom did he kill?"

"Astrea told me you've been having trouble sleeping," Orion ignored the question. "When you do, she says it looks like you suffer from nightmares. Judging from how violently you were tossing about just now, I'd say someone or something is invading your sleep."

"Orion."

"Roan … for once, could you please not be a pain in the ass?" Orion asked with a tired sigh, rubbing his eyes with his free hand as he hunched over and rested his elbows on his knees. It had obviously been a long few days and Roan noticed his older brother looked his age more than usual. There were already streaks of gray in his brown hair. Orion looked over at Roan, who leaned forward. He set the syringe off to the side, rubbing his raw hands together.

"Chance massacred the Lair. He killed some rebels, wounded a lot more. If it weren't for Jack, Isis, and Coop, it would have been much worse," Orion explained wearily, sniffing. "Brindy and Devlin were killed in the attack."

Roan leaned back, watching his brother fiddle with the watch on his wrist. "I saw traces of follower blood on Alex when they questioned me about Chance. Must have been brutal, if he was involved."

Orion squeezed his hand when a tremor went through it. His gaze became distant and for a moment, Roan thought his brother might have one of his debilitating panic attacks. Leaning forward, Roan snapped a couple times, hoping to keep Orion in the present.

"Orion, look at me," he commanded, waiting until his older brother complied. "Don't think about the past. Focus on what happened at the Lair, all right? Talk to me."

Orion swallowed and began wringing his hands, unable to quell the shaking. Roan waited patiently for him to continue, keeping his older brother's focus on him.

"He — he used followers and a werelion," Orion began, his brow furrowing. "What has me worried is he disintegrated them once the fight was over. He would have had plenty of time to retreat and escape into the night, but he burned them."

Roan whistled, straightening up. It was a very clear statement when Grenich didn't feel the need to conserve their power. Killing allies was not a good sign for the protectors.

Orion rested his face in his hands, softly saying, "Of all the people Grenich could have called on … why him?"

"They never cared much about collateral damage," Roan mentioned, almost feeling sorry for his brother. "Still, Chance is a risky move, even for Set and Pyra. I thought for sure he would try to win some more shape shifter allies, most likely the rebels, but to attack their home and then kill his own allies? Not the best way to win over hearts and minds, is it?"

"Unless he wants to stir up fear, which he might use to turn people against Jack and Isis, not to mention the other experiments." Orion paused and looked over at Roan. "Why do you think he brought in Chance?"

Roan scratched his chin. "There are a number of reasons. If I had to guess, I'd say it's mainly because Set needs someone to lead his armies. Someone with no mercy, no compassion or empathy, a unique ability to instill fear in others, and a desire to dominate and destroy everyone and everything. Chance is the best candidate for the job. Actually, it was probably the position I was being groomed for before I turned against the Corporation. If Chance killed two of the Monroes' children, that sends a very clear message."

Roan glanced at his brother's hands when he noticed the tremor go through them again. Orion had been in bad shape after Chance had finished with him. Truth be told, Roan had been surprised he pulled through. He probably wouldn't have were it not for the Grenich doctors. After he recovered, Orion became a very different man. Much less likely to smile and more on edge; there was a distinct coldness to his personality after his encounter with Chance. When Roan had been recovering from his own wounds, there were times when he was woken up by Orion's screams in the room down the hall. Then there was the constant cleaning. After the nightmares, Orion would clean whatever small space he inhabited from top to bottom. Roan would never forget the overpowering smell of the chemicals Orion used or how his hands looked afterward. He wore gloves when he cleaned, but after he removed them, he would scrub his hands until he had practically removed a layer of skin. After that, he would take a shower so hot the steam would often set off the smoke alarms. *Set knows exactly what he's doing by recalling Chance*, Roan realized as he studied his brother's shaking hands. He looked back to Orion's face, but Orion was looking off to the side again.

"Orion." Roan waited until his older brother was looking at him. "Talk to the guardians about giving me a temporary leave. Remington wouldn't see reason, but maybe you will. Nobody knows Chance like I do. I'm one of the only people he's scared of and it will throw him off his game. I'll put him down and come right back, I swear it."

Orion looked contemplative, studying his brother. He leaned back and grabbed the syringe, checking the level inside. Roan held out his arm, waiting for the stab of the needle. He was confused when he felt the gentle swab on his flesh. Orion was never gentle when giving him inoculations. He just jabbed the needle into the flesh and that was that.

"I don't know how they figured out how to dream walk, but they did. At least Tracy and Set are able to," Orion explained as he injected the solution. "Our ally says this will shield you from them. They'll still be able to enter your dreams, but they won't be able to see you, where you are, or get past any mental walls you put up. There shouldn't be any side effects, but if there are, tell Astrea and I'll see what I can do."

Roan pulled back his arm, flexing his fingers a couple times. Orion tossed the used syringe into the bag and closed it again. He stood up, straightening his suit.

"Will you talk to the guardians?"

"No," Orion said after a moment, his shoulders dropping. "It's the easy way out, letting you go and kill the man. If it comes to that, I would prefer an experiment do it."

Roan was quiet for a moment, regarding his brother. He felt a strange sense of concern for Orion, who looked as though he hadn't slept in months. Orion had always been the one to shoulder the responsibility in the family. After their father had died in the field, the eldest Deverell had helped the Deverell women raise all of his siblings. When the brothers were old enough to go off on their own, Orion had kept them together and watched out for them.

"I have to go," Orion stated, glancing at his watch. "The service is going to start in another half-hour."

Orion started to make his way out of the cell, bag in hand, pausing when he heard his brother's voice.

"You're a good man, Orion. Better than I ever was."

Orion shook his head. "No. I'm really not."

Then he was gone.

~~*~*~*

Isis stood with Coop and Jack in the entryway of the mausoleum, watching as the guardians and protectors filtered in. Messengers accompanied the diplomats from the different supernatural races who had come to pay their respects. Isis' eyes were sharp as she observed each individual. They disappeared in the room at the end of the hall, where the ceremony would take place.

Electra stepped outside the mausoleum and approached Isis. She glanced over her shoulder before turning her attention back to her sister. A cold breeze swept over them. Isis' cropped hair barely moved and her glowing green eyes regarded Electra.

"You're going to be around after the service?" Electra asked. "When we return to the mansion?"

"I am still under strict orders not to leave the grounds without an escort," Isis replied. Electra gestured off to the side and Isis followed her, watching as the Deverells passed by.

"There is something I need to tell you about, but we can't talk about it here," Electra whispered. "Can we talk at the mansion?"

"If you wish," Isis answered. Electra gave her a small, sad smile.

"I know you don't think it's a big deal, but you should be allowed to attend the remembrance ceremony. Despite what anyone else thinks, you're still a protector," she stated with conviction. Isis stared at her, wondering what was so important to normals about funerary services. She understood their need to acknowledge their loss, but they assumed everyone needed to do so. Electra turned and headed back to the mausoleum, disappearing inside the marble structure. Isis waited until she was out of sight before approaching the other two experiments. Jack was standing, looking out toward the vast forest below. Coop was lying on his back, his glowing eyes fixed on the silver stars above them. They both looked over at Isis when she approached.

"There is something on your mind," Jack observed. Isis leaned back, watching as the doors of the mausoleum closed. The melodic sound of guardian chanting soon drifted out from the stained glass windows.

"We can go back to the mansion now," Isis stated. Coop sat up, his gaze never moving from her. She glanced over at him and then looked pointedly up at the sky. Both experiments followed her gaze.

"It is the new moon tonight," she observed. "A

celebratory day for the followers of Set. They say when Selene fell in battle, the moon went dark for a time."

Jack's eyes turned back to her. "The nests will be crawling with followers. We don't know where they are."

"They like the cold and damp, they are drawn to caves more often than not. However, they have on occasion been known to settle in abandoned quarries, until they fill up with water. There's a quarry just across the border that has been abandoned for years, but has yet to fill up with water. They haven't been able to figure out why," Isis explained. "It should be a lake by now, but no matter how much rain falls, the water always seems to dry up."

"You think there's a nest," Coop said.

"I do. The followers who attacked the Lair had traces of rock dust on their clothes and feet. Some of it was from minerals found only in that quarry," she explained, looking back to Jack. "Chance killed the group who came with him, probably at least half the pack who lived down there. With their decreased numbers and celebratory ecstasy, they will be weakened and easy to destroy."

Jack turned his attention back out across the lands. A guerilla attack without any kind of backup was a risky strategy. Followers were known for being unpredictable and brutal.

"It being an observed day, there will be a high demon there," he mentioned. "Hand-picked by Grenich and he will not be as easily killed."

"I have thought of that. High demons, while formidable, are still no match for an experiment," Isis replied, looking back to the mausoleum. "I don't need either of you to come with me, but your help would provide an advantage. The service will last approximately three and a half hours, maybe four. They will then return to the mansion for the more informal gathering. We can attack the nest, destroy it, and return."

Jack looked over at Coop when he rose to his feet. He brushed off his hands and the back of his pants.

"I assume you want to return to the mansion first," the L-series said. "For firearms?"

"We can, but firearms will present a drawback. The noise will give away our position," Isis remarked, but Coop shook his head.

"Once we start killing, they'll be drawn to us anyway. Guns will save time. If we're going to bring the fight to them, we need to be prepared."

Isis shrugged and looked back to Jack. He still looked unsure as he rubbed the back of his neck. Isis knew he was struggling with his own instincts. He was intrigued by the normals, perhaps even desired to be one of them. However, he could not hide his true nature. Jack was an experiment, a 7-series, modified for action and killing. Just like them. Even if he wanted to, he could never be a normal.

"Jack, these are not normals and they aren't innocent. They are part of Set's army, which exists only to kill. If we don't strike back, they will continue to pick away at the protectors until they can't put up a good fight," Isis explained. Jack scratched the back of his head.

"I understand the strategic benefits, but you are forgetting something. Such an act of aggression will result in further retaliation. We got lucky with the recruitment team, but if you target his allies, Set will have no choice but to escalate his attack on the protectors."

"He is already escalating," Coop pointed out. "Jack, I don't like this action any more than you do, but we have to be realistic. Soon we'll be attacking a Grenich laboratory that will be filled with experiments and revenants. I would prefer they not have a couple hundred followers backing them up."

Isis looked over at Coop. Since she had been brought to the mansion, Coop was a bit of a mystery. Not a normal, but he never quite seemed like an experiment either. He was a man in two worlds. This was the first time he had ever sounded like an actual experiment.

Jack looked between the two and eventually nodded. In a few seconds, all three experiments had vanished from the Meadows in a flash of light.

~~*~*~*

The quarry sat on the edge of town, forgotten and abandoned. Some old faded graffiti decorated the high stone walls and there were beer cans scattered on the ground, but for the most part it was empty. There were signs around it, warning of the treacherous footing. A few years ago, a high school senior had fallen to his death after a night of partying. In response, the city had put a fence up around the empty quarry and only a few scientists were allowed inside to study the rock formations. The current quandary being investigated was why no water seemed to pool in the deep quarry, which remained bone dry. Though it remained empty, people walking past the fence claimed to hear strange noises. Most assumed it was wildlife, but a few claimed the quarry was haunted by restless ghosts.

A glimmer of light started to form in the center of the quarry and within seconds, three human shapes stood where the light had been. The woman lifted her head, inhaling the sweet night air. Gesturing with one hand, she began moving forward and the two men followed. In the shadows of the quarry, only their glowing eyes could be seen.

Gravel crunched under foot as the three experiments continued forward, scanning the rock walls surrounding them. Isis held a fist up and the three of them stopped. She tilted her head to one side, her sharp hearing picking up the distant sounds of rasping and scraping. She moved over to a large boulder, motioning for Coop and Jack to follow her.

"They're two clicks north," she reported, looking at the two men. "Chances are there's a cave nearby and that's where the noise is coming from. A traditional approach would be best."

"One stays near the entryway to push the stragglers back inside, the other two eliminate the ones inside," Jack said, nodding in agreement. "Probably the best strategy we have."

Coop adjusted his grip on the heavy bag he held. "I'll stay by the entryway. You two have the most recent experience with close-quarter combat."

"I don't expect many will get past us," Isis mentioned. "You'll have plenty of time to set up the explosives. Leave the high demon to me."

Jack and Coop exchanged a puzzled look before turning their attention back to Isis.

"I have my reasons," she said. "Let's move out."

The three of them swiftly moved out from their cover and ran toward the faint celebratory sounds. The trees rustled in the breeze and howled through the rocky formations.

Isis spotted the cave entrance, even in the pitch black. The faint flicker of light gave it away. No one but an experiment would have spotted the way the shadows moved differently. Isis scanned the rocky ledges for guards and lookouts. There were none. The followers of Set had spent so many years underground, hidden from the world, that it made them sloppy. They had yet to understand the value of sentries. Looking over at Jack and then at Coop, she nodded toward the cave and the three started forward. A steady stream of adrenaline began to pump into their systems in anticipation of the fight.

Reaching the mouth of the cave, Isis peered inside. The fetid smell of dampness hung heavy in the air, as did the chalky scent found in most quarries. The strange hissing and screeching noises were louder, as were the heavy footsteps. They pounded the ground as the creatures danced rapturously deeper in the cavern. The cave was dark and stretched back further than the experiments' sharp eyes could see.

Isis ducked inside, followed by Jack and then by Coop. Coop hung back by the entrance, placing the bag down by a rock. Drawing his gun, he nodded at the two other experiments. They turned to face the shadows of the cave and started moving forward. As they moved, their bodies melted into the lean sleek bodies of panthers. Black fur sprouted all over their flesh as their limbs grew and stretched. Their eyes rounded and became glowing yellow. The two big cats padded down the long stretch, turning down into another cavern. After a few more feet, they came upon a crude stairway that led further down. There was a torch at the bottom. The two panthers swiftly and agilely moved down the rock steps, which were somewhat slippery due to the dust. The squealing and hissing grew louder the further down they went.

Reaching the torch, there was another flight of rock steps. There were more torches lighting the way. The panthers glanced at each other and one started down the cavern, ignoring the steps. There was an opening off to the side, which she trotted through. The other followed close behind. The sounds of the followers filled the air as they entered the sacred space of the altar. Their rancid smell invaded the experiments' sensitive noses.

A herd of followers in brown robes danced and hissed below. They raised their arms to the likeness of Set, which was carved into one of the rock walls. Both panthers flattened their ears and pressed their bodies to the floor as they crept forward, observing the scene before them. The likeness of Set stood proud and tall, obviously modeled after his guardian appearance. At his feet was a wealth of shiny objects. Stolen watches and jewels, coins, and glassware glinted in the torchlight. Sand was sprinkled generously on the offerings.

A strange rasping sound drew the panthers' attention to the right. Perched on a rocky outcropping was a creature that resembled a man, except for the massive leathery wings at his back. His face was more bat-like than human. His flesh was maggot-colored and as leathery as his wings. Coal-dark eyes watched the celebration below and one knee was up so he could rest his arm on it. Around his throat was a collar of interlocking iron rings with a glass sphere of sand at the end of it. His feet were claws, including one on the back of his ankle. What little hair he had was brown and tied back.

Isis looked over her shoulder at Jack. He caught her gaze, turned, and left the way they had come. She listened to his paw pads whisper across the stone as he made his way down the rocky steps. Watching the demon to make sure he stayed put, Isis waited for Jack to emerge. Glancing over the celebrating hooded figures, she estimated there were about fifty. Maybe a few more.

There was a loud snarl moments before a black figure dove in through the rocky opening, tackling two of the celebrating followers. Isis didn't hesitate as she leapt out from her rocky hiding place. As she descended, she allowed her body to melt back into its usual human form. Her muscles shrank and expanded, stretching out until her joints were in their normal place. The black fur disappeared, leaving only pale flesh and then shiny black. She hit the floor in a crouching position and stood up, lashing out with a powerful kick that sent a follower crashing backward into two others. Spinning around, she reached out and dug her fingers into the throat of another. Ripping out his throat, she tossed the scaly flesh away and withdrew her sais. She lunged forward and buried them in the chest cavity of a rushing follower, spraying yellow blood everywhere.

Strong talons grasped her shoulders and lifted her off the ground, throwing her backward. Isis collided with the enormous rock carving of Set and fell to the ground, looking up at the demon. A smile crept across his face as he held himself up to his full height. He towered over her, standing at least seven feet. Isis grabbed her sais and stabbed another follower who had rushed at her, keeping the demon in her peripheral vision. Twisting, she stabbed the second sai in the center of another follower's face. Further back, she could hear Jack roaring and tearing open flesh. Isis rushed past a line of followers, slitting their throats as she went by.

The demon flapped his wings and Isis saw Jack narrowly avoid getting skewered by his talons. He shifted back into his human form, throwing himself to the ground when the demon flew back. A couple followers had run out, but most remained. They weren't the most intelligent creatures, but they could put up a decent fight. Jack drew his gun and fired, killing a few of them. He met Isis' gaze and nodded that he was okay.

The rasp of a weapon being drawn caused Isis to arch back, narrowly avoiding being smashed in the head with a club. A few followers had retrieved their weapons from wherever they had hidden them. Isis leapt backward when the club was swung again and kicked out at the creature, knocking it away from her. She leapt on top of him, pinning his wrists and stabbing him in the face. Glancing over at the club, she noticed the wicked-looking spikes jutting out of it. The sound of air being sliced made her roll out of the way of another weapon. She threw her sai, and it sank into the center of the attacker's face. Flipping back to her feet, Isis retrieved her sai and slipped it back into the sheath she wore on her belt. Leaping forward again, she wrapped her legs around the neck of another creature, swung around, and forced it to the ground. Drawing her gun, she shot it in the back of the head and holstered the gun again.

Hearing a familiar leathery flapping, she dove into a forward roll. Isis saw the flash of pale flesh as the demon's weapon missed her. Standing again, she sprinted toward the rock with Set's likeness carved in it. As she anticipated, the demon gave chase. Isis ran up the wall until she was parallel to the ground. Spinning around, Isis launched herself at the demon. They collided in midair and fell to the ground in a heap. Quickly scrambling over him, Isis grabbed one of his wings and snapped it. She repeated the action on the second and then drew a throwing knife and buried it in the back of the creature's knee.

"Stay," she ordered the now howling demon as she ripped her knife free. She whipped it at a follower who was sneaking up behind Jack. Distantly, they could hear the echo of a metallic whisper. Coop was taking care of any followers that tried to flee. Isis ducked under a rock that was thrown at her. Grabbing the club of a fallen follower, she smashed in the skull of a creature to her right. The follower who had thrown the rock launched itself at her and she swung the club, burying it in the creature's face. Bones crunched under the heavy weapon and the follower fell. Tossing the club away and pulling out her sais again, Isis proceeded to fight off the few remaining followers. She punched one in the face, back kicked another, and followed through by front kicking the one who was rushing her. Isis proceeded to gut the first, thrust the longest prong of the sai through the second, and eviscerate the third.

Soon, the only sound in the cave was the howling of the fallen demon. Jack fired his last round, killing the last follower. The ground was sticky with yellowish blood and the overpowering stench of it filled the area. Jack stumbled and Isis noticed a large gash running across his ribs. The demon had managed to graze him with its talons, but the skin was already knitting back together. He would be fine in another few minutes or so. They were both dusty and streaks of chalk decorated their clothing and hair, as did the blood that had sprayed up in their faces.

Isis turned her attention to the snarling demon and walked through the bodies, crossing the space to where it was dragging itself along the rocky ground, his ruined knees trailing grayish blood in the dust. She crouched down and watched him for a moment. He lashed out at her face with his talons, but Isis leaned back and out of reach, unbothered. Leaning forward again, she grabbed the heavy iron links and viciously twisted them. Yanking the demon up to his knees, she held him close to her so he would see her glowing green eyes.

"I know you're linked to Set or Pyra," she began, leaning away from the claws that thrashed about. She tightened the chain around his neck as a warning. The demon quieted down, but still glared at her.

"What do you want, 7-299?" he growled, his voice like dried leaves on pavement.

"I want them to know that attacking the Lair was strategically unwise," she began. "It has forced my hand. Every time they attack an ally, I will respond in kind. They think they own me and the others. They do not and that should scare them."

"Rabid dogs need to be put down," the demon hissed, looking back at Jack. The experiment watched him, unimpressed. Isis took out a throwing knife and sliced it across the creature's tendons, causing him to howl and shriek. She threw the demon down to the ground and began moving out of the cave, sliding the knife back into her belt.

"Beware of what's behind the doors you're unlocking, seven series," the demon warned. He began to cackle, an unpleasant rough sound.

Isis ignored him as she continued moving out of the cavern. Jack frowned as he looked between her and the demon before hurrying to catch up to her.

"Aren't you going to put him out of his misery?" he asked.

"To do so would suggest that I am merciful," Isis responded as they continued down the cave entrance to the stairs. "That would be unwise and inaccurate."

As they ascended the rocky steps, the air began to grow cleaner. They stepped around a few bodies of followers, all leaking blood from bullet or stab wounds. Their long forked tongues lolled out of their mouths and their lips were pulled back in a snarl, revealing mouths of curved triangular teeth.

Isis glanced up at the walls, smelling the explosives. It wasn't long before she spotted the first gray brick with wires running out of it. Soon after, Coop came into view. He was outlined in the moonlight streaming through the cave's entryway. Isis passed by him, accepting the detonator he held out to her. The three experiments ducked down and slipped out of the cave. They began to walk down the long empty quarry. Once they were a safe distance away, Isis pressed the button on the detonator. The explosion echoed throughout the quarry, travelling to the nearest town. The ground shook beneath their feet and the sound of rocks caving in shattered the quiet. None of the experiments looked back and, after another moment, they disappeared in a bright flash of light.

CHAPTER FIVE

Sly draped herself across the steps, bored. She was wearing dress pants and a top, which were uncomfortably stiff. Glancing at the clock on the wall, she groaned. It would be another forty-five minutes before the memorial gathering at the mansion. The halls were filled with the sounds of frantic steps as last minute preparations were attended to. Most of the noise originated in the kitchen, but a few housekeepers were draping gray veils over the last bare sculptures. Sly's eyes wandered over to the tapestry of Selene in battle. The tapestries wouldn't be covered, but the portraits would. Sly didn't understand the protectors' grieving customs at all.

A sudden light in the front room drew her attention down the hall. *Odd,* she thought as she straightened up. Her hand drifted down her leg to where she kept a throwing knife strapped to her calf. After a moment, Isis emerged from the room. Sly noticed her dusty appearance and her curiosity was peaked. Aside from dirt and grime, Sly noticed the coagulating yellowish blood — which smelled faintly of rot — splattered across the shiny black catsuit.

"Where did you run off to?" she asked and the

experiment's glowing green eyes turned to her. As usual, the woman's face betrayed no emotion. *Wouldn't want to play poker with her,* Sly thought as she suppressed a shudder. Jack and Coop both stepped out into the front hallway, looking equally filthy. Sly arched an eyebrow when she noticed Jack's bloodied torn shirt. She could see no wound, which meant he probably healed already. Their glowing eyes fixed on her and Sly couldn't help but feel a little intimidated. She could only imagine what it would be like to face a large group of them at night when only their eyes would be visible.

Jack and Coop stepped past Isis and moved toward the stairway, swiftly ascending. Isis remained where she was. Sly moved down the steps, taking her time. She reached the bottom and leaned against the banister, pursing her lips. It intrigued her how Isis could switch to her Blitz persona so easily. Sly was sure the protectors didn't see it, or pretended they didn't, but she did. There were times when the woman was Isis and other times when she was Blitz. Right now, Sly saw the latter.

"Don't think you're supposed to be off the property without a supervisor," she mentioned. "And I *know* you're not supposed to engage in fisticuffs."

"You have no evidence I was off the property," Isis countered. "And I'm not supposed to engage with normals unless it is in self-defense. Should you not be at the service?"

Sly smiled, impressed with her easy dodge. "I am not a protector. I'm sure Aneurin made you aware of the strict rules regarding who enters the mausoleum."

"He did," Isis responded simply, moving forward to the stairs. Sly glanced to the side as the experiment glided past her. She shivered when she noticed she didn't hear the woman's footsteps.

"That's just plain creepy," Sly laughed to herself, shaking off the chills she got. Moving a few steps down the hall, Sly paused in front of a frame of pictures of

Brindy and Devlin. A couple of them were set up next to the pillars in the hallway. Studying their smiling faces, Sly wondered how many more services she would have to go to. Shape shifters dying had never bothered her. It occurred regularly, almost as often as humans dying. It was war and that was what happened in war.

"Sorry, kids," she said to the pictures. "It's always the innocent who fall first. You're not the first to be caught in the crossfire and you sure as hell won't be the last. Such is life."

Turning her attention to the noisy kitchen, Sly made her way to the closed door. She intended to pour herself a large glass of wine.

An hour later, the guests began to Appear in the main hall. Shape shifters, guardians, and diplomats from the other worlds gathered and looked around at the magnificent dwelling. The ones who called it home quickly broke away from the large group, going about their hosting duties. Servers began to circulate with glasses of fine wine, attending to the newly-arrived visitors.

Jensen and Nero moved off to the side, watching the gathering from the edge of the hallway. A knock at the door drew everyone's attention down the hall as a footman moved to answer it. Lilly moved forward to greet whoever was at the door.

Alpha stepped inside, nodding in greeting to Lilly. "A few of us wanted to pay our respects."

"Thank you," Lilly said, gesturing inside, welcoming them. Alpha entered, rotating her wrist a couple times. Wylie and Amber followed her and behind them were about ten rebels. Jensen recognized the twins who took the coats at the Lair. Many of the guests were looking at the rebels in barely disguised contempt. They hadn't exactly dressed appropriately. Most were wearing club attire and many of them had neon-colored hair. Brightly-colored elaborate tattoos of animals and plants decorated most of their exposed flesh. Jensen grabbed a glass of wine from a passing server. The rebels were showing respect in their own way. They wore darker colors and braided ribbons in black and white were tied to their upper arms. Each of them had likely had a small dove tattooed somewhere on their body, a sign of remembrance for those who were lost. Jensen looked down at his polished shoes, as his thoughts strayed back to the mausoleum, where he had visited the final resting place of his sister and parents.

"You must be the last Aldridge."

Jensen looked at the stern-faced man who stood in front of him. He was wearing a plum-colored tunic and a gold circlet around his brow. He had long light brown hair, which was pulled away from his face. Jensen looked to his ears, which were rounded, indicating he wasn't from the Seelie Court. There was no shimmer to his flesh, so he wasn't a guardian, though he held himself and dressed in a similar manner.

"That would be me," Jensen responded, sipping his wine. He noticed Jack come down the stairs. The experiment slipped into the crowd and soon disappeared from Jensen's sight.

"I am Gethin from the Magic Orders," the man introduced himself. "The loss of your family was a great tragedy."

"Yes, yes it was," Jensen said, not paying much attention to Gethin. He frowned when he noticed Coop come down the stairs. Why had the experiments been upstairs? Scanning the crowd, he noticed Isis was missing. His hand strayed to his pocket where he still kept her necklace, a habit he had been unable to break. Jensen planned on returning it to Isis but it kept slipping his mind.

"It is fortunate you survived," Gethin continued. "You may be able to restore your family's bloodline one day."

Jensen looked back to the man, wondering if every race knew about his background. If they did, how many were waiting for him to reproduce? Just thinking about it made him uncomfortable. Nero draped his arm around Jensen's shoulders.

"Don't know if that's very likely," the youngest Deverell put in with a suggestive wink. Jensen hid his smile behind his wine glass.

Gethin turned when Jack passed by them, moving silently among the crowd. His eyes were alert and Jensen could tell the experiment was surveying his surroundings. The experiments moved like sharks through crowds, never staying still.

"Animals," Gethin muttered, sipping his wine. Both Jensen and Nero turned their attention back to him. Nero's arm dropped from Jensen's shoulders and when Jensen looked over at his friend, he noticed his expression had hardened.

"We were warned about them after the services. I don't understand the High Council's decision to allow them to run wild," Gethin continued with a shake of his head. "There is no wisdom in letting dangerous creatures like that run loose."

"They were being held prisoner by a madman," Nero replied, sounding a little annoyed. "They're shape shifters, just like the rest of us."

"From what I understand, they're little more than wild animals designed to kill. They don't even look like normal shape shifters anymore. At least the Corporation sterilized them so your world doesn't have to worry about their reproducing," Gethin remarked, unbothered by Nero's tone. "And that hybrid? The power of a guardian and a shape shifter mixed with whatever was done to them. It's a disaster waiting to happen."

"You probably won't feel that way when they save you from whatever Grenich throws at us. If you'll excuse me," Jensen said calmly, as he moved to set his wine glass down only to realize he was no longer holding it. Jensen's brow furrowed as he looked around, spotting the glass on the table he was standing next to. He had no memory of putting it down. Jensen stared at it for a moment. There was a dull throbbing behind his eyes and he felt as though he was missing something.

Shaking his head, Jensen put the strange feeling out of his mind as he moved away from the man from the Magic Orders, wandering through the crowd toward where he had seen Jack go. He turned when he felt a hand on his shoulder and found himself face-to-face with glowing brown eyes.

"You were attempting to find me," Jack stated. His soft voice was almost lost among the quiet murmuring of the crowd. Jensen looked around them, noticing Jet and Lilly standing by one of the pillars. Passion and Electra stood next to them. Jet had been practically catatonic ever since returning from the Lair. Jensen hadn't heard him speak since then. His normally bright blue-green eyes had gone dull and Jensen wasn't sure how aware of things the protector was. It concerned him. Jet had been like a second father to Jensen; his late parents had entrusted their children to the Monroes. To see him so devastated broke Jensen's heart.

"How did you — never mind," Jensen massaged his brow. The lingering ache in his head was swiftly dissipating and his mind didn't feel as foggy as it had moments ago. "Where's Isis?"

"If she is not down here, her room is the most likely place you'll find her," Jack answered. "She wanted to take a shower before the gathering."

"Thank you, Jack," Jensen said and turned toward the main stairway. He weaved his way through the murmuring crowd, attempting to keep his face down. The last thing he wanted was another awkward exchange with a stranger.

~~*~*~*

Isis leaned against her dresser, attempting to will the

excess adrenaline out of her system. It still coursed through her veins, making her more on edge than normal. A hot shower hadn't helped and neither had a cold one. Push-ups and crunches hadn't done anything. She was too on-edge to even attempt meditation. Curling and flexing her fingers, Isis rolled her neck. Her entire body was tingling like a live wire and she had to find some way to expel the excess energy before going downstairs. The follower horde had been much smaller than expected, which caused the build-up of adrenaline. She adjusted the towel she had wrapped around herself after the most recent shower and let out a breath. Digging her toes into the soft carpeting, Isis closed her eyes and turned her face to the ceiling. The room was dark since she hadn't bothered turning on any lights.

Her eyes snapped opened when she caught the faint scent of a familiar soap and deodorant. Isis listened for the quiet footsteps, her body beginning to tremble. Without thinking, she went to the door and pulled it open. Jensen stood on the other side with his hand poised to knock.

"Hey, are you—"

He was cut off when she grabbed his tie and yanked him inside the room, practically tossing him onto the bed. Jensen turned around as she closed the door, staring at her in surprise. Locking the door, she dropped the towel to the floor and was on top of him in two steps. She kissed him deeply, feeling his body respond to her.

"Wait, wait, wait," Jensen said as she pulled the belt out of his pants and tossed it to the side. "What in the name of the guardians are you doing?"

"We need to have sex. Actually, I need to have sex but I imagine you will benefit as well," she replied.

"Um, why?" Jensen asked, trying to hold her at arm's length. She stared at him, puzzled. Normals were so strange and contradictory.

"Don't you want to have sex?"

"It's a little odd when there's a memorial service going

on," Jensen paused, frowning as he ran one of his hands up her arm. "You're shaking."

"There is an excess of adrenaline in my system and I have to find an outlet for it. Sex is the most logical means," Isis explained, looking to his hand and then back to his blue eyes. "I've tried all other methods and I cannot go downstairs if I'm as on edge as I am right now. It would be dangerous."

After a moment, Jensen sighed and removed his jacket, tossing it to the side. He loosened his tie, pulled it off, and then undid the buttons of his shirt.

"When we're done, you have to explain how you built up so much adrenaline," Jensen stated, pulling his shirt off and tossing it to the side. Isis jumped forward again, tackling him on the bed. He trailed his hands over her soft flesh, turning so she was on her back. Looking at her, he ran a hand through her short hair. She undid the button and zipper on his pants, as he continued to explore her body with his mouth. The lights in the room flickered briefly.

As passion overcame them, Jensen gently nuzzled her collarbone. Isis could feel his warm breath against her sensitive flesh. Their breathing quickened as they rolled over in the bed so she straddled him. The moonlight caught her and her flesh glistened in the dimness. She looked at her lover and for the first time she could remember, Isis didn't feel like a simple killing machine. Jensen wasn't scared of her and he didn't look at her as though she were a monster.

Grenich had underestimated her and she would make sure it was their undoing.

~~*~*~*

Orion stood among the mourners, sipping his wine. He recognized many faces — most of which looked at him with suspicion. There were several he didn't recognize, but he knew what lands they were from. Having studied the supernatural races recently, Orion was able to distinguish them from guardians and shape shifters. The lycanthropes were the most at home among the shape shifters, being a similar species. They were also dressed the most plainly, their clothing made to last. They wore no makeup and their hair was very long.

The representatives from the Magic Orders and Seelie Courts were dressed in their finest clothes and looked the most out of place. The diplomats from the Magic Orders seemed to be taking offense to just about everything. *They might be worse than the guardian men,* Orion thought with a quiet laugh.

"There's a sound I never thought I'd hear again," a soft feminine voice came from his left. Orion turned, recognizing the voice. A woman in an elegant black dress with gold trim stood beside him. Perrin — his mentor. She turned her gaze toward him and smiled faintly, pushing a strand of hair away from her face.

"I thought you never left the Sanctuary," Orion mentioned as he sipped his wine.

"I came to pay my respects," Perrin answered, her voice gentle as always. "It's also one of the few times I will be able to see my sister."

"Ah, so Gwendolyn is still studying in the Magic Orders?" Orion asked.

"She is. She has achieved the rank of sorceress," Perrin said with a nod. "I believe she is here as a liaison."

Perrin looked pointedly at his raw hands. "What is troubling you?"

"A number of things," Orion answered, lifting his chin in Jet's direction. "Not the least of which is him. He's devastated."

Perrin looked over to the protector leader, who was listening to a representative from the lycanthropes. He nodded when appropriate, but his gaze was distant. Lilly and Passion stood next to him, both looking much more alert.

"He and Lilly have lost two children. That would devastate anyone," Perrin pointed out. Orion was quiet for a moment, thinking over all that had happened. Looking up again, he noticed how much dimmer the mansion seemed to be.

"I wish I understood the wisdom behind letting Chance out into the world," Orion stated, turning his attention back to Perrin. "They had a werelion with them. According to the rebels, slugs didn't affect it in the slightest. Isis managed to kill it with guardian silver bullets."

"You require more?"

"If we have any hopes of surviving," Orion said, placing his half-emptied glass on a passing tray of empty glasses. "I know he won't be thrilled about the prospect, but the protectors and their allies need effective weapons."

"Are you the Deverell everyone thought had perished?" one of the fey delegates asked as he approached Orion. The protector shook his head.

"No, that would be him," Orion said politely, pointing to where Ajax was conversing with a rebel. "It's a common mistake."

The fey turned and moved through the crowd to Orion's younger brother. Perrin chuckled as she looked over at him. She reached into her sleeve and withdrew a thin stick of light blue chalk, which she handed to Orion.

"If you want more weapons, you will have to talk to him yourself. I trust you remember where the gateway to the Sanctuary is," Perrin said, her gaze traveling across the main hall. "Bring Hunter with you. Something seems to be troubling her and there is a strange aura about her. A visit to the Sanctuary will do her good."

Orion followed her gaze to where Hunter was standing with Declan. They were speaking with a couple rebels and a representative from the Magic Orders. Hunter was absent-mindedly massaging her arm. Orion took another glass of red wine from a passing tray as Perrin moved away, watching as she approached her sister. Gwendolyn was wearing a maroon dress with silver trim. She had blonde hair and lighter eyes than her older sister. Orion had never met her. What little he knew about her was from what Perrin had told him.

"You look rather lonesome," Electra observed as she approached the eldest Deverell. Orion shrugged and sipped his wine. He glanced to the side when he heard the heavy metal ringtone of Alpha's cell phone. She answered the phone and moved toward the kitchen.

"How many guardians are here?" Orion asked.

"At least two from each land," Electra answered. "Mom's here, of course, and Donovan came with his apprentice. Why do you ask?"

"Just making conversation," Orion responded.

"Have you seen my sister? I was looking for her," Electra said. Orion looked around, noticing Isis' absence. *That can't be good,* he thought as he scanned the muted colors of the attendees. He turned to look behind him and spotted her approaching. She was clad in her shining black catsuit, the cat charm gleaming at her throat.

"Where have you been hiding?" Orion asked when she stopped beside him. He lifted his wine glass to his lips.

"I was not hiding. I was having sexual intercourse," she replied and Orion choked on his wine. She was unbothered by his gagging and hacking while Electra just looked stunned. The young guardian knew people processed grief in different ways, but she had never heard of someone having an amorous response. Isis looked over to her twin as Orion tried to quell his coughing. Most of the guests were staring at them.

"You told me you wanted to speak with me after the ceremony," Isis mentioned. "Would now be an adequate time?"

"Um, yeah, I think it would," Electra responded, glancing over at Orion. "Let's go to the library."

The two moved away from Orion, who had managed to get his coughing under control. He straightened up, cleared his throat, and smoothed his suit. Ajax approached him, holding his hands behind his back. Orion looked at him expectantly, noticing his irritated expression.

"Is this about the fey?" he asked. A fake smile was plastered on Ajax's face.

"You're better at speaking to people," Orion stated, spreading his hands. "The last thing Jet and Lilly need is me causing some kind of interdimensional incident."

Ajax opened his mouth, closed it, and studied his brother for a moment. "You know, I hate it when you're right."

"Orion?"

Orion turned to look at Alpha. She was tapping her phone against her palm and looked concerned. Orion felt a sinking feeling in his stomach.

"I just got a call from Sabina. Before you jump to conclusions, don't worry. Ace is fine," Alpha said, raising her hand to prevent Orion from asking a hundred questions. "There was a similar attack at her club. Less followers, no wereanimals, and fewer casualties. They lost two rebels and maybe ten were wounded."

Orion rubbed his brow, not bothering to hide his relief. "Did Chance make an appearance?"

Alpha shook her head. "No, but someone matching his description has been visiting the club the past week or so. Apparently he showed an interest in Ace."

"Of course he did," Orion grumbled. "You have told her to be on her guard?"

"I've warned all rebels of the situation," Alpha replied, sounding offended. "We look out for each other. I'd thank the protectors to keep in mind that it wasn't just Brindy and Devlin who lost their lives."

She turned and walked off, nearly bumping into a guardian.

"Quite the effect you have on people," Ajax

mentioned. Orion just dropped his shoulders, feeling slightly dizzy. There were so many fronts to the war with Grenich and he was having trouble keeping track of them all.

~~*~*~*

In the library, Isis and Electra sat across from each other in one of the window seats. It was a clear night. Hundreds of stars dotted the night sky, but the moon was absent. Shadows clung to the walls of the library. The only sound was the quiet murmuring from the gathering out in the main hall. The subtle scent of the books danced about the room.

Electra was fidgeting with her hands, trying to figure out how to broach the topic. She didn't even know if Isis would be able to tell her anything, but she wanted her twin to be aware of the situation. She noticed the faint glimmer in Isis' skin, identical to her own. It identified them as being descended from guardians. Electra felt a sense of relief when she saw the subtle shimmer. She had been worried the Grenich Corporation would find a way to remove it. *I still don't know if she has any guardian abilities aside from Appearing,* she realized.

Electra decided to just come right out with it. "There might be a mole in the Meadows."

Isis didn't appear bothered at all as she looked back to her twin.

"Do you have evidence to support your theory?" she asked. Electra bit her lower lip and shook her head.

"Not a lot. I don't understand how it's possible. The Meadows have always been peaceful. We are born to care for the Earth and her inhabitants. To ally with a place like Grenich is beyond reprehensible," Electra replied, speaking quicker than she usually did. "I don't even know what would be gained by it."

"Guardians are unconcerned with monetary currency," Isis observed, still calm. "The price would be something more valuable. Perhaps their life."

"How would Set even be able to contact the guardians? He was banished. He should have no ties to—"

"I cannot give you answers unless you show me evidence of your suspicions," Isis interrupted. Electra lifted the small hat off her head, reached inside the brim, and pulled out a folded bit of paper.

"Our sacred texts have been altered, censored," she explained as she handed the papers to her sister. Isis unfolded them and laid them next to her, studying them.

"All mention of Pyra has been erased," Electra continued. "Just torn out. What's weird is we already know the stories so censoring the texts is pointless."

"What am I looking at?" Isis asked, ignoring her sister's explanation.

"Phoenix and I decided the best place to start would be the library, where our histories are kept. We looked up the last person to check out the tome and it turns out it was Aneurin," Electra pointed to the older looking paper. "That's the record. The other one is a recent letter from him to Adonia. Can you compare the handwriting?"

Isis didn't look up from the papers. "Handwriting analysis is useless. There are too many factors that can corrupt the samples. Different inks and paper textures, for example. Calling it a pseudo-science is being generous."

"Can you tell me anything?"

Isis lifted up the papers, looking from one to the other. "This record is odd. There's a blank space where there should be a name."

She pointed on the thin tan paper and Electra leaned forward, noticing the small space just before Anuerin's name.

"He also pressed his seal much harder on this one, but he could have been in a rush when he did the other one," Isis mentioned as she handed the papers back to Electra.

"You don't think he's a traitor?"

Isis looked over at her sister. "He's too dedicated to the rules and laws. The status and title is enough of a reward for him. There is nothing Set could offer him that he would accept, from what I've seen."

"Who do you think censored the texts?"

Isis lifted her thin shoulders. "I don't know, but I have a couple ideas. The first being someone related to Pyra who couldn't live with the shame of her betrayal. If not that, my guess would be someone younger who would be easy to threaten or intimidate. It would have to be someone who had been to Earth at some point because Set doesn't have access to the Meadows."

Isis stood up and rolled her neck, stretching her arms over her head. Electra watched her, thinking over what she had said. She folded up the papers and put them back in her hat, hoping she would be able to return the one before Athena discovered it was missing.

"How have you been?" Electra asked, looking over at her sister. Isis was looking out the window, but turned her attention back to her twin. She sat across from her again.

"Do you want to engage in small talk?" Isis said. Had anyone else asked that question, it would have sounded mocking or dismissive. Electra knew the experiments were not accustomed to things like socializing and conversation, so the question was probably genuine. Isis leaned back against the wall behind her, looking out the window again.

"We haven't seen each other since the Changing of Seasons celebration and even then we didn't really have a chance to catch up," Electra replied. Isis still looked a little puzzled.

"I am functioning normally. I'm at peak physical health and my abilities appear to be intact," she said. Electra smiled, a little entertained by the blunt answer.

"Do you think Jet will be all right?" she asked, wondering about the protector leader. He had barely moved or spoken during the interment and at the memorial, he had yet to utter a word.

"I do not understand. He is not injured or sick," Isis responded, frowning. Electra adjusted the netting on her face, wondering how much longer she would have to wear it.

"You understand grief, right?"

"I know of the concept. It is a temporary emotional state of distress usually caused when a bond is severed, typically by death. Normals experience it in varying degrees," Isis answered, crossing one leg over the other.

"Experiments don't?"

"Not to the best of my knowledge."

Isis looked up when Jade poked her head in the door. She approached the two women, glancing once over her shoulder.

"I need to borrow Isis," Jade said under her breath. "Jet's not in any state to see diplomats and we have to start organizing meetings with the other supernatural races. Lilly has asked for our help."

"I think I would be more of a detriment. Your guests are wary of experiments," Isis pointed out.

"Well, they're going to have to get used to you if we are to have any chance of defeating Grenich," Jade replied, brushing a strand of long hair behind her shoulder. Isis rose in one fluid movement.

"Very well," she agreed, waiting for Jade to lead her back out to the main hall. Electra followed behind them. Alex and Shae were waiting just outside the door. Both Jade and Electra blinked at the onslaught of light, but Isis was unaffected. Electra nodded to her sister and went to rejoin her mother and the Monroes. Isis turned her attention back to her three teammates.

"Okay, Lilly and Raven are going to speak with the Magic Orders. According to Hecate, the vampire representative didn't show up, which was expected due to their sensitivity to ultraviolet light. They did agree to a meeting though," Jade explained.

"So that leaves the fey and the lycanthropes?" Alex asked.

"Right. You and I will speak with the fey. Shae and Isis will approach the lycanthrope diplomats," Jade said. *Lycanthropes are much less likely to take offense at speaking with an experiment,* she refrained from adding. The older protector had seen the looks the representatives from the Magic Orders and the fey had been sending to the experiments. They were uneasy with the strange shape shifters. Lycanthropes were the species most closely related, and the most similar, to shape shifters. Unlike shape shifters, lycanthropes could only shift into one animal form. They were the only mortal supernatural species, with a life span of up to two thousand years.

"The lycanthropes are over there, across the hall," Jade mentioned, nodding. "The fey are over on that side, toward the front door. Looks like they're speaking with Devin and Malone at the moment. Let's get to work."

Alex and Jade moved toward the fey. Isis followed Shae toward the lycanthropes, who were wearing blue clothing, which was very plain compared to everyone else. They had long black hair, which fell past their shoulders. The lycanthropes had dark complexions and dark eyes. Unlike the other supernatural races, the lycanthropes had sent two women. When one spotted Shae and Isis, she smiled politely. The other woman was a little taller and her eyes traveled around the open space. She was holding a glass of red Bordeaux.

"Hello," Shae greeted, shaking the hand of the first woman. "Thank you for coming. My name is Shae and this is my cousin, Isis."

"Ah, two members of the Four. Don't we warrant all of you?" the first woman asked as Shae shook the other woman's hand. Shae looked over at Isis, who stood by patiently.

"Don't mind Beatriz. She loves to take the piss out of everyone," the second woman said, wrapping her arm around Beatriz's waist. "I'm Marisol. We are from the lycanthropes."

"You are from the leopard family," Isis observed, nodding to the small pin on the woman's collar before looking to the second woman. "And you are tiger."

"That's us," Beatriz said. "We heard you're very observant. Is it true you're a living weapon?"

"I was modified to be a superior warrior, yes," Isis answered, her eyes traveling about the hall. Her mind was humming with the information her senses were processing. She had already tuned out most of the conversations. Isis didn't care for large crowds due to the sheer amount of information she had to process. For every benefit a large crowd offered, there were quite a few drawbacks.

"Can we have a demonstration?" Beatriz asked, finishing her wine. She put the empty glass on a passing tray. Isis turned back to her. She could smell the subtle sweet hint of dirt and plants on her, but no perfume. Both lycanthropes had been working before attending the interment ceremony. Lycanthropes were known for being an agricultural society and one without strict socioeconomic classes.

"Beatriz, she can't just open a can of whoopass in the middle of a memorial," Marisol chided, turning back to Shae and Isis. "What would the Four ask of us?"

"The protectors need allies for the fight against Grenich," Shae began. "Their army grows larger and stronger every day. We are here on behalf of the Monroes to ask for an audience with your leaders."

Beatriz and Marisol exchanged a look. Shae waited patiently and straightened the sleeve of her dress shirt. She was wearing black like most of the other shape shifters, save for the two experiments. Both Jack and Coop still demonstrated a strong aversion to the color black, whereas Isis did not.

"We will have to consult them, but it should be easy enough to arrange," Marisol agreed. "The Monroe family has long been an ally to Diego and Ella. I'm sure they would be open to honoring their alliance."

Isis glanced over to Shae, who was obviously pleased with how the conversation had gone. Isis was more wary. She wasn't used to things being so easy.

"Out of curiosity, how many experiments will Jet and Lilly have on their side?" Beatriz asked. Shae opened her mouth to answer, but Isis responded first.

"At least three, most likely four."

Shae stared at her, but Isis ignored her. After some more small talk, the two lycanthrope representatives stepped away and Shae turned back to Isis.

"Who's the other experiment on our side?"

"An experiment who escaped the same time as Coop did," Isis stated, looking off to the side when a member of the Seelie Court passed by them. "Coop has been talking to Jack and I about him. His name is Shocker and he is an early E-series prototype. If we can convince him to join the fight, he would be a worthwhile asset."

"Do you think he will fight?"

Isis was quiet for a moment, thinking over her answer. "It is difficult to say. If I were him, I would not. The risk would appear to outweigh the benefit. However, he is an experiment, and fighting is what we do."

Shae looked around the crowded hall. Isis turned her attention back to the crowd, observing them.

"You are curious about the other races," she mentioned.

Shae grinned. "I am or at least I was. Judging by the looks the Seelie Court and Magic Orders are giving you and me, I don't think the same can be said about them."

"They feel unsure around experiments. We were designed to be intimidating. Fear is a natural evolutionary response in normals," Isis stated. "And as I understand it, memorials are meant to be solemn events. Their aloofness is appropriate, given the circumstances."

Shae looked at her in a way Isis had grown accustomed

to over the past few months. Normals had a very distinct look when they wanted to argue something but couldn't find the words to do so.

"It's Isis, isn't it?"

Shae and Isis both turned at the smooth voice behind them. A tall black guardian stood there, dressed in a dark blue tunic. There was a twinkle in his eyes and he smiled when the shape shifters turned to him.

"You must be Donovan," Shae said, turning to Isis. "One of Passion's lovers, he also sits on the High Council."

Donovan let out a bark of bitter laughter. "Please don't remind me of that. I just wanted to meet the woman I've heard quite a lot about."

"Why?" Isis asked. She still didn't understand the normals fascination with her, other than her superior abilities, which many of them had never seen. It might have been the glowing eyes, but even the novelty of that should have worn off.

Donovan seemed amused at her response. "I have been told you have a cynicism that could rival my own. I wanted to meet the competition."

Shae snorted and turned away to hide her laughter. Isis was saved from answering by the sound of a glass shattering. Looking over Donovan's shoulder, she spotted a younger guardian man sputtering out apologies as he attempted to help a server clean up the mess of broken glass. Donovan looked up to the ceiling, shaking his head and closing his eyes. He massaged his brow in exasperation.

"That would be my imbecilic apprentice," he grumbled, glancing over his shoulder. "He still hasn't quite got the hang of walking yet."

Shae leaned to the side to get a better look at the younger guardian, whistling. "*Ooh*, he's a *looker*. That must be the infamous Lucky whom Electra and Phoenix have told me about."

Lucky straightened up, almost colliding with Jack. It was only the experiment's quick reflexes that prevented a collision. Lucky raised his hands as an apology, but Jack didn't seem to notice. The younger guardian's clumsiness was very unusual, an anomaly Isis noted. Most of the guardians had a natural grace and moved effortlessly. Lucky seemed to be the exact opposite. Isis watched as Lucky was cornered by a fey, dressed in green. He was still obviously embarrassed about the racket he caused. He ran a hand through his short, curly black hair, nodding and smiling uncomfortably at whatever the fey was saying to him.

"Good, maybe that will keep him out of trouble for the time being," Donovan said, turning back to the two women in front of him. "I understand the four of you are preparing to go to war with Set and Pyra."

"Their aggression will only escalate if we do not," Isis mentioned. "The shape shifters are all that's standing between Set and the Meadows."

"It will not be an easy task, bringing them down. I wish you the best of luck for it sounds as though you'll need it," Donovan observed. "If you should require anything, please don't hesitate to call on me. Passion will be able to reach me. You do have allies within the High Council, even if it doesn't always seem like it."

Shae and Isis watched as he moved around the edge of the hall, back to where Passion stood. The atmosphere was heavy, but the experiments didn't experience it. Isis could tell Shae was nervous about fighting experiments. When they practiced sparring, none of the protectors could lay a hand on them. The experiments were too fast and skilled.

"Shae?"

Shae turned when Jade and Alex approached. Isis continued observing the crowd, not enjoying remaining sedentary. Experiments didn't often stay in one place too long, especially in a crowd.

"Did you speak with the lycanthropes?"

"We did and they agreed to speak with their leaders. They seemed optimistic about scheduling a meeting," Shae reported. "They'll probably respond through Hecate."

"That's good. The fey also seem open to having a discussion," Jade said. "We can tell Lilly and Jet after everyone has left."

"Do you think any of them will agree to an alliance?" Alex asked, putting her hands on her hips. "We are kind of asking a lot."

"If they want to ensure their survival, it's not asking a lot," Jade answered, playing with a silver cuff bracelet on her left wrist. "Set wants to wipe us out so he can conquer the Meadows. If he succeeds, he will be able to destroy their worlds. They're as much at risk as we are and I think they're smart enough to recognize that."

~~*~*~*

Shortly before dawn, the last guest left. The housekeepers swept up what little mess remained and the kitchen was alive with the sound of dishwashers. Jet had retired to the master bedroom a few hours earlier. Most of the inhabitants had gone to bed, but the few who were awake were in the main entertainment room.

Lilly was sitting in a large chair near the front of the room. Velvet and Raven, Jet's twin sister, were standing toward the middle of the room. Isis was sitting in the window seat, staring out at the brightening sky. Coop stood in the doorway, as did Jack. Jade, Alex, Jensen, and Nero were sitting on the couch. Orion was silent in a corner of the room, scrolling through his phone. Shae was sitting on the ground, reclining on her elbows with her long legs out in front of her. She tried to hide a yawn behind her hand. It had been a very long night.

"I expect to hear from the supernatural races next week," Lilly began. "Once I do, Jet and I will assign who will speak to whom. I think it would be in our best interest to arrange meetings as soon as possible. First we have to convince the leaders from each race to agree to a meeting on Earth. Then we have to convince them to take an active part in this fight, which will not be easy."

"You can assume the lycanthropes will help us," Raven spoke up. "The Magic Orders will only speak with the guardians, so their assistance is probably going to be the hardest to get."

"We also need to speak with the other experiment escapee," Coop put in. "I think I know where to find him."

"That's not a good idea," Orion said without looking up from his phone. "Shocker is volatile and unpredictable. That's on a good day, of which he has *very* few."

"What can he do?" Jensen asked, elbowing Nero when he noticed him drifting off. Nero jolted awake and ran a hand down his face, mumbling something about being awake.

"He's an E-series prototype," Coop answered. "He can control electricity through simple touch and with his mind on occasion."

"Dude's a living electric chair?" Nero said, waking up completely as he twisted back to look at Coop. The experiment glanced over at Orion when he snorted. His expression was one of irritation.

"More or less," Orion grumbled. "He's also not shy about demonstrating his abilities. He almost killed me the last time I tried to approach him."

"He was probably unaware that you weren't affiliated with Grenich anymore," Coop pointed out. "If you're serious about going to war with Grenich, you need all the help you can get. I will go with whomever you like to speak with Shocker."

"That will be up to Jet and Lilly, but I would recommend at least one other experiment," Orion said, looking over to Lilly. "I am going to have to go out of town for a couple days, maybe a week or two."

"Where are you going?" she asked, raising an eyebrow. Orion slipped his phone back into his shirt pocket.

"To Perrin's sanctuary. I'm going to ask for Copper's help," he explained, an unusual hesitance in his voice. "We need special weapons, ones only he can make."

Raven frowned and straightened up. Like her brother, she got her looks from her mother. They all had dark hair and clear blue-green eyes. Like her mother, Raven also had a curvaceous form and a shrewd mind.

"Copper? The banished guardian?" she asked, crossing her arms over her chest. "How do the guardians feel about that?"

"I don't think they would be thrilled if they knew," Orion answered with a small shrug, turning his gaze to Lilly. "I'm sorry, but there are some rules we're going to have to bend. Copper was banished for taking human lovers. He never plotted against the guardians and never did anyone any harm—"

"That's inaccurate," Isis mentioned from over by the window. Jensen and Nero smothered their chuckling at her statement. The directness of experiments was often rather amusing.

"Any *direct* harm," Orion amended his statement, glancing over at Isis. "He could be a beneficial ally, one we shouldn't be so quick to write off."

Jensen looked over at Isis. "So that's where the weapons are from?"

Isis glanced at him, nodding once. She then turned her gaze back outside to the brightening landscape. Orion turned his eyes back to Lilly, who looked exhausted. Her normally perfect hair was coming out of the braid she had tied it in.

"Perrin suggested I take Hunter to the sanctuary," the eldest Deverell began, hesitating again. "She thinks it will do her good."

Lilly smoothed her dress, a thoughtful expression on

her face. She tucked a stray strand of golden hair behind her ear as she looked back to Orion.

"If Hunter agrees to it, she may go with you. But you will take Remington along as well," she spoke in a firm voice. "I do not want her going without an escort, one whom Jet and I trust."

Jensen looked over at Nero, whose expression reflected his surprise. It was very unusual for Lilly to be so blunt, even when the situation warranted it. Orion seemed unbothered as he turned his attention to Jack.

"Jack, would you be willing to accompany us as well? I'd feel better with you watching our backs."

Jack, who had been looking at his feet, glanced at Orion. His glowing brown eyes regarded the doctor for a moment and then he nodded. He had never been to the Sanctuary before, but Perrin had sent him numerous books after he had been extracted from the Grenich facility. The books had always had a sweet woodsy scent, like everything from the Sanctuary.

"The four of us can go with Coop to find Shocker," Jade offered. "He might be more willing to listen with two experiments there."

"That is a good suggestion," Lilly agreed. "You can plan everything tomorrow. Right now, I think we are all tired. It's time to call it a day."

She rose from her seat and moved out of the room, disappearing into the hall. One-by-one, the other shape shifters followed until only Jensen and Isis were left in the room. Jensen got up from the couch and moved over to the window seat where Isis was still sitting. She didn't seem to notice his presence as she kept her gaze outside. Jensen leaned forward, interlacing his fingers in front of him.

"I think you should tell Orion where you were during the interment ceremony," he mentioned. "You should probably tell Jet and Lilly too."

"No," Isis replied. "They would be forced to put the

three of us back in the dungeons. Right now, the protectors can't afford to lose any of us."

"I don't think the repercussions will be so severe. Give us normals some credit," Jensen said with a small smile. Isis turned so she was facing him, her brow furrowed.

"The nest was a lot smaller than it should have been," she mentioned. "Even if they're using followers to attack rebel clubs, Set would have ordered Chance to leave at least half the horde there. There were barely a fourth of them in the cave."

Jensen sat up straighter, looking over at her. "You think the rest are somewhere else?"

Isis lifted her shoulders. "I don't have enough information to theorize. Chance could be going after a larger target and using the attacks on rebels as a diversion."

Jensen stifled a yawn, attempting to hide how tired he was.

"You need sleep," Isis observed. Jensen almost envied her ability to go without sleep. *Though I don't think I would enjoy being so alert constantly,* he thought as he looked over at her.

"Will you be able to meditate soon?" he asked.

"Yes, in another few minutes," she answered, looking back outside. Jensen got to his feet and began to make his way out of the room.

"I'll see you later on today," he said before leaving the room. Isis leaned closer to the window, studying her glowing eyes in the glass surface. The low number of followers was troubling her. She knew it was significant, but she had to figure out why exactly.

Outside, the morning mists were snaking through the grounds. It looked like it would be an overcast day.

CHAPTER SIX

A week later, Orion was packing a bag in his room. The supernatural races had all agreed to hold an audience with an ambassador from the protectors. They were scheduled for different days so they could give each appointment their undivided attention. The fey had requested the first meeting and Hecate had given Lilly everything they would need to cross into the different worlds.

Orion could feel a dull headache building behind his eyes. He didn't know how long he would be at the Sanctuary. Copper was obstinate and a misanthrope. He didn't care for Orion at all and it had taken forever to convince the exiled guardian to make weapons for the experiments. Orion didn't know how he was going to approach the topic this time. *Perhaps if I introduce him to Jack. He did express some interest in the experiments,* Orion thought but dismissed the idea. Copper was a man who was interested in having less people in his life, not more.

Orion turned toward his dresser and was surprised to see Isis standing in his doorway. He thought he had shut the door, but a closed door never deterred experiments. Her glowing eyes were blue and they were fixed on him. Orion moved over to the dresser and opened the drawer containing his shirts, pulling out a couple for the trip. He didn't know what his niece wanted, but she would tell him eventually. Though it was morning, Orion had drawn all the shades so his room was cloaked in shadows. The only light came from the small lamp on the bedside table and the hallway outside the open door. Even in the dim light, her catsuit and the charm at her throat gleamed.

"You are leaving today?" Isis asked, watching as he returned to the bed where his bag was. Orion placed the shirts inside, making sure they lined up perfectly.

"I am," he answered, trying not to think of how much dust would accumulate in his absence. Orion had woken at dawn just to clean his room from top to bottom one final time before he left.

"How long do you expect to be gone?"

Orion frowned as he turned and sat on the bed, smoothing the comforter absent-mindedly. Decades of being entrenched in Grenich had given him a sixth sense about experiments. He could often pick up on the subtle changes in their voices and body language that others would miss. Isis' face betrayed no emotion, but her tone indicated some apprehension.

"I don't know," he admitted. "Is something wrong?"

Isis crossed her arms over her chest. Her attention remained on him. The shadows seemed to soften her features and Orion was reminded of why experiments preferred the dark. It gave them an advantage in the form of concealment.

"You're a good asset," she answered. "It is unwise to leave for an undetermined amount of time to an unsecure location."

Orion chuckled. "I think that may be the nicest thing you've ever said to me."

"If something happens to you or you die, it will be a severe detriment. You have indispensable intel on Grenich."

Orion looked at her skeptically. "Please, with the

compliments, my ego can't handle it."

"I'm not—"

"I know, Isis. I was teasing you." Orion rubbed his eyes, trying to will the building headache away. "If something were to happen to me, Perrin knows all that I do. She would be able to help you finish what we have started. You'll also have Roan at your service. I don't know whether or not I should apologize for that."

"I don't know Perrin or Roan," Isis responded. Orion squinted at her, finally understanding what her uneasiness was about.

"This is the first time I've left since you've come to stay at the mansion," he observed gently. "You've never been left alone with the normals before, not like this."

"I'm not concerned with normals."

"Not about them, about being around them. Are you worried about hurting them?"

Isis, who had been doing her best to look at everything but him, turned her attention back to Orion. He saw the mix of hesitance and confusion dancing in the glowing depths. *Never thought I'd see the day she was unsure of something,* Orion thought, trying to figure out some way to reassure her.

"I prefer having someone I know watching my back," Isis stated.

"You'll have the Four and Coop and Jensen," Orion said, standing after a moment. "I'll have Jack watching out for me. Nothing is going to happen, I promise. Just remember that you're not in Grenich anymore."

There was quiet for a moment as Orion looked about the room, trying to remember if he missed packing anything. He was a thorough packer, but he always had a nagging feeling that he was forgetting something. Looking back to the doorway, Orion noticed Isis still watching him. Though he wouldn't admit it, Orion felt a large amount of anxiety about leaving but it wasn't completely about her being around normals. Set was obsessed with finding the

Key, which Isis could potentially be. There was no telling how far Set would go to retrieve her. Orion had already thought of numerous worst case scenarios, each more nightmarish than the last. He had no doubt Isis and Jack could defend themselves, but it was the collateral damage that concerned him the most. *We already lost two young protectors and chances are we're going to lose so many more*, he thought. Turning, he smoothed the sheets again.

Orion approached Isis, lowering his voice to a whisper. "If you encounter any more Grenich lackeys or followers of Set, show them the mistake they made keeping you prisoner. He's scared of you, Isis. Never forget that and make sure he doesn't either."

Isis looked up at him, nodding after a moment. Orion turned back to his bag, zipping it closed. He had another hour or so before they were scheduled to set out. They would have to appear in a redwood forest. Orion grabbed the chalk Perrin had given him at the memorial and stuffed it in his pocket. He knew Isis was watching his every move and his thoughts turned to Nick Chance. According to his sources, Chance was known to have a particular interest in the potential Keys and he was always looking for ways to win Set's approval.

"Your hand is shaking," Isis pointed out with her characteristic bluntness. Orion noticed a tremor go through his hand and flexed it a few times, willing it away. *Quit being such a child. Chance is just a regular sociopathic Grenich minion, not the goddamn boogeyman*, Orion chastised himself. He hated how scared he was of the man. The mere mention of his name brought up memories Orion would prefer to keep buried.

He was shocked when Isis crossed the room and wrapped her arms around his neck in a very cautious embrace. Hesitantly, he returned the embrace, unsure of what else to do. In all his years around experiments, Orion had never seen one offer any kind of physical affection. They avoided contact like it was the plague unless it was required for a mission. Even Coop had trouble with a simple handshake.

After a moment, Isis stepped back and turned her gaze off to the side. Orion stared at her, unable to conceal his amazement at the gesture. Even after returning to the mansion, Isis was withdrawn and aloof, more so than the other experiments.

"I've observed normals using that gesture to reassure each other," she explained, looking back at him. "Particularly when they are experiencing negative emotions."

"Yes, it's a common way to show empathy," Orion said. "Normals often use physical contact to assure each other of their presence and support."

"It's an easy way to get stabbed."

Orion couldn't help but smile tiredly at the statement, looking to the ground. Experiments were nothing if not straightforward. He grabbed his bag, still smiling, and slung it over his shoulder. Reaching down, he picked up the walking stick that doubled as a staff. Like the experiments, Orion never went anywhere without at least one weapon. Isis stepped back, out of Orion's way. He moved out of the room and started down the hall toward Hunter's room. Remington would likely be in the main hall, waiting for them. The old trainer always seemed to be early wherever he went.

When he reached the door to Hunter's room, Orion paused and knocked. He could hear loud rock music from inside the room, which was turned down slightly. The door opened and Hunter looked up at him. She was wearing her usual dark colors, her baggy shirt hanging off one shoulder.

"You're early," she said as she opened the door wider and stepped back into her room. The angry music continued inside as Orion stepped through the door. Hunter tossed a shirt inside her bag, not bothering to fold it, which made the older protector cringe. It looked like she had tossed most of her clothes inside. She moved across the room and took a couple books off her dresser, both of which were worn from repeated readings. Orion watched as she tossed them over to the bed and resisted the strong urge to straighten them. He didn't think Hunter would appreciate his tidying up. The thought of how little she dusted made Orion straighten up so he no longer leaned against the dresser.

"Yes, but we can leave earlier if we wish," Orion answered, moving away from the dresser. "I just wanted to check in."

"Should I bring some kind of gift or offering?" Hunter called over her shoulder as she walked back toward her bathroom.

"No," Orion replied, straightening one of the paperbacks on the bed. "Those seeking sanctuary are not required to offer any payment or gifts. It's a safe haven and you're not under any kind of obligations."

Hunter walked out from the bathroom again, carrying a clear bag filled with different containers, bottles, and a brush. "Good to know."

She stuffed the bag inside the larger bag of clothes. Grabbing the books, she stuffed those inside too, causing Orion to cringe again. She pulled the drawstrings shut and then pulled the flap over the opening, buckling it closed. Hunter turned back to Orion, her crystalline blue-green eyes studying him expectantly.

"Hunter, you've been through a lot," Orion began, trying not to focus on the disarray of her room. "If you wanted to stay here with your family, I'm sure Perrin would understand. Her request was just that: a request."

"If I stay here, will my brother and sister magically not be dead anymore?" Hunter asked in a bitter tone. She leaned back, looking up so she met Orion's gaze. Out of all Jet's children, Hunter had always been the shortest. It didn't make her any less formidable.

"I need to be away from here," Hunter continued. "I

don't care for how long, but I have to get away from this place. It's suffocating me."

"Very well. I'll be in the front hall. We leave in an hour."

Orion turned and left the room, closing the door behind him.

~~*~*~*

Jet sat on the edge of the bed, watching as Lilly adjusted her green velvet dress. Her hair was braided so it would stay out of her face. A thin silver chain was wrapped around her waist. She was preparing for her meeting with the fey, which was scheduled for later in the afternoon. Jet ran a hand over the rough stubble decorating the bottom of his face, debating whether or not he would shave that day.

"Jet?" Lilly asked, looking at her husband in the mirror. "Are you all right?"

Jet almost laughed at the absurdity of the question. "Does this have to happen today?"

Lilly turned and moved back to the bed, sitting next to the haggard protector. "This was the day the fey agreed to. Grenich will not stop just because we are grieving. We need the fey to attend the summit. They are important allies."

"We just lost our son and daughter," Jet whispered, looking down at his feet when he felt tears well up. He still felt the agony of their loss as acutely as he had when he first entered the rebel Lair after the attack. He felt Lilly gently rub his back and looked over at his wife. Her dark blue eyes were also filled with tears.

"I know," she murmured. Jet looked forward to the window across the room. The sunlight felt warm on his face, but he couldn't enjoy it. Everything seemed to remind him of the children they had lost.

"Since the memorial, I've been questioning why we

fight," he confessed. "There's part of me that just wants to let the world burn. Let Grenich have the corrupt hell-hole, whatever they don't already control."

His fists clenched and unclenched a few times. Lilly laid her hand over his left hand, intertwining her fingers with his. She pressed her lips to his temple and ran the fingers of her other hand through his black hair.

"You are grieving, as am I," she reassured him. "We fight so others won't have to feel the pain we are experiencing. We need to remember the countless shape shifters who are still being tormented in Grenich laboratories. Who will fight for them if not us?"

"Ask Orion," Jet answered bitterly. He still felt a certain amount of anger at Orion for going into hiding and letting Grenich remain a secret. Lilly rested her head against Jet's.

"Blaming him won't help anything," she reminded him. "We need all the allies we can get. Like it or not, we need Orion."

Jet sighed and closed his eyes briefly. He wanted to see Hunter before she left for the Sanctuary. Though Jet wasn't wild about the idea of her leaving with Orion, he understood her need to be away for a little while. Grief still haunted the mansion and it was even felt in the Meadows.

"Who is going with you?" Jet asked after a moment.

"Ajax and Sly have agreed to accompany me," Lilly responded. Jet stared at her.

"Sly? Really?"

"She is more than capable of the job and volunteered for it. She seems rather ... interested in the different worlds."

Oh I bet she does, Jet thought as he looked up at the ceiling. The fey were known to have a land rich in jewels and precious stones. He had a feeling that was the main reason their shady informant offered to act as a guard for Lilly. Though Jet wasn't sure he much cared. Sly was an infamously fast draw and proficient with a number of weapons and fighting styles. Not even assassins dared to mess with her. He knew she was more than capable of watching Lilly's back. For one of the first times, Jet was thankful for Sly's questionable morals. He didn't want to take any chances with his wife's safety or any other member of his family.

"I expect we will be back later tonight," Lilly mentioned. "Orion is unsure when he will return. Copper is apparently not very welcoming of visitors."

"Being exiled has that effect," Jet responded. "Though Orion doesn't exactly bring out the best in people."

Lilly gave him a small sad smile and stood from the bed again. She approached the mirror and unbraided her hair. Reaching toward the mirror frame, Lilly pulled down a few evergreen ribbons and re-braided her hair, weaving the ribbons in among her golden hair. It was a small acknowledgment of fey tradition. Fey women often decorated their hair with ribbons or jewels and it was considered polite for guests to do the same. The fey were notorious for having aesthetic appreciation and attraction.

Lilly turned back to Jet. "How do I look?"

He smiled thinly. "Like the most beautiful woman in all the worlds."

Lilly moved over to him and took his hands in hers, helping him to his feet. "Come. Let's see Hunter off."

Jet kissed the back of her hands. He didn't dare tell Lilly of the dark thoughts he had recently had. During the funeral of his children, Jet had begun to contemplate letting the experiments wage the war against Grenich on their own. Isis, Jack, and Coop were more than proficient when it came to fighting. They saw the world differently than other shape shifters. They approached everything like a battle strategy, unconcerned with collateral damage as long as the mission was completed. If Grenich was going to employ similar tactics, Jet wondered if the protectors shouldn't just fight fire with fire. He had already decided Nick Chance needed to die, preferably slowly and painfully. There had been numerous times during the week when Jet had thought about approaching Isis and just telling her to do what needed to be done. He had even contemplated requesting temporary leave for Roan in order to let the assassin kill Chance. However, he knew Lilly would never agree with nor approve such actions.

As he followed his wife down the hall toward Hunter's room, Jet glimpsed Isis lingering around the main stairway. She often seemed to pop up in random places in the mansion, like a ghost. Her attention was on the main hall, but she looked over her shoulder at Jet and Lilly when they passed by. Jet caught her glowing eyes, which were a brilliant shade of silver-blue, and looked at her. She was wearing her normal house clothes, pants and a tank top, made of the same material as her catsuit. The sunlight shone on the shiny material. Isis straightened up and twisted when Jet looked at her, watching him. In that moment, Jet wondered if she somehow deduced what he was thinking.

He turned down the hall, stopping in front of Hunter's door. Jet looked back toward the staircase. Isis had disappeared.

~~*~*~*

Jade, Alex, and Shae were sitting in the library. Jack was somewhere among the bookshelves, picking out some books to read while at the Sanctuary. Shae was sitting in the window seat, enjoying the warm sunlight, while Jade and Alex were on the chaise lounge. Alex had her nose buried in a book about shape shifter history. Jade was reading an article on her phone, her gaze fixed on the screen.

Jack stepped out from the shelves, glancing over at Shae. He tucked a small book into the pack he had over his shoulder. Shae smiled at him, leaning back.

"Where is the entrance to this Sanctuary?" she asked.

"The one we'll be using is in Sequoia National Park," Jack answered as he closed his pack again. He adjusted it so the pack rested on his back, leaving his hands free.

"Is it safe to tell me that?" Shae asked, glancing over at Jade when she turned her face toward the ceiling. Jack's glowing brown eyes wandered over to the lounge before turning back to Shae.

"Just because the Earth is a crossroads doesn't mean there are literal doors out in the middle of nowhere," Jade answered. "You need to have certain materials to reveal the gates and there are gatekeepers who have to open said gates from their side. So even if you know where an entryway is located, it doesn't mean you'll be able to find or use it."

"It doesn't mean someone can't ambush the site," Isis remarked as she stepped into the library, looking over at Jack. "Are you armed?"

"Always," Jack replied, twisting so Isis could see the shoulder holster he was wearing. Both Alex and Jade looked over at the two experiments.

"I assume you are also carrying a couple blades and at least one other firearm," Isis stated, her voice firm. Her body was rigid and she stood in front of the door, her hands clasped behind her. The sunlight reflected on her shiny black clothes.

"Of course. I also have a few back-up weapons and magazines in my pack," Jack responded. "Nothing is going to happen, Blitz."

The others caught the slip from Jack — he still sometimes mixed up her aliases and Orion's as well. However, he did not do it as frequently as when they had first come to the mansion.

"If anything goes wrong, you need to find some way to contact me," she demanded. "We cannot lose Dr. Deverell and if Jet loses another daughter, he will be even more compromised. It will make him useless to us."

"Guardians have mercy," Jade muttered under her

breath as she rested her feet on the coffee table. Alex looked back to her book. It still disturbed them how cold and detached their teammate could be. Her calculating nature was unsettling at times.

"I will not allow anything to happen to them," Jack promised, adjusting the pack on his back. "I have already thought of every ambush Set would attempt. I have planned for every scenario."

Isis was quiet for a moment, studying him. "You know you are not safe until you are physically inside the Sanctuary and the gate is closed? Don't let your guard down at the gate."

Jack stared at her, his posture becoming a little rigid. "Are we capable of that? Letting our guard down?"

"It would appear not, which is good," Isis responded.

"I'm sorry," Shae interrupted, raising a hand slightly. "Isn't Sequoia National Park enormous? What's the likelihood of Grenich knowing the exact spot of the gateway to the Sanctuary?"

"Underestimating Set is a dangerous and foolish mistake," Isis told her before turning her attention back to Jack. "I should go with you."

"That's an unwise strategy. They need your help retrieving Shocker," Jack pointed out. "We're both seven series, Isis. I learned the exact same things you did, have almost the exact same skill set as you do. I know how to—"

"I don't want you to get killed," she interrupted him in her usual flat tone.

Shae, Alex, and Jade all stared at Isis. The random statement sounded downright bizarre coming from her. Even Jack seemed a little taken aback. Isis looked around the room.

"If you die ... I will have to kill a lot of people at Grenich. They — the normals — don't like it when I eliminate threats," she explained. "I think they refer to it as a murder spree, which is inaccurate."

Jack turned his eyes over to Shae. She looked between the two, unable to hide her happiness. It was the first time since returning to the mansion that Isis had demonstrated something close to concern about another individual. *She can try rationalizing it all she likes, but she's worried about something bad happening to Orion and Jack,* Shae thought as she smiled over at Alex and Jade. Alex looked over at Jade, shrugged, and turned her attention back to her book.

Isis turned and left the room. Jack watched her and then looked back at Shae.

"If something does happen to Orion or me, you won't be able to stop her from going after the Corporation," he mentioned. "I wouldn't recommend trying."

"Then you damn well better come back," Shae responded, beaming as she stood up. "I will be so pissed if you don't."

"If I'm dead, I don't understand how your anger would affect me," Jack said, glancing over his shoulder. "Shae, please be careful when you go after Shocker. Coop has been on the outside too long and I fear he underestimates the danger an experiment like Shocker poses. He has been alone for a very long time and isn't accustomed to normals. He will see you as a threat, so be on your guard."

"We'll have Coop and Isis," Shae reassured him, leaning forward. "And we've been training long enough to know not to let our guard down. Don't worry, we'll be fine."

Jack looked somewhat unsure, glancing back at the lounge. Shae placed her hands on her hips, still grinning.

"Jack, we'll see each other again," she tried to reassure the tense experiment. Jack turned his gaze back to her and Shae wondered if he was stalling. Jack didn't seem keen on leaving and she got the distinct impression the experiments didn't like separating. They probably saw it as creating an exploitable weakness.

"In case we do not, the rest of my weapons are in my room," Jack told her. "They are made of pure guardian silver, which will kill anything Grenich sends after you."

"I'll keep that in mind," Shae grinned. "Good luck, Jack."

He turned and started moving toward the door, pausing just before it. Jack turned around and moved back toward Shae, capturing her lips with his own. Alex glanced over her shoulder at them, her eyebrows rising before she turned her attention back to the book she was looking at.

"Finally," Jade declared, raising her hands to the ceiling. Jack pulled out of the kiss and Shae grinned.

"We'll definitely have to do more of that when you get back," she said, a little breathless. Jack nodded once before turning and exiting the library. Shae moved over to the lounge, hopping over the back and sitting between the other two protectors. She leaned over and rested her head on Jade's shoulder.

"I miss him already," she stated melodramatically. Jade snorted and shook her head. She had always enjoyed Shae's lightheartedness.

"What's got you so interested, bookworm?" Shae asked, looking over to Alex when she brushed her hair over her shoulder.

"I wanted to double-check something," Alex explained, running her finger down the page she was looking at. "Yeah, I was right. The Deverells helped hunt down the last of the wereanimals back in 1910. We should talk to them about that so we know what to expect."

"I also helped hunt those things down you know," Jade reminded her. "They're not too difficult to put down. Guardian silver will do it. Nasty things, wereanimals. Not the brightest creatures, but they were fast and they always traveled in absurdly large packs."

She shuddered, not enjoying the memories she had of the monsters. The werelion at the rebel Lair had been at least double the size of any recorded wereanimal. Shae glanced over at Alex when she closed the book and set it down on the table in front of the lounge and chair.

"Think Lilly will be able to convince the fey to attend the summit?" Alex asked as she sat back. Shae straightened up and stretched her arms out across the back of the lounge.

Jade shrugged. "The fey aren't the ones who will be the most difficult to convince to attend. The leaders of the Magic Orders are the ones who will be a pain more likely than not. They're the most isolated of the supernatural races. But even if they do come, that's not going to be the hardest part. I don't know how Jet and Lilly will be able to convince these races to fight and die alongside us."

Jade looked at the empty fireplace again. Out of the four of them, she was the most pessimistic about the chances of such alliances doing any good. From what Orion had told them, Set already had a sizeable advantage over them. He controlled most of the world's wealth and his army grew larger every day. Shape shifter and human disappearances had doubled over the winter and continued to increase. The three women glanced over to the door when Isis strode back inside the room. She moved through the bookshelves, disappearing somewhere among the rows of books.

~~*~*~*

In the late afternoon, Lilly, Sly, and Ajax Appeared in a small cottage. There was no furniture or decorations, nothing to indicate anyone lived there. Sly frowned when she heard sheep bleating somewhere outside.

"Where the fuck are we?" she asked warily, looking around at the ancient cobwebs decorating the corners of the tiny house. Everything was dusty and dirty. Surprisingly, the smell was rather pleasant. It had a distinct scent of dew and trees.

"Scotland, in the countryside," Lilly replied, smoothing

the front of her dress. "The farmer who lives here is a protector. His family has been protecting this gateway for millennia."

"Uh huh," Sly said, glancing over at Ajax as he moved about the small space. He checked around every corner and peered out the windows.

"He prefers dog form, like most of his family, but sometimes takes on human form to tend to the animals he keeps," Ajax explained, his attention never wavering from checking the house. As if on cue, there was the faint sound of a dog barking outside, followed by more sheep bleating. Sly adjusted the holster about her waist. Streaks of sparkling purple gleamed on her black top and her jeans even had a faint glisten. She and Ajax were both armed, but Lilly was not. They were all dressed nicely, as per fey custom.

"Looks like we're all clear," Ajax reported, reaching into the inner pocket of his dark blue suit. He produced a handkerchief and handed it to Lilly. She unwrapped the stick of sparkling purple chalk contained within it. Stepping forward to one of the bare walls, she crouched down and drew a line. Releasing the chalk, Lilly stepped back. The chalk remained pointed against the wall. After a moment, it began to scribble rapidly on the wall, drawing an elegant gate. When it was finished, Lilly stepped forward and caught the chalk when it fell away from the wall. She knocked twice in the middle of the gate and then stepped back again.

A gold line appeared toward the base of the gate, flowing upward through the chalk lines until the gate became three-dimensional. A bright glowing light began to grow behind it. Sly and Ajax both squinted at the onslaught of light. There was a soft squeaking sound and when they looked back, the gate was open. A tall black woman clad in green clothes stood just inside the gateway. An impressive bow rested across her back and a sword was on her hip. Her hair was braided so it was away from her face and brown boots rose to her calves. Her face had a youthful look to it and there was a delicate point to her ears.

"You are the protector ambassadors?" she asked, her voice assertive. Sly looked over her shoulder to the bright lands behind her. The gate opened somewhere elevated and the blue sky stretched for as far as the eye could see. Sly glimpsed the tops of what she assumed were trees in the distance. It looked as though it were autumn in their world. The leaves were a rainbow of colors.

"We are," Lilly answered, dipping into a curtsey. "I am Lady Lilly Monroe and I have an audience scheduled with Queen Titania and King Oberon."

The tall woman bowed to Lilly. "I'm Deirdre, part of Queen Titania's personal elven guard. She sent me to greet you and bring you to the palace. Please come this way."

She motioned inside and Lilly stepped forward, followed by Sly and Ajax. They stepped onto a rocky mountain path. Sly glanced back at the gate when it began to close. A stocky man dressed in light blue moved away and sat on a small wooden stool near the gate. His hood was up, concealing his features. There was a large iron key resting on his chest. Smoke drifted up from the pipe in his mouth. He didn't even look up at them as he turned his attention back to a small book he held.

"Never let it be said the fey lack hospitality," Sly muttered under her breath. She lifted her face to the bright sky, breathing in the sweet air. There wasn't pollution in the lands of the Seelie Court, which made the air fresher than it was on Earth. Deirdre led them down the mountain path. Sly walked near the edge, peering down to the ground far below. There were a few strange looking birds flittering between the trees. One particular creature had rainbow-colored feathers.

"We will take Nimue's path. It is the easiest way to reach the palace from this gateway," Deirdre's no-nonsense voice brought Sly's attention back to her. *Still more normal than experiments*, Sly thought as she looked around. They soon began to descend a long narrow stairway and Sly could hear the soft splashing of water. When they reached the bottom, there was a woman in the water harnessing two smoky gray horses to a boat that looked similar to a gondola. The horses were standing on the water, unbothered. One tossed his head up and snuffled, while the other bowed his head to drink some water. The woman had long black hair and blue eyes. She was half in the water and glanced up when Deirdre approached, smiling and waving in greeting. The woman was topless and had what looked like sapphires and pearls in her dark hair. As they approached, Sly glimpsed the blue iridescent fish tail under the water.

"May I introduce Fiona of the mer-people and keeper of the kelpies," Deirdre stated as she moved over to the long white wooden boat, which was decorated in a variety of jewels. The nearest kelpie pawed at the water, splashing it around.

"It is a pleasure to meet you," Lilly said politely, nodding to the woman. The mermaid smiled shyly and waved.

"Thank you, my lady," she replied in a sing-song voice.

"Fiona shall lead the kelpies along Nimue's path to the harbor," Deirdre explained as she stepped into the boat and sat on the elevated seat in the back. Ajax offered a hand to Lilly as she held her dress in one hand and stepped onto the boat.

"If you don't mind my asking," Sly began as she approached the boat. "How are two horses able to stand on water?"

"They're not horses, they're kelpies," Fiona answered as though it were the most obvious thing in the world. She swam over in front of the two kelpies. "They can live either under or above water. Right now they're wearing a special shoe, which keeps them above water."

Sly wasn't reassured, but stepped onto the boat and sat

across from Lilly and Ajax. Fiona whistled and the kelpies started forward, smoothly pulling the long boat through the calm blue water. Trees of all different colors grew along the banks and multicolored leaves shuddered above them. There were a few rocks on which different merpeople reclined, sunning themselves. Their tails were an assortment of colors and each had iridescence to them.

"On the west bank, you will see the banners of the different races of the Seelie Court," Deirdre told them as she reclined in her seat.

Sly glanced over her shoulder when she heard giggling. In the distance, a group of women had wrapped ribbons around a tall tree and ran about the trunk, holding brightly colored strips. Squinting, Sly was amazed to see a few of the women had wings. Mostly clear with just a hint of color, they were similar to a butterfly's wings and many had colorful swirls and lines running through them.

Looking to the west bank, they soon saw the banners. Each had a family crest on it and gems hanging from the ends. They were an assortment of colors and many had mottos beneath the crests. Sly knew next to nothing about the Seelie Court, much less how many races were found there. Judging from the number of banners, there were quite a few. She glanced over to where Lilly was chatting amicably with Deirdre. Ajax was studying each banner as they passed by, enthralled.

Sly looked up to the trees when she heard rustling. A couple of people sat in the branches, hiding among the purple and blue leaves. They waved at the boat as it past beneath them. As they continued forward, more people appeared in the trees. Some of the bolder ones hung from their arms or upside down to study the new arrivals. Sly looked into the depths of the forest when she heard squealing, watching two women and a man chase each other through the trees. Every now and again, she would catch a glimpse of a mermaid or merman swimming alongside the boat. None of the Seelie Court citizens looked the same and were just as colorful and bright as their surroundings.

After what seemed like an hour or two, the kelpies pulled up alongside an outcropping of beige stones where a large group stood. They were clothed finely in shades of pinks, purples, and blues. The women's long hair was done up in complex styles and decorated with small flowers and gemstones. The couple who stood in the middle of the group were clothed in white and gold and wore silver circlets of leaves at their brows. *Well, this is almost certainly going to be boring,* Sly thought as she watched the mermaid bring the kelpies to a halt. She noticed the group had feathered wings, similar to birds' wings. Their wings were jointed and folded flat against their backs.

"Lady Lilly, welcome to the Seelie Court," the man in the middle greeted in a strong voice as he and the woman descended the stairway. They both had light brown complexions and bright eyes. Deirdre stepped out of the gondola and held out her hand to Lilly, helping her out of the boat. She did the same with Ajax and Sly.

"King Oberon, Queen Titania," Lilly said as she curtsied. "Thank you for agreeing to meet with us."

"It is our pleasure," Titania replied as she bowed her head. Sly looked behind them as Fiona led the kelpies and the boat away. Deirdre stood near the fey leaders, her back ramrod straight. Sly noticed a few other elves standing in the hallway, dressed similar to Deirdre. Their bladed weapons were sheathed and they stood still as stone.

"We shall be meeting in the dining hall. It is this way," Oberon told them as he turned and started to make his way back up the steps. Sly noticed the folded wings on his back were royal blue with streaks of gold and silver among them. When Titania turned, she revealed her own wings, which were emerald green with streaks of glistening purple. The group that had gathered remained off to the side, a few soft whispers exchanged among them.

"Funny, I never thought I was so interesting," Sly

muttered under her breath to Ajax as they followed Lilly and the two leaders of the Seelie Court.

"Really? I always thought you were a bit too interesting," Ajax responded with a small smile. Sly rolled her eyes over to him.

"Said one of the infamous Deverell brothers."

They were led down a grand hall. The colors were all subdued and created a calming ambiance. Sunlight streamed through the numerous open spaces and flowers surrounded them. Vines ran up the pillars, which were decorated with numerous jewels, and it was difficult to tell where nature ended and the palace began. The walls were decorated with paintings of different important fey in natural settings, mostly forests. There was a pleasing symmetry to everything in the open castle and almost no corners.

Deirdre and another elf walked ahead of the fey leaders and when they came upon a pair of doors with curvy handles, each elf grabbed one and pulled them open. They were led into an open room, which overlooked a vast forest. A large round table sat in the center of the room, surrounded by intricately carved wooden chairs. A number of tall elves and fey were setting food out on the table. When Titania and Oberon entered, they stopped what they were doing and bowed to their leaders.

"Please have a seat," Titania said, gesturing to the table. Her voice had a stoic quality to it, which reminded Sly of Adonia's. The three of them sat at the table as did the two fey leaders. Sly sat near the open area, where she could see the door they came in through. She looked behind her when she noticed movement out of the corner of her eye. Hidden among the plants outside were a group of younger fey, clothed in light pinks and purples. Their hair was short and the same color as their clothing. Their faces sparkled and gleamed in the light. Small jewels decorated the corners of their eyes, catching the sunlight and their clear iridescent wings glistened. When Sly looked over, they giggled and tittered, turning their faces away as if to hide.

"Who are they?" Sly asked, nodding over her shoulder. Oberon leaned to the side, looking over to where she was indicating.

"They're pixies," he answered, waving his hand as he addressed the pixies. "Run along."

Sly turned back when she heard a rustling sound. The pixies were gone.

"You must excuse the young ones," Titania said, smiling a little. "They have never seen people from the Unseelie Court before."

Ajax looked over at Sly, anticipating her question. "Species not part of the Seelie Court."

"I figured," Sly stated, looking over to the door they had entered through. Deirdre and another elf stood at attention, their gaze fixed across the room. Sly looked back at the table, studying the food set out for them. There were numerous vividly-colored fruits, some of which she recognized and others she didn't. Her gaze was drawn to a particularly strange fruit that looked like a cross between a melon and a flower. The ring of fruit was in the center while purple petals folded out from it. There were a few loaves of bread on the table and a crystal glass of red wine sat before each person.

"We were sorry to hear of your recent losses," Oberon stated. "There is no greater loss than that of a child, no matter how young or old they are."

For a moment, Lilly didn't seem to know what to say. She swallowed and folded her hands on the table in front of her. Sly looked to the side, noticing the attendants were standing a few feet away, decanters held at the ready. Looking back to the table, Sly reached forward and plucked a grape from the nearest bowl. The minute she bit into it, an overpowering sweetness invaded her senses and she had to struggle not to gag. Reaching for the glass of wine in front of her, Sly took a sip and again fought not to spit it out. *What is with the sweetness? Wine shouldn't taste like pure sugar,* she thought as she blinked a couple times.

"Thank you for your condolences. It was most kind of you to send diplomats to the service," Lilly said, recovering quickly.

"It was the least we could do," Titania began. "But as to your purpose, Doyle and Oona mentioned some kind of summit."

"Excuse the interruption," Sly spoke up, turning to Lilly. "Would you mind if I took a short walk? Diplomacy is more yours and Ajax's area of expertise."

Lilly turned her attention to Titania and Oberon, who laughed softly. He waved a hand.

"Of course," he answered, his dark eyes twinkling with amusement. "I remember what it was like to be young. You are more than welcome to explore our lands."

Lilly nodded and Sly stood from her seat, nodding in respect to the two fey leaders. She moved toward the entrance, ignoring the muted conversation continuing behind her. The shape shifter had decided to let the age comment slide. One of the few rules Sly followed was to never start a fight when the opponent had the home field advantage.

"Do you require a guide?" Deirdre asked as she opened the door for Sly. "Our lands are vast and it is easy to get lost if you've never been here before."

Sly shrugged. "I'm used to open spaces. I won't get lost."

Deirdre gestured down the empty hall. "There is a stairway to your left. It will take you outside and onto the grounds."

"Much obliged," Sly said as she started down the way Deirdre had indicated. She found the stairway, jogged down the steps, and found herself in another open hallway. She could see the purple, blue, red, and yellow trees across the way and was tempted to jump off the balcony. Walking down the long pathway, Sly looked up at the jewels decorating the pillars and walls. She examined how embedded they were to the wall and when she couldn't pluck them out of the stone, she turned her attention to the great portraits depicting fey in natural scenes, which adorned almost every wall. When she reached the end of the hall, Sly turned and sauntered down another flight of stairs, happy when her feet touched the vibrant green grass. She closed her eyes and inhaled the sweet clean air. *I don't know. I think I might be able to live in one of these forests. The food and drink is terrible, the clothing is boring, the fey are uptight, but there are no humans,* Sly thought, nodding in agreement with herself. She moved among the scattered trees, trailing her fingers over the different barks. Some felt like thin sheets of paper and others felt velvety to the touch. The leaves and bark were a variety of colors, some not found on Earth. Looking to the side, she watched a herd of deer grazing nearby. A few were blue and pink. Ajax had mentioned something about the fey being a completely vegan culture. *Would have been nice to warn me about the overly sweetened food,* Sly thought, irritated, as she continued on her way.

"No! They're just going to stick their heads in the ground like they always do! In the great and noble tradition of their ancestors, they are going to do *nothing!* They can't find an answer by just looking, so there must not be one!"

"Saoirse, will you just hold on for a moment?"

"No, Conner. I'm a healer, not a sheep!"

Sly turned her attention toward the argumentative voices. It sounded some distance away, but the angry steps were getting closer. It was the first non-serene thing she had noticed since arriving and Sly was intrigued. She moved around another tree, leaned against it and waited. A few moments later, an irate woman stormed down the path, followed closely by a flustered-looking red-haired man. The woman's skin was light brown and her long hair was as dark as her eyes. Her clothing was a pale lavender color and much more androgynous, similar to what Deirdre was wearing. The woman had no weapons, but carried a satchel over one shoulder. Sly noticed the tips of her ears were pointed, but she didn't have wings so she wasn't fey. The man wore all green and was a little taller than the woman.

As they approached, Sly cleared her throat and they both looked over at her. Their eyes widened and they stared at her as if she were an alien. Sly snickered, amused by their bafflement. *Wonder if this is kind of like how the experiments feel,* Sly thought, imagining how many times Isis and Jack had encountered similar wide-eyed stares.

"Saoirse and Conner, I take it," Sly said when it became apparent neither of them would say anything. Conner looked over at Saoirse before turning his green eyes back to Sly. She looked at them expectantly.

"You are from Earth? One of the shape shifters?" Saoirse asked, curious. Conner continued to stare at her suspiciously.

"That I am," Sly answered, looking the woman up and down. "Surprised you didn't refer to me as someone from the Unseelie Court."

"The term is too broad to serve any purpose. Only fey nobility use it," Saoirse responded, looking to the side. "What are you doing out here? I thought you had an audience with Queen Titania and King Oberon."

Sly almost rolled her eyes at the formality. Titles were so archaic and meaningless. She didn't understand why some people were nostalgic for such traditions. She had never used them, even when it had been common practice. Sly turned her gaze to Conner.

"Cat got your tongue?" she asked, trying to figure out what the man was. He didn't have wings, so he wasn't a fey. His ears were slightly pointed, but nowhere near as obviously as the fey and elves. He straightened up, his mouth set in a thin straight line. Sly clicked her tongue and turned her attention back to Saoirse, who was the more interesting of the two.

"I'm here in a guard capacity," Sly answered. "The

other guard has remained with our diplomat, so I was given leave to explore by your leaders. I've answered a few questions and my answers aren't free."

"What does that mean?" Conner asked, suspicion dripping from every word.

Sly smiled. "The silent man speaks. For a moment there, I thought I might be losing my touch."

"What do you want from us?" Saoirse asked.

"Yet another question. Perhaps if I knew to whom I spoke, I'd be more inclined to answer," Sly suggested. The woman wrapped the fingers of one hand around the strap of her satchel, which was a greenish-brown color.

"I'm a sprite and a healer," she answered, nodding over her shoulder. "Conner is a leprechaun and my occasional assistant."

"No shit?" Sly laughed. "Seriously? A leprechaun? Tell me, what does a leprechaun do in the Seelie Court?"

"We're gardeners and harvesters," Conner answered proudly. "I take care of the plants near the hospital where Saoirse works."

"Uh huh," Sly said, crossing her arms over her chest and turning her eyes back to Saoirse. "So what's got you so angry?"

Saoirse bit her bottom lip and looked back over her shoulder at Conner, seeming to debate answering the question. He shook his head, but she turned her attention back to Sly.

"I'm sure you know of the richness of the Seelie Court," she began. "Our land is abundant in jewels, but there are only two races who can work in the mines. The dwarves and the goblins."

"I always thought leprechauns were associated with gold," Sly mentioned as she looked at Conner. "Why can't your people mine?"

"Dwarves and goblins are the only races who don't need the natural light of the sun to survive," Conner said, sounding offended. "The other races die when hidden away from the light. Goblins and dwarves prefer the shelter offered by caves."

"They don't need as much sunlight as we do, but they still need a certain amount of it, so they live in cottages near the mountains," Saoirse added. "A month ago, the goblins started getting sick. They developed pustules, coughed up blood, and their skin turned a horrible shade of purplish-black. Once they started showing symptoms, they were dead within days. No matter what we tried, nothing worked. We couldn't even slow the sickness. The last goblin died just two days past."

"The entire race just died?" Sly asked. "There are no more goblins?"

"Not in the Seelie Court," Saoirse confirmed. "There may be a few abroad. The head healers believe it was a natural occurrence and don't want to cut open any of the bodies."

Conner raised his hand to massage the back of his head. "Saoirse thinks they're mistaken, but they won't listen to her because she is still young."

"You don't think it was natural causes?" Sly asked.

"The evidence doesn't support that conclusion. True, the goblins dug deeper than most of the dwarves do, but none of the dwarves showed *any* symptoms of the illness. A few of them have gone as deep as the goblins, possibly deeper, but they were unaffected by this sickness. In the history of the Seelie Court, there has never been a single instance of illness affecting one race and not any another."

Conner swallowed and looked off to the side. "Then there were the stories."

Saoirse and he exchanged a look. Sly resisted the urge to shake them. The air seemed to still around them. Saoirse looked at the ground, tucking some hair behind her ear.

"A few goblins, in their delirium, babbled about a figure with glowing eyes," she said. "I would have brushed it off as fevered dreams, if it weren't for a dwarf who brought in a goblin. He told me that one night, he caught a glimpse of glowing blue eyes deep in the tunnels, where the goblins had been working. They disappeared so fast that he wasn't sure if it was real or his imagination."

Conner looked at Sly. "Our ambassadors spoke of shape shifters with glowing eyes at the memorial service."

Sly almost laughed at the insinuation. "Are you suggesting one of them is the cause of this illness? Sorry to break it to you, but the experiments who live at the mansion can't travel between worlds. No one can without specific supplies, which only the guardians possess. And you have a gatekeeper. Nobody gets in without their knowing."

"No, they don't," Saoirse admitted, shooting Conner an annoyed look. She opened her satchel and dug around in it. Sly glimpsed a few scrolls and some parchment in the stuffed bag.

"There is one thing that you, or your experiments, might be able to help us with," she said as she pulled out a sturdy-looking box and handed it to Sly, who accepted it. She slid back a tab on the top, revealing a small window. Sly couldn't help but be impressed with the well-designed object. Looking through the clear glass, she studied the round gray object contained inside. It looked advanced, some sort of gadget. There was a symbol carved on top, but Sly couldn't quite make it out and she didn't want to open the box to study it closer.

"The dwarf I mentioned, he investigated the area where he thought he saw the eyes and found this. He didn't recognize any of those materials and neither did any of our other metal-smiths. It's not made of anything found in our lands, so perhaps you could identify it."

"I can't, no," Sly said, not missing the disappointed looks of both Saoirse and Conner. "But if you would allow me to borrow it, I think I know someone who could."

"Keep it," Saoirse replied, crossing her arms over her chest and shaking her head. "Nobody deserves to die the way the goblins did."

Sly looked over at her. *Finally met a member of the Seelie Court who isn't stuck-up, and a cute one at that,* she thought as she raised an eyebrow.

"Your rulers won't object to my taking this with me?" she asked. Saoirse adjusted the strap over her shoulder. She knelt down and pulled a flower from the ground, studying it for a moment. Conner smiled, obviously amused by the question, and looked over at his friend.

"Tell them it was a gift of friendship, if they ask," she said, looking up. "They won't. That box is not precious and they don't care about what happens among the healers."

"Healers are valuable, yet every culture seems to take them for granted," Sly observed with a shake of her head. "Strange the things we place value on."

Saoirse tucked the flower she plucked into her bag, gathering a few more of the blue blossoms. She looked at one as she straightened up. After a moment, she held it out to Sly.

"Though I love my home, there are times I envy those who dwell on the Earth," Saoirse admitted. "From what I read, it sounds like an exciting place to live."

Sly took the proffered flower. "Don't know about that. Our resources are dwindling and we share the place with humans."

She decided to leave out the part about the power-hungry necromancer who was consolidating his power and gradually taking over the Earth. Sly had begun to wonder how many more days of freedom the shape shifters would enjoy.

CHAPTER SEVEN

Isis stopped pacing the room to look up when she heard a clock strike midnight. She resumed almost immediately. Jade and Coop both looked up from the map they were poring over in the study. Alex and Shae were sitting in the chairs across from the desk. Isis hadn't been still since Orion left. She had first occupied her time with one of the most intense workouts Jade had ever witnessed. After a quick shower, she had explored the entire mansion from top to bottom again. She had started pacing three hours ago.

"Is she going to be okay?" Jade asked Coop.

"She will be," Coop answered, looking back to the map. "The first couple years out of the Corporation is always the most difficult. Our bodies produce excess adrenaline in high-stress situations, such as a sudden change in environment. We often have to keep moving to use it all up. I used to run forty-five miles to get rid of it."

Coop paused and held his hands behind his back. "It served a dual purpose since I was also trying to stay off the Corporation's radar. I never slept in the same place twice."

Isis changed her direction and moved straight at the desk, causing Jade to lean back. "Why are you discussing me? What about the abandoned plant? What should I expect from Shocker?"

She turned back and continued pacing, but now watched Coop. Both Shae and Alex looked from her to the other experiment. Coop was unbothered by her sudden demanding tone. He turned his attention back to the map.

"From what I remember, Shocker keeps all the main entrances rigged with electricity," he began. "We can't just go in through the front door, not without risking a severe and possibly fatal shock. He also keeps a lot of buckets filled with water on hand."

"For what purpose?" Alex asked.

"Water is an excellent conductor of electricity," Isis answered from behind her. "He'll create a large puddle and wait for someone to step in it."

"That's reassuring," Shae yawned and closed her eyes, resting her head against the chair's arm.

"Couldn't we just knock on the front door?" Jade asked. Coop shrugged.

"We could try, but I don't trust him not to shoot a couple volts through the door," Coop answered. "Shocker is very territorial. He believes if he stays removed from civilization, Grenich will lose interest in him."

"That's borderline delusional and assumptions are foolish in general," Isis commented. "What's our best approach?"

"I'll go first. He knows me and will be more likely to hear me out," Coop said. "We have to avoid making him feel cornered, so no aggressive tactics."

"Should we just hang back until you give us an all-clear signal?" Jade asked.

"That would be my recommendation."

"It is unwise to approach a hostile alone," Isis remarked. Coop leaned forward, resting his hands on the desk. His glowing blue eyes fixed on Isis.

"If we treat Shocker like a hostile, he will react as such. As you or I would."

Isis regarded him for a moment before she resumed her pacing. Jade looked between the two experiments. She also questioned the wisdom of sending Coop alone to approach what sounded like a very dangerous experiment.

"Also, it would be wise to go without firearms," Coop continued.

"No," Isis responded almost before he finished speaking. Her intense glowing green eyes turned back toward him.

"Isis is right," Jade put in. "We can't approach this experiment without a single weapon. Even if he's not hostile, there are a number of other things that could happen. I would prefer not to be ambushed while unarmed."

"If that's your decision, you should at least keep your weapons concealed," Coop stated. "If Shocker sees a gun, he will react badly and chances are he will kill at least one of you, probably more."

Isis turned her attention toward the door, which opened to reveal Sly. She smiled as she looked around the room. Both Coop and Isis looked to the wooden box she held under her arm. The lacquer had a sheen even in the dim lamp light.

"How did the meeting with the fey go?" Jade asked, straightening up.

"You'll have to ask Lilly and Ajax," Sly answered. "Diplomacy is boring, so I took the opportunity to go exploring. Beautiful place, the Seelie Court. I could live there if it weren't for the fey. They're uptight, like you protectors. They also use titles, which is a complete turn-off."

"You and titles," Jade chuckled, shaking her head. Her lover had always believed titles to be one of the root causes of superiority complexes and had no tolerance for them. Sly looked over at Jade and her smile grew. She held up the box.

"I come bearing gifts of a sort. I know Orion's not

around, but I figured maybe the experiments could take a crack at identifying this mystery object," Sly continued as she moved into the room. She ran her fingers through Alex's hair as she passed by her. The other shape shifter looked up, frowning as she smoothed her hair again. Sly winked at her. Isis took the offered box and examined it. Coop approached and peered over her shoulder. She slid back the tab on top and inspected the contents of the box. She turned her neck a little, tilting the box as she examined the object inside.

"It's a viral containment device, designed by Grenich. You can just make out the symbol of the Corporation on top," Isis said, turning the box. "It holds a virus in a gaseous state. There's a timer on top, easy to use. Set the timer, up to twenty-four hours, and then it releases whatever virus is inside. It's similar to a landmine but used for bio-warfare."

"That is not good," Sly said, leaning against the side of the desk. "It seems a virus has wiped out every goblin in the Seelie Court."

"Guardians have mercy," Shae breathed, looking over to Jade. The elder shape shifter looked puzzled as she crossed her arms over her chest.

"How the hell could Set have gotten into another world?" Jade asked. "Only the guardians have the materials required to cross planes."

"When I was in the Corporation, I wasn't even aware there were other worlds," Coop mentioned, looking over at Isis. "What about you? Are the seven series aware of the supernatural races?"

Isis opened her mouth and then closed it again, looking away for a moment. Placing the box on the desk, she closed her eyes and held her hands in front of her, her fingertips subtly moving as if sifting through memories. After a moment, Isis opened her eyes and dropped her hands, looking back to Coop.

"I have no memory of the Seelie Court or any of the

other races, just a basic general knowledge of their existence," she began. "There are a couple gaps in my memory, so I could not say for sure whether or not I have ever been to these other lands."

Isis rested her hands on her hips. "That is a Grenich viral container, though. Someone from the Corporation must have figured out how to get things into the other worlds."

"Why kill off the goblins?" Alex asked. "If Set's invested so much time into Earth, why would he start advancing on the Seelie Court?"

Isis looked back at the box. "It could be viral testing."

"Someone should warn the Seelie Court," Sly mentioned, crossing one long leg over the other. "If Set is able to cross planes."

"It is unlikely," Isis responded, looking up again. "Orion mentioned something about the supernatural races crossing over to Earth?"

"That's true and the members of the Seelie Court are the ones who do it most often, or used to, from what I understand," Jade said.

"The most likely scenario is someone was being careless," Isis stated, her eyes wandering back to the box again. "If I wanted to release a virus in a place I couldn't physically infiltrate, I would use a carrier and disguise the container as something useful. There's a small light on top of this device. Chances are it was disguised as an illumination device for mine work."

"That still leaves the question of why target them," Alex pointed out.

"The fey I spoke with said there's never been an instance of a virus affecting a race in their lands without affecting at least one other," Sly put in. Isis ran a hand over her forehead, wondering how normals got anything done. They seemed incapable of focusing on a single task. Isis was good at multitasking but she couldn't do it when she had to stop and explain every last action and thought.

"I don't have answers to these inquiries," she said, glancing over at Coop. "We're supposed to approach Shocker tomorrow. Perhaps that's what we should focus on."

Sly leaned back and looked at the sketches of the abandoned plant where the experiment lived. She yawned and straightened up again.

"Have fun with your diagrams. I'm calling it a night," she said as she moved out of the room. Shae stretched, raising her arms over her head and resting them on the back of the chair. She glanced over at Alex when she yawned and rested her head against her fist. Even Jade looked rather tired.

"We should call it a night," Coop stated, straightening up as he looked at the three women. "We can sort out last minute details tomorrow. We've done all the planning we can do."

Isis glanced over at him and he gestured with his head toward the three protectors. She studied them, noticing their tired appearances. *Normals require so much sleep,* she thought. The last time Isis had experienced anything like tiredness had been when she was suffering from the Omni virus. It had been unpleasant.

"Very well," she agreed. "But we should go early in the day. I don't want him to have any advantages over the normals."

~~*~*~*

Electra sat in the training room of the Meadows, bouncing her leg impatiently. She watched as a few younger women left followed by a couple messengers and turned her attention to the door. It had been almost an hour, but Electra was waiting for a particular guardian. The woman had a schedule she stuck to like clockwork and Electra showed up early to think over what to say. The guardian she planned to speak with was one of the older ones in the Meadows, older than Artemis. Though she wasn't as cold as Athena, she was still intimidating. *Which is why she is the head guard of the Meadows,* Electra thought as she leaned back when the door to the training room opened again.

A tall woman entered, her long black hair tied back. She was wearing pants and armor made from a leather-like material, one that was flexible and allowed full range of motion while still protecting the wearer's vital organs. Brown boots covered her feet, stretching up to her calves. She carried a long wooden staff at her side. Her face had an aquiline quality to it, but was still beautiful. Her skin was reddish brown and her sharp earth-colored eyes fixed on Electra. She dipped her chin to her chest briefly, resting one end of the staff on the ground.

"Lady Electra," she greeted. Electra paused, wondering if she was the last guardian woman who still used titles when not in formal settings.

"Lady Nemesis," Electra returned the greeting and got to her feet. "I was hoping to have a word."

"If it is about prisoner visitation, I only head the guards. I have no say over the rules and regulations of the dungeons," Nemesis said, glancing over to the windows where the afternoon sun streamed in.

"No, it's not about that," Electra responded, toying with the charm she wore at her throat. "It is common knowledge that you are the best warrior in the Meadows. I wanted to ask if you would consider training me."

Nemesis studied Electra. "You've had basic self-defense, as have all guardians your age. Why do you need more?"

"I often visit my sister on Earth and most of the self-defense we learn in the Meadows is inadequate and outdated. I need to learn something better than just disappearing when I spot a threat," Electra half-lied as she dropped her hand away from her throat, hoping Nemesis would be satisfied. The elder guardian looked skeptical.

"Retreating is often the best tactic in dangerous situations," she responded, resting her free hand on her hip. Her gaze was scrutinizing as she observed Electra.

"You've never run from a fight and neither have any of your ancestors," Electra pointed out. Nemesis looked over her shoulder and then back to Electra.

"I'm not a neophyte, Electra," she began sternly. "You're worried about your sister and you want me to train you so you can fight by her side when the protectors launch an attack on the Grenich Corporation."

Electra put her hands on her hips and held Nemesis' gaze. "What would you do, if it were your sister?"

"What my elders and the High Council told me," Nemesis answered without hesitation, lifting up her staff and stepping around Electra.

"The protectors are all that's standing between us and Grenich," Electra called after her and Nemesis paused. "This fight is all of ours. Guardians, shape shifters, and all other supernatural races. When are we going to stop allowing protectors to get slaughtered and help them as we have in the past?"

Nemesis was quiet for a moment, her back rigid. She turned around and walked back to Electra. "If I agree, there are going to be a few conditions. The first one is that you don't go looking for trouble. You will follow the same rules and regulations, including the one that states you must have a protector escort while on Earth. A *protector*, not an experiment."

"Of course," Electra agreed, waiting for the other terms.

"Next, you will not take part in the protectors' assault on Grenich," Nemesis continued, raising her hand when Electra opened her mouth to protest. "My terms are non-negotiable. Set and Pyra are dangerous foes, one whom we have not encountered in many years. The guardians may have a role to play in this battle, but it is not in attacking Grenich laboratories. At least, not yet."

Electra's eyes narrowed, but she managed to nod once. Nemesis lowered her hand again, her gaze never moving from Electra's.

"I understand your desire to protect your sister, but you must recognize that she does not need your protection," Nemesis stated, putting one end of her staff on the ground and leaning it against her shoulder. "If anything, she would be a more knowledgeable instructor than I.

"My final condition at the moment, and I may think of more later, is that you read up on the history of guardian fighting techniques. There are two tomes of it in the library," Nemesis stated, pulling a pair of gloves off her belt. "You will read both in their entirety. Tell Athena you have my permission to check them out and if she wishes to speak to me about it, she knows how to reach me."

Electra stared at her incredulously. "You must be joking."

"I am not. Fighting is not just physicality, it is also about knowledge. Much of the information you will probably already know, but it never hurts to refresh your memory," Nemesis said, pulling on her gloves. "I suggest starting as soon as possible. Some of our ancestors were a bit dry in their writing and needless to say, quite dull in their lengthy descriptions. We will begin training at the end of the week."

Nemesis moved past Electra and into the arena, spinning the staff she held. The air howled as the staff swept through it. Electra watched her for a moment before turning and leaving the exercise arena. She had a lot of reading to do. *Better get some tea or coffee first,* she thought as she pushed open the door and left the arena.

~~*~*~*

Hunter tried to hide a yawn behind her hand as she

continued trudging behind Orion and Remington. It was pitch black in the middle of the forest they were traversing. Glancing over her shoulder, Hunter was unsurprised to see Jack had gone missing again. They had been walking ever since they had Appeared and at random intervals during the hike, the experiment would vanish. He always came back though.

"Is there any reason why we couldn't just Appear in front of the gateway?" Hunter asked as she adjusted the pack on her back. Looking up to the sky, she noticed she couldn't even see the tops of the trees. They were enormous. Had she not been grieving her sister and brother, Hunter would have marveled at the sheer size of the trunks. Her thoughts turned to Declan and her father. Declan hadn't spoken a word since the massacre at the Lair and it worried her to no end. Her father was also withdrawn and it seemed a part of him had died with her siblings.

"The fresh air will do us good," Orion responded. "Also, I've never been able to Appear at the exact coordinates of the gateway. Before you ask, I haven't the faintest idea why."

"Perhaps Perrin put a spell of some sort on the entryway to the Sanctuary," Remington suggested. He waved a large hand at a small bug that flew about his head. The two men began a quiet conversation, which Hunter tuned out. They talked about the dullest things and she was bored. Jack hadn't been much of a conversationalist, but then experiments rarely were. Hunter almost felt bad for trying so often. She could tell he wanted to participate, but just didn't quite know how.

I smell them. They're over this way.

Hunter's head shot up when she heard a strange disembodied voice. It was rough and scratchy, unlike any other voice she had heard before. Reaching to her hip, she rested her hand on the large knife she had taken from the mansion's weapons room. Hunter didn't have much experience with guns and felt more comfortable with a blade. Squinting, she thought she saw a gauzy silhouette, grayish in color, almost glowing in the night. Hunter tightened her grip around the grip of the knife, pulling it out of its scabbard. Her attention was glued to the indistinct shape and she couldn't turn her gaze away from it.

"Do you have any idea when we'll get there?"

"Shouldn't be more than another few hours, dawn at the latest."

I smell their blood. Warm, coursing shape shifter blood. I'm so hungry, so very hungry.

Hunter dropped her bag and sprinted through the forest, ignoring the hissing protestations of Remington and Orion. Darting around the thick trunks, she tackled the shape behind the tree. They tumbled partway down a small hill and Hunter wound up on top of the creature. The glow that had drawn her attention vanished and Hunter saw the chalk-colored face of the being she had tackled. He resembled a hairless man, but his eyes were much bigger and rounder than normal. Hissing, he opened his mouth, revealing rows of sharp pointed teeth. Hunter hesitated for a moment, startled by the hideous creature's appearance. When a forked tongue slid out of his mouth, she plunged her knife down into his throat. Foul-smelling blood sprayed up in her face as she plunged the knife down again and again. She could hear air hissing out of the wounds each time the knife pierced flesh. The hot liquid made the grip slippery and she soon struggled to keep hold of her weapon. The stench was overpowering, but Hunter ignored it as she continued plunging the knife into the creature, her movements bordering on frenzied.

Hunter wasn't sure how many times she stabbed the creature. The hackles rose on the back of her neck and she whipped her head around, looking over her shoulder. A tall figure was approaching and Hunter found herself unable to move. Her eyes were fixed on glowing white circles that seemed to swirl around her. The forest drifted away and Hunter felt as though she were floating. Time seemed to freeze and it felt as though she were gradually being wrapped in a cocoon of nothingness …

The sound of a familiar soft metallic whisper yanked her back into the forest and Hunter leapt to the side when the shadowy form fell frighteningly close to her. The blade the mysterious figure had been holding gleamed in the moonlight.

"Hunter? Are you all right?"

Hunter barely heard Remington as he hurried down the small incline. He slipped on the ground when he was a few feet away and fell backward, but quickly scrambled to his knees and crawled over to where she was. Hunter could feel her chest rising and falling rapidly as she panted for breath. Each intake of air stung her dry throat and she grimaced when she swallowed. She looked up to where Jack stood near the top of the incline and the experiment lowered his gun. His unnaturally luminous brown eyes were the only part of him the young protector could see in the night.

Hunter felt like she would be sick. The fetid odor of the creature's blood was strong and it made her stomach lurch. Sticky coagulating blood coated her arms and some had sprayed up in the young shape shifter's face. It covered her shirt and was splattered across her jeans. Hunter looked at the body she still straddled and moved away from it, still trying to catch her breath. The young protector forced herself not to vomit and wiped the back of her hand over her sweaty face. She cleaned her blade on the ground and shoved it back into the scabbard, wishing more than anything for a shower. Hearing more rustling, Hunter looked up and noticed Orion cautiously approaching.

"Hunter!"

Remington's stern voice brought her attention back to him. Even though she couldn't see his expression, Hunter could tell he was concerned. One of his hands rested on her shoulder and he positioned himself so she couldn't see the body of the man she had killed. *If that's what it was,* Hunter thought. Looking down at her shaking hands, she knew they were covered in blood and gore.

"I'm okay, Remington," she reassured him, struggling to her feet. Her legs felt as though they were made of rubber and it was difficult to find her balance. The trainer stood when she did, holding out a steadying hand each time Hunter wavered.

"My hands are really gross," she stated sheepishly and he handed her a handkerchief. Wiping her hands off as best she could, Hunter took a step forward and craned her neck to better see the bodies. Jack approached Orion, who crouched by the one Hunter had killed. The experiment glanced at the two approaching protectors before turning his attention back to the bodies. He still had his gun out, but pointed it at the ground. Every now and again, his eyes would scan their surroundings.

"This one looks to be a standard low-level sanitizer, used mostly for easy wet jobs," Orion observed, almost to himself. "I know Carding sold a couple to Adara some years back. They can be taught fairly simplistic torture methods, but for the most part they just kill low-priority targets."

Orion stood and took a couple steps back, motioning for the other two to do the same. A moment later, the body exploded in a mess of jellied insides, which soon crumbled into dust and blew away into the night.

"Some of their lower creatures disintegrate after they expire," Orion explained. "It's less work for cleaners."

Hunter looked over at the other body, which didn't seem to be disintegrating. "That one did something with his eyes. It sounds crazy, but I swear, I couldn't move."

Jack tucked his gun in the back of his pants as he jogged over to the body and turned it onto its back, leaning over the head.

"This one is an experiment," he called back to them. "The eyes have a luminescence, but the pupil and iris are unusual."

Orion quickly moved over to where he was and crouched on the other side of the body, examining it for a moment. "I have seen experiments who can exert a limited hypnotic stare. They can paralyze a mark for a few seconds, maybe half a minute if they're experienced. The Corporation could never make it last long enough for a significant benefit and abandoned the idea for more profitable ventures and abilities."

"Hunter, what were you thinking?" Remington asked and Hunter turned to look at him. She lifted her shoulders and spread her hands, unable to think of a response. Thinking back on the incident, Hunter felt uneasy. She didn't know what had happened or how she had known about their would-be attackers. A dull ache flared up in her arm and she rubbed it absentmindedly.

"I don't know," she admitted. "I thought I saw something and I went after it. I'm sorry, Remington, I wasn't really thinking."

The sound of switchblade being flicked open drew Hunter's attention back to Orion and Jack. The experiment was cutting into the strange body and after a moment, he straightened up and moved over to a fallen log. Placing something on the large branch, he brought the butt of the knife down and ground it against whatever was there.

"We need to keep moving," Jack stated as he closed his switchblade and put it back in his pocket. "That body won't take care of itself. I destroyed the tracking chip, but we can't know how much information the Corporation was able to glean from it. There's a good chance they know the general location of this experiment and if they do, they will send cleaners."

"The gate shouldn't be too much further," Orion said, brushing his hands off. "But Jack's right. We should pick up the pace a bit."

Remington and Hunter started back up the incline. Orion moved to follow, stopped by Jack's hand on his arm. He turned to the experiment, a little surprised by the physical contact.

"There's something different about the Monroes' daughter," Jack whispered, his eyes never moving from Hunter. "She spotted the sanitizer at the same time as I did, maybe a little sooner."

"Are you sure?"

Jack furrowed his brow as he turned his eyes back to Orion. "I always am, but what bothers me is not that she spotted him so quick. All normals are lucky every now and again. It looked like she … heard him."

Orion gave him a skeptical look. "Jack, most sanitizers don't make noise. Grenich removes the vocal cords of the ones they keep to assure that."

"I'm aware of that, doctor. I'm telling you, her body language and reaction suggested she heard something. She ran right at the sanitizer, indicating that was what she heard."

"Maybe he snapped a twig or something."

"*I* would have heard that."

Orion looked back up the slope to where Remington and Hunter were waiting. He was becoming increasingly aware of why Perrin wanted to see Hunter. Something was going on with the young protector and Orion wasn't sure if it was a good thing. Hunter seemed to become uncomfortable with his gaze and rubbed her arm, looking off into the woods. Orion looked around, noticing how quiet everything had gotten. There were no more birds or insects, not even a quiet wind sweeping through the leaves.

"Her arm appears to be causing her discomfort," Jack observed. "It has since that night at the rebel Lair."

Orion turned his attention back to the seven series. "Standing out here isn't going to help. We need to get to the Sanctuary. If something is wrong with Hunter, Perrin will be able to figure it out."

Jack started making his way back up the slope. Orion quickened his pace so he was walking right next to the experiment.

"Don't go wandering off anymore and keep your eye on Hunter. Guard her with your life," he whispered under his breath before they reached the other two shape shifters. Jack didn't respond or look at him, but nodded once to indicate he understood.

~~*~*~*

At dawn, two cars traveled down a long abandoned road. The grass had overgrown most of the dirt path beyond the rusting sign warning away trespassers and what was left of the path was bumpy. The only thing that worked in their favor was the ground was dry. Nero, Jensen, and Coop were in the first car and the Four followed close behind them.

"I can see the old plant up ahead," Jade said, gritting her teeth when the car rocked back and forth over a rough part of the nonexistent road. It felt more like they were driving on a hiking path meant for walking.

"Copy that," Nero replied through the earpiece. "Coop said to avoid harming any of the animals on this property. Apparently this Shocker has a soft spot for friends of the four-legged variety."

"That explains the recent spate of shelter thefts," Isis mentioned from the passenger seat, turning a page in the book she was reading. She had picked up the mansion's copy of *Frankenstein* before they left and her glowing eyes had been glued to the small print ever since. Both she and Coop were hiding their eyes with their special sunglasses instead of their usual lenses. Alex and Shae exchanged a look in the back seat.

"I thought experiments were unable to experience

emotion," Jade mentioned. Isis didn't respond or look up from the book, resting one foot on the dashboard. Jade couldn't help but notice the throwing knife tucked snugly in the black boot. It was one of the only visible weapons Isis wore, though she had more hidden on her person.

Soon, the first car came to a stop. Isis glanced up without moving her head, closing her book and lowering her leg back to the floor. She unbuckled her seatbelt when the doors opened and the men got out of the vehicle. Coop moved through the overgrown grass, pausing to stroke a large gray pit bull who popped out of the brush. Nero and Jensen approached the second car. Isis removed her sunglasses and put them up on the dash.

"Coop says to give him five minutes to talk to Shocker alone," Nero reported as he leaned down and rested his elbows on the open window. Isis opened the door on her side and stepped out of the car, moving around a large black cat. Jade glanced over at her teammate when she closed the door.

Jensen undid a button on his suit and leaned down to the now empty window, nodding to where Isis was standing at the edge of the overgrown grass. "Better vantage?"

"Probably," Alex answered from the back. Nero frowned and looked around, moving to the side.

"There are fucking dogs and cats *everywhere*," he observed, shaking one leg. "Thankfully, they seem to understand vehicles are to be avoided, otherwise it would have been a bitch to get up this far."

"None of them are shape shifters?" Alex asked and Nero shook his head.

"None that I've seen so far."

Jade glanced to the windshield when she heard a quiet thump. A large orange tabby stood on the hood of the car. It sat down and began to clean itself. Outside, she could hear all kinds of barks and yips and meows.

"Okay, I'm keeping this one."

Jade looked over her shoulder, noticing Shae had opened the door on her side and was now cuddling a small gray cat with white paws. It mewed in her hands, closing its eyes when she stroked its head.

"Shae, get it out of the car, please," Jade groaned. "We've got more than enough animals back at the mansion."

"But are they this wittle? Look at his face," Shae said, thrusting the kitten forward into Jade's face. Jade looked over at it and the kitten sniffed her nose. She could hear Alex snort quietly behind her.

"If she gets to keep that one, I get this one."

Jade rolled her eyes over to Nero, noticing he was now holding a small furry white dog. It looked like some kind of terrier mix, but Jade wasn't an expert on dog breeds. The dog licked Nero's face and its stumpy tail wagged ecstatically.

"Jade?"

"Guardians have mercy, Jensen, if you found some kind of bird or pony, the answer is no," Jade snapped, exasperated. Jensen looked over at her.

"First of all, no way in hell I'm dealing with an animal while wearing this," he gestured at his nice suit. "Second, Isis seems to have disappeared."

"What? Oh dammit, where did she go?"

Jade looked around, noticing the stillness of the grass. Isis was nowhere to be found. Jade swore and opened the door, forcing Nero to take a large step back. The wind whipped through her long black hair, rustling the grasses surrounding them. Jade rested a hand on top of her head, contemplating the best course of action. Looking for an experiment would be a waste of time. If Isis didn't want to be found, she wouldn't be. Jade hadn't been wild about letting Coop go to the abandoned plant on his own, but allowed it due to the possible volatile nature of Shocker. An unpredictable experiment with the abilities of an electric eel wasn't something Jade was keen on dealing with on her own.

Jade turned when she heard the car door open. Alex stood from the car and looked over at her. Jade lifted her shoulders, indicating she had no idea what to do.

"She can't have gotten far," Jensen offered. "I think we all know she's going for the power plant."

Jade bit her bottom lip, considering their options. "We were going to head up there anyway. We'll go a bit early, scope out the place from afar. Bring no more than two weapons. We know how easily experiments can disarm us. Try not to engage if it's at all possible."

"This should be fun," Alex muttered as she leaned down to the still open car and retrieved a knife in a sheath. Jade approached the vehicle again, leaning down and pulling out her shoulder holster. She pulled it on and tightened it so it fit snugly. Jensen and Nero returned to the Jaguar, retrieving their own weapons. Five minutes later, the five shape shifters stood on the edge of the overgrown field, studying the power plant in the distance. Jade glanced over to the men.

"You two, go around the back. You might want to take on dog or coyote form until you get closer," she suggested. "We'll stake out the front. Don't leave the cover of the grass unless it's a matter of life or death."

Nero and Jensen began to shift. Their bones cracked and popped and fur sprouted all over them. In a moment, a large black lab and a Border Collie stood in front of the women. The two galloped off to the right, disappearing in the overgrown grass. Jade turned her attention to Alex and Shae.

"We could cover a greater area if we split up, but since this is an experiment, we should stay close," she said.

"No argument here," Shae replied. Jade motioned forward and they started to make their way through the overgrown grass, which provided excellent cover. They glanced to the side when they heard rustling, noticing two mixed-breed dogs wrestling a few feet away.

"The animals seem to have a number of uses," Alex observed. "The constant rustling makes it easy for someone to sneak up on intruders."

"Thanks for that, Alex," Shae snickered, looking behind them. Jade shushed them as they continued forward. They reached the edge of the grass and the enormous decrepit structure of the abandoned plant towered over them. The walls were steel gray with long brown trails of rust below the windows and around the doors. Surprisingly, most of the glass remained intact. More than that, it looked new. There was a fenced-in garden off to the side and it looked like multiple vegetables had been recently planted.

Jade got down on her stomach, crawling forward with her elbows. Her sharp eyes were peeled for any kind of suspicious movement. Shae and Alex followed her lead. Wind howled through the grass. A number of animals were sunning themselves in the open space before the enormous structure. Jade could smell the faint scent of rust even from where they were. There was no sign of Coop or Isis anywhere.

"Maybe we should find a door and knock," Shae suggested from her left.

"Remember what Coop said about the place being rigged with a number of electrical traps," Alex warned from her other side. Jade ran her thumb over her lower lip, trying to figure out their options. Her attention was drawn to the right when she saw movement out of the corner of her eye.

"God dammit," she whispered.

Jensen and Nero came out slowly, moving oddly. They were both in human form. Judging from their stiff gaits, Jade surmised something was wrong. It wasn't too long before she spotted the man behind them, using the two shape shifters as living shields. A hand rested on the side of each of their throats and neither man looked thrilled with the situation.

"All right, come out! I know there are more of you," the man called out with a distinct London accent. "Two cars, four birds in one, three blokes in the other, all shape shifters. Come out now unless you want your friends returned to you extra crispy. Don't let the posh voice fool you. I can be rather violent when the situation calls for it."

Jade stood up and stepped out from the cover of the grass with her hands held up. She ignored Jensen subtly shaking his head. Piercing luminous silver eyes peered out from between Nero and Jensen, ducking back behind Jensen's head again. *Shocker,* Jade realized as she swallowed, trying to figure out what to do.

"Look," she began calmly.

"And the others," Shocker snapped, cutting her off. Jade looked behind her and gestured for the other two to come out. The grass rustled as Alex and Shae came out into the open, both their hands raised as well.

"We're just here to talk," Jade began.

"Save it! You have nothing to offer me," he snarled.

"We know what happened to you," Alex tried.

"You know nothing, normal," the man cut her off. A couple sparks appeared behind Jensen and Nero, causing them both to flinch.

"Stop," Shae yelled.

"You're trespassing," the man responded just as harshly. "I want you gone. Now."

"Fine, just—" Jade began.

A distressed yelp drew all their attention to the left. Standing a few feet away from the plant was Isis. She held a small gray and white dog by the scruff of its neck, the sharp point of a sai pressing against its throat.

"For godsakes, Isis," Jade hissed between her teeth, cringing when Isis pressed the blade of the weapon even more against the dog's throat. *Taking a dog hostage, well that's a new kind of fucked up,* she thought with a shake of her head. Isis ignored her, her glowing green eyes narrowing at Shocker.

"Hurt that dog and I kill your mates," Shocker warned, gripping the back of Jensen's and Nero's necks. Both men cringed and grimaced.

"Hurt those men and I kill this dog," Isis countered, ignoring the dog as it whimpered and squirmed. "And all the other animals running around here."

"You don't want to get in a standoff with me, dearie. You *will* lose."

There was quiet for a moment, broken by Nero clearing his throat. Jensen looked over at him. He cringed in pain when Shocker sent a low level electric charge through his body.

"Could we maybe all just take a moment and calm down?" Nero suggested, yelping when Shocker sent an electric charge through his body. The dog whimpered when Isis tightened her grip, squirming even more. Both Jensen and Nero let out cries of pain when Shocker responded by shocking them again.

"Hey, Isis, could you not antagonize the experiment who is threatening to electrocute Jensen and Nero?" Jade said, trying to defuse the tense situation.

"He shouldn't antagonize *me*," Isis responded, pressing the sai tighter against the whimpering dog's throat, her gaze still glued to Shocker. Jade could see the dog was trembling and ran a hand over her face. She couldn't believe she was in a standoff where a dog was being held hostage. Looking back to Alex and Shae, she could see they were also at a loss about what to do.

"Shocker, let them go."

Jade breathed a sigh of relief when Coop's soft voice came from behind them. The three women all looked over to where the other experiment stood in the entrance of the abandoned plant. He leaned against the frame of the open door, unbothered by the scene in front of him.

"Isis, put the dog down," Coop said, still laid back. Neither experiment moved to comply. Isis kept her eyes on the man in front of her but Shocker was looking back at the other experiment.

"Coop?" he finally said. "I'd heard you were dead."

Coop almost smiled. "Just off the grid for a while. Would you mind letting those two go? They have a proposition for you and I can vouch for them."

Shocker turned his attention back to Jensen and Nero. Removing his hands from their necks, he took a step back. Both men scrambled away from their captor. Isis lowered the dog back to the ground. The dog whined as she ran toward Shocker, moving around behind his legs, still trembling. Shocker reached down and scratched the dog's large pointed ears, soothing her.

"You took a *dog* hostage?" Nero asked his niece when she approached. "That's some supervillain-level shit, Isis."

Isis spun her sai and slid it back into her belt, unbothered. Jade approached them, looking at the new experiment. He was dressed plainly in a t-shirt and jeans. His hair was a light blond, almost silver, and he had a square build. Like the other experiments she had met, Jade noticed he was more on the wiry side. After a moment, Shocker shrugged and moved inside the building. Coop turned his attention back to them.

"He'll hear you out," the experiment reported. "You can come in. I took care of most of the traps so no one will have an advantage over anyone else."

"Reassuring," Jade said as Isis stepped past her. She followed her inside the large building. Inside it was cool and quiet. The bright lights illuminated towering walls decorated with paintings, most of them recognizable. Jade moved over to a canvas of the Mona Lisa, squinting as she examined it. It was remarkably authentic, a perfect replica. The paint and frame even looked aged.

"Where did you get all this art?" Shae asked, leaning down to stroke a large brown tabby.

"I made it all," Shocker called back. All the shape shifters, except for Isis and Coop, stared at him in disbelief.

"No fucking way," Alex said, pausing to examine a Rossetti reproduction. Shocker looked over his shoulder, pausing to watch them. Isis approached Jensen, who was marveling at a reproduction of Botticelli's *Birth of Venus*.

"Well I can't wander down to a museum now can I? Grenich made sure of that," Shocker stated, leaning against another doorway. "Can't go out into the world and I have to find some way to pass the time. In case you hadn't noticed, my kind isn't exactly suited to a sedentary lifestyle. Painting and sculpting has proven to be an adequate outlet."

"Does it help?" Isis asked, her eyes not moving from the painting in front of her. Jade turned away from the painting to look over at her teammate, wondering what she was talking about. Jensen was also studying her.

Shocker shrugged, apparently understanding the question. "It doesn't hurt. I may not understand the motivations of normals when it comes to their visual arts, or any of their arts for that matter. Still, there is something quite ... pleasant about such things. I enjoy looking at these, even though I don't understand why."

Isis looked over at him and Jade could see something similar to curiosity in her expression. She glanced to the side when she heard a soft thumping. A large black and white Border Collie with a snowy white face was curled up with a sleeping Golden Retriever, his brown eyes watching the visitors.

"Why do you steal animals?" Shae asked, petting a German Shepherd mix who was sniffing at her shoes. The dog's tail swished on the ground as he sat down and pawed at her leg.

"I don't. You normals, you discard your domesticated pets like garbage. You don't care how many of them are put down, so long as you don't have to worry about them anymore," Shocker responded. "You can't steal what has been thrown out. I like companion animals. They're not afraid of me."

Shocker turned his attention back to Isis. "Blitz, right? You sense their fear, the normals, don't you? They think they hide it, but you know they're afraid of you."

Isis didn't respond, but looked back to the paintings. Shocker looked back to the other shape shifters.

"That's a yes, in case you have difficulty translating our language and cues," he said, a sharpness to his tone.

"That's enough, Shocker," Coop stated as he stepped forward. "They need your help."

Jade stepped up next to Coop. "We're planning to attack the main laboratory in this state. Coop tells us it's one of the bigger Grenich facilities and there are a number of experiments being kept there, including the last of the three Key possibilities. We're going to release the experiments and shut the lab down for good, which will neutralize an important Grenich facility."

Shocker stared at her for a moment, not making a sound. Jade waited, trying to read his expression, but could not. Shocker looked over at Coop and then Isis before turning his gaze back to Jade. Then he laughed loudly. It was so sudden, Jade flinched. Of all the possible reactions she had expected, that had not been one of them.

Shocker howled with laughter, his voice echoing off the walls. Jade looked over at Coop and Isis, but neither of them moved or reacted.

"Well he's not killing us," Nero mentioned quietly behind her. "I suppose that's a good sign."

Shocker's laughter died down and he regained his composure, chuckling and wiping his eyes. "Oh that's *brilliant.* You normals are very entertaining. Let me get this straight. You're planning an assault on an underground lab, which is impenetrable, with a few normals and two experiments in a town Grenich has basically already conquered and controls."

"Three experiments," Coop corrected and Shocker almost starting laughing again.

"Two of whom are Key possibilities, correct?" He

nodded at Jensen. "Will you be bringing the last Aldridge along too?"

"He is a capable fighter," Coop answered.

"Good god, you are asking for a massacre. I'm tempted to agree just to see this entire thing blow up in your face," Shocker said.

"Excuse me," Alex spoke up. "You mentioned Grenich has already conquered this town. What do you mean by that?"

Shocker looked over at her. "You're one of the Four, I take it. You've got a whole rah-rah sisterhood vibe to you. Normals never see it, blissful state of ignorance you lot live in. Grenich is like a virus, sweetheart. It plants its RNA in a town and that RNA spreads. First, some people go missing. Then a bunch of abandoned buildings start popping up. Small at first, tiny farms and foreclosed houses, but they steadily get bigger. This town already has an abandoned factory, this plant, and there's a school that just became abandoned yesterday."

"That school has been abandoned for at least a decade," Jade pointed out from where she was admiring a recreation of Donatello's David. A little smile danced across Shocker's face.

"Of course it has," he said, humoring her as he knocked on the wall. "This plant was thriving about six years ago and then, practically overnight, it was buried under decades of dirt and detritus. Most of the employees vanished, erased from existence. As it gains power, Grenich is able to fuck with normals' sense of time. You don't see the population go down because it happens so gradually. As the abandoned buildings start increasing, the surveillance also starts going up. Eventually you're left with a little shell of what was once a town, one always under surveillance, and sweetie, this town has just about expired. It'll be a ghost in about five years, maybe even sooner."

"Why don't the guardians notice this?" Shae asked.

"Not entirely sure of that, but my understanding is that

guardians are more aware of the macro. Grenich tends to stick with the micro."

"All the more reason to target the main laboratory," Coop pointed out and Shocker snorted, looking back over at him.

"How are you going to get in? There's only one entrance — the rotunda — which is a killbox. You'll be slaughtered on the stairs. There are at least fourteen guards down there, round the clock."

"If we had someone knock out the power, it would provide a small window of opportunity," Isis put in.

Shocker whistled. "The amount of juice in that place? Tricky. Not impossible, but not probable either. You'd still have the problem of the guards. How do you expect to get the experiments out of there before the kill switch is activated? Coop and I barely knew what to do when our cells were opened. They're not going to just follow you out. They're not ducklings. I suppose you could just leave them in there and activate the kill switch. That would be the most merciful course of action."

Jade put her hands on her hips, wondering what it would take to convince the experiment to help them. Shocker didn't seem interested in being cooperative and she was disturbed by the idea that the town was disappearing right under their noses. Looking around the space, Jade was impressed with how tidy he was. There wasn't a speck of dust to be seen and the experiment had obviously done a massive amount of renovation. It looked more like a museum wing than an abandoned power plant. *Except with a lot of animals*, Jade thought when a calico rubbed up against her legs.

"You will harbor some of the freed experiments here, the ones who wish to help fight against Grenich," Isis stated as she moved around the open area. "They will be able to help you with your animals."

Shocker turned to stare at her. "I'm sorry, when did I agree to have any part in this suicidal plan of yours?"

Isis didn't look at him as she examined a short bookshelf near a large window. Sunlight gleamed on the shiny catsuit she wore. She crouched down to read the titles on the shelves. Jade glanced over at Shae and Alex, wondering if another confrontation between the experiments was inevitable.

"You may have lived on the outside longer than I, but you still retain your instincts," Isis mentioned, straightening up again and looking over at Shocker. "This is about survival. If we don't win this fight, we face extinction. Grenich is not fond of things connected to the guardians or of malfunctioning products. Sooner or later, Set will come for you. You said it yourself: this town is falling under Grenich control, as are many others. When he does come for you, he will destroy any living thing you've been in contact with. That includes your dogs and cats."

Shocker narrowed his eyes at her. "You do enjoy threatening, don't you?"

"I don't threaten. I observe and I occasionally warn," Isis replied, looking around at the art surrounding them. "Set will burn every last book, every last painting. He will annihilate any trace of beauty in this world."

Shocker started making his way to the doorway leading to the back. "You can show yourselves out."

"Nick Chance," Isis called after him.

The reaction was immediate. Shocker froze and turned his now wide eyes toward her. A couple sparks fell from his spikey hair and the lights in the plant flickered. A dog whined somewhere nearby. Shocker looked over at Coop and it was the closest to fear Jade had ever seen in an experiment. She exchanged a look with Alex, who seemed rather concerned.

"He has been recalled," Isis continued. "He led the assault on the local rebel Lair, killed a few shape shifters and wounded even more."

Shocker looked around the open space and Isis moved

closer to him.

"We can't run and hide, not anymore," she told him, crossing her arms over her chest. "There's nowhere to run, nowhere that Set and Pyra won't be able to find us. It's time to fight back."

Shocker stared at her and then at the other shape shifters, his shoulders dropping. "If Chance is in town, we're all fucked. That lunatic will have all our heads on pointed sticks outside the entrance to the Grenich laboratory."

"You can control electricity," Nero pointed out. "Why not just shoot him with a thousand volts?"

"Chance has a knack for anticipating the moves of experiments," Coop answered. "Shocker would have to get within a certain range to do him any damage. Getting in that range would be dangerous."

"Believe me, mate, I've considered doing it. Many, many times before. However, I find I value my life," Shocker added, running a hand through his hair and closing his eyes. "When are you planning to attack the laboratory?"

"End of the month," Isis answered. Shocker opened his eyes, studying her for a moment.

"There are some rather unsettling stories about you, you know. The killer in the shadows," he mentioned. "Word is you're quite cold-hearted and ruthless, even by experiment standards."

"My heart is a normal temperature and I am no different from any other experiment."

Shocker shook his head, frowning. "No, you're definitely not like other experiments. There's something … different about you, but I don't know what exactly."

Isis turned from him and moved further away, looking up at the assortment of paintings on the wall. Jade glanced over her shoulder at her and then looked back to Shocker. He dropped his gaze to his feet before raising his eyes back to her.

"If something happens to me, one of you needs to take care of my animals," he stated. "There's a book of instructions in the back room, under the pillows. Medicines and foods are in the kitchen area."

"Fine," Jade agreed, wondering how many animals the experiment had collected. They all looked well-cared for and incredibly healthy. There was no smell, surprisingly, and they all seemed to be very friendly. Even the cats were affectionate. She looked back to Shocker, who picked up a tortoiseshell cat and massaged the animal's ears.

"Well, as you normals are so fond of saying, better to die on your feet," Shocker said, letting the large cat climb up onto his shoulders. "Count me in, I guess."

CHAPTER EIGHT

Orion, Remington, and Hunter stood behind enormous redwood trees, allowing the large trunks to conceal their presence. Orion had his gun out and pointed to the ground, his eyes never moving from the open valley. The sun was beginning to rise, coating everything in a strange grayish light. The blades of grass were beginning to appear green as the sky lightened and the sweet scent of the forest was soothing.

Hunter stifled a yawn, trying to keep her exhaustion at bay. They had walked all night and she hadn't slept much the past few days. The young protector understood the need for caution, but she wanted the journey to be over. Hooking her thumbs in the pockets of her jeans, Hunter looked out into the forest and observed the numerous trees stretching as far as the eye could see. After a moment, Jack stepped out from behind another tree, adjusting the pack he carried on his back. Sunglasses were concealing his luminous eyes.

"There's one more following us, but he's staying out of my sensory range," Jack reported. "We should move now. I'll take care of our tail."

Orion holstered his gun again, taking something out of

his pocket. Hunter followed him and Remington out into the valley, looking around. Jack had the uncanny ability to inspire paranoia. Hunter didn't even want to think about what it was like in his head. Glancing over her shoulder, she watched Jack bring up the rear. He didn't remain in line with them, but walked off to the side and his gaze never moved from behind them. Hunter turned her attention to Remington's back.

Orion stopped in front of another redwood. Crouching down, he pressed the object he held against the enormous trunk. Hunter peered over Remington's shoulder and noticed it was a stick of blue chalk. Orion started to draw a straight line, releasing the chalk after a moment. The chalk remained pressed against the trunk for a moment before it started rapidly scribbling the shape of a simple arched door. Hunter watched in amazement as it even drew wood panels and a circular doorknob before dropping back into Orion's hand. A thin line of silver began to fill in the chalk outline. Hunter stared in amazement as a door gradually took the place of the chalk drawing. Orion stepped forward and knocked three times, stepping back again.

Jack darted forward and reached out. Hunter turned when she heard a hiss of air, jolting when she saw the bolt Jack caught in his fist, inches away from Orion. In one fluid movement, the experiment tossed the bolt to the ground and pointed his gun, firing two shots. The sound was so quiet, it didn't even echo. Hunter turned back when she heard something crashing through the canopy. She watched a shape plummet to the ground, twisting back when she heard the door creaking open. Jack yanked off his sunglasses and took a couple steps forward, squinting as he looked toward the trees.

"Tail's gone," he reported. Hunter turned back to the doorway, trying to see who had opened it.

"Hello, William," Orion greeted as he stepped through the door, unbothered by the attempt on his life. Remington called Hunter's name and gestured for her to go through the tree. As she stepped through the door, Hunter looked over at the gatekeeper and felt her eyes widen.

William was on the shorter side — shorter than most people Hunter had met — and very sturdily built. He had a mop of grayish-black hair on his head and gentle blue eyes. His skin was a bright shade of green and he had a prominent hooked nose on his otherwise thin face. His fingers were quite stubby and he wore tan clothes, which had colorful tulips sewn on them.

"Hullo, Dr. Deverell," William greeted in a melancholy voice. His eyes widened and he shrank back when Jack came through the door. Hunter thought the gatekeeper would start trembling. The experiments were intimidating and many people became uneasy around them, but she had never seen anyone outright petrified by one before.

"The threat has been neutralized," Jack confirmed as he slid his sunglasses back on, ignoring the terrified creature in front of him. William ran forward and pushed the door shut, staying as far away from Jack as was possible. Hunter looked over at Orion, waiting for him to introduce them. Behind her, she could hear a key turning in a lock.

"Hunter, Remington, Jack, this is William, the gatekeeper of the Sanctuary," Orion introduced when William returned, his brow furrowing. "William, what's wrong? You sound rather sad."

"Just received word yesterday, sir. I'm the last goblin," William explained, turning to the other shape shifters and bowing. "Pleasure to make your acquaintance. Perrin is expecting you."

"William, hold on. What do you mean, the last goblin?" Orion asked. Hunter adjusted the pack on her back as she followed Orion and Remington. She looked up at the bright blue sky above her. It was already well after dawn in the Sanctuary. Looking around, Hunter noticed there were wildflowers as far as the eye could see. Vibrant colors of all different shades stretched on for an eternity. Foxes chased each other through the trees and plants, flowers waving as they dashed through them. Hunter could see people reading books high in the branches of the trees and some were painting on easels on the ground. The air felt clean and refreshing in her lungs; a subtle sweet scent from the flowers seemed to chase away some of the tension Hunter had been carrying throughout the trip.

"A sickness, sir," William answered Orion. "It killed 'em all. The last of 'em died a few days back, which means I'm the last one, sir."

Hunter noticed the fearful glances the goblin cast over his shoulder as he continued leading them onwards. His square-shaped body quaked every now and again when his eyes fell on Jack. She looked back to where Jack was following a short ways behind her. He had holstered his gun and now his gaze traveled around the lands.

"Why is he so scared of you?" Hunter asked, turning around so she was walking backward. Jack turned his face toward her, his eyes shielded by the reflective lenses.

"Who?" he asked.

Hunter nodded over her shoulder. "Don't tell me you didn't notice how frightened the gatekeeper is of you. If you sneezed, he'd bolt."

Jack furrowed his brow. "I don't sneeze."

"You haven't answered my question."

The experiment shrugged. "I'm frightening to normals of all species. It is a natural evolutionary response to danger. You're about to walk into a tree."

Hunter turned around, stopping just before she collided with the rough bark of a large tree. She glanced up when she heard giggling. A woman with short pink hair sat up in the branches. She wore a white dress and held one hand over her mouth, amusement dancing in her violet eyes. Hunter grumbled under her breath and continued following Remington.

After an hour of walking through the scenic lands, they

came upon a large stone structure. To Hunter, it resembled Raphael's painting *The School of Athens*. She had seen it years ago when she and Brindy had been traveling around Italy. The painting had been her older sister's favorite and her face lit up when she saw the actual one. The memory brought a lump to Hunter's throat and she looked down at her feet, fighting back tears.

"Orion, it is good to see you again."

Hunter looked up when she heard a throaty voice. A tall beautiful woman with long brown hair stood a few feet before them. Her dark eyes turned to Remington and her smile grew as she approached them. She had long legs, which gave her a lengthy stride. When she reached Remington, she kissed him passionately. Hunter stared at them, surprised. She knew Remington had companions and lovers in the past, but she had rarely seen him with any. Hunter couldn't help but be impressed with the ardor of the two shape shifters and began to feel a little voyeuristic. She looked back to the stone structure, happy to focus on something else. Wind rustled through the leaves.

Remington smiled. "It has been a long time, Perrin."

"Much too long, dear Remington. We will find some time to catch up later." She grinned suggestively as she ran a hand down the side of Remington's face before turning her attention to the experiment. "Jack, it is good to finally meet you in person. Orion has written to me often about you and Isis, I feel as though I already know you. While you are here, feel free to explore the lands. I know you were always looking for something to read, so I recommend the library. It is quite extensive."

"Thank you," Jack responded, looking a little confused. "I enjoyed the novels you sent when we were first extracted."

"I thought you would," Perrin replied, turning to Hunter. "Jet and Lilly's youngest daughter, it is a pleasure to meet you."

"Likewise," Hunter replied, adjusting the strap on her shoulder as she looked around. "Orion said you wanted to speak with me."

"I would like that very much, but I have some matters to discuss with Orion first," Perrin said, gesturing with her arm. "Feel free to explore the Sanctuary. There are plenty of residents who can direct you to whatever you need or want."

"I'm kind of tired right now," Hunter admitted, rubbing her arm when the dull ache flared up in it. "Are there any rooms where I could sleep?"

"Of course. Follow the stone path down to the stream. You'll find a small dormitory. There are plenty of empty rooms on the second floor," Perrin directed, gesturing down the stone path leading away from them. "You'll pass the library on your way there, if you desire a way to pass the time."

Hunter started down the pathway, happy to be alone. She kept her gaze down as she followed the smooth stones. *Perfect for skipping,* she thought as she focused on the gray rocks. Around her, she heard a number of natural sounds, mostly animals. Occasionally, Hunter would hear quiet laughter or voices, but she wasn't interested in what others were doing in the Sanctuary. The protector just wanted to be alone.

Soon, she came upon a babbling stream. A number of small orange fish dotted the water, swimming around the rocks. Hunter spotted a modest wooden building ahead and quickened her pace, jogging up the creaking steps. She opened the door and noticed a room full of cots off to the side. Moving down the short hall, she stood in the large entrance of the room. Sunlight beamed down from the high windows on the left side, casting shadows of the frames across the empty beds. There were a few privacy curtains toward the back, likely concealing more cots. The room had a pleasant aroma and was quite welcoming. Hunter looked to the right and noticed a couple closed doors. Turning her attention back into the room, she noticed one bed was occupied.

A dark-haired man slept in a cot halfway down one of the rows. His bare chest rose and fell shallowly. A large bandage was peeking out from under the blankets that covered him up to his abdomen. The bright sunlight enhanced his pallid complexion. Hunter glanced back over her shoulder, wondering if she had taken a wrong turn. She turned back and the cot was empty, the blanket on the floor. Hunter took a cautious step forward, looking around the bright room. *Okay, I know I didn't hallucinate just now*, she thought, feeling more than a little unsettled.

"Hello?" Hunter called out. "I think I might—"

An arm around her throat choked off her words and she gagged when it tightened. The pressure applied to her windpipe made breathing difficult and Hunter flashbacked to the massacre at the Lair. Her heart began hammering in her chest and she started to thrash around but stopped when she felt the sharp end of a scalpel press against her chest.

"Just a little pressure, I puncture a lung and you'll drown in your own blood. Understand?" a deep voice spoke softly behind her. The warm breath brushed against her ear and Hunter let out a steady breath. In one fast move, she drew the knife she had in the sheath at her waist and pressed it backward, estimating where the man's groin was. She felt him stiffen in surprise, but the grip around her neck didn't loosen.

"Stab me and I cut it off. I may drown in my own blood, but before I do, I'll either castrate you or sever your femoral artery. You'll bleed out right along with me. Is that a risk you really want to take?" she threatened, pushing the knife further back to drive her point home. "Trust me, I've got *nothing* to lose at this point."

The stranger was quiet for a moment. He pressed his nose against her hair, inhaling. Hunter closed her eyes in disgust and annoyance, but kept the knife pressed against her captor. The grip around her throat vanished as did the scalpel pressed against her chest. She turned around, narrowing her eyes at the stranger. Hunter kept her knife out, her knuckles turning white with the intensity of her grip.

"Apologies, I didn't realize you were the Monroes' daughter," the man said, spinning the scalpel around his fingers. He had black hair and expressive brown eyes with flecks of green in them. The stranger was handsome despite the pallor of his skin. Hunter again noticed the bandages winding around his abdomen. They were fresh as though they had been recently changed. Hunter couldn't help but stare at the multitude of scars decorating the man's torso. There were some that looked as though they should have killed him.

"Who are you?" Hunter growled, her knife still held at the ready. The man, who had been looking all around the room, glanced over at her, the scalpel still twirling around his dexterous fingers. His alertness reminded Hunter of Jack and Isis.

"No threat to you," the stranger replied, grimacing.

"That's debatable at best," Hunter said. A twinkle of amusement appeared in the man's eyes and he tapped the flat of the scalpel against his palm.

"Fair enough," he conceded with a nod, squinting against the bright sunlight. "The alias I frequently use is Anubis. You may call me that if you wish."

"You threaten to kill me and you won't tell me your real name?" Hunter said, flexing the fingers of her free hand. Anubis moved back into the room, tossing the scalpel onto a nearby table. It clattered against the smooth surface.

"Why is my name so important to you?" he asked, not turning around as he made his way to the cot he had been sleeping in. Hunter followed him, more curious than anything. She re-sheathed her blade, resting her hand on the grip just in case.

"I don't know. I find it wise to know the identities of would-be assassins," she replied with a nonchalant shrug. "I'm assuming you're a shape shifter, since you know who my parents are."

Anubis glanced over his shoulder at her as he retrieved the blankets from the ground. Hunter could tell from the stiffness of his movements that he was trying to conceal how much pain he was in.

"Interesting assumption, seeing as how you don't have much evidence to base it on. However, in this case, you're partially correct. I'm half shape shifter," Anubis stated as he sat on the cot, grimacing again. Reaching over to the nearby table, he retrieved a glass of water and took a sip.

"What's the other half?"

Anubis gave her a thin, half-smile. "Not shape shifter."

Hunter crossed her arms over her chest and turned her gaze to the window across the way. "Look, it's been—"

"My condolences on your recent losses," Anubis interrupted. "Perrin told me about the attack on the Lair."

Hunter turned her attention back to him. He held one arm protectively over the bandages around his stomach. His expression reflected genuine sympathy without a hint of pity, something she found refreshing. Hunter looked down at her feet, quickly raising her eyes to Anubis' again. She didn't want anyone to see her grief, especially not a stranger, but she didn't want to appear weak either. Rubbing her arm, Hunter wondered when the dull throbbing would go away. It was a constant reminder of the night she lost her sister and brother. Hunter didn't know how much longer she could deal with it. Part of her just wanted to cut the damn thing off.

"Could you—"

"What's wrong with your arm?" Anubis interrupted her again, looking pointedly at the offending limb. Hunter dropped it to her side, hiding it.

"Nothing," she mumbled.

"Did a demon bite you?" Anubis continued, ignoring

her response. He gingerly lifted his legs up onto the cot, stretching them out in front of him. Hunter stared at the peculiar man, more curious than ever what the other half was.

"There's no such thing," she responded. He leaned back, drumming his fingers on the mattress.

"You may have another name for them. Experiments do, but they're the same vermin," he explained. "Orion probably refers to them as followers of Set or just followers."

Hunter toyed with the strap over her shoulder. "Are you a friend of Orion's?"

"Wouldn't say a friend, doubt the good doctor has any of those. Ally would be a more accurate term," Anubis answered, grunting as he shifted his position. He muttered a couple colorful curse words before flopping back against the headboard.

"Are you all right?" Hunter asked, glancing over her shoulder behind her.

"Just dandy," Anubis replied, clearing his throat. "If you're looking for an empty room, they're upstairs. Just go around the corner, you'll see the stairway."

Hunter hesitated, torn about what to do. On the one hand, she wanted to take a nap and just forget the past few weeks. On the other, she didn't like leaving a shape shifter so obviously in pain. Sure, he was kind of an ass, but he was also somewhat interesting. *If nothing else, he might be a good distraction,* she thought as she chewed her bottom lip.

Anubis leaned his head back, his eyes closed. "You're still here."

"Well you look inches from death's door," Hunter pointed out. A small smile played on Anubis' lips.

"Been a fuck lot closer, if you can believe it," he replied, opening his eyes slightly to look at her. "I'll be fine, Ms. Monroe. Please don't stick around on my account."

Hunter shrugged and turned to leave the room, when

the throbbing in her arm started to intensify. She blinked and the walls began to wobble, as if they were melting. Hunter clenched her eyes shut and shook her head once, trying to rid herself of the strange tunnel-vision. She thought she heard someone calling to her, an echoing whisper.

When she opened her eyes again, Hunter found herself in a shadowy room with smoky walls. The lack of substance made her head spin, but she resisted grabbing hold of anything for fear it would vanish. A bright white light snapped on above her, illuminating a nude man tied up on a rack. He was suspended by his arms, which were bound above his head. Even though she could only see in black and white, Hunter could tell his eyes glowed. The man was an experiment. He looked in her direction and stared directly at her for a moment. *Does he see me?* Hunter wondered, glancing behind her before looking back to the experiment. He dropped his gaze again.

The sound of a whetstone sliding down a blade drew her attention to the right. Hunter felt her heart start to hammer against her ribs when she saw the man from the Lair, Nick Chance. He was smirking as he slid the whetstone over the curved shining blade he held.

"7-082, you have been one naughty guinea pig in my absence. Gambling, hustling, sneaking out, fornicating," Chance said, clicking his tongue. "What are we going to do with you?"

The experiment licked his lips, but didn't respond as he kept his eyes downcast. Chance tossed the whetstone to the side, where it clattered noisily on the surface of the table. The sound echoed through Hunter's mind and she cringed at the noise, putting her hands over her sensitive ears. Chance spun the curved knife a few times as he walked around to face the experiment.

"Now, I can't kill you. Short of that, your punishment is up to my discretion," Chance continued, running the flat of the blade up the experiment's side. "You know, I'm not quite sure the pelt I collected from you last time was up to my standards for display. I've been dreaming of collecting another ever since I was sent away."

Hunter thought she would be sick. Blood was thundering in her ears and she felt like the room was spinning. Chance twisted his body, his gaze fixing on where Hunter was standing. She stiffened and struggled to remain still, wondering if he could see her. Glancing to the side, she saw the table where a variety of knives were laid out. *Can I reach them before he reaches me?*

"Ever have the feeling you were being watched?" Chance asked, squinting as he continued looking in her direction. After a moment, he gave a small shrug and turned his attention back to the experiment. "No matter. I've always enjoyed an audience."

Without warning, he started slicing the flesh off the experiment. He cut and peeled off a large chunk of flesh from the nude man's back. The experiment didn't flinch but closed his eyes, clenched his fists, and gritted his teeth. Hunter started forward when her surroundings became blindingly bright. She lost her footing and fell hard on her knees. Beneath her palms, she felt the familiar smoothness of hardwood. Blinking a few times, she tried to force her eyes to adjust to the sunlight.

For a moment, Hunter was certain she was going to be sick to her stomach. She became aware of steadying hands on her back and arm. Quickly as she was able, Hunter scrambled away, raising a protective hand up to shield her face. Her vision began to clear and she found herself face-to-face with Anubis. He was crouching in front of her, concern apparent in his expression. Swallowing, Hunter tried to find her voice but her throat was dry and scratchy. She noticed her body was shaking and tried to stop.

Anubis rose and approached the table next to the bed he had been sleeping in. He lifted the decanter and poured water into a glass. Returning to where Hunter was still trying to get her bearings, he crouched down and held out the glass. She accepted it and drained it in a single gulp, wiping her mouth with the back of her hand.

"What is happening to me?" she asked, not expecting him to answer. Anubis sighed, lowering himself to the ground so he was sitting across from her. She noticed a light pink stain on his bandages.

"I'm sorry, but I think your life is about to get a lot more difficult," he answered after a moment.

~~*~*~*

Isis sat in the library in front of the towering bay windows, sunlight streaming down on her back. Numerous files were opened around her, papers spread out messily. There was a map behind her, most of it shaded with a red grease pencil and dotted with black circles. Her glowing eyes darted back and forth over Orion's illegible handwriting. Being used to his awful script and various codes, Isis was able to decipher what he had written. She didn't understand Orion's desire to keep hardcopies of everything when digital was a much more efficient and sensible method of storing information. Hard copies couldn't be hacked, but they could be stolen or lost.

On her left, Jensen was sitting beside another set of windows. His nose was buried in a worn copy of *The Canterbury Tales*. Toward the front of the library, Shae was curled up in one of the large chairs with her tablet. She had earbuds in and would occasionally touch the screen to select something. Though she was aware of their presence, Isis was focused solely on the papers in front of her. She had spent most of the night working on the map, tracking the steady spread of the Grenich Corporation. Last night, she had talked Alex into going for a late night walk through town. While walking the empty streets, Isis had taken note of the increase in security cameras. There was one on almost every lamp and streetlight. It had been difficult to avoid them and Isis had to rely on her counter-surveillance experience to hide from the cameras. Grenich had eyes everywhere.

The sound of Nero's voice brought Isis out of her thoughts, but she immediately re-focused on Orion's notes. The main hallways were alive with activity. Jetta, Jet and Lilly's eldest daughter, was going to meet with the heads of the lycanthropes later that afternoon. Malone and Devin were going as bodyguards, which was troubling Nero for some reason she didn't understand nor had any interest in figuring out. It was likely to be the easiest diplomatic mission as the lycanthropes had always been loyal to the shape shifters and to the protectors in particular. Familial love was a concept Isis was having trouble understanding. It caused undue stress and worry, yet was considered of the utmost importance to a normal's well-being. To her, it seemed to be a constant distraction. *Distractions cause death* — a lesson from Grenich popped into her head. She kept sorting through papers, closing her eyes for a moment and forcing the memory out of her mind.

"Nero, I've told you a hundred times, we'll be fine. We'll be back before you know it. Go find a rebel to sleep with or something." Malone's voice came from out in the main hallway. To her left, she heard Jensen chuckle as he turned a page in his book.

"How can I be expected to perform when at any minute I could be that much closer to being the last male Deverell? I'll be like Jensen and I can't pull off the mopey emo persona," Nero protested, his voice closer than Malone's. "No offense, man."

"None taken," she heard Jensen call back. Judging from the muffled volume, he hadn't looked up from his book. Isis listened to Nero's footsteps approach the library, but her attention was drawn to a sheet of paper poking out from under a couple others. She snatched it up, her eyes sweeping over Orion's shorthand. Looking down to her right, she moved a couple papers around, searching for something she had seen earlier.

"Isis, isn't it a strategically bad idea to send only two Deverells on a mission like this?" Nero asked from the doorway. She heard Devin's footsteps approach, pausing at the library entrance.

"Aw, Nero, you're worried about your brothers. That is so adorable," Shae commented from where she was sitting.

"For a low-risk diplomatic mission, the danger is minimal," Isis answered without looking up from the papers. "Orion believes the supernatural races will be beneficial in the fight against Grenich. It is one of the few things we are in complete agreement on. Normals need the numbers, especially since you'll only have four experiments on your side. This facility has approximately three hundred fifty experiments on site and at least double that number of guards, maybe triple."

"Nero, it'll be fine. We've been in more dangerous situations before," Jensen mentioned from where he sat. "Remember Crete?"

"But we've always had each other's backs," Nero protested.

"We'd never leave you, little brother," Devin commented. "And don't worry, you'll always have Roan. Nothing's going to happen to him in the Meadows."

"Real comforting," Nero grumbled. "Malone, you're bringing guns right?"

"For the love of the guardians! Ajax, would you *please* deal with him?"

Devin and Nero's footsteps faded as they left the library. Isis snatched up another sheet of paper, looking at the scribbled address. Looking back at the first sheet, she read the address she had found there. Every now and again, Orion had written down the address to a bank and under a couple of them, a three-digit number. What caught her attention was their proximity to different Grenich facilities. Turning her attention to another stack of papers, she dug through them until she found another map, a smaller one that Orion had marked up. Looking back to the first sheet she had taken out, Isis examined the address. Her glowing green eyes turned back to the map, her gaze drifting between the two sheets of paper. After a moment, Isis looked up to where Jensen was sitting. Rising to her feet, she approached him and stuck the paper in front of the page he was reading. He looked up at her and she pointed at the address. Jensen gave her a quizzical look, but turned his attention to where she was indicating.

"Orion still has atrocious handwriting I see," he observed with a small grin.

"The bank, next town over, do you know it?" Isis asked. He toyed with the cuff of his sleeve and nodded once.

"Actually, I do," he answered. "I keep some heirlooms in a safe deposit box there. Bought it quite some time ago, when it first opened. Haven't thought—"

"We need to go there," Isis interrupted him, looking over to Shae. She had taken her earbuds out and was looking over at them.

"What's going on?" she asked, her green eyes sparkling with interest.

"The Grenich Corporation has a safe deposit box in a nearby bank," Isis explained, massaging her brow. "It's not in a designated drop site, so it's not meant for deep cover missions. I have overheard Orion speak of personal boxes the Corporation keeps. There's a good chance that box contains sensitive information, which could prove to be worthwhile to us."

Jensen shut the book and exchanged a look with Shae. Isis began to pace around the library, rubbing her palms together as her mind raced.

"Wouldn't they keep sensitive information on site?" Shae asked.

"It depends on what kind of information it is," Isis answered, looking out at the sunny day. "In the event something happened to one of their facilities, Set and Pyra would want to have some kind of back up so they could rebuild and start again."

"If you're right, surely they would have eyes on that bank around the clock," Jensen pointed out.

"Undoubtedly," Isis replied. "Our window of opportunity would be small, but I believe it is a risk worth taking."

"How would we infiltrate a bank?" Shae asked. "Besides Grenich, we would also have to worry about their security. The Monroes' only have so many contacts and operatives. How would you even gain access to the box?"

"Jensen would go in with Coop," Isis explained, a plan taking shape in her mind. "As a Lock series, he can open any lock, including the ones on safe deposit boxes. He could pose as your bodyguard. It would be wise to take Shocker as well. Being able to control the electricity would be useful."

"We barely got him to agree to help us attack the laboratory," Shae mentioned. "You think he would help us infiltrate a bank that's being watched by Grenich?"

"The four of us can keep watch outside," Isis continued, ignoring her. Shae looked over at Jensen again.

"Snipers might be a concern, but they would draw too much attention," Isis kept thinking aloud. "No, they'll probably use low-value products, but those will still be dangerous. Jack would be useful, but that's out of the question. Three experiments will have to be enough."

Isis paused and looked up at them. "We should do this as soon as possible, ideally in the next day or two, right when the bank is opening. I'll have Coop contact Shocker. You two should talk to Jade and Alex. We can discuss a plan over dinner tonight."

She swiftly and silently moved out of the library, not giving the two protectors a chance to protest. Isis didn't have the time for it and neither did the normals, though they were less aware of it. They would be attacking the Grenich facility in the next couple weeks and they were still at a severe disadvantage. Set had the numbers and the experience. By sending out his followers to attack the rebel clubs, he was chipping away at the protectors' allies. Orion could bring back more weapons, but it wouldn't be enough.

As she made her way up the main stairway, Isis' thoughts turned again to Nick Chance. He hadn't been seen or heard from since the attack on the Lair and that bothered her. Chance needed to kill and torture, needed to cause chaos. If he wasn't acting on his impulses and needs, it meant he was plotting and nothing positive would result from that.

~~*~*~*

"Of course the gateway was located behind a waterfall. Why not?" Malone grumbled as he tried to shake the excess water out of his hair. Devin squeezed one eye shut as he tried to get the water out of his ear. Like his brother, he was also sopping wet.

"I warned you two to bring a raincoat," Jetta mentioned as she pulled off her bright yellow rain jacket. She closed her eyes and raised her face to the sun.

"Aren't you a little dressed up," Devin asked, looking at her elegant clothing as she smoothed it with her hands. She was wearing a beige pantsuit with pointed shoes.

"Devin, I've been working as a lawyer for more than a hundred years and I frequently have to update my wardrobe," Jetta responded with a wide grin. "I don't have plain clothes."

Devin looked back at Malone, who just shrugged. They were both dressed plainly. Lycanthropes were farmers and wore clothes that were meant to last. They viewed fashionable clothes as ridiculous and frivolous. From what Malone read, their culture was quite different from shape shifters in some ways.

"Shall we?"

Malone looked at the tall long-haired man who was to be their guide. He was from the jaguar clan, judging from the symbol tattooed on his upper arm and sewn onto his clothing. Jetta smiled brilliantly and allowed him to lead the way. Devin and Malone hung back a few steps as was customary during diplomatic missions. Jetta made small talk with the guide, who would occasionally point something out, while the two Deverells observed their surroundings. It was a sunny day and vibrant shades of green surrounded them on all sides. The crops grew well over their heads and stretched as far as they could see. In the distance, they could hear fiddles and other stringed instruments. As they continued walking past endless fields of various crops, they would often glimpse lycanthropes working among them. A group of young children dashed across their path, squealing in delight and pointing at the strangers. They were herded off by two older women with long silver hair. Looking off into the distance, Malone couldn't help but think Orion would probably feel right at home in the lycanthropes' rustic world. *Well, except for the part where he would have to farm the land,* Malone thought, snickering at the thought of his oldest brother trying to learn how to harvest.

They soon came to a large hall built of wood. Symbols of animals were carved into the walls. Like everything else, it looked as though it had been constructed by hand. Their guide opened the door for Jetta and the Deverells. They stepped inside a long hall, at the end of which sat Diego and Ella, dressed in plain clothes, both husking ears of corn. They had long manes of hair — Diego's was black and Ella's was fiery red. Their skin was dark tan from the hours they spent outdoors. Though they were technically the leaders of the lycanthropes, they worked in the fields like the others.

"Jetta Monroe, welcome," Ella spoke as she put a husked ear in a wicker basket, rising from her seat. "It is good to connect with the protectors again."

"Thank you for agreeing to this meeting," Jetta said, stepping forward and kissing Ella on both cheeks. "Allow me to introduce Malone and Devin Deverell. They are loyal allies of my parents."

"It is a pleasure to meet you both," Ella greeted as she shook each of the Deverell's hands before turning her attention back to Jetta. "Our ambassadors mentioned Jet and Lilly's plans to hold a summit. Might I inquire what the summit concerns?"

"Of course. Your ambassadors undoubtedly mentioned Isis and Jack," Jetta began.

"They spoke of three strange shape shifters with glowing eyes," Diego replied, continuing to husk corn. "They heard some rather unsettling rumors about them, but were unsure how much was just conjecture."

Jetta held her hands in front of her. "Jack and Isis were taken by a corporation called Grenich. They were experimented on and modified to be the perfect weapons. We don't have a lot of information on the Grenich Corporation, but what little we do have paints a very disturbing picture. The corporation is owned and run by Set, who once went by a different name: Chaos."

Both Diego and Ella's expressions reflected a certain amount of fear at the name.

"The guardian who tried to conquer the Meadows?" Ella asked, glancing back to Diego. "I thought he perished in the war."

"So did we, but we were mistaken," Jetta continued. "He is amassing an army, abducting shape shifters and turning them into weapons. If we don't stop him, there's no telling how much damage he'll do. He already controls most of the wealth in our world and has allies in the highest offices of government. My parents wish to hold a summit at the end of the month with the heads of all the supernatural races in the hope of creating an alliance to challenge Set's empire. I come on their behalf to request your presence at this meeting."

"At the risk of sounding callous," Diego began as he stopped husking. "Why should we be concerned with matters on Earth?"

"Because we have evidence Set may be able to cross planes," Jetta replied. "We don't know how, but he might have found a way into the Seelie Court. Even if he did not, his ultimate goal seems to be conquering the Meadows. Should he accomplish that, all worlds will be in danger. Chaos was never known for mercy and neither were those who followed him."

Ella's eyes narrowed at the mention of the Seelie Court and Malone struggled not to cringe. The fey and the lycanthropes didn't get along. There was strife between them that went all the way back to the War of the Meadows. If the fey were involved in something, the lycanthropes would be less open to participating.

"Will the fey be at this summit?" Diego asked, his tone becoming colder and less congenial. The husking became a bit rougher, the tearing a little louder in the mostly empty hall. Malone rubbed his eyes when Ella crossed her arms over her chest. *This really isn't going well,* he thought. He looked over to the windows, admiring the sunlight and vibrant shades of green. He could faintly hear the music of string instruments outside.

"They will, as will leaders from the Magic Orders, the vampires, and the guardians," Jetta answered without missing a beat. "The threat of Grenich concerns all of us. I know there's bad blood between lycanthropes and fey, but is it worth risking the survival of your world over a feud? No place is safe while Set is free."

Malone glanced over at his brother and Devin looked back at him, his expression reflecting how impressed he was with Jetta's quick save. She had her mother's diplomatic and persuasive skills, which made her highly respected among the protectors.

Ella moved over to one of the windows, sunlight

streaming down on her and gleaming in her long red hair. Diego looked over to her, waiting for her to speak. She glanced back at him and he shrugged, turning his attention back to husking ears of corn. Ella turned her attention back to Jetta, interlacing her fingers.

"Very well, we shall attend this summit," she agreed, returning to her seat and picking up a fresh ear of corn. "However, I make no promises about the willingness of our people to fight alongside the fey."

"Understood. Thank you," Jetta said, bowing her head in respect. She turned and made her way out of the hall. Devin and Malone followed her. Once they got outside, Jetta raised her face to the sky, resting the backs of her wrists on the top of her head.

"Good save," Malone complimented. Jetta dropped her arms back to her sides.

"That was the easy part," she replied as she started down the path. "Convincing them to fight and die in this battle against Grenich is going to be the challenge."

~~*~*~*

What are you up to, seven series?

Isis ignored the smoky form lingering around the corners in the dark hallways. Part of her wanted to figure out what it was, but she had more pressing matters on her mind. Whatever the shape was, it had no corporeal form and therefore wasn't a threat to her. It was a mere annoyance she was learning to ignore.

I'm going to burn them all. They will fall and you know this. There is no way they can defeat me. They don't have the numbers or the means. You will die alongside them, but I will bring you back. And I will turn you into the monster you are destined to be.

Reaching the door to the second floor of the library, Isis opened it and stepped inside. She closed the door behind her and blinked a few times, her glowing eyes traveling over the shelves. Glancing behind her, she waited a few moments to see if the form would follow. When she was sure it wouldn't, Isis stepped away from the door. She noticed a warm light coming from the first floor. Isis moved forward to the railing, looking down.

Jet was sitting in one of the large chairs, his gaze fixed on the empty fireplace. He twisted a half-full glass of red merlot, his blue-green eyes haunted. Isis noticed he had shaved, but the dark rings under his eyes remained and his face still looked gaunt. She moved over to the stairway, gliding down to the first floor. Approaching the chair, Isis stopped when she was standing next to it. Jet sipped his wine, unaware of her presence.

"You are up late," she observed. He jolted, nearly dropping the glass, and looked up at her. A thin smile that didn't reach his eyes crossed his face. His heart rate had jumped up, but soon went back to normal.

"We need to get you some kind of bell to wear," he laughed, watching as she moved over to the chaise lounge. "I'm often up late at night."

"Is that how normals grieve? Isolation and insomnia?" Isis asked as she folded her body onto the lounge. Jet took another sip of wine.

"Sometimes," he answered. "We all have different ways of grieving."

Isis folded her hands on top of each other on the arm of the lounge, turning her glowing gaze to the fireplace. Her sensitive nose picked up the faintest trace of alcohol on his breath, nowhere near enough to be inebriated. She wondered if that was his intention. Normals often used alcohol and other narcotics to dull pain, both emotional and physical. It was a weakness that was easy to exploit.

"I grieved you as well," Jet mentioned, drawing her attention back to him. "We all did, back when you were taken by Grenich. Guardians, I wish that hadn't happened to you."

Isis stared at him, puzzled. "But … I'm a more efficient soldier and an invaluable asset to the protectors."

Jet rubbed his brow with his other hand. "Whatever happened to you was done without your consent. No one should have their rights taken away like that."

Isis was quiet for a moment, her brow creasing as she mulled over his words. "Maybe only an experiment can help the other experiments."

Jet looked over at her. "You sounded a lot like Passion just now."

Isis turned her eyes down to her hand, observing the faint guardian glisten in her flesh. In the Grenich Corporation, it made her stand out and she had to find different ways to conceal it. She hadn't known what it was, but she always thought it was important somehow. Looking up again, Isis returned her attention to Jet.

"I need some information from Roan," she stated.

"I imagine it has to do with your planned bank heist. Lilly mentioned something about that to me," Jet replied, sipping his wine. "You think he knows what's in the safe deposit box?"

"Unlikely, but he might have some idea about how Grenich watches the bank," Isis explained. "It would be useful to know what to expect."

"You understand we are bound by the laws of humans?" Jet warned. "The protectors have no contacts in that bank. If you are caught and arrested, I can't help you."

"I am cognizant of the risk," Isis replied. "But the potential benefits outweigh the risks. If nothing else, it will send a very clear message to Grenich that we are capable of finding whatever they try to hide."

"Is that a message we want to send?"

"Yes. The necromancers believe shape shifters to be weak, little more than cattle. You want to show them otherwise," Isis explained, going quiet for a moment. "I heard Jetta was successful in her mission."

"Diego and Ella have agreed to attend the summit, though they are less than thrilled about the fey being there," Jet said, drumming his fingers on the arm of the chair. "I don't know if they'll agree to fight alongside them. Truthfully, I think Lilly and I will be lucky to get through the summit without there being bloodshed."

"I read about the supernatural races two days ago. The Seelie Court has a history of questionable practices. The legend of the changeling is based on a partial historical truth. The fey cross planes more often than any of the other races and they used to do so in order to capture the children of other species, whom they would then put to work as servants. They ceased the practice centuries ago, after the protectors threatened go to war with them, but the lycanthropes and vampires are still angry with them," Isis explained, her gaze turning to the half-empty wine bottle on the table in front of her. In the shadows, the green bottle almost looked black.

"Yes, trafficking tends to bring that out in people," Jet remarked, finishing his wine. He obviously wasn't keen on dealing with the Seelie Court. His father, Caedmon, had also had an uneasy relationship with the fey and the few times he had to deal with them, they had been an unending headache.

"The fey believe lycanthropes are beasts of burden and used them as such, which is the main reason there is such acrimony between the two races," Isis continued, watching as Jet poured himself another glass of wine. "It will be difficult to negotiate an alliance between the two, but it is important to do so. They are both superior warriors with many useful abilities."

"Not as superior as you," Jet pointed out, sitting back with his glass. He swirled the wine around a little.

"I am modified for war, but even I have my limits," Isis replied. "I cannot fight Grenich on my own. Set will be able to anticipate my strategies and will therefore have me at a severe disadvantage. Normals are going to be crucial in taking down the Grenich empire. You are difficult to predict and that can be used to your benefit."

A comfortable quiet fell over the two for a short while.

Jet continued sipping his wine and Isis just watched the empty fireplace. Their surroundings remained quiet and the dim lamplight gleamed on the spines of the numerous books surrounding them.

"The surveillance in town has increased, more cameras have been installed," Isis stated, drawing Jet's attention to her. "Set will turn his focus to privatizing the police and fire departments while also chipping away at the populace."

Jet stared at her and for a moment, Isis found it difficult to read him. She could see the tiredness in his expression and wondered if his resolve was wavering. He was likely trying to process the information.

Jet put his glass down on the table and sat back in the chair. "How do we win this war, Isis? Is it even possible?"

She thought over the question, her gaze fixed on the empty fireplace. Isis was unsure of how to answer. Grenich had plants in the highest offices of governments around the world, which meant Set already had a great deal of control. Set and Pyra were conquerors and they were good at what they did. The normals were very uncomfortable with assassination, so she had dismissed that option for the time being. Isis planned to revisit it in the future.

"Liberating the experiments will do a great deal of damage to Set and will weaken Grenich," Isis answered. "It will probably take years since he has facilities all over the globe. As for how to deal with the plants in governments, I do not know any ways that protectors would readily agree to."

She turned her gaze back to him. "If you desire victory, you must focus on this summit. Bring together the supernatural species and you will have a powerful alliance, one that could rival Set."

Jet sighed and looked back at the fireplace. She could read the indecision and exhaustion in his face and it was not reassuring. His mind wasn't fully on the task at hand.

Isis had more faith in Lilly, but Jet was also a respected leader. They worked best as a team and at the moment, the protectors needed the best.

"If you want to avenge your children, put aside your sorrow," Isis said, drawing his attention back to her. "I do not understand grief, but experiments know how to use it against those who experience it. The necromancers will use similar tactics against you."

Jet was quiet for a moment. He ran a hand over his face and through his hair, leaning his head back and closing his eyes.

"Brindy was never afraid of the experiments, you know," he began. "Guardians, I know she would have been fighting there with you on the front lines. She always had a soft spot for underdogs and could see the good in everyone. I'm not going to lie. I had my concerns about you and Jack coming to live here."

A watery smile crossed Jet's lips. "I don't think my daughter was ever more disappointed in me. She knew experiments were dangerous, but she didn't believe in quarantine. 'Dad, if we treat them like prisoners, we're no better than Set.' That was Brindy."

He cleared his throat and looked away. Isis waited, looking up to the railing on the second floor. She wondered if she and Jet were close when she was a normal, back before Grenich. There were vague memories of kind blue-green eyes, but nothing substantial enough for her to recognize.

"Nick Chance, he's a monster?" Jet asked. Isis looked over at him.

"I don't know what he is for certain," she answered. Jet turned his eyes to her and his expression was colder than she had ever seen it.

"He is a monster," Jet stated. "Isis, I've never had dealings with assassins and I never will. But I don't want that man brought in. He needs to be put down."

Isis studied him, wondering if normals were aware of

their frequent contradictions. She didn't mind it, but found it odd how reviled the notion of hypocrisy was. Still, she had already planned to kill Chance and the heads of Grenich. There were just some individuals who were too dangerous to be captured and imprisoned.

Isis nodded once and Jet seemed to relax a little, looking back to the empty fireplace. They sat in an easy silence while the peaceful night continued to pass by.

CHAPTER NINE

Hunter scrunched her nose up and groaned when she felt the sunlight on her face. Rolling onto her other side, she could find no shelter from the brightness. Grumbling, she opened her eyes and turned onto her stomach, resting her chin on the thin pillow. Outside the window, she could see a pair of bright red birds dancing around each other on the small tree near her room. Running a hand through her short hair, Hunter tried to will away the lingering headache from the previous day.

Turning her head to the side, she scrambled up to a sitting position when she saw Jack sitting on the short desk across the small room. Hunter narrowed her eyes at him, annoyed at the invasion of privacy. He didn't appear to notice her. His attention was focused on a thick book he held in front of him. He turned one of the thin pages.

"What the hell, Jack?" she snapped. "Do you have any notion of personal space or the right to privacy?"

Jack looked up from the book, his expression puzzled. "I told Orion I would keep an eye on you. You did not have dinner yesterday and when I looked for you, I found you asleep in here. I didn't want to wake you."

"I don't need a damn babysitter. You were here all

night? That's *unbelievably* creepy," Hunter grumbled, rising from the bed.

"Orion, Perrin, and Remington are having breakfast in the gazebo near Perrin's personal quarters. Your presence is requested," Jack reported, closing the ancient-looking book. Hunter rolled her eyes, not desiring company.

"Can I shower first? Alone?" she asked.

Jack stared at her. "Why wouldn't you shower alone?"

"Never mind," Hunter muttered under breath. "Don't suppose you know where there's a shower."

"Just around the corner," Jack replied. "I did a sweep of the floor last night to make sure it was secure."

"Good to know," Hunter grumbled, grabbing her bag from where she had stuffed it under the bed. She left the room, heading down the tiled hall in the direction Jack had indicated.

A half-hour later, Hunter was following Jack through the Sanctuary toward Perrin's personal quarters. She saw plenty of shape shifters throughout the land. They were in a variety of forms, both human and animal. Ahead of her, Jack remained silent. Every now and again, he would glance over his shoulder, as if checking to make sure she was still following. Hunter wondered what he would do if she just bolted. Truth be told, she wasn't sure she was steady enough to run anywhere. Her legs still felt a little unsteady, but the headache was gradually clearing up.

After ten minutes of walking, Jack led her through a pergola, soft petals drifting down from the flowering trees surrounding the path. Hunter soon heard Remington's dulcet brogue up ahead. They emerged into a gazebo and Hunter paused when she saw the stranger from the previous day sitting across from Orion. Anubis still looked quite pale, enhanced by the midnight blue clothing he wore, but appeared much stronger than he had been when they first met. His expressive eyes were fixed on Orion, who turned when Jack entered the gazebo.

"Ah, Jack, Hunter, good morning," Perrin greeted as

she rose from her seat at the front of the table. The three men at the table all looked up to the two standing in the entrance. Hunter moved to the empty seat between Remington and Anubis. Jack sat across from Hunter, next to Orion and near Perrin.

"Sorry if I kept everyone waiting," Hunter said, observing the plates of food on the table. There was a rainbow of fruits and breads. She noticed what looked like waffles further down the table.

"It is perfectly all right. We were just catching up," Perrin reassured the young protector as she sat down again. Hunter glanced at the dark-haired woman, wondering what she was. She didn't smell like a shape shifter. Perrin was tall and graceful enough to be a guardian, but she didn't have the shimmer unique to guardians.

"Please help yourself to whatever you like," Perrin's voice interrupted her wondering. "We're expecting one more for breakfast, but he could be some time yet."

Hunter didn't miss the slight scowl from Orion. She reached across the table to a plate of toast, helping herself to a couple slices.

"Hello, Jack," Anubis said. "You're looking well."

Jack turned his attention to the stranger. Gradual realization spread over his normally expressionless face. For the first time, Hunter saw his glowing brown eyes light up with something like disbelief.

"It's you," Jack murmured. "You extracted us from the laboratory."

Anubis smiled sadly. "I wish I could have extracted all the other experiments too."

"Wait, you're the one who rescued them?" Remington asked the question on Hunter's mind. She stared at the man, somewhat impressed.

Anubis sipped his tea, shaking his head once. "I wouldn't say rescued. I merely took them out of the laboratory. Orion gave them a safe haven. The rest they did on their own."

"We owe you our lives," Jack stated.

"You owe me nothing," Anubis replied, sitting back in his chair. "Seeing you free is thanks enough."

Perrin smiled as she folded her hands in front of her, watching the two.

"How did you get them out?" Hunter asked. "How did you even manage to get *in*? Grenich doesn't strike me as a place that would be lax on security."

Anubis sipped the steaming mug of tea and licked his lips. He looked over at Orion, who sat back and raised his hands.

"It's up to you," the eldest Deverell said. "Tell them whatever you like."

Anubis turned his eyes to Perrin, who spread her hands indicating the choice was his. Hunter waited. It was a pleasant day. As they sat out in the gazebo, Hunter felt some of the tension leave her body.

"My name — my real name — is Milo and I told you yesterday that I'm half shape shifter. My mother is a shape shifter. My father is a necromancer; Vladimir Carver, Set and Pyra's eldest son."

Hunter moved her chair away from him. Milo didn't seem surprised or offended. He looked amused as he reached for his tea, taking another sip. Placing the mug back on the table, he turned his eyes back to Hunter.

"I turned against the necromancers more than a century ago," he explained. "I've had a price on my head ever since, hence my use of the alias Anubis. A sniper caught me with a lucky shot a week ago. I barely managed to reach the Sanctuary's entrance, almost bled out in front of the tree. Thank the guardians for the superior hearing of goblins."

"It's not the first close call you've had," Orion mentioned as he took a sip of coffee. Milo rolled his eyes over to him.

"And where would you be if I didn't take risks, Dr.

Deverell?"

"I took Milo in after he turned against the line of Set. He was much younger back then," Perrin explained, interrupting the two as she looked over at Milo.

"It feels like a lifetime ago," he said, a hint of nostalgia in his voice. "I can hardly remember it."

"He has insights into the inner workings of Grenich and the necromancers that have proven invaluable," Perrin concluded, turning her gaze back to Remington. "His experience and knowledge will be of great use to you in your fight against Set and Pyra's empire."

Hunter stared at Milo suspiciously, but relaxed a little. She turned toward Remington, noticing his intrigued expression. She glanced back at Milo, who was focusing on his tea again. He stirred his small silver spoon around in his mug.

"Is the headache gone yet?" he asked, without looking at her.

Hunter pretended not to hear him and picked at a slice of toast on her plate. Milo reached out and gently, but firmly, grabbed her arm. She tried to disengage his grasp as he pushed back the strap of her tank top.

"Guardians healed you? After the incident at the Lair?" Milo asked, studying her shoulder.

"Yeah, so I'm fine. Let go of me," Hunter growled, reaching for her fork with the intent of stabbing his hand.

"Guardian healing tends not to leave scars, correct? And yet . . ." He ran a finger over her flesh where the creature had bitten her. Hunter stopped reaching for her fork and looked to where he was indicating, noticing the thin white line.

"Perrin tells me Nick Chance was the ringleader of the attack," Milo mentioned. Orion's hand shook so violently that he almost spilled his coffee. He carefully put the mug down and hid his hand under the table. Milo looked briefly at him before turning his attention back to Hunter's shoulder.

"That is correct," Jack confirmed.

"You've been experiencing strange flashes? You blink and your surroundings change for a short amount of time, right? You see things that aren't there, people and objects?" Milo asked, as he met Hunter's gaze.

Hunter didn't answer, focusing on the nearly invisible scar. She was trying to figure out how she hadn't noticed it before.

"Hunter?" Remington asked. Hunter glanced over at him, biting the inside of her cheek. The trainer looked to Milo, who stirred his tea with a small spoon.

"Chance is the illegitimate son of Set and Pyra's other son, a necromancer, and as such, he has some of their abilities," Milo explained, tapping the spoon on the edge of his mug. "He will sometimes use followers as surrogate eyes. When he's connected to a creature in such a way, it can pass that vision onto another. I think that's what's happening to you, Hunter. You're seeing what he does."

Hunter stared at him. "How do I get rid of it?"

"You don't, at least not while Chance is still alive," Milo answered, pausing to sip his tea. "The visions will become less intense over time. It might be possible to learn to control them, which would be quite useful. You could see where he is and what he's doing, perhaps even know some of what he does."

"Oh good. I've always wanted to watch a psychopath skin living shape shifters," Hunter said sarcastically.

Milo looked over at her. "Is that what you saw yesterday?"

Hunter was saved from answering by a rustling sound from the opposite side of the gazebo. She looked over toward the sound and watched a tall man stride down the path. He was buttoning up a blue shirt with his long fingers. As he approached, Hunter noticed he had dark blue eyes and dark hair. His features were sharp, almost aquiline, and he didn't look happy to be there. Sweat glistened on his brow and his shirt was a little damp. The way he held himself reminded Hunter of the guardians. The man swatted a branch away from his face, grumbling irritably as he continued moving toward the gazebo. The stranger didn't appear to care about the nice weather or surroundings. To Hunter, he seemed to be in an overall sour mood.

"Perrin," the stranger greeted, nodding to her as he stepped up into the gazebo. "I'd apologize for being late, but the truth is, I really don't care. I didn't want to come in the first place."

He pulled out the chair on the opposite end of the table. Reclining in the seat, he looked over at Milo and frowned.

"You look awful," he commented, reaching across the table for the pot of tea, pouring himself a cup. "Are you dying or recovering?"

"Recovering," Milo answered, reaching for a clean mug.

The man dropped a couple cubes of sugar in his tea followed by some milk or cream. "What was it this time? Harpoon? Spear? Whatever it was, you must have lost a lot of blood. You're pale as milk. You look worse than the last time I saw you and you were comatose then."

"Sniper," Milo answered as he reached across the table for the coffee pot. The stranger chuckled as he stirred his tea.

"They're a rather odd bunch, aren't they? Always modernizing when it comes to weapons, but regressing in every other aspect of life," the man remarked as his gaze flicked over to Hunter. "You look almost as bad as him, whoever you are."

Leaning forward, he crossed his arms over each other and squinted, studying her face. Hunter turned her face away, annoyed with the stranger's scrutiny.

"Jet and Lilly's daughter. You've got your father's features," the man concluded, sitting back and nodding toward Remington. "And his manservant."

"Copper, can you ever make an effort to be civil?" Orion asked, massaging his brow. Copper turned his eyes and then his head toward Orion, a bitter smile crossing his features.

"Let's see — I was exiled from my homeland and family for daring to fall in love with those who weren't guardians, which didn't stop the High Council from exploiting my abilities when it suited them. A tradition you are here to nobly continue. So no, I don't feel the need to be pleasant."

Milo tried to hide his smile behind his freshly poured cup of coffee. Copper sat back again, stretching his long legs out in front of him. He looked back to Hunter, who was picking at some fruit on her plate. Pulling his steaming cup of tea closer to him, Copper picked up a spoon and stirred the hot liquid. His gaze never moved from her.

"Your mother is a former guardian, is she not? The youngest daughter of Viridia, a legendary beauty from what I've heard. She goes and falls in love with a shape shifter, *huge* no-no in guardian culture, but it was lucky for her. She had immortal children and an immortal husband. The loves of my life were two humans, a man and a woman. I had children with the woman. We had a happy little life, the three of us with our children. But my lovers were mortal so they grew old, their bodies decayed, and they died."

Just when I thought I couldn't be more depressed, Hunter thought as she looked over at the flowering trees, watching small birds dance about in the falling petals.

"Guardians," Orion grumbled, running his hands down his face in exasperation. Hunter looked around the table. Perrin and Milo seemed accustomed to Copper's directness and Milo even seemed amused by it. Jack and Remington both appeared neutral toward the former guardian. If anything, Remington appeared to be rather sad by Copper's story.

"Got to watch my children wither and die too," Copper

continued. "And my grandchildren, a couple great-grandchildren. But Orion thinks I'm just being a miserable cu—"

"My sister and brother were murdered," Hunter interrupted, wanting the former guardian to stop talking. She had close friends who were human and didn't enjoy being reminded of the limited time she had with them. Hunter had seen too much death in the past couple weeks and was tired of it. Copper crossed his arms over his chest.

"I heard something about that. I would offer my condolences, but I imagine you've heard that shite so many times you're sick and tired of it. Empty words meant to make the speaker feel better, right?"

"Copper," Perrin said, drawing the former guardian's attention. "Orion is here to request your assistance."

"Oh I bet he is," Copper remarked, smiling with mock pleasantness as he ran a hand through his short dark hair. Leaning back and craning his neck, he looked at Jack.

"Are you one of the modified shape shifters?" he asked, grinning a little when Jack nodded. "How are the weapons?"

"They are remarkable," Jack replied. "The best I've ever handled. The balance on the blades is amazing and the accuracy of the firearms is impressive."

"A craftsman always enjoys hearing his work is appreciated, doubly so in this case. The only thing worse than the protectors and guardians are those damn necromancers," Copper said, glancing at Milo. "No offense, half-breed."

Milo chuckled and sipped his coffee. "None taken."

Copper reached forward and grabbed a large red and gold apple from a nearby bowl. He tossed it up and down, looking to Orion.

"What do you want from me, Deverell?" Copper asked as he pulled out a knife and allowed the apple to drop onto the sharp blade. He pulled the knife out of the fruit and began cutting into it. Hunter looked over at the weapon, which gleamed in the sunlight, and marveled at the beautiful craftsmanship. Wavy designs were etched toward the top, the same as those found on guardian blades.

"We're going to need more weapons," Orion explained. "A lot more. Guardian silver is the only thing that works against Grenich wereanimals, which leads me to believe it's the only thing that will work against the higher ups."

Copper slid an apple slice into his mouth, chewing for a moment. "Do you want me to make you a nuke while I'm at it? Maybe a few tanks just for good measure? How about a flame-thrower? Do you need some of those too?"

"There it is," Orion muttered, frustrated. Copper slid another apple slice in his mouth and focused back on his fruit.

"May I ask something?" Remington asked, drawing Copper's attention to him. "How are you able to make guardian silver when you're not a guardian?"

Copper chewed on another apple slice. "The manservant asks an interesting question. I'm not *technically* a guardian anymore. Because I left peacefully and of my own volition, I was allowed to keep some of my abilities. The High Council would lead you to believe it was a gift, since my weapons were a huge part of what won the War of the Meadows. But I think it's more likely insurance, in case something ever happened to their smiths and they needed more weapons. Bunch of manipulative, self-serving pricks."

At any other time, Hunter would have found the former guardian's resentment entertaining. It reminded her of Passion and Electra, though he was a lot more forthright with his disdain. At the moment, Hunter found it grating and debated faking a headache so she could go back to her room. Using her fork, the younger protector pushed some food around on her plate. She noticed a couple butterflies fluttering near one of the flowering trees and focused on them.

"Is there a forge in the Sanctuary?" Jack asked.

"Of course," Copper answered, setting his apple core down and slipping the knife back into the sheath on his hip. "Perrin was kind enough to allow me to construct one when I decided to make my home here."

Reaching forward, Copper grabbed a large orange and began peeling it. His sharp blue eyes turned back to Orion.

"How is Silver doing these days? Still bound by the laws of the Meadows, poor dear. That woman has *so* much talent and she's trapped in that bureaucratic nightmare. Such a waste," the former guardian mused, turning back to the fruit.

"Copper, please. The protectors need weapons. The guardians' sacred laws forbid them from actively participating in Earth conflicts. They cannot make us weapons," Orion explained, pleading. "You made weapons for the experiments."

"Ah, but I actually care about what happens to them," Copper pointed out. "They're honest about their intentions. No politics, no games, no bullshit. Also, they were being exploited. Exploitation rubs me the wrong way. What you're asking me now is to choose a side in this war, which I have no interest in doing. As usual, the guardians are using archaic laws to hide the fact that they majorly fucked up. And now they're expecting the protectors to fix it for them. Well the guardians made this mess, they can damn well clean it up."

Copper leaned forward, looking at Jack. "You know you're a damn fool if you agree to help them, right? The guardians will use you, and the other shape shifters, as cannon fodder. They expect you to shed your blood without any intention of doing the same. You're being used as drones."

Jack looked over at Orion, puzzled. Hunter watched him and wondered if he understood the problem. Having been used as a weapon for so long, Jack probably expected to be used as such. The experiments still had trouble understanding the concept of liberty and human rights. Hunter looked back at Copper, who was focused on his orange again.

"If you don't help us, won't you be just as complicit as the guardians?" Hunter asked, looking at the croissant in front of her. "If we had weapons, at least we'd be able to defend ourselves. We might even have a fighting chance against Grenich."

Copper sat back, staring at Hunter. A cool breeze swept through the gazebo, rustling through their clothes and hair. Hunter frowned as she continued to pick at the breakfast pastry, studying the pattern of sunlight on the table. She watched Copper, trying to figure out what he was thinking. The former guardian was studying her with an unreadable expression, probably still on his high-horse.

"You're against exploitation, right? That's against your morals or something? It seems to me the Grenich Corporation is going to keep exploiting shape shifters if we don't stop them."

"You can be certain of that," Milo affirmed, sipping his coffee. Copper crossed his arms over his chest, glancing over at Orion and then to Perrin.

"Hunter does have a point," Remington added. "We're fighting for our very survival and we are greatly outnumbered, not to mention outgunned."

Copper reached for his tea, stirring the still steaming liquid for a moment. He set the spoon off to the side and sipped the hot liquid. Looking over at Hunter, his expression seemed to be impressed.

"Copper, please," Orion attempted again. "Set and Pyra are close to finding which of the three experiments is the Key. When they do, it will be too late. They will be able to take the Meadows and if they do, they won't just conquer Earth. They'll destroy this world and many of the others."

Copper looked over at him, his eyes narrowing. "And what's your brilliant plan to stop them, hmm? Are you going to use the Key against him? Because I will not help you fight fire with fire."

"I don't care about the Key. I want to release the shape shifters trapped in their torture facilities and then destroy those facilities once and for all," Orion replied. Hunter looked down the table at him. There was something in his voice, an edge that she hadn't heard before. Copper drummed his thumb on the arm of his chair and he put his tea down, chuckling.

"Sounds like you have a bit of bloodlust there, Dr. Deverell," he mentioned, looking back to Hunter. "What *is* wrong with you, by the way? There's something … off, but I can't figure out what."

Hunter looked down the sun-dappled path, almost afraid to blink. Her headache was gone and the throbbing in her arm was barely noticeable. The thought of being somehow linked to the man who had murdered her sister and brother made her sick to her stomach. Hunter glanced over at Copper, noticing he was still studying her. His expression had softened and the resentment wasn't quite as blatant.

"Copper?"

Copper looked back to Orion, the bitterness returning almost instantly.

"Fine, I'll make your damn weapons, if only to get you to leave sooner," Copper agreed. Hunter felt a little shocked that he had actually agreed to help. The former guardian closed his eyes and lifted his face up toward the sun, stretching out in his chair.

"Thank you," Orion said.

"Oh, don't for a second think I'm doing this for you," Copper warned, not bothering to look at the shape shifter. "You lucked out. I hate Set only slightly more than I do the guardians."

Orion looked back to his coffee, his jaw clenching in frustration. Hunter wondered how Perrin had convinced the two men to talk in the first place. It was quite obvious Copper wasn't fond of the eldest Deverell. She made a mental note to research Copper when she returned home. She knew Silver had apprenticed under him, which was one of the few times a guardian woman had trained with a man. Beyond that, Hunter didn't know much about him.

"Write down what you need and I'll get to work this afternoon," Copper grumbled as he straightened up again and reached for a croissant. Ripping it into two halves, he dipped one half in his tea. Hunter looked across the table, noticing Orion pulling out a small writing pad and pencil. Jack was observing everything in silence. He was the only one who hadn't touched any food. Thinking back on it, Hunter realized she had rarely seen experiments eat or drink. Then again, they often stuck to the shadows and always seemed to be on the move.

"If you should need anything else, you have allies in the Sanctuary," Perrin mentioned to Orion. "Some who call this place home would gladly fight alongside the shape shifters."

Hunter looked over at Milo, who was quiet. He was still sipping his coffee, also watching their surroundings. Next to her, Hunter could hear Perrin and Remington speaking softly. Orion tore a sheet of paper from the pad he had been writing on, leaned over, and held it out to Copper.

Copper leaned forward and took the paper from him, his eyes darting over it. He gave a half-smile and shook his head once.

"You're underestimating," he said, folding the paper and sticking it in his pocket. "You're going to need a hell of a lot more than this. If I'm going to help you, we're going to do this right. You're not going to half-ass this fight, Deverell."

"I'm thinking of logistics in regards to travel," Orion explained. "There are only four of us and we can only carry so much. Even with Jack."

"I'll make these and then send more to the mansion," Copper stated, wiping his hands on a napkin. Hunter poured herself a glass of water, swirling the clear liquid around in her glass a couple times before sipping it. Out of the corner of her eye, she noticed Milo look over at her. He soon turned back to his own drink.

"Thank you," Orion said. Copper's response was a noncommittal grunt as he turned back to his croissant. Orion cleared his throat and turned toward Perrin. "There was one other matter I wanted to discuss with you."

Perrin smiled knowingly. "The Sanctuary is open to all who seek it, including experiments."

"Are you certain? Perrin, they are a handful in the beginning," Orion warned. Perrin laughed softly, waving him off.

"Orion, I've been fighting Grenich as long as you have, longer technically. You forget, Coop stayed here for a short time after escaping from the Corporation."

Hunter wondered how she had not heard of the Sanctuary before. She had never been all that interested in the history or politics of protectors. Those were more Jetta, Brindy, and Devlin's interests. Hunter had always been more interested in the stories and legends of protectors and guardians. After her experience at the Sanctuary, she found she was more curious than ever about the other supernatural races. *Well, we'll probably be heading home soon. I can ask my sisters about them when I get back,* Hunter thought.

~~*~*~*

Jet glanced back at Isis and Alex, who sat on a bench in the dungeons of the Meadows. He looked to Astrea again, who stood at her post looking less than thrilled. Jet smiled politely, to which she just arched a suspicious eyebrow. Dressed in the traditional guard's uniform, which included leather-like chest armor, Astrea was intimidating like all guardian guards. Jet rocked on his heels, glancing at his

242

watch.

"The weather's nice," he commented, not knowing what else to say. Astrea remained silent, watching him. She had glanced at Isis and Alex when they first arrived, but didn't seem as scrutinizing toward them. Jet looked back to the two shape shifters again. Isis was paging through one of her own books, which Steve had given back to her shortly after she returned to the mansion. Isis didn't read quite as much anymore. Her attention was solely on the battle with Grenich, but every now and again, Jet would glimpse her with a book. The sunlight sparkled in her hair and on the catsuit she wore.

"When did Passion say she would meet us?" Alex asked, running a hand through her sleek hair. Her left leg was crossed over her right and she picked at a thread on her black slacks then smoothed her teal-colored top. Both Jade and Shae were back at the mansion, training more likely than not.

"She said to send a messenger when we arrived, which I did," Jet replied. He had sent the messenger almost ten minutes ago. Passion being late wasn't anything new. In the long time they had been friends, Jet couldn't remember her ever being on time.

"Humans have interesting ways of looking at non-humans," Isis stated, turning a page in her book. "They seem to both desire and fear becoming non-human. It is very odd."

All three people looked over at her as she turned another page, seemingly unaware of their attention. Both Jet and Alex knew she was aware of everything going on around her. Isis was just choosing to disregard it since it was unimportant and therefore not a threat. Astrea crossed her arms over her chest and looked back to Jet.

"I'm sure she'll be here in a minute," Jet mentioned, looking around. "Any minute now."

Alex looked over at him and he spread his hands. Isis closed her book and craned her neck, her attention fixing in the direction of the stairs.

"The Strange Case of Dr. Jekyll and Mr. Hyde," Alex read the title of her book. Isis looked back at her and handed her the novel. Alex opened the book and flipped through a couple of the thin pages.

"Steve said it was one of my favorite books. When I was a normal," Isis explained, turning her eyes back to Jet. He stroked the back of his neck, wondering how much longer he should wait for his friend. Almost as soon as he finished the thought, he heard the soft whisper of bare feet against the smooth marble floor.

"I'm here. I'm here," Passion's voice preceded her as she jogged down the stairs. Her wine red dress was in slight disarray as was her honey-colored hair. There was a rose flush in her cheeks and she was out of breath. In one hand, she held a pair of sandals and she used her free hand to smooth her hair, brushing it away from her face.

"Guardians, Passion, it took you long enough," Jet said under his breath as she skidded to a stop next to him. Grasping onto his shoulder, she slid one sandal on her foot.

"Sorry," she apologized breathlessly, slipping on her other sandal. "I was … working out, lost track of time. Good morning, Astrea. I'm here to escort them to speak with Roan Deverell."

Astrea gestured toward the door leading to Roan's cell block. Passion smiled and started for the door, pausing when she saw Isis and Alex.

"Ladies," she greeted as they stood, looking back over her shoulder to Jet. "Shall we?"

Passion reached the door and held it open for the three shape shifters, following in after them. Jet watched as she hurriedly tied her hair back with a band she had been wearing on her wrist. She glanced at him out of the corner of her eye. Their footsteps scarcely made a sound as they continued down the hall.

"Working out?" he asked skeptically. Passion smiled

her typical suggestive smile.

"Meztli came for a visit. Many guardian women have a certain amount of sensuality, but the night guardians," Passion paused and shivered. "Let's just say silver tongues don't just refer to speaking."

Jet let out a soft laugh. Passion looped her arm around his as they continued down the hallway.

"What are you going to ask Roan about?"

Jet grimaced, hesitating as he tried to think how best to answer. "Isis thinks Grenich might have something valuable stored in a safe deposit box in a bank in Bellville. She wanted to see if Roan had any information about it."

Passion stared at him. "Isis wants to carry out a bank heist? You're going to let her attempt a *bank heist?*"

"Passion—"

"No, Jet. You're not going to let her walk into a bank, armed to the teeth, around who knows how many guards and Grenich personnel."

"I wouldn't be armed to the teeth," Isis mentioned from in front of them, without turning around. "And it would not be carried out like a robbery. It would be executed similar to a covert retrieval. Countries engage in espionage all the time, which I have first-hand experience in. This is an easy mission compared to infiltrating a Grenich laboratory."

Jet looked over at Passion and shrugged, spreading his hands. She narrowed her eyes at him and then turned her attention back to the hall as they came upon Roan's cell.

He was shirtless, doing push-ups in the middle of the cell. The stones enhanced his pale complexion and reddish blond hair. Looking over his shoulder, Roan's green eyes traveled over all of them. The assassin pushed himself to his feet and approached the glass, grabbing his shirt off the chair next to the desk. He nodded in greeting to Passion.

"You're looking well, though a little flushed," he said, a hint of teasing in his voice. "Who's the lucky man? Or woman?"

Passion crossed her arms over her chest and didn't respond. Jet cleared his throat, drawing Roan's attention to him. The small smile didn't leave the assassin's face.

"Don't suppose you've come to your senses about letting me take care of Chance for you," Roan said, his voice smooth and relaxed. "Wouldn't take more than a day."

"No," Jet answered and Roan shrugged, resting an arm against the glass.

"Your loss," he replied, turning his eyes to Alex. "What can I do for the protectors on this beautiful day?"

"Grenich keeps safe deposit boxes," Isis stated, standing in front of the glass. Roan studied her curiously.

"It does, for missions. Usually they have some currency and passports, sometimes a weapon or two. I'm sure you've used them in the past."

"I'm not talking about drop sites," Isis clarified. "They keep boxes not meant for experiments or missions, like the bank in Bellville."

Roan's eyes widened as he looked back to Jet. "You're not considering going after the Corporation's personal boxes, are you? Does Orion know about this?"

"What's in these boxes?" Alex asked. Isis was studying Roan and Jet recognized she was observing his tells. She often watched people discreetly, which Orion had explained was how she read them. Experiments were always absorbing information and storing it away for later use. Jet sometimes found himself wondering what they had deduced about him.

"None but the higher ups know for sure, but I can tell you what it most likely is," Roan answered, drawing Jet out of his musings. "Records of missions, clients, experiments, and a lot of other sensitive information tied to the laboratories. It's probably a kind of insurance policy as well as blackmail material to control their powerful clientele. If anything ever happened to one of their facilities, they would want to rebuild as soon as they could."

"Why hasn't any member of the resistance tried to retrieve this information?" Isis asked. Roan looked back to her, drumming his fingers on the glass.

"Because it would be suicide," he answered. "With information like that, you don't think Grenich has taken precautions? Aside from the usual unbreakable encryption that is."

Isis watched him and Roan took a step back, running his hands through his hair. Jet could see the apprehension in his expression, which was a first for Roan.

"If the information is so valuable, it makes sense we at least make an attempt to retrieve it," Jet put in and Roan dropped his hands, shaking his head.

"Maybe, *maybe* after you liberate the first laboratory. They'll take some time to regroup, reassure investors that they're still in control, and you will have a miniscule window of opportunity," Roan suggested. "But if you try before that? You're going to be walking into a death trap."

He moved over to the desk, leaning back against it. "You mentioned Bellville? Aside from the usual bank security, which granted is a hassle but manageable for an experiment, you're going to have at least two Grenich plants working there. They'll appear completely normal, probably average worker drones, but it's a ruse. They'll be experiments from one of the newer lines, likely an eight series. They'll also have a patrol team watching the perimeter. The members of this team will take turns checking the bank, probably using the excuse of using the bathroom to get inside. They watch and note every car and patron that enters the bank, as well as how long they're inside."

"Retrievers or wet workers?" Isis asked.

"Wet workers."

She clasped her hands behind her back. "What kind of encryption?"

"I don't know for sure. Chances are you'd need a

modern E-series to break it, not the outdated one Orion and Coop know," Roan answered, looking between all four people on the other side of the glass. "Look, I was an enforcer in the Corporation, but I also helped with a lot of their security strategies. I helped come up with the idea of how to safeguard important information. Believe me, there is no way to retrieve what's in that box."

Jet looked back at Passion and could see the concern in her expression. She looked over at him, her eyes bright green. He bit the inside of his cheek, wondering if it was possible to talk Isis out of attempting to get the contents of the box. He looked over at Isis, who appeared unbothered by Roan's warnings. It was one of the first times Jet was willing to take the former assassin at his word. He had seen too much of Grenich's brutality to question the lengths the necromancers would go to protect their assets.

"How large would the patrolling team be?" Isis asked.

"My guess? Probably six or seven."

Isis glanced over at Alex, who was leaning against the wall. She turned and walked away from the cell, back down the hall. Roan ran a hand over his face.

"Jet, don't let her near that bank," he warned, glancing over at Passion. "You risk losing her again, and a few other shape shifters if she brings a team with her. She's good, there's no doubt about that, but she has limits, whether or not she realizes it."

"Answer me this," Jet began. "Could that information help bring Grenich down?"

Roan was quiet for a moment, looking contemplative. "If it could, Set would not react well to any attempt to grab it. He might send Chance to finish what he started."

Jet felt his throat clench, but forced his expression to remain neutral. He could almost feel Passion's ire next to him as he turned away from the cell. Once again, Jet wondered if he could talk Isis out of attempting such a dangerous retrieval. *Do I want to?* Jet wondered.

He glanced to his left when he heard the soft scrape of Passion's sandals. She looked over at him and he was reminded of the promise he made her so many years back. He had sworn he would protect her daughters, no matter what the cost. *If only they didn't make it so damn difficult,* he thought.

~~*~*~*

Late at night, nine shape shifters gathered in the training room of the mansion. Most of the inhabitants had turned in, leaving the dwelling dark and silent. The only lights were the ones in the training room. The faint buzzing from them prevented any quiet in the enormous room.

Isis' glowing green eyes observed the seven normals who stood around in a circle. Next to her, Coop stood in a similar stance with an almost identical blank expression. They had spoken earlier and it had been a disagreement. Coop didn't see the possibility of success, especially with only a few normals. They would never be able to pull off the retrieval on their own, but the normals didn't have much experience fighting with experiments. *They struggled with followers,* he had argued. Isis pointed out his constant insistence that normals had some strength and usefulness.

Coop turned away, whispering to her, "I just want to make sure you understand how much danger you're about to put them in."

Isis looked over at him. "Do you understand how much danger they're already in?"

Coop stared at her for a moment before turning back around to face the shape shifters who were looking at them. Isis' eyes traveled around the circle. The other members of the Four were there, as were Jensen and Nero. She noticed Jensen was dressed in his usual high-quality clothing. Steve was there, his mop of black hair messy as though he had just woken up. Sly stood near Jade, her arms crossed over her chest, a smirk playing on her lips. She examined the nails on her left hand for a moment.

"After speaking with Roan this afternoon, I have a better idea of what's in the box and the security we can expect to encounter," Isis began, clasping her hands behind her back. "They're not insignificant. We'll probably encounter a wet work team, meaning they're not interested in recruiting shape shifters for experimentation."

"Is that just a nice way of saying they're going to kill us?" Nero asked. Isis looked over at him and nodded once. He shrugged and put his hands on his hips.

"Are there going to be experiments on the premises?" Jade asked.

"According to Roan, there will be at least two," Isis answered. "There might be more on the perimeter. Grenich sometimes changes tactics to avoid routine."

"Roan also mentioned this is very unlikely to be successful," Alex added. "Grenich will go to extreme lengths to protect whatever is in this box."

"We stand a better chance if we work as a team," Isis continued. "The danger is still the same though, which is why I wanted to offer the opportunity to back out."

The shape shifters looked around at each other, but none moved to leave. Isis waited, watching them.

"I think we're all in," Jensen mentioned from her left. She glanced at him and then looked back to the group.

"It would be beneficial to have Shocker's assistance," Isis mentioned, her gaze landing on Coop. He rolled up his sleeve a little more.

"I'll see what I can do," he said.

"So what's the plan?" Shae asked. "Who's doing what? And can I wear a catsuit too?"

Isis rubbed the side of her neck, thinking. She already knew what she wanted everyone to do, but she was having trouble figuring out how to maneuver normals. In the Corporation, normals were mere collateral damage, good for distraction but little else. Actually seeing them as individuals was something Isis still struggled with. Trying to keep them all alive was an added challenge to an already complicated mission and she wasn't sure if she could do it.

I will burn them, all of them, the strange form had said. *Not if I burn you first,* Isis thought as she continued to watch the shape shifters debate among themselves.

CHAPTER TEN

In the depths of a dank cave, four shape shifters stood in front of a smooth rock wall. Two held yellow lamps and one stood off to the side. The one woman watched as the stick of chalk drew an elaborate door on the face of the rock. She held out her hand and caught the stick as it fell, curling her fingers around it. A moment later, a thin line of gold traced over the chalk outline as a door began to take form.

The hair on the back of Coop's neck had been standing on end since they entered the cave. Jet and Lilly had requested the experiment accompany their daughter and two sons on the mission to the realm of the vampires. Out of all the supernatural races, the vampires were the ones the protector leaders trusted the least. The vampires never traveled to earth due to their severe allergy to ultraviolet light. As a result, not much was known about them. Even the guardians had minimal contact with them. The Monroes probably would have asked Isis, but she was too preoccupied planning the bank infiltration. Coop wasn't keen on entering another world — one which he knew little to nothing about — but agreed to it. He felt he owed the leaders of the protectors, a strange concept he still had trouble understanding.

Coop looked over to Robin when she knocked on the newly formed door. She was an interesting hodgepodge of both her parents. She had her mother's features and dark blue eyes, and her father's dark hair. She was wearing a blue dress, which was tastefully simple. Reading up on her and eavesdropping on different conversations had given Coop a general idea about her background and character. Robin lived in Australia and worked as an actress, mostly theater work. She had always been artistically inclined, but also dedicated to the protectors. She was her parents' liaison to the protectors in Australia.

The cave was quiet, except for the distant dripping of water and the occasional squeaking of bats. The door didn't open. Coop noticed the puzzled look on Robin's face as she stepped forward and knocked on the door again. He turned to the door, glancing over at Cassidy and Declan. Cassidy was tossing the glowing yellow rod up and catching it, obviously bored. Declan stood next to his older sister, looking at nothing. He was still distraught over his twin brother's death. Since the interment, Coop had observed him wandering the halls a few times late at night. The experiment kept his distance from the younger protector, who still harbored some anger toward those connected with Grenich.

"Is it supposed to take this long?" Cassidy asked, tossing his lamp up again. He put a little too much arc in it and the lamp sailed over his head. It would have shattered on the rocky ground had Coop not reached out and plucked it from the air.

"I don't know," Robin answered, brushing a strand of hair away from her face. "Maybe the gatekeeper is away from his post?"

"He would have left someone at the post," Coop mentioned. "There is always someone watching the door or gateway. According to your histories and lore."

"Something you learned at Grenich?" Declan asked

darkly.

"No. When Jack and Isis were awaiting sentencing in the Meadows, I was in the guardian library," Coop answered, using Cassidy's lamp to illuminate the door. "There's a wealth of knowledge in that place."

Running his fingers over the smooth metal of the door, Coop felt a strange chill go through him. He didn't know what the metal was. The material was similar to iron, but much lighter. It was plum colored with the occasional spot of silver or gold, most likely representing the night sky. Vampire culture was lunar-centric and revolved around the night. Wrapping his hand around the knob, Coop attempted to turn it but it didn't budge an inch. The experiment let go of the doorknob and massaged his chin, his brow furrowing.

"Can't you kick it down or something?" Cassidy asked.

"It won't open from this side," Coop explained, taking a step back. "You are certain the vampires agreed to this meeting?"

Robin reached into her pack and withdrew a letter from one of the pockets. "According to their response, yes."

She handed the letter to Coop, who examined the parchment. He sniffed it and touched the letter to the tip of his tongue. He could taste the blood and ink mixture vampires wrote with and the smell was old. As far as he could tell, it wasn't a forgery.

"The only other way to enter is through the Meadows," he explained, handing the letter back. Robin took it lightly, her expression mildly disgusted. Coop assumed it was due to the possibility of contact with his saliva.

"Guess we have a date with Hecate," she said. "Come on, guys."

Coop watched as they disappeared in bright flashes of light, which illuminated the cave. He hesitated, turning back to the door, which was already disappearing. Something about the absence of a gatekeeper was bothering him, but Coop knew the protectors needed more allies. He closed his eyes and focused on the Meadows and the lands of night in particular. There was a brilliant light and he opened his eyes, blinking a few times.

His surroundings had changed to mountains and the atmosphere was much lighter and cleaner. A wind swept through the dark fields, rustling the grass. Coop turned and spotted the large hall. Running through the grass, he could hear various animals growling. They wouldn't attack him, but the presence of an experiment did put them on edge. Coop soon reached the steps leading up to the entrance and bounded up them two at a time. He pulled the door open and found himself in the middle of a number of messengers, most in dark robes. They scurried out of his way and he ignored their fearful glances.

"Coop, over here."

Coop looked to the right, spotting Cassidy. He moved across the floor, following the younger shape shifter into the throne room. Hecate looked over at them when they stepped through the doors. She was sitting at a large round table, which was positioned a few feet away from the moon-shaped throne at the back of the room. Hecate was wearing a long black dress, which matched her eyes and curly hair. Her hair was held back from her face by a long gold band. She rubbed her palms together methodically as she observed the two men.

"I thought the protectors had a meeting with the vampires," the guardian said, her regal voice smooth as satin. She looked back over to Robin, who stood next to the chair she was sitting in. Robin glanced over her shoulder to Declan, who stood a few feet behind her. He had switched off his lamp, as had Cassidy. Coop looked around the large room, observing the beautiful arched ceiling. His heightened senses were absorbing everything about the surroundings. Numerous stars were suspended high above them, illuminating the entire hall with their bright silver light. Night-blooming flowers wrapped around the pillars, their subtle sweet scents drifting around him.

"The gatekeeper didn't answer," Robin explained. "We were hoping to use the doorway in the Meadows."

Hecate looked between all of them. "You know that is *highly* unusual and right on the edge of going against protocol."

"I know," Robin agreed, brushing a strand of hair behind her ear. "We wouldn't ask, but given the situation, I thought you might make an exception."

Hecate laid down the pen she had been writing with and sat back. "I think this is a situation best handled by the Four. Let them go through the gateway in my realm, make sure everything is okay, and then you may proceed with your mission."

"The vampires won't be happy with that," Declan mentioned from where he stood behind Robin. "They might take offense."

"They should have thought of that before leaving their gate unattended," Hecate replied, shuffling the parchment in front of her. "Find the Four, bring them, and we shall find out what is going on."

~~*~*~*

Isis walked down the long hall, a few steps behind Jade and Shae. Her gaze wandered over the smooth sand-colored stones. The walls were decorated with banners and tapestries, most depicting important moments from the history of the lands of night or different family crests. Looking up toward the sky, Isis observed the floating stars. As she watched the stars, a streak of silver shot through the plum-colored sky.

Isis looked back as they continued down the long hallway to the tall wooden doors. Behind her, she could hear Coop following. He had Appeared at the mansion a little more than an hour ago to explain what was going on.

Isis had read the uneasiness in his demeanor and suggested they arm themselves.

"This has to be a first," Alex mentioned next to her. "Going into a diplomatic mission while heavily armed."

"I was under the impression all diplomatic missions involve guards, who carry weapons," Isis replied as they stepped into the throne room. She took note of all the entrances and exits, as well as the number of people inside the room.

"Most diplomatic missions involve diplomats," Shae pointed out. "Which we technically aren't."

Sitting on the steps leading up to the throne was Hecate herself. She smiled when the Four entered and rose to her feet. She was tall and elegant, as most guardians were. Isis glanced to the right where Jet's children were sitting at the long table. Robin and Cassidy were playing a card game while Declan watched. He glanced up when the Four entered before turning his attention back to the game. Isis had noticed a change in his demeanor since his twin's death. He avoided the experiments and whenever he had to speak to them, it was usually curt and without emotion. He hated everything connected to Grenich, which seemed to include the experiments. Isis disregarded it, but made sure to avoid him all the same. She didn't trust a hostile at her back, particularly one with the potential to be unpredictable. The normals would probably have an opinion on Declan's distrust of experiments. *Normals have opinions on everything,* she thought as she looked back to Hecate.

"Coop mentioned there might be a missing gatekeeper," Jade said, putting her hands on her hips. "You want us to go through to the lands of the vampires and make sure everything is on the up-and-up?"

"That is the agreed upon procedure," Hecate answered as she approached them. "I trust all of you have weapons to defend yourselves, should a situation arise?"

"Are we expecting there to be trouble?" Alex asked.

"I don't think it likely, but it is always wise to be prepared," Hecate responded. "The gatekeeper probably stepped away from his post temporarily and forgot to appoint a stand-in. However, the vampires have had trouble with warring families in the past. If one group has attempted or carried out a coup, the situation might be volatile. They are unlikely to attack protectors though. They fear the wrath of guardians too much. This way please."

Isis followed her teammates as Hecate led them through a door a few feet behind the throne. Turning, she opened another door that led to a narrow flight of stairs. They proceeded down with Hecate leading. Isis looked up at the sconces, each of which contained bright silver light enclosed in glass. She had read the lands of night were lit solely with star and moonlight. Continuing down the winding stairs, the light never dimmed.

"I'm sure you're aware that I help watch over magic in the Meadows, which includes matters of the supernatural," Hecate explained, her voice clear and strong. "My castle contains doorways to each of the lands, doors only I can open. Normally, they remain closed and locked. The only time I'm to open them is when a situation such as this arises."

They soon reached the bottom of the stairs and stood in a long hallway of wooden doors. Each had an iron ring with a lock underneath. Isis heard the jingle of keys and watched Hecate take down a large key ring from a hook on the wall.

Hecate stopped in front of a door and slid the ring onto her wrist. Withdrawing a dagger from a sheath worn on her hip, she dragged the sharp silver blade across her palm. Sliding the ring off her wrist again, she grabbed a large brown skeleton key and dipped it in her blood. When she had coated it with her silvery blood, Hecate stuck it in the keyhole.

"Blood is at the center of vampire culture and this key

wouldn't work without it," she explained as she turned the key. The guardian grasped the iron ring and pulled the door open. Isis craned her neck to better see what was behind the door. It looked as though there were a curtain of black on the other side. There was a distant rumbling, thunder perhaps, and Isis could smell rain on the air. There was a coppery scent as well, much more subtle. She would recognize the scent anywhere. It was the smell of blood.

Isis turned her attention back to Hecate, watching as she produced a spool of golden thread from a pouch around her waist. She tied it to the iron ring on the Meadows side.

"The door will be difficult to see once it's closed," she explained, tossing the spool into the blackness. "Use this thread to lead you back. The royal dwelling of the vampires is about thirty minutes due north."

The guardian handed Jade a compass. Isis squinted and approached the opening, listening to the rain on the other side of the door. It was just a drizzle, but the heaviness of the air indicated it would soon become a downpour. Behind her, Isis heard Hecate wish them luck but she was too focused on the scene in front of her. Tilting her head, she tried to listen for anything out of the ordinary. Aside from the rain, there was no sound, which was unusual. According to her research, there were night birds in the vampire realm. She should have at least heard them, even if the vampires were silent. Something was very, very wrong.

Ignoring the instructions to wait, Isis stepped into the blackness and allowed it to envelop her. Her boots touched soft grass and her senses sharpened. Rain fell from above, plastering her short hair to her skull. The entire land was engulfed in blackness. The land of the vampires was one of endless night.

A rustle to her right caused Isis to drop into a crouching position, her hand hovering above the gun at her hip. Her glowing green eyes scanned the shadows in front of her, but could find nothing. Scooting forward a bit, she heard Shae curse when she almost stepped on Isis.

"Dammit, it's raining," Shae groused. "Not cool. No one said to bring an umbrella."

"I doubt we get weather forecasts from the other worlds," Alex responded.

In her peripheral vision, Isis could see the lamps of starlight Hecate had given the other three. Though they had superior night vision, they hadn't experienced the kind of darkness the vampires lived in. It was so thick it was almost a solid mass.

"It's rather quiet," Alex observed, holding her lamp out in front of her. Isis straightened up and watched the tall grass flatten when a strong wind blew through the land. Thunder boomed from somewhere in front of them and the rain picked up. The scent of blood and fire was strong to her sensitive nose. Isis looked back to the other three.

"It's this way," Jade said, glancing over at Isis. "You see anything?"

Isis looked back over her shoulder, focusing behind them. "No, but I'm hearing rustling. We should be on our guard. Something has taken notice of us."

"Think it's the vampires?" Shae asked.

"Vampires are a culture that prides itself on hospitality," Alex mentioned. "If it were them, we'd know it."

"We should move," Isis stated, looking over the land. She was feeling very uneasy and it wasn't helped by whatever was following them. It knew enough to stay just outside her field of vision, but close enough that she could hear it. Another thing that was making her uneasy was her ability to see so clearly. Isis had superior vision, but Earth had nothing like the kind of darkness they were currently in. By rights, her vision should have been moderately impaired, which would have made her other senses compensate. But it wasn't. *Have I been here or somewhere similar before?* Isis wondered, shaking some of the rain out of her hair.

"I agree," Jade said as she started in the direction Hecate had indicated. Alex followed behind her and then Shae, who unbuttoned her jacket and held it over her head as a makeshift umbrella. Isis covered their backs, glancing back over her shoulder every now and again. They moved through the land, not saying a word in the hopes that their presence would go undetected. Lightning split the sky open with an electric glow and the thunder became even louder as the storm increased in intensity. The four women continued making their way toward the vampire's castle as rain beat down on them.

After nearly a half-hour of walking, Isis noticed a large castle in the distance. She jogged up to where Jade was still leading. The rain steadily poured down as the storm continued.

"The castle's just up ahead," she stated, nodding in the direction. "I'll go first and make sure there are no traps or troops waiting to ambush."

"What if there are?" Jade pointed out. "You'll need back-up."

"Not if it's regular vampires. I've read up on the culture. Vampires value honor above all else. They have never attacked from behind because they view it as an act of cowardice. This strategy benefits me."

"If the rain continues, we're going to be standing in the middle of a swamp," Shae observed from beside them. Isis watched as she picked up her foot and shook it in a vain attempt to get rid of the excess liquid. Isis had noticed the damp ground when they arrived, which was getting wetter as they got closer to the castle. It could have been on account of the rainstorm, but that wouldn't account for the coppery smell. She scratched the back of her head, already having some idea of the cause of it.

As Alex crouched down to study the wet ground, Isis slipped away from them and made her way through the tangled trees and shrubs. Thorns jutted out from every twisted limb. Almost everything in the vampire's world was dangerous in some way. The trees offered limited protection from the rain and Isis dragged a hand through her cropped hair, pushing some of the liquid out. Leaping over a fallen log, she paused in front of a stick rising out of the ground. There was a head stuck on the top, a few inches over her head. Stepping closer, Isis looked at the slackened features of the man. The point of the sharpened stick was somewhere inside the skull. Even in death, the symmetrical features were attractive. A long mane of blond hair tumbled down behind his head, sticky with coagulated blood and dripping with the newly fallen rain.

Leaning closer to the stick, Isis examined the blood staining the wood. Touching a thick streak of blood, she rubbed her fingertips together as she observed the residue. Most of the blood was dry, which told her it wasn't a recent kill. Looking back up to the head, she noticed blood around the mouth. Reaching up, Isis pushed the lips back, noticing the absence of sharpened canines. They had been yanked out while the vampire was still alive, indicating he had been tortured to death. That would not have been an easy feat. Vampires were well-known for their military prowess. Looking around, Isis noticed a number of other sticks set up among the trees. It was a forest of the dead. Turning her gaze upward, she could see more dismembered heads and limbs hanging down from the branches of the trees. Thunder rumbled in the sky, and Isis could feel it in her bones. The rain dripping down from the trees was tinged with blood.

"What the fuck?"

Isis glanced to the side when Jade came up next to her, shining her light toward the head on the stick. They had to yell to be heard over the storm. Wind whipped through the trees and Isis heard one of the limbs fall from the heights. The storm would probably knock the rest of the limbs down before it was done. Isis looked back, watching as Alex and Shae approached. Shae almost lost her footing on the slippery ground and grabbed onto Alex to keep herself upright.

"Isis, did you know the ground is—" Shae stopped when she saw the head.

"It's soaked in blood," Isis finished. "There has been a massacre here."

"Maksim or Pelageya must still be alive," Alex mentioned, shining her light around as she took in the gruesome scene surrounding them. "Otherwise Hecate would see this land register as dead. We need to find them."

"Perhaps," Isis muttered under her breath.

"Under no circumstances are we to separate," Jade ordered. "Whoever or whatever did this might still be around."

They are, Isis thought, glancing behind them. She looked to the castle, surrounded by dead vampires impaled on sticks. Glancing up to the windows, Isis thought she glimpsed eyes for a moment. She looked at the banners hanging from the arched windows, stained with blood. Looking back to the shadows of the window, she started to make her way toward the castle. Isis had seen worse at Grenich — had been the cause of it on occasion. If something or someone attempted to attack her, it would be at his own peril.

The four women crossed the drawbridge with Isis leading the way. Jade motioned for Isis to come back, which she did. Even outside, Isis could smell charred flesh. It was old, not a recent scent. Jade had drawn her gun and motioned for the other three to do the same. Shae and Alex did, but Isis didn't. At the moment, she didn't see the necessity for her firearms.

"You want to lead us in?" Jade whispered, pointing her gun at the opened door. Isis glanced behind her, noticing the ashen remains of a vampire just inside the door. Isis approached the door without hesitation and leaned to the side, peering around the corner. Her nostrils twitched as she absorbed all the information she could. Holding out a hand to tell them to hang back, Isis stepped inside the castle.

Emerging from the alcove, she saw the torches on the wall, illuminating what had once been the main hall. There were dead vampires everywhere, all curled up and charred to a crisp. It was very difficult not to step on the numerous bodies. Studying the walls, Isis noticed the blackened spots where there had once been paintings or tapestries. The destruction of historical relics told her it was unlikely other vampires had done this. They wouldn't have destroyed their own cultural achievements, even if it had been a coup. Conquerors tended to replace art with their own or appropriate the pieces they liked. Isis' eyes turned to the ground, which had been white tile at some point. Splashes of brown coated it where blood had spilled. There wasn't much; most of the dead in the room had been burned. Glancing back over her shoulder, Isis noticed Jade make her way inside. Isis turned her attention back to the gruesome scene, trying to piece together what had happened. All that she had read at the mansion indicated the vampires were a strong race of warriors. Their military prowess was impressive and nothing indicated they would have been easy to conquer.

There was a strange faint wheezing sound originating from behind a door at the end of the main hall. Isis looked up to the second floor when she heard a soft scraping sound. Without taking her eyes off the landing of the second floor, she nimbly stepped through the bodies and approached the other three.

"I hear a noise I can't identify," she reported to Jade, leaning back to see if she could get a better view of the second floor. "I'm going to go investigate. I suggest the three of you stay out here and watch each other's backs. There's something upstairs and whatever it is, it knows how to stay unseen, even by an experiment."

"You have three minutes before we follow you in,"

Jade stated, following her gaze up to the second floor. Isis turned and made her way across the hall, her hand hovering over her hip by her gun. She didn't smell any other scents aside from her team and the remains of the vampires, along with the ashes of their culture. Glancing down at the ground, she would catch the occasional glimpse of broken glass or stone.

Once she reached the door at the end of the hall, Isis put her hand on the knob. The wheezing sound was more pronounced. Pausing for a minute, Isis listened for anything out of the ordinary. There was nothing, no sound or scent. She turned the smooth knob and pushed the door open. The hinges squealed loudly in protest as the door swung inward.

Standing in the doorway, Isis observed the room. The only light came from the contraption in the center of the room. The bright yellow-green light cast an eerie glow around the room. Tubes extended out from the center glass cylinder, pumping liquid through the whole set-up. As Isis approached, she could see the beating heart in the center of the tube, wires extending from the organ. She recognized the advanced technology from Grenich. The system was keeping the heart alive and beating. It was designed for long-term use and could keep an organ viable for an almost unlimited amount of time. Looking up to the corner, Isis recognized the Grenich Corporation symbol of the backward "P" and the cuneiform at the bottom. It was a symbol she would never forget.

"We meet again."

The voice froze Isis for a split second, but it was enough time for Chance to hit her in the jaw with the weighted end of his cane. The blow sent her sprawling and Isis felt her jawbone snap, her vision going wavy briefly as she hit the floor. She struck out with a side kick, catching him in the knee and arched back, striking him under the chin with the top of her foot. Her jawbone snapped back into place and repaired itself before her feet touched the ground again.

Isis straightened up and backed away, watching as Nick Chance got back to his feet. He swung his cane around. His cream-colored suit stood out in the gloom. A tremor went down her spine, but Isis pushed the sensation to the back of her mind. Chance smirked, baring his pearly white teeth, and began to walk around the contraption. Something shimmered in the darkness and he disappeared. Isis looked around for the man frantically, turning around a couple times. The coils of a whip wrapped around her throat, cinching tightly and cutting off her oxygen. Isis' hands flew up to the tight braided leather and she struggled to pull it loose. She was yanked off her feet and her back slammed to the hard stone ground, driving the breath out of her body. Somewhere in the room, Isis could hear Chance laughing, a deep growling sound.

~~*~*~*

Jade looked over to where Alex was sifting through one of the ash heaps. Shae stood watch, her gaze never moving from the second floor. Jade glanced at her watch, considering following Isis. Her eyes were drawn over to a sculpture, blackened from fire. It was an odd-looking thing and Jade couldn't quite make out what it had been. It was either a very short man or a crouching one. It was up on a granite pedestal.

"Think we should follow Isis?" Shae asked, her attention not moving from the floor above them. "Got to be honest, I'm feeling *really* exposed right now."

"Give her another minute," Jade said as she approached the sculpture. Examining it, she reached out and touched it. The smooth material was icy to the touch, flesh-like and pliable. Looking at her fingertips and rubbing them together, she frowned when she saw there was no soot or residue from the sculpture.

A loud screech was the only warning Jade had when the sculpture lunged at her, tackling the protector to the ground. Once they hit the floor, the creature's flesh turned pale. Jade heard her gun clatter across the floor as they rolled backward and Jade wound up on top of the creature. She drew her second gun, pointed it at the face of the creature, and fired. It shuddered and went still, its mouth slackened. Staring at rows and rows of sharp triangular teeth, Jade stood and backed away. She didn't have time to figure out what the hell the thing was. Shae shouted a warning over to her and Jade looked up, noticing the walls were crawling with strange pale creatures. They were swarming over the second floor balconies, launching themselves at the three protectors in the large hall. Jade ran back over to her two teammates, firing a few shots at the attacking creatures and ducking under one that launched itself right at her.

"What are these things?" Shae asked as she fired at one of the creatures. Both she and Alex twisted when one landed on the table near them. Jade turned and shot it down.

"No idea, but I'd really like Isis to get her bony ass out here right about now," Jade replied as she aimed at another creature and fired. They were everywhere, crawling all over the walls and surrounding the three women in the hall. Thunder rattled the windows as the rain continued beating down outside.

~~*~*~*

Isis drew a throwing knife and severed the leather coiled around her neck. She inhaled deeply once the whip fell away, gasping as she struggled to get her breath back. Looking around, Isis tried to find a target. Her senses detected nothing, which was impossible. Massaging her throat, she pushed herself up on all fours and climbed to her feet.

"Do you remember me, seven series?" Chance's disembodied voice spoke from all around her. "I remember you. I remember carving into your flesh, peeling it back from your muscles. I remember the sweet scent of your blood, washing my hands in it. The taste of it on my fingertips. Your beautiful pelt still hangs above my bed in my home. Oh how it sparkles in the moonlight."

"You can't be here," Isis said, turning around as she tried to catch a glimpse of him again. "It's impossible."

"Am I here? Or is this just a nightmare? Are any of us really ever anywhere?"

Out in the main hall, Isis heard gunfire. A strange smell, ancient and decrepit, invaded her nose. Distantly, Isis heard thunder and glass rattling. The storm was still raging outside. She began to back up toward the door, her eyes sharp as she watched for Chance. The feeling of an icy blade stroking her cheek made her lash out with a spinning kick. She hit nothing but air.

"You'll have to do better than that, lab rat."

Isis closed her eyes, relying on her other senses to tell her where her opponent was. She could hear the cane slicing through air again and leapt back, narrowly avoiding a blow that would have broken a few ribs. Striking out with a side kick, she hit the soft abdominal muscles and heard the air rush from his body.

A screeching growl behind her preceded a strong grasp on her shoulders. The talons almost cut into her flesh and she felt the hot breath of whatever it was on her neck. Isis leaned back and threw her leg up, striking the creature in the forehead with a high kick. Spinning out of its grasp, Isis kicked it away from her. Drawing her gun, she fired into its skull and the creature went still. Pointing the gun back inside the room, Isis looked and listened for Nick Chance. When she was satisfied he wasn't there, she approached the creature and examined it. It had chalky grayish flesh, dark gray eyes without sclera or pupils or irises, and the blood was gray. Leaning forward, Isis pushed the lips away from the mouth. It was full of needle-like teeth. There was no hair on the creature, nothing to indicate a gender. The creature also lacked a scent, meaning it might have come from Grenich. More gunfire drew her attention out into the main hall. Isis stood up and drew her other gun, striding out to where she had left her team, firing at a few of the creatures that were in front of her.

"Isis, look out!"

Isis heard Shae's warning, but was already moving. She crouched low, under the creature who lunged at her, and straightened up again while firing her guns. Isis killed the first creature and shot at a second without even glancing in its direction. She moved toward where the other three were struggling to hold off the swarming creatures.

"Aim at their heads," she called out. "It's their weak spot."

"What are they?" Alex asked when Isis reached them. The experiment released her empty magazines and reloaded without looking, pressing her guns down on her thighs to lock the magazines in place.

"Mutations or maybe failed experiments," Isis answered. "They don't know how to use modern weapons, but they make up for it in aggression and numbers. They'll tear a shape shifter apart using their bare hands and teeth. They may have some regenerative capabilities, but a head shot will kill them."

Isis fired at a couple more, moving forward as she shot them down. Looking around, she estimated how many were left. There were at least fifty, and very likely more. Spinning around, she kicked a creature in the face, sending it crashing to the ground. She fired a round into his skull. Glancing up, Isis noticed two more back away when they spotted her. Their eyes weren't glowing, therefore, they weren't mutations or failed experiments. Isis found she didn't know what the creatures were, but shooting them in the head seemed to be an effective strategy.

"We have to retreat," Jade shouted over the pandemonium. Lightning lit up the sky outside, shortly before another bang of thunder.

"Can we Appear without a hitchhiker?" Alex asked, firing at another creature. She leaned to the side and knocked another back with a powerful side kick.

"Not in here, too risky. There aren't as many outside," Isis stated. "Make for the way we came in. I'll cover you."

"Isis, there are too many," Shae yelled, firing at a creature who leapt away and hid behind a pillar.

"You don't have a choice. I've fought more skilled combatants in greater numbers," Isis called back, slipping her guns back into the holsters on her upper thighs. "I'll be right behind you. Now go!"

She drew her sais in one fluid motion and stepped away from the other three, spinning the sharp weapons once. The dim light shone on the silver blades. A large group of the creatures congregated toward one end of the hall, hissing and snarling. One stood at the center and the others gathered around him. A small motion of his clawed hand and two creatures ran right at her. Isis dashed forward and stabbed one in the gut before leaping up and striking the other with the top of her foot. Pouncing on him, she buried the longest prong of her sai in the center of his skull.

Backing up, she kept her attention on the creatures while listening for her teammates. They had reached the opened door easily enough. Isis quickened her pace as she continued backing away, noticing the eyes up on the second floor. They were following her progress, but they weren't advancing on her. That was rather peculiar. Another motion from the strange beast and four creatures ran at her. Isis turned and ran toward the wall near the alcove, noticing an iron lever and ran straight for it. Slipping her sais back into her belt, Isis pulled the cold heavy lever down and ran for the alcove, sliding under the portcullis as it crashed to the ground. Glancing back when she heard shrieks and hissing, Isis noticed the spikes had gone through the throats of two creatures who had lunged for her. Looking around in the alcove, she spotted the second iron lever and scrambled back to her feet. She pulled it down before rolling under the second rapidly falling portcullis.

Noticing the other three women standing at the end of the drawbridge, Isis jogged over to them, her feet splashing in the growing puddles. They were all drenched in rain, which continued to fall. Another crash of thunder made Shae flinch. Jade brushed some hair away from her face.

"They'll figure out how to use those levers, so we have to go now," Isis explained as she glanced back over her shoulder. Jade nodded once and the Four disappeared from the drawbridge.

~~*~*~*

Jet hurried down the hall of the Pearl Castle, hearing Jensen's anxious steps just behind him. Lilly was right beside him, her lips set in a tight thin line. Robin and her brothers had Appeared at the mansion moments earlier to tell them what had transpired. An emergency session of the High Council had been called and the protector leaders were expected to be there with the Four. Robin had told her parents the Four looked banged up and were soaked to the bone, but nothing serious. Still, Jet couldn't help but worry. Nero had also wanted to come along, but Jet insisted he stay at the mansion and protect the inhabitants with Sly and Alpha. The leader of the protectors didn't want to take any chances. The Monroes would have insisted Jensen stay as well, but they knew nothing would keep the last Aldridge from accompanying them.

"Jet, Lilly, over here."

Jet turned when he heard Electra's voice, picking up his pace as he continued to the Healing Wing. She was standing just before the door. Her lustrous hair was damp with sweat and she was wearing tight workout clothes.

"Are they all right?" Jensen asked when they reached the young guardian. Electra brushed a sweaty strand of hair out of her face as she looked up at him.

"Minor cuts and scratches, nothing serious," she reported, turning to the Monroes. "The High Council will be ready for you in half an hour."

"Thank you, Electra," Lilly said with a small smile of gratitude as they followed Jensen inside the healing rooms. Isis was standing just inside the doorway, dripping wet, and Jensen approached her. Isis looked up at him, not saying anything. Jensen looked back at her, questioning, and she shook her head. Jensen closed his eyes in relief, his shoulders dropping a little, and he leaned forward, resting his forehead against her temple. Jet felt himself tense up and he exchanged a quick look with Lilly, waiting for Isis to chuck the shape shifter over her shoulder. Isis merely turned her head toward Jensen, resting her head against his, and closed her eyes for a moment. Her glowing green eyes opened again and fixed on the Monroes.

"Oh we're fine, Jensen. Thank you so much for asking," Shae's chipper voice came from behind them. Jet stepped around Jensen and saw the three other women sitting on one of the beds, also drenched. Jade, Alex, and Shae looked a little worse for wear. Aside from their ripped and stained clothing, they had their fair share of scrapes and bruises. Shae was running a large towel through her sopping wet hair, trying to wring out the excess water. Jet looked back to Isis, who had no wounds, not even superficial ones.

Jensen straightened up, turning to the other three. "My apologies. Are the rest of you okay?"

"They're fine," Amethyst reported as she approached

the bed. "It's all superficial wounds, but that one won't let me examine her."

"It is unnecessary and even if I were wounded, you would be unable to heal me," Isis responded. Amethyst shook her head and moved over to Alex, beginning to heal her wounds. Jet and Lilly approached the bed and he leaned down on the frame.

"The High Council convenes in half an hour. What the hell happened?" he asked, looking at Jade for an explanation. Jade shrugged and she spread her hands.

"I haven't a clue. We got there, everyone was slaughtered and then these creatures attacked us," she said, nodding over at Isis. "She probably knows more."

Jet looked to Isis and she gazed back at them. "Isis?"

Isis put her hands on her hips. "Some of them might have been dead at least a month, maybe less. Vampire blood differs in coagulation times from most normals, so it's difficult to estimate an exact time. Most had been tortured and their remains were displayed. The creatures that attacked us resembled a primitive species of vampire; one thought to have died out centuries ago."

"Well, we thought the same of wereanimals, and yet," Shae pointed out as she continued drying her red hair with the light-colored towel.

Isis paused, her brow furrowing. "I think the vampires have been wiped out, unless a few made it to Earth."

"But how is that possible?" Alex asked. "If all the inhabitants of a land were dead, Hecate would know about it."

"There was a machine keeping the heart of one of the head vampires alive, thereby giving the illusion they were still living," Isis explained, her green eyes turning once more to Jet and Lilly. "It was Grenich technology."

Jet felt a chill go through him and he glanced back at his wife when Lilly tightly gripped his hand. All the color seemed to drain from Lilly's face and he could read the concern in her expression. What Isis was saying was impossible. There was no way a single man could have an army large or organized enough to wipe out an entire species. Jet glanced over to where Amethyst was now healing Shae. The older guardian was focused entirely on her task.

"Are you certain?" Lilly asked, looking back at Isis. The seven series crossed her arms over her chest and looked at her, nodding once. Jet turned his attention to Jensen, who looked dapper as always in a three-piece suit. He cleared his throat and straightened one of his already straight sleeves, toying with his cufflink.

"So it looks like Set can cross planes," Jade mentioned. "I guess the only question left to answer is how."

Jet ran a hand through his hair. "I really wish you had brought evidence."

"We were kind of preoccupied with being ambushed," Shae chimed in. Jet straightened up again and moved across the healing wing.

"When you're ready, come up to the High Council room. Lilly and I will be waiting outside," he instructed as he strode toward the doors with Lilly beside him.

A half-hour later, Jet and Lilly sat at a long table with the Four in front of the High Council. Jensen sat behind the gates with Passion and Electra, who were allowed to observe the proceedings. Jet briefly looked over at the Four. The three women still looked a little worse for wear, but much better than they had when the Monroes had first arrived. Isis sat at the end, silent as always. When they first entered the High Council chambers, he noticed her hesitate for a split-second. There were no shadows in the chamber — everything was brightly lit. Such environments seemed to make experiments extra cautious. Jet noticed Isis' gaze roaming over the guardians, but for the most part, she was still. She hadn't bothered to conceal her glowing eyes, which had raised the eyebrows of a few of the older guardians. Jet wasn't sure what was raising the ire of the older guardians more, her eyes or the slinky catsuit she still wore. *If they knew her lover was a shape shifter, their heads might actually explode,* Jet thought with morbid amusement as he looked back over his shoulder. Astrea and Nemesis were standing at the door to the High Council room, acting as guards. Astrea stood at attention, her back ramrod straight. Nemesis looked a little more at ease, though no less formidable.

Looking back at the guardians in front of him, Jet tried to identify the ones in attendance. He knew all the heads of the various lands, but their apprentices were a lot trickier to identify. Aneurin continued reading through the hastily written incident report Jade had jotted down for the emergency meeting. She had written it in the healing room just before they left for the council meeting. Lilly slid her hand into his and Jet raised it to his mouth, gently kissing her knuckles.

"Hecate, you were there, were you not?" Aneurin asked, his gaze traveling over to the night guardian, who sat near Adonia. She looked puzzled at the question.

"No, I wasn't present where the actual incident took place," she responded. Aneurin chuckled quietly. Donovan, who was sitting at the far end on the guardian men's side, rolled his eyes and started scribbling something on the parchment in front of him. He had never been able to conceal his contempt for Aneurin and from what Jet understood, often appeared bored during High Council sessions. Lucky, his apprentice, sat behind him. The young guardian fidgeted as he tried to get in a more comfortable position. He lost his grip on his writing tablet, which clattered to the ground. Everyone looked over at him and he mumbled apologies as he retrieved the tablet.

"I meant when they came back," Aneurin clarified after one final disapproving look in Lucky's direction. "It says here one of the unidentified creatures nearly came through the door with them."

"That's correct," Hecate responded. "The creature grabbed hold of Shae as they came back through the door, but Isis managed to take care of it. I sealed the door shut after that."

There was some murmuring from the council members. Donovan remained silent as he glanced up at the Four. He looked quite impressed. Aneurin turned his attention back to the protectors in front of him.

"I'll try to make this quick. I know it has been a very long afternoon and evening for the four of you," he said calmly. "Your claim that these were Grenich allies — I assume that theory comes from young Isis, correct?"

"In all due respect, it's not a claim," Jade remarked. "None of us had ever seen these creatures before and they weren't normal vampires."

"I guess I'm just having trouble understanding how this could be connected to Grenich. Neither Set nor Pyra has access to the doorways and if they entered any realm, the guardians of magic and the supernatural would know about it. Hecate would most certainly know about it," Aneurin responded. "The vampires have long had problems with the stability of their society. Clans were always at war, fighting for power—"

"You are wrong," Isis said softly, looking up to Aneurin. "Your logic is flawed and it makes your conclusion incorrect."

Jet almost cringed at her interruption and noticed his wife had a similar expression as she briefly grit her teeth. The head guardians would not be happy with such an interruption. Her flat-out telling the king of the guardian men he was wrong was not going to win her fans on the High Council. Jet could see quite a few older guardians glaring at her, stunned by what they saw as blatant impudence. Donovan was the only one who appeared to be close to laughing. Most of the women seemed less offended, though a few of the older ones didn't look pleased. Aneurin was relatively unbothered.

"I see. Please educate me, then, on how you're so certain this was the work of Grenich," Aneurin requested, folding his hands in front of him.

"Aside from the technology and the symbol, I recognized the method of the attack," Isis replied.

"How?"

Jet looked down the table to her when she didn't respond right away. Normally, she was forthright to a fault when it came to explaining why someone was wrong. Isis hesitated, looking over her shoulder to the three sitting behind them and then at the others sitting beside her. She looked back to Aneurin, who was watching her expectantly.

"Because it showed evidence of similar methods I employed when I was sent out on missions," she answered.

"Right, your past at the Grenich Corporation," Aneurin said, nodding. "Did you ever kill an entire race?"

"Aneurin," Adonia interrupted. "That is unfair and not what we are here to discuss."

"Aneurin is making a point that we only have the word of an admitted killer," Merrick, the current head male guardian of water, spoke up from near Aneurin.

"And the three other women," Donovan pointed out, not looking up from whatever he was writing. "Oh, and Hecate."

"Which doesn't alter the fact that Set *cannot* enter other realms," Aneurin continued. "If he or his followers got inside, it was because someone opened the gate for him."

"Aneurin, two races have been decimated in a short span of time," Adonia said. "The guardians can't just stand by and do nothing."

"We shall send out messages warning against opening the gates to strangers," Aneurin stated as he sat back. "Something they should have been doing already. I'm not sending out guardian forces to different realms. They wouldn't do any good and I am uneasy acting as an occupying force."

"The summit is supposed to take place at the end of

the month," Jet mentioned, drawing the guardians attention back to them. "We have one more race to contact and I would appreciate not walking into another trap if it's at all possible."

The guardians spoke among themselves for a moment, except for Donovan who continued writing or drawing on the parchment in front of him.

"The last race is the Magic Orders and they will not speak with shape shifters unless they have a guardian with them, so the Council has to go the extra mile this time," Donovan spoke without looking up. A few guardian men threw annoyed looks in his direction. He smiled but still didn't look up from his drawing. Lucky leaned forward to peer over Donovan's shoulder. His eyes widened significantly and he sat back, looking forward again. Jet found himself wondering what was on the paper. Judging from Lucky's reaction, it was something lewd or graphic.

"We will do our best to ensure your safety, Jet," Adonia stated. Jet wasn't always fond of the guardians' occasional isolationist ways, but he trusted the women implicitly. Like all protector leaders, he had been around guardians his entire life and the guardian women were the closest with the protectors. He glanced over at Lilly, who still looked very concerned.

"Well, if there's nothing else," Aneurin said. "Hecate, make sure you permanently seal that door. Have your apprentices keep their eyes out for any vampires who may—"

"You're making a mistake."

Jet almost didn't hear Isis' soft proclamation. He looked down the table to her as did the other three. She had folded her hands in front of her on the table and raised her gaze to look at the members of the High Council again.

"If Set were let into the vampire realm, it means he can talk his way into the other realms," she continued. "If he can do that, he can reach the Meadows. The guardians should take a more active role in fighting Grenich."

"I thought that was what you were for," Aneurin commented. Isis watched him for a moment, her gaze scrutinizing. Jet looked back to Aneurin and was surprised to see the guardian appeared somewhat unnerved.

"I am one seven series," Isis replied. "Set has hundreds of experiments at his disposal, maybe even a thousand, and he's constantly creating new products, improving on the old series. A day will come when I'm obsolete and when it does, I will not be much use to you. Your battle strategies and tactics are flawed. I do not understand your reluctance to update them for the very real danger you are facing."

"And what would you have us do, Isis?" Ocean asked from where she sat near Hecate. Lilly's eldest sister, Ivy, sat beside her as she always did in meetings of the High Council. Ivy caught the Monroes' eyes and smiled in a reassuring way.

"I have been studying your texts and legends and histories," Isis answered, her gaze roaming across the members of the High Council. "You are capable warriors. I would ask you to fight."

"We'll be attending Jet's summit and we can further discuss our involvement there," Aneurin stated dismissively. "For now, we err on the side of caution. I thank you ladies for your bravery, service, and bringing this incident to our attention. You have done the Meadows a great service and you have the gratitude of the guardians. Adonia, do you have anything further to add at this time?"

Adonia sat back. "I do not."

"All right, meeting adjourned," Aneurin declared, smiling at the Four one last time before standing and making his way out of the council room. The shape shifters stood as the guardians filed out of the room. Soon only Adonia, Artemis, Donovan, Lucky, Passion, and Electra remained with the shape shifters. As soon as the guardians left, Jensen stood from his seat and smoothed his suit. Jet ran a hand over his forehead, disappointed.

Lilly rested her elbows on the table, her chin on the back of her hands.

"I don't know what I expected," Jet muttered, sitting back. "It's not directly affecting all of the Meadows so why should the guardians get involved?"

"You made the mistake of assuming they have scruples," Donovan mentioned from where he still sat behind the elevated desk. His dip pen continued scratching across the paper in front of him.

"At the very least, we should have sent out a few troops to destroy those creatures," Electra stated.

"We couldn't risk guardian lives for what might be a pointless endeavor," Artemis explained. "Guardians will not go to war again, not without a tangible threat to our existence."

"This threat seems fairly tangible," Jet pointed out, looking over at Isis. She was silent, her chair turned a little so she could watch the shape shifters and guardians converse. Jensen stood near her, on the other side of the smooth gate.

"I agree with you, Jet," Adonia said. "I have ordered Hecate to seal the door to the vampire realm and extra guards will be posted in the hall of doorways, but that's the best I can do at the moment."

"I guess we'll just have to continue the fight on our side," Jade put in, leaning back in her chair. Passion looked over at Jet and Lilly.

"Has Orion returned yet?" she asked.

"No, we haven't heard from him," Lilly replied.

Isis stood from her seat. "We shouldn't sit around. There's work to be done and we can do nothing more here."

Jet watched as she made her way through the wooden gates and out of the High Council chamber. He and Lilly stood from their chairs as did the other three.

"I guess we should be on our way," Jet said. "Please let us know if there's any further trouble."

Adonia smiled and nodded. Lilly said goodbye to Passion and Electra, kissing each on the cheek, before turning to her husband and nodding. Jet motioned to the other three and the protectors exited the High Council chamber, following Isis. Jensen slowed his step so he was just behind Jet and Lilly.

"That could have gone better," he said under his breath.

"You can say that again," Jet replied just as quietly and Lilly nodded in agreement.

~~*~*~*

Set sat behind the desk in Nick Chance's office, rotating the chair back and forth. He looked over to where Tracy lay on the couch, staring up at the experiment pelts the bastard necromancer kept. Set glanced at them. Chance was fairly adept at preserving the trophies he collected. Most of the skins looked as though they were only days old. *One of the few things he's actually good at,* Set thought.

The soft rumble of wheels drew Set's attention over to the double doors of the large office. Out of the corner of his eye, he saw Tracy push herself up on her elbows and watch the doors. After a moment, they were pushed open with the typical flourish that Chance often showed.

Nick Chance entered, a small group of followers on his heels. The followers were dragging a cart behind them, a curtain draped over the object being wheeled in. Chance took his bowler hat off, bowing low to Set. His blue gaze traveled over to Tracy and he stuck his index and middle finger up in a vulgar sign. She gave a half-smile, unbothered by his childishness. Set couldn't help but be pleased at her self-control and professionalism. He always knew he made the right choice in making her a revenant.

"Took some doing, but I can report that all vampires have been eradicated as per your orders," Chance reported, his grin becoming almost feral. Set turned his attention back to Chance, unimpressed.

"Yes, but I understand you went back to toy with the seven series despite my implicit instructions not to," he remarked. Chance's grin faltered.

"The P.V.s were going to have all the fun. It wasn't fair," he protested, sounding like a petulant child. Set crossed his arms over his chest, not enjoying the back talk. He narrowed his eyes at his illegitimate grandson, debating how useful he really was. Chance recognized his mistake and dropped his gaze as he moved over to the covered object.

"I thought you might be a little upset, so I brought you a gift," he explained as he took hold of the white sheet. With the embellishment of a matador, Chance threw the sheet off to reveal a cage containing a dark-haired vampire. She blinked against the onslaught of light in the white room, gradually rising to her feet. Set recognized the crest sewn into the woman's regal clothes, identifying her as royalty. *He brought me back a leader. That is somewhat impressive,* the necromancer thought as he approached the cage.

"She was good at hiding and her people were loyal to a fault, but we finally managed to flush her out," Nick bragged as Set continued to watch the caged woman.

The vampire woman noticed him and she stopped blinking, recognition apparent in her fearful expression. She took a step back, looking around the rest of the room at the other individuals before her attention turned back to Set. He smirked as he looked up at her, his mind dancing with possibilities.

"Pelageya, I take it. Your clothing is much too fine to be just another mistress. You're the whore who became a queen," Set said, not speaking to anyone in particular as he circled around the cage. She stared at him, not answering.

"I knew a vampire once," he continued, never looking away from her. "An opera singer, lovely creature. Used to lure her out of your realm in the night and have her sing for my wife and me. That one got carried away and slit her throat one night."

"Her screeching was giving me a headache," Chance spoke up from where he was pouring himself a drink. Set noticed the blood on her dress, which also stained her hands. A smile spread across his face and he stopped in front of the cage again.

"You left Maksim's heart beating, correct?" Set asked, still watching the vampire queen in the cage.

"We did, sir," Tracy replied. Set stuck out his bottom lip as if he were pouting.

"That must've been traumatic for you, poor lamb," he spoke to the vampire woman. Her expression flashed with rage and her mouth set in a thin line, but she didn't physically react. Set found he was actually impressed with her. It was almost a shame he had to kill her.

"A true queen to the end, I see. Ever the noble and dignified woman, they trained you well," he complimented, leaning closer to the bars. "I'm going to let you in on a little secret, sweetheart. Bravery is admirable, but futile. You will be forgotten, your people will be forgotten, and in the end, your bravery, your very existence will be completely meaningless. The word vampire will forever be associated with some ridiculous fanged boogeyman hiding under the beds of children."

Set turned away from the cage. "Take her away, drain her dry, have the scientists figure out if they can do anything with her blood. If they want to dissect or experiment on her organs, they can have at it. Once they're done, dismember the corpse and toss it in the incinerator."

Nick Chance smiled and waved at the vampire as the cage was wheeled out of the room. One of the followers turned back to shut the doors.

"Another species down," Set said to himself, smiling victoriously. Closing his eyes, he inhaled the sweet artificial air. The smell of sterility was positively heavenly. He couldn't wait until he got his hands on his Key. Then the real fun would begin.

CHAPTER ELEVEN

The Four lay on their stomachs atop a hill in a forest preserve, looking down to the bank. Isis turned to check that Coop was still on guard. Shocker was refusing to leave the backseat of Jensen's car. It had been difficult convincing him to cooperate and Isis had considered taking another of his pets hostage. In the end, Coop and Jade had managed to bribe him into helping. He insisted on someone staying behind with his dogs and cats, a job that had fallen to Cassidy and Jay.

"The bank's going to be opening in a few minutes," Jade mentioned, peering through her small binoculars to the plain building below.

"Traffic's starting to pick up," Alex observed. "On the plus side, I haven't seen any people with glowing eyes or any other suspicious individuals."

"The jogger who passed by ten minutes earlier and the woman sleeping on the bench," Isis pointed out as she scooted back out of the shrubbery. She brushed the dirt from her hands and looked down the quiet path. The other three followed her. They were all dressed in plainclothes, except for Isis who wore her usual guardian-made shirt and pants. Sly was reclining on the hood of the car the

Four had borrowed from the mansion. The sun shone in her black hair.

"How do you—" Alex began.

"Her hands are clean and the clothes, though torn and threadbare, fit as though they have been tailored," Isis explained. "Grenich is meticulous about most things, but certain small details can escape their notice."

Steve, Nero, and Jensen were leaning against the Jaguar. Isis saw Shocker in the back seat, his arms crossed over his chest. He didn't look at any of them, but stared straight out to the horizon. Jensen had cracked the windows for him; a gesture the experiment didn't acknowledge.

"It's not too late to go on our way," Coop whispered. Isis glanced at him, knowing he had been against the idea from the get-go. It didn't dissuade her. The guardians weren't going to help and their resources were limited. At the very least, retrieving whatever was in the safe deposit box would give her something to hold over Set. If she could get some kind of leverage, Isis was willing to take the risk.

"How are we going to do this?" Steve asked. "Keep in mind that I would like to keep my job as a detective."

"I have an idea," Shocker said from inside the car. "Why don't we not do this? Maybe commit the dominatrix who is demonstrating what normals consider suicidal tendencies?"

"Can I request we use the cowardly Brit as a living shield?" Sly suggested. Shocker looked over at her. Isis turned her attention back to the shape shifters in front of her.

"We'll need at least two other shape shifters in the bank, to act as lookouts," Isis said, turning her attention to Jade. "You and Sly are the best qualified for that position."

"Jade's the best qualified for many things," Sly responded with a suggestive grin.

"I am not referring to sexual interactions," Isis said,

causing Nero and Shae to crack up.

"This is the best conversation *ever*," Nero laughed. Isis stared at him, wondering if normals ever thought about anything other than sex. Once again, she couldn't figure out how they continued to survive. A cool wind swept through the trees and Isis tried to detect any unusual scents. When she was satisfied nothing was out of the ordinary, she turned her attention back to the normals.

"Coop and I need to be in the bank as well, but I don't know how to get past the Grenich plants inside," Isis explained. "Coop should not attract their attention. He has been gone for some time."

"A plant will still be able to detect me," Coop reminded her.

"You pose no significant threat to the Corporation. You're low-risk. They'll be too distracted by my presence," Isis stated, taking in his appearance. He was dressed in a dark suit and mirrored sunglasses, which made him look like hired muscle.

"Just maintain your cover as Jensen's bodyguard," she said. "Shocker is going to send a charge through their security system, which will take care of the cameras."

"Won't that trip all kinds of alarms?" Shae pointed out.

"Their vault will go into lockdown, but since we're unconcerned with its contents, it is no matter to us," Isis replied. "Shocker, you can knock out the cameras without affecting the rest of the security system, correct?"

Shocker grumbled something under his breath before responding, "That is accurate."

"I'll have to sprint through the door," Isis said, scratching the back of her head.

"If you were to shift into a bird," Shae began, but Isis shook her head.

"My eyes glow even in animal form and the lenses I wear will slip out if I'm in animal form. It would draw too much attention and the plants would still be able to detect me," she said, looking off down the hill.

"Isis, how skilled are the lookouts?" Alex asked.

"More skilled than the average normal, but still manageable," Isis answered, moving over to the Jaguar. She walked around the car, opened the door to the backseat, and slid in next to Shocker. He continued looking straight ahead, his arms crossed over his chest. Like her, he displayed no visible emotion. Looking at him, Isis could see small tells that indicated his nervousness.

"You know this is suicide. I may be one of the earliest E-series, but I know a lot of the same strategies you do," he muttered, not looking at her.

"I need you to do your job," she said, ignoring his statement. "After you knock out the security feeds, you have to help the normals. Watch their backs. They can handle themselves for the most part, but they're still inexperienced and outmatched when it comes to Grenich."

Shocker stared at her, studying her for a moment. "You're concerned about them."

"Our numbers are pitiful as it is," she replied. "The last thing we need is for the necromancers to kill our more capable fighters."

Shocker snorted. "You lot are supposed to be merciless killers and you're worried about a couple of normals? What happened to that cold-as-ice demeanor the seven series are so infamous for?"

Isis glanced at him before opening the car door and rising from the backseat. The sun felt warm on her face, a pleasant sensation. Her mind was racing again and Isis didn't know whether or not she was concerned for the normals. The thought of something happening to one of them caused an unpleasant constricting sensation in her chest. Isis forced her mind to remain in the present, focusing on strategy instead of possibilities. Coop approached her and she looked up at him.

"I do not understand the motivation behind this foolhardy endeavor," he said under his breath. "Even if we are successful — which is very unlikely — whatever is in that box will be useless to us."

"To us, it might be useless. To Set and Pyra, it won't be," Isis responded. "We are going into battle with inadequate numbers and, for the normals, inadequate training. They think we can protect them, lead them to victory, but we cannot do that on our own. Four experiments against an entire laboratory? That is folly. We need some kind of leverage. It is a small advantage, but it is better than nothing. The contents of the security box will give me something to hold over Set's head."

Isis looked over the roof of the car to where Jensen was talking to the other members of the Four. He noticed her and gave her a small half-smile.

"You care for him."

Isis turned her back and leaned against the Jaguar. "Whatever you think I feel is irrelevant. The plants detecting the last Aldridge is a concern. Watch out for him. Don't let him out of your sight, not for a minute."

"Are we going to do this sometime this century?" Sly called out from where she still lay on the hood of the car. The experiments all glanced over at her.

"I thought you would be watching him," Coop mentioned. Isis looked up into his mirrored sunglasses, studying her reflection for a moment. She was wearing the specially-made contacts that hid her glowing eyes. It was odd, having eyes like a normal. Isis almost didn't recognize herself without the glowing irises. Coop was also wearing the lenses, in case his sunglasses slipped off. Seeing an experiment without the glowing eyes was a little unsettling for other experiments.

"I will do my best, but the plants will become aware of my presence very soon after we're inside. I could be waylaid," Isis explained, remaining vague. "We have to go now, before the bank becomes crowded."

Coop nodded and she moved around the car, back to where the shape shifters had congregated. Looking down the bare stretch of road, Isis wished they had another experiment on the team. It would have been beneficial to have one hang back and do a sweep for hostiles. Snipers would draw too much attention and the risk of using one far outweighed the benefit, but Isis preferred to have a solution for every possible danger.

"What are you thinking?" Jensen asked, coming up next to her. The subtle scent of his soap and deodorant had become an almost comforting aroma. The Grenich Corporation had conditioned her to despise familiarity and routine, but being on the outside, Isis had begun to see the value in both.

"Whether Grenich will try to kill me or just capture me," she answered. "The more advanced series are more difficult to predict."

"Hey, Isis," Nero called over. "Don't get stabbed. Again."

Isis' brow furrowed and she watched Shae smack Nero's arm. "When did you witness me getting stabbed?"

"Your uncle has an idiotic sense of humor," Jensen mentioned. Isis looked up at him. She felt the strange tightening in her chest. Opening her mouth to say something, she closed it again when she couldn't find the words. A cool wind slid past them, brushing some stray debris on the side of the road.

"Stay alert. And don't get killed," she told Jensen before turning and making her way back to Jade's car. She sank into the backseat of the car and turned her face up toward the roof. Her other senses drank in the information surrounding the car, her mind humming as it processed everything. She heard the car doors open and close, the engine start, and the car move away from the side of the road. *An eight series is going to be difficult,* she thought as she turned her gaze to the road passing by.

"So Isis, how hard is this wet work team going to be?" Sly asked from the front seat.

"For normals? You'll need to work in pairs," Isis answered. "They're likely to have been handpicked by one of Set's sons. Don't hesitate to use underhanded tactics when fighting them because they won't."

"Best advice I've heard in quite some time," Sly said.

Five minutes later, they pulled into the bank's parking lot. Rounding a corner, Jade pulled over and parked. Isis climbed out of the car, looking around for the wet work team. When she was satisfied they weren't there, she picked up her pace and jogged to the bank. Isis caught a glimpse of Shocker in the lot. He was wearing a baseball cap and a pair of sunglasses. He looked as nondescript as a person could be. Looking up at the sky, Isis wished it were overcast. Nice weather usually meant more people.

Isis moved to the far end of the lot, noticing Coop and Jensen were already half way to the bank doors. Jensen buttoned up his suit, looking every bit the wealthy customer. Isis' legs tensed up and she bent her knees. When Coop reached the door, she dashed across the parking lot and was through the door before he had fully opened it for Jensen.

Running around another corner, Isis made her way for the women's bathroom. She slowed her speed when she was halfway there and jogged the rest of the way to the door. Once inside, Isis looked around for any unwanted company. She could hear the regular sounds of the bank outside: heeled shoes, computers, idle chatter, and other sounds. There was an unusual rhythm to the noise. Isis approached the door, putting her ear near it. The rhythm wasn't natural. It was much too uniform, too ordered. The lights flickered once and she wondered if Shocker had overestimated his ability.

The sound of shoes approaching the bathroom made Isis back up. She entered one of the empty stalls, closing the red swinging door and pressing her back against the side. The door opened and she smelled the metal of a weapon. The sound of the heels stopped just inside the bathroom and it took Isis a second to realize the owner had taken off her shoes. Waiting for a moment, Isis kicked the stall door as hard as she could. It swung open, nearly coming off its hinges, and slammed into an experiment. Isis stepped out of the stall as the experiment — an eight series — flipped back to her feet. Isis grabbed hold of her wrists, forcing her backward as she wrestled for control of the knife the woman held. The two women collided with one of the hand driers, which buzzed loudly as warm air flowed out from it.

The eight series kneed Isis in the stomach and threw her weight forward, tossing Isis over her knee to the hard ground. Isis lost her grip on the knife and scrambled to her feet, narrowly dodging out of the way of the knife blade. The woman thrust the knife forward and Isis grabbed her wrist again, trying to force the weapon out of her grasp. With her free hand, the eight series grabbed the back of Isis' hair and slammed her head into the nearest wall. Isis thrust one elbow back into the woman's throat. The eight series responded by tossing her to the ground again and Isis slid across the floor. She leapt to her feet, holding her fists defensively in front of her. The eight series adjusted her grip on the knife. For a moment, the two women circled each other.

Isis wasn't sure she could beat an eight series. Her opponent seemed to be able to anticipate her every move. The eight series lunged for her, thrusting the knife forward. She managed to graze Isis' ribs, but got close enough for Isis to elbow her in the face and follow through with a strong roundhouse kick that broke a couple ribs. Isis leapt up and followed through with a knee to the face, knocking the eight series backward. The woman adjusted her grip on the knife again and Isis took a large step back, holding her fists in front of her. The eight series lunged at her, feinting and slicing into her back. She followed through with a strong kick that sent Isis sprawling. Isis barely had time to react when the eight series pounced on her again, knife poised for the kill. Isis gripped her wrists, keeping the knife away from her heart.

The eight series was strong and put all her weight on the knife handle, trying to force the sharp point down. The knife dipped a little more as Isis struggled to keep it from plunging down.

"I will burn them all."

"You can't give up. Not now, not when you've come so far," she heard her ghost whisper.

Changing tactics, Isis pulled the knife up and allowed it to sink deep into her shoulder. Punching straight up, she broke the eight series' nose and sent her sprawling back. Isis yanked the knife out of her shoulder with her good hand and adjusted her grip as she scrambled back up to her feet, ignoring the pain in her wounded shoulder. She had to beat this eight series. It wasn't just instinctual self-preservation that was driving her. Isis felt something else, a need to protect the normals. It made no sense to her, but she didn't have time to ruminate on the odd new motivation.

The eight series also got to her feet and wiped the blood from her nose and lip, both of which had already healed. Her eyes fixed on Isis and the two women circled each other again. Above them, the lights buzzed. Isis could feel warm blood crawling down her arm as her shoulder wound sealed up and repaired itself. The eight series moved first, aiming a fast high kick at Isis' head, which she barely managed to dodge. Isis lunged forward with a side kick, which the eight series shoved away. The eight series grabbed Isis' wrist and latched onto the back of her neck with her free hand, shoving her head first into the mirror, breaking it, before tossing her to the ground.

Isis climbed back to her feet, dodging a roundhouse kick aimed at her face. She kicked at the other woman's stomach, and when the eight series deflected, aimed a snap kick at her head. The eight series stumbled back a couple steps. Isis noticed the knife she had dropped and retrieved it. Isis adjusted her grip on the knife again, holding it in a defensive position. The weapon was a last resort. Killing the experiment would cause more problems than it would solve. The hand drier gradually died down as it automatically turned off. The eight series leaned forward and hit the button with a back kick, turning the drier on again.

Isis narrowly avoided an elbow thrust to the throat and when the eight series lunged at her again, Isis leaned forward and struck her in the head with a scorpion kick. The other experiment stumbled back and Isis tossed the knife away. The eight series looked from her to the knife, holding her fists in front of her. *Come on. Take the bait,* Isis thought as she aimed a jab at her face, which the eight series blocked. When the eight series punched forward with a strong cross, Isis grabbed her arm and spun her around. Grabbing hold of her brown hair, Isis smashed her head into the sink counter twice and then threw her back into a stall. Leaping in after her, Isis slammed her elbow down on top of the woman's head. She felt the skull crack and the experiment dropped heavily to the ground. Reaching into the back of her pants, Isis removed a zip-tie and bound the experiment's wrists.

Leaning against the stall door, Isis took a moment to catch her breath. The hand-drier went quiet again. She leaned forward and rested her hands on her knees. The fight had required a lot of energy, but not as much as she had anticipated. It was strange since the eight series was a more advanced product. By all rights, a seven series shouldn't have been able to best a more advanced experiment. Isis looked over to the bathroom door, wondering about the other plant. She had to get out into the main part of the bank and rejoin the others. Turning her attention back to the woman, Isis estimated her size, which was almost the same as her own. There was some blood on her clothing, but not a noticeable amount. The woman's hair was a similar shade, on the shorter side, and her eyes looked similar.

A few minutes later, Isis adjusted the woman's clothes

on herself and slipped the glasses on, which were ordinary glass like she had expected. The eight series had been a little smaller than her and didn't have quite so many weapons, so the clothes were tight. Isis glanced over her shoulder to the stall door, behind which was the bound experiment. She turned and made her way out of the bathroom, heading for the main part of the bank.

Isis took a moment to observe the main area of the bank, hoping to spot the other plant. There was a mechanical atmosphere in the bank, as though everything was programmed. The tellers were in synch with each other and the people in the bank moved as though they were choreographed. The colors were all drab neutral tones, lending to the lifeless feeling in the building. On the far side of the bank, Isis saw Jade and Sly sitting across from an adviser. Their fingers were intertwined and they were acting like a couple in love. The adviser was busying himself with paperwork. Isis crossed him off the mental list of suspects. Turning her attention to the tellers, the majority of whom looked blank-faced and robotic, she crossed them off her list as well. She spotted Jensen sitting across from another adviser. Coop stood behind his chair with his arms crossed in front of him, looking quite intimidating.

Moving across the bank, attempting to conceal her smooth gait, Isis stepped up next to the adviser. Coop and Jensen didn't react to her presence, both knowing better than to do so.

"Ms. Burrows can show you to your box, Mr. Aldridge," the adviser said without looking at her. Isis glanced over to the windows, noticing Steve struggling with a very large man. Shocker sauntered up behind them, pressed a hand on the man's back, and the man started shaking violently. He smashed into the glass with a loud thump, causing most of the people in the bank to slowly raise their gaze from whatever task they were working on to look at the windows. Shocker and Steve had dropped, so there was only the sunny day outside. The sounds of the bank soon resumed. Isis looked around, feeling uneasy about the mechanical rhythm. It was unnatural and therefore a potential danger.

"What was that?" the adviser asked.

"A bird," Isis answered. The adviser looked back to the computer, saying something about the damn flying nuisances under his breath. Isis gestured to the door leading to where the safe deposit boxes were. Coop and Jensen followed her as she made her way across the bank. Stepping through the doorway, Isis led them down a long flight of stairs.

"I assume those are the plant's clothes," Coop spoke under his breath.

"They are, an eight series," Isis responded, answering his unasked question.

"Isn't it a little risky to pose as her?" Jensen asked as they reached the bottom of the stairs. Isis moved through the hall, keeping her bearings. Banks were often difficult to navigate and it was hard to get the blueprints. Banks outside drop zones required a lot of improvisation, which experiments didn't enjoy.

"We have very similar builds and features," Isis answered, turning down a hall. "Normals aren't as perceptive as they think. It's easy to slip by them unnoticed."

Isis stopped in front of the barred door and Coop moved to the lock, pressing a finger against it. It soon formed into the shape of a key. He unlocked the door and three of them entered the room with the safe deposit boxes. Jensen pointed to his and Coop opened it up, bringing the box over to the counter. Isis pulled off the glasses and jacket, tossing them near the box. Coop handed one of his guns to Jensen, who tucked it in the back of his pants.

"The Grenich box is in the area across from this one," Isis mentioned, nodding over to the other barred door.

"Box 757."

Coop made his way out of the room, pausing only to open the barred door across the way. When the door closed, Isis began to do a sweep of the room, her eyes sharp for any suspicious movement.

"There's blood on your shirt," Jensen observed, stopping her sweep.

"It's the plant's. We fought. I was stabbed in the shoulder, but the wound's already healed," Isis stated, stepping around him.

"What? Isis, are you sure you're okay?"

Isis looked back at him. "Yes. I am still functioning—"

Isis heard the rustle of a gun being drawn and ran toward Jensen, shoving him to the ground. Bullets pierced the boxes near them. Isis dashed forward, slamming the door backward and into the second plant, who was wearing a security uniform. He stumbled back and she leapt up, slamming her elbow into his face. Pulling the knife from behind her back, Isis thrust for his heart. He grabbed her arm and tossed her against the bars of another wall. Isis crashed to the ground and the plant, another eight series, kicked her mercilessly in the ribs. She felt a couple give under his foot as she slammed into the solid bars again. He grabbed the back of her neck and Isis leaned forward, throwing up her leg into a solid kick that connected with the back of the eight series' head. His grip vanished from her neck and Isis dropped to the ground, scrambling to her feet. He cracked his neck and Isis looked around for any weapon she could use against him.

Hearing something behind her, Isis dove to the ground and Jensen fired a couple shots at the eight series, who dodged out of the way while returning fire.

Isis bolted after him and slid under a kick aimed at her face. She leapt to her feet again and threw a right hook at the eight series. He caught her fist, punched her in the face, and followed through with an elbow to the throat, which knocked her down again. Isis scurried back up and the eight series pounced on her, swinging out with a right cross. Pushing the punch past her face, Isis leapt up, grabbed his ears, and yanked his face down to connect with her knee. He grabbed her throat and slammed her up against the nearest wall. She clapped her hands over his ears, bursting his eardrums, and spun out of the weakened grasp. Grabbing his shirt, Isis slammed his face against the wall he had held her against. The eight series weaved about unsteadily, disoriented and dazed. Isis lunged forward and kicked him under the jaw, snapping his head back and knocking him out cold.

Once she had zip-tied the wrists and ankles of the eight series, Isis jogged back to where Coop was kneeling next to Jensen, who was writhing on the ground. Isis could smell blood and saw it pumping from the bullet wound near his abdomen. He was bleeding out. Her eyes darted around the room, searching for something to help slow the bleeding. Isis noticed the knife she had dropped. Looking down at her own hands, an idea began to form in her mind. Retrieving the knife, Isis hurried back over to the men.

"Did you get the contents of the box?" she asked Coop as she sliced open her palm and pressed it against Jensen's wound, ignoring his protestations. Closing her eyes, Isis visualized the healing properties in her blood fixing the damage done to the protector.

"Isis, he's losing too much blood," Coop stated, frowning. "What are you doing?"

"Saving him. Did you get whatever was in the box?"

Coop tapped his breast pocket and opened his mouth to repeat his question. The words died in his throat and he stared at her hands when they started to glow with a soft purple light. Isis opened her eyes and looked at her hands, puzzled. She was not descended from healers and had never done any kind of healing before. Isis really didn't know what she was doing. It had only been a hunch, a desperate attempt to help the last Aldridge.

After a moment, the glowing stopped and Isis took her hands away from the wound. Jensen stared down in shock when the bullet fell from the wound, which sealed itself up.

"What the hell?"

"Isis, what did you do?"

Isis looked to the ground briefly, feeling dizzy and unsteady. Her head swam a little and there was a faint sense of nausea. She cleared her throat and helped Jensen to his feet, forcing herself not to waver. Next to her, Coop rose with them and Isis knew he was staring at her in bewilderment. Jensen stared at his healed flesh in amazement. His expression morphed into mild irritation when he noticed the amount of blood on his suit.

"Are my eyes going to start glowing?" he asked after a moment, looking at Isis with a teasing grin. She exchanged a confused look with Coop.

"You're not an experiment," she answered, massaging her brow. "We need to go. The plants will be waking soon and we can't be around when they contact their handlers."

Isis turned and made her way out of the room. She heard Coop closing the doors behind them. Looking down at her hand, Isis flexed her fingers a few times. Though her hand shook a little, the deep cut had already healed. She still felt a little weak, more drained than she had in quite some time. The eight series groaned and Isis moved over to him, stomping on his head a couple times until he was unconscious again.

"Remind me never to piss you off," Jensen commented. Isis stared at him, wondering why he wasn't scared of her. He was a normal and had witnessed her efficiency more than once, yet he didn't seem frightened by her at all. The last Aldridge was a very peculiar man. Coop exited the room, grabbed the ankles of the eight series and dragged him inside the room with the safe deposit boxes. He exited a minute later and shut the door.

The three shape shifters ascended the stairs.

~~*~*~*

In Perrin's Sanctuary, another perfect day was taking place. As usual, Orion didn't notice it. They were leaving soon and he was checking again to make sure he had packed everything. He'd spent most of the morning folding his newly cleaned clothes and then it took another couple hours to put everything in its proper place in his pack. The eldest Deverell was preoccupied with thoughts of the experiments back at the mansion and hoping they were okay. Looking up, he wondered where Jack had gone off to. The seven series had looked in on Orion earlier that day, asking if he needed any help. After Orion assured him he didn't, Jack wandered off. *Probably to the library,* Orion thought with a smile and a shake of his head.

"Never thought I'd see the day when you actually smiled."

Orion looked over to the open door where Milo leaned against the frame. He looked stronger than he had a couple days ago at breakfast, but was still a little pale. As usual, he wore midnight blue garb with black boots and gloves. Orion could see the grip of a sword on his left hip and a holster on his right.

"Are you headed out?" Orion asked as he zipped one of his bags shut. He turned his attention to the box Copper had sent him and opened it, counting the gun magazines inside.

"I am," Milo answered as he stepped inside the room and moved across the space to the windows, opening them. "I'm coming with you."

Orion looked up sharply, staring at Milo in disbelief. "You're what?"

Milo closed his eyes and inhaled the fresh air. He turned and leaned on the ledge, studying Orion for a moment.

"You need all hands on deck, Doc. Especially now that you've got a shape shifter who can see inside the Corporation. You've got a new and valuable asset, the first in a long while, and I'm not going to let you squander it."

Orion stared at him. "I'm not going to use Jet and Lilly's youngest daughter as bait or a weapon or anything else. They have already lost two children and would have my head if anything happened to Hunter."

"I think they would be more angered by their daughter slowly going insane, because that is what will happen if Hunter doesn't learn how to control that ability," Milo mentioned, unbothered. "I can teach her, but it might take a little time."

"You do understand the mansion is protected by the guardians, right?" Orion asked as he turned his attention back to counting the gun magazines.

"Yes, Orion, I do know some things," Milo answered, sounding a little offended. "What does that have to do with anything?"

"Milo, you're part necromancer. The sworn enemy of guardians and protectors," Orion pointed out, looking up at the man. "They're not going to welcome you with open arms. You'll be lucky if they don't toss you in the dungeons next to Roan."

A small smile crossed Milo's face as he crossed his arms over his chest. "So the good I've done doesn't matter? I'm only to be judged by my bloodline? You protectors can be very prejudiced."

"You are the grandson of—"

"Your brother is the most notorious assassin in the world," Milo pointed out. "We all have skeletons in the closet, but sometimes those skeletons have their uses. You said it yourself: nobody knows Grenich better than I do. The protectors want to defeat Set and Pyra, reduce their empire to ashes, as do I. We're going to need each other if we wish to accomplish that. I'm going with you when you leave and that's all there is to it."

Orion sighed, knowing he wouldn't be able to stop Milo from accompanying them back to the mansion. "Very well. I'll contact Jet and Lilly before we Appear back at the mansion and have them prepare a room for you."

Milo started to leave, pausing and raising a finger as he turned to face Orion again. "Just one more thing. I received word from sources late the other night. Apparently, Set managed to get his greedy talons on a vampire."

Orion scratched the back of his head, confused. "Why would he give a damn about vampires?"

"Same reason he gives a damn about rebels. Weakening the Monroes' potential allies," Milo replied. "He's going to try knee-capping the protectors before the war escalates. Set enjoys chaos, but only when he's in control of it. What's more concerning is *how* he managed to get his hands on one and when."

"You don't think he was laying a trap for the protectors?"

Milo shrugged. "You and I both know Nick Chance doesn't care about collateral damage. Set wouldn't mind taking more of the protector leaders' family. Grief can be a very dangerous distraction."

Orion straightened up, putting his hands on his hips. "Set can't cross planes and the gatekeepers would know better than to let him in."

"You really think Set does his own dirty work?"

"William mentioned he was the last goblin. Apparently some kind of disease killed his people," Orion mentioned, remembering the Sanctuary's gatekeeper. He could feel the cool fresh air flowing through the room, which made him start to worry about pollen.

"That doesn't bode well for us, Doc," Milo said, turning to leave. "All the more reason we need to get this show on the road."

Orion watched him until he disappeared down the hall. The older shape shifter sat on the bed he had slept in for the past couple days, dragging his hands down his face. A songbird chirped near his window and the wind swept through the branches of a nearby tree. Orion's mind was racing with the information he had just received. How was Set able to target the other worlds? Grenich had much control over Earth, but surely it didn't extend to the other worlds.

"Isis, I hope you haven't gotten into too much trouble in my absence, because we desperately need you," Orion spoke to himself as he stood up again and turned his attention back to the bags on the bed. He paused and looked out the window, taking a moment to admire the beauty of the Sanctuary. In the distance, he could hear a waterfall. Orion hoped one day he would be able to appreciate the serenity of the place. Whenever he visited, it seemed as though he was always troubled by matters concerning Grenich.

Maybe I should speak with the High Council about letting Roan out on temporary leave, Orion thought. It wasn't the first time he had considered his brother's offer and Orion knew it wasn't going to be the last.

~~*~*~*

Electra stepped into the training room, looking around. She soon saw Nemesis, who stood at the far end of the room. Her chin lifted slightly as she watched the young guardian, her arms crossed over her chest. They had been training every day and there wasn't a single part of Electra's body that wasn't sore. Even her brain seemed to ache with the amount of information she had crammed in it.

Electra started to walk forward, pausing when she noticed the large circle in the center of the room. The younger guardian looked up to where Nemesis stood, still as stone. Her lustrous black hair was tied back from her face, as it always was, and her earth-colored eyes never moved from Electra. The younger guardian squared her shoulders and walked into the circle, waiting.

"What do you fear, Electra?" Nemesis asked. A quiet whoosh was the only warning Electra had before a large punching bag swung down at her. She managed to drop into a forward roll and avoid getting hit. Maneuvering around the bag when it swung back, Electra looked around for any more falling hazards. She froze and gritted her teeth in frustration when she felt the flat of a cold blade against the back of her neck.

"And you're dead," Nemesis said behind her. "You're going to have to do better than that if you want to go toe-to-toe with a necromancer."

"I'm fairly certain they're not going to throw bags at me," Electra pointed out.

"No, but Set and Pyra might throw an army at you. You must never focus solely on one threat, but neither must you ignore it. You need to learn how to properly divide your awareness," Nemesis said, sliding her sword back into its scabbard. "Very rarely will you encounter a one-on-one fight in a war. There will be chaos around you and multiple enemies will come at you at once. You must learn to use that or at least counter it."

Electra turned and watched Nemesis walk over to the wall, removing two staffs. She approached the younger guardian again, tossing one staff to her. Electra caught it and held it in the proper two-handed grip. Nemesis swung hers around a couple times before grasping it in a similar grip.

"My grandmother fought Set's forces in the War of the Meadows. She lost many of her loved ones and friends in that war, including her personal protector," Nemesis began, striking out with a high blow. Electra deflected the strike and Nemesis followed through with a swing aimed at her leg, which the guardian blocked but a little less easily. The only sound in the training room was the staffs cracking together.

"I know more about him and his tactics than most guardians today," Nemesis continued, swinging her staff again. Electra blocked but Nemesis struck her with a side kick, knocking her back a few steps. Electra spun her staff once, watching Nemesis as the older guardian began to circle her.

"I know that he will try to get under your skin and will probably succeed in doing so," she continued, batting away Electra's staff when she went on the offensive.

"I'm not as sensitive as you seem to think," Electra stated, blocking a blow aimed at her leg. Their staffs cracked against each other as each struggled for the upper hand.

"I do not believe you are overly sensitive. There is a strength you inherited from your mother, but there is also vulnerability. You feel emotions more intensely than many others, but you attempt to bury the ones you deem weak. Fear, for example," Nemesis continued. Their staffs met again and they stood there. Sweat began to bead on Electra's forehead as she fought not to stumble.

"Acknowledging your fear takes away the power it has over you," Nemesis continued as Electra gritted her teeth. Nemesis swung her staff down, which caused Electra to lose her balance. The head guard hit her in the back of the legs, knocking Electra down on all fours, and then smacked her on the back with the staff. Crouching down next to the younger guardian, Nemesis leaned her head against the staff, studying Electra for a moment. Electra looked over at her, slightly out of breath, muscles quivering.

"You don't need a weapon to be strong, daughter of Passion," Nemesis began. "I can read the fear in you. You are afraid of Set and Pyra taking everything from you and you are afraid of being helpless. But you will never be able to out-brutalize them. You are a capable warrior, but you're also clever. Use your wits against the necromancer's forces as well as your physical abilities."

"He has more experience than me, they both do," Electra protested, pushing herself over so she was sitting. Nemesis had the unnerving ability to deduce what she was thinking and feeling.

"They may have more experience, but they also have more arrogance," Nemesis mentioned, rising to her feet again. "Set has been targeting those he sees as weaker than him. He will underestimate you. Do not make the same mistake."

She offered a hand to Electra, who took it and allowed the head guard to help her back to her feet. Nemesis kicked under Electra's staff, lifting it off the ground and up into her waiting hand.

"A great warrior is a wise one," Nemesis stated, moving back to the weapons wall. "I rely more on my mind than on my weapons."

Electra watched Nemesis put the staffs back up on the wall. The head guard moved over a couple sections to where the bows hung. She took two down and returned to Electra, tossing her one. The younger guardian caught it and waited as Nemesis retrieved a couple quivers of arrows. She handed one to Electra.

"I remember you being adept with a bow, almost as skilled as your grandmother," Nemesis mentioned, taking a few steps back. Electra drew an arrow from the quiver, nocked it in the bow, and let it fly. The arrow soared past Nemesis' face and embedded deep in the punching bag behind her. Nemesis twisted to look at the arrow, unbothered.

"Impressive," Nemesis complimented. "Know your strengths, Electra."

"Bows aren't very effective against modern firearms," Electra pointed out. "And believe me, Grenich has plenty of those."

"Firearms are dangerous, but they also instill a degree of overconfidence in those who rely too heavily on them,"

Nemesis said. "If I am not mistaken, your sister went into a manor of armed assassins and emerged relatively unscathed."

"I am not my twin."

"No, but you are not helpless either. Recognize your strengths and weaknesses and modify your strategies accordingly," Nemesis replied. Electra looked over at the enigmatic guard, who watched her.

"If the protectors are victorious, what do you think will happen to the experiments they release?" she asked. Nemesis shrugged as she picked up her quiver of arrows, sliding it over her shoulder.

"I imagine they will do what shape shifters do every day. Make a life, survive day-to-day," Nemesis responded, pushing one of the punching bags so it swung back and forth. Electra nocked another arrow in her bow, easily hitting the moving target.

"You think the High Council will be fine with all those experiments on the loose?" Electra asked. "The only reason they released my sister and Jack was because they might be our best chance against Grenich."

Nemesis put a hand on Electra's wrist, making her lower the bow. Electra looked over at the head guard, who was again giving her a scrutinizing look. The sunlight glistened in her hair and highlighted the gleam in her flesh.

"I know you don't hold a high opinion of the High Council and I don't always disagree with such feelings, but they are not going to imprison shape shifters without good reason," Nemesis said, looking back to the still swinging target. She nocked an arrow to her own bow and let it soar. It pierced just above Electra's arrow.

"Besides, I do not think the fight against Grenich will end any time soon," Nemesis continued. "I believe it will take many years to fight against Set and his influence. And I think before this fight is over, the guardians will have to take a more active role."

Electra watched as she nocked another arrow in her

bow and shot it at the target. It pierced the bag right next to the first arrow. Nemesis lowered her bow, never looking away from the target.

"Is that why you agreed to train me?" Electra asked, sweeping a sweaty strand of hair out of her face.

"I agreed because I know you will have an active role in this war, likely without permission from the High Council. I would rather you at least have a fighting chance instead of running in blind," Nemesis replied. "And like your mother, I believe guardians need to make their own decisions."

"Didn't really take you for a progressive," Electra mentioned. Nemesis shrugged.

"I am the Head Guard of the Meadows, a station the women of my family have always held. It is not my place to make decisions for others."

Electra let another arrow fly. It pierced the small space directly between Nemesis' two arrows.

~~*~*~*

Sly swirled the whisky in her stout glass, pausing to sip the tawny-colored liquid. She looked up at the fully lit bar area of the rebel Lair. Alpha was sitting next to her, resting her elbows on the bar. She had parted with her ordinary black attire and wore an aqua blue tank top, exposing the elaborate and colorful tattoos of animals running up both her arms. There was a new flock of small doves on her left shoulder in memory of those lost in the massacre. Alpha had always seen her skin as a canvas on which to paint beautiful works of art. Wylie and Amber were behind the bar, preparing for the night. The sun was setting, casting orange rays through the large window at the end of the bar.

"This place is nowhere near as interesting in the daytime hours," Sly mentioned, resting her glass against her temple. She rubbed her sore jaw with her free hand, which was sporting a good-sized bruise. The wet work team had been even tougher to subdue than she had anticipated. Sly had expected some highly-trained ex-military types. What she hadn't anticipated was people — or shape shifters — who seemed incapable of feeling pain, which made them more difficult to deal with. They also seemed to pop out of nowhere and since they had no scent, it was difficult to track them. They had attacked shortly after Sly and the others left the bank, nearly running them off the road. Only the experiments had been unbothered by them, taking them out with the frightening ease they all seemed to possess.

"Business has been slow as of late. Apparently, a brutal massacre scares most people away. Go figure," Alpha grumbled, grabbing her own glass and downing the whiskey. She motioned for Amber to refill the glass, which the skilled bartender promptly did.

"I'm sure your women and men still bring in plenty of customers," Sly mentioned suggestively. The temperature in the Lair was cooler than she had ever experienced. It got warmer when there were crowds. Sometimes it was downright sweltering.

"There is always a market on desire," Alpha agreed with a wicked smile.

"Speaking of rebels, any word from the other clubs?"

"Jet and Lilly are going to have a lot more rebel allies. Set fucked with the wrong group of shape shifters. I've been getting calls from rebel leaders all over the country who want to know when the raid on Grenich is going down."

Sly smiled, which turned into a grimace. "Rebels are always great in a tight spot. An assassin is a little better, but you always need to have your guard up around them."

Alpha looked over at her lover. "So you mentioned going on a heist?"

Sly sipped the whisky. "Isis wanted to get her hands on the contents of a safe deposit box Grenich was keeping.

That woman is terrifyingly good at pretty much everything, but she has knack for violence in particular."

"Good thing she's on your side."

"Maybe. Kinda makes me worried about what else Set has up his sleeve," Sly said, glancing over at the bartenders.

"What was in the box?"

Sly laughed humorlessly. "A flash drive that is pretty much useless to us. The encryption on the drive is unlike anything found on Earth."

Alpha grinned. "That must be driving you up the wall."

"Guardians, it's *got* to be something interesting for that level of encryption," Sly agreed, turning her glass on the bar.

"Do you want me to send over one of our techies, perhaps a hacker? They're pretty good at unbreakable encryption," the rebel leader offered. Sly turned her attention to Alpha.

"Trust me, Alpha, even *your* hackers couldn't break this thing."

Alpha shrugged. "The offer stands."

Sly sipped her whisky, shaking her head. "I don't know what's more unnerving. The experiments or the efficiency Grenich has cleaning up after them."

Alpha raised her eyebrows and Sly could tell she understood what she was referencing. There had been no news reports of a theft at the bank, indicating Grenich hadn't reported the contents of the box as stolen. A teller and a guard knocked out and bound should have raised some red flags, but Sly wouldn't be surprised if none of the employees noticed anything amiss. The entire bank had a very strange atmosphere, which Jade had also noticed. It was more than everyday drudgery and people loathing their jobs. The employees in the bank had been nearly lifeless, going through the motions and almost never looking up from their computers. The financial adviser they met with was one of the most normal people in that bank and even his responses were off. It took him longer than usual to answer simple questions, for which he needed his computer. *Everything was muted and gray, even the humans,* was how Sly had described it to the others. Thinking back on it, Sly felt a tremor creep down her spine and she sipped her whisky, trying to push the thought of the bank out of her mind.

~~*~*~*

Isis was stretched out on the window seat in the library. It was late at night and most of the other shape shifters were asleep. She was wearing her shiny black plain clothes, made from the same material as her catsuit. The windows were open, allowing the pleasant warm spring air inside. Isis had one knee curved up and her other leg straight out in front of her. She rested her wrist on her upraised knee and in her hand, Isis held the flash drive. Turning it around and around in a slow methodical motion, she examined it. To the outside observer, she would have appeared hypnotized by the small device. In reality, she was fully alert to her surroundings, as she always was. Looking over at her free hand, Isis flexed her fingers a few times. She was wondering what else she could do. *What if I'm the Key he's looking for?* Isis put the thought out of her mind. She didn't want to be the Key, didn't even want to entertain the notion. It was a death sentence. No, Jack or the other possibility was more likely to be the mythical Key Set and Pyra were hunting for.

The team had done well and they hadn't suffered any casualties, which was a relief. Isis had been concerned at least a couple shape shifters might get killed, but thankfully that hadn't happened. The bank was a very strange place. It felt like a Grenich simulation, but off the grounds of the corporation. The other shape shifters had noticed something unusual about the bank too, but couldn't put what it was into words. Isis was still trying to figure out why the environment was so strange. Humans did tend to become rather blank-faced and robotic after being exposed to Grenich for a while. It was a strange phenomenon and one she had only seen in the laboratory. There hadn't been many humans working there, they were too fragile a species, but the few she encountered had a similar demeanor to the employees in the bank. Was Set starting to experiment off the facility grounds?

Isis stopped turning the flash drive in her hand and tapped it against her knee, unconsciously running a finger up her chest where her clothing hid her only scar. She had no memory of receiving it, but the length indicated it was a fairly severe wound. It would have been fatal, even to an experiment. Her attention remained fixed on the flash drive. When the protectors found the encryption was unbreakable, she had borrowed it to examine the device. It was fairly ordinary, though it was obviously manufactured in Grenich. The corporation's symbol was etched near the top on one side. The amount of data it could hold would be astronomical, greater than anything the normals had seen.

"You're still awake?"

Isis looked over to the doorway where Shae was. She looked tired — the protector had confided to Isis some time ago that she suffered the occasional bout of insomnia. Judging from her appearance, Isis assumed she was experiencing it now.

"I don't sleep," Isis reminded her. Realization dawned on Shae and she crossed the library, sitting across from Isis. She gestured at the flash drive.

"Have you cracked it yet?"

"Why would I intentionally damage it?"

Shae's shoulders dropped a little. "I meant, have you figured out how to decode the encryption?"

"Grenich encryption is beyond my skills. However,

what is on this drive is unimportant to me. It is to be used as leverage in case the fight doesn't go our way."

"But if there's information on the experimentations and missions, couldn't that be used to destroy Grenich?"

Isis shrugged. "It would be a last resort. Exposing Grenich means exposing shape shifters. Most humans aren't even aware shape shifters exist. Why would they care about what Grenich does to them? Most humans aren't concerned about what happens to other humans, much less other species."

Shae looked out the window. "You have a very bleak view of humanity."

"I hold no opinion on it. I merely observe," Isis replied, looking over at Shae. "When I was a normal, did I have an opinion on humanity?"

Shae snickered. "Yes, you certainly did. It was a rather cynical one."

Isis frowned, puzzled at the nostalgia in Shae's voice. She followed her gaze out the window, observing the peaceful night. Normals were very strange creatures and Isis questioned whether she would ever understand them.

CHAPTER TWELVE

Jet paced up and down the main hall of Hecate's castle, once again waiting on Passion. His twin sister, Raven, and Steve sat at the long table in the middle of the hall, as did Hecate herself. Hecate was paging through a book, paying no attention to the agitated leader. Jet began to rub his palms together, his mind racing. It had been difficult to find the energy to shave and put on a suit, but he had done so. He really didn't feel up to diplomatic missions, but knew it was his duty.

"Hecate?" Steve waited until Hecate looked over at him. "The Magic Orders are related to the guardians, aren't they?"

"Some are," Hecate answered. "After the War of the Meadows, some of our people could no longer find peace in our world. A land was created for them and some of the members of the Magic Orders are their descendants. They are no longer guardians, but they do retain some forms of magic."

"They also have the most rigid hierarchy known to any of the races," Jet commented, looking over when he heard the soft click of shoes. *Oh thank the guardians, she's wearing shoes,* he thought. Passion entered the main hall and Jet couldn't help but stare. She was wearing a tastefully cut dress, bright red with gold inlay. Her hair had been styled neatly, framing her face perfectly. A silver circlet sat on her brow, marking her as a guardian of the royal line. Her eyes were a beautiful shade of emerald green and her skin glimmered in the morning light. A simple gold necklace sat at her throat with a small ruby in the center. Passion looked every inch the royal guardian she was.

"I apologize if I'm late," Passion said as she approached Jet, fixing her dress. "I couldn't find a proper dress. Well, I needed Artemis' help figuring out what to wear. My mother has always known more about proper decorum and dress than I have. Also, the hair took some time and then I had to dig this damn circlet out."

Raven shook her head and hid a smile behind her hand. She was dressed in a blue pantsuit and looked very professional. Raven's usual job was as a covert operative and she was very quiet by nature. Passion approached her and kissed her cheek in greeting, moving over to Steve to greet him as well.

"You look lovely, Passion," Hecate complimented when Passion turned back to her.

"I feel like a primped show dog," Passion replied, kissing Hecate on the cheek. "But thank you for the kind words. We're off to see Ifan and Meirionwen, correct?"

Jet smiled and offered his elbow, which she accepted. "How long did you have to practice those names?"

Passion chuckled as the group followed Hecate out of the hall and toward the stairs. "I'll never tell."

They entered the hall of doors and Hecate moved over to the one gold door near the front of the hall. She slid the key into the lock and turned it. She knocked three times and the knob turned, the door opening inward. Jet peered inside, noticing a number of tall people in different colored robes. Some of them looked ageless, while others appeared quite ancient. A few wore laurels on their heads. There was a cold feeling due to the towering white walls in the hall, which seemed to stretch on forever. There seemed to be an almost hazy quality to the scene before them.

"Good luck," Hecate stated as Jet passed by. He nodded his gratitude before stepping into the realm. Passion let go of Jet's elbow and moved forward, standing at the edge of the steps. Jet looked back to the man who had opened the door. He was on the larger side and had his nose buried in a massive tome. The gatekeeper barely spared them a second glance.

"You are the ones with an audience with the lord and lady?"

Jet turned his attention to the small voice, noticing the mousy man standing at the foot of the steps leading up to the gate. He was wearing off-white robes and was holding his hands clasped in front of him. Jet cleared his throat and moved to stand next to Passion.

"We are," he said. The man glanced over at him with a trace of disdain and turned his attention back to Passion. She looked at Jet and then to the man.

"They are," she responded and the man smiled.

"Right this way, please," he said, turning on the balls of his feet and starting down the long hallway. Passion glanced over at Jet and shrugged. He gestured to follow and then motioned for Steve and Raven to follow them. It wasn't a good start to the diplomatic mission and Jet wasn't sure what had happened. The Magic Orders were notoriously isolated, but everything he read indicated their culture and philosophies were similar to the guardians.

They were led to a small room connected to what Jet assumed was their meeting room. Their guide gestured toward a bench.

"Would you like me to show your servants to the servants' space?" the man asked Passion, causing them to all stare at him.

"Excuse me, sir, these are not my servants," Passion began and Jet could hear the offense clear in her voice. "You are addressing one of the leaders of the protectors,

Jet Monroe, whose family has been loyal to the guardians before your race even *existed*. I am here as a formality because the guardians respect your customs. However I will not sit here and let you disrespect my friends—"

"Okay, Passion, let's not alienate the Magic Orders before we even get started," Jet whispered under his breath. He glanced back to Raven, who looked quite annoyed at being called a servant. Steve appeared unbothered as he observed the people around them. Jet looked around at them, noticing none of the passersby even acknowledged the presence of the diplomatic group.

"I apologize, my lady. I did not mean to cause offense," the man stuttered, nervous. Passion waved him away, watching as he scurried off before turning back to Jet.

"I can tolerate many things; bigotry is not one of them," she stated, looking around. "What is with all the white and gray? The Pearl Castle has more color than this. I feel like I'm in some kind of elaborately designed glacier."

Jet followed her gaze up to the ceiling high above them. She was right. The entire decorating scheme revolved around shades of gray and white, with the occasional gold flourish. It was a very cold place and the architecture reminded Jet of old monasteries. There were arches everywhere. Jet frowned when he noticed something missing.

"Where is the art?"

"Pardon?"

"I see a few banners and the coat of arms at the end of the hall there, but no paintings or tapestries. Everything I read indicated they were just like the other supernatural races in regards to the arts," Jet explained, looking up when the doors opened to the room they were sitting near. The group of four rose, patiently waiting. A young man in dark purple robes stepped out from the room.

"Lady Passion, it is an honor to make your acquaintance," he said, bowing his head. "Allow me to introduce myself. I am Gawain, son of Ifan. We will hear your protector's proposal now."

The man leaned to the side a little, his expression becoming less cordial. "I'm afraid his companions will have to stay out here. We only agreed to listen to the protector leader and the guardian who accompanied him."

Jet could picture Passion's eyes turning bright red and put a pacifying hand on her elbow when her body went rigid. He removed it just as swiftly when he saw the look of disapproval that crossed Gawain's features. Jet turned back to Raven and Steve.

"Do you mind waiting until we're done?" he asked. The two protectors exchanged a concerned look.

"Jet, is that wise?" Steve asked.

"What if there's trouble?" Raven added, nodding over at Gawain. "We don't know them. This is not a good idea."

"Trust me, the leaders of the Magic Orders aren't going to make an attempt on our lives. Not with Passion here," Jet reassured them.

Steve looked unconvinced, but acquiesced. He sat back down, as did Raven, who still looked concerned. Jet let out a breath and turned back to Gawain and Passion.

"Lead the way," Jet said.

"If you can give us one minute," Passion requested. Gawain stepped away to give them their privacy. Passion smiled and turned to Jet, her smile disappearing immediately.

"How recent is your information on the Magic Orders?" Passion whispered, glancing over her shoulder to make sure Gawain was out of earshot. Jet shrugged, adjusting the cuff of his suit. Briefly, the memory of Remington teaching him how to affix a cufflink properly flashed in his mind.

"I'm not sure. Why?" he asked.

"I was doing a little research in the Meadows yesterday. Ifan and Meirionwen had an older daughter, Olwen. She was their original heir, but left more than twenty years ago. No reason was given — none that the guardians know of — but from what I read, the subject is a *very* sensitive one in the Magic Orders. Her name is no longer spoken and has been stricken from the family trees," Passion paused, nodding up toward a large banner. "I haven't seen a trace of her symbol anywhere in the castle. So I would avoid using that name, if I were you."

"Thank you, Passion. I wasn't planning on asking after any missing family members, but it is good to know all the same," Jet said, sharing a smile with his friend before nodding to Gawain when he looked over to them. The young-looking man gestured for them to follow. Gawain led them into a small room where two short chairs sat across from a long table. Behind the table, sitting in tall decorated chairs, were Ifan and Meirionwen along with another woman Jet didn't recognize. Gawain took his spot at the table. Behind each of the leaders stood a person of the opposite sex dressed in much plainer clothing, whom Jet recognized as their nagas. Each member of the Magic Orders grew up with their own naga who served them as mentor, protector, and confidant. Oddly, there was no naga behind the woman Jet didn't recognize, which was strange. *Unless he was killed,* Jet thought, remembering that nagas were irreplaceable.

"Lady Passion, Mr. Monroe, welcome to the Magic Orders," the man greeted. "I am Ifan, to my left is my wife, Meirionwen. You have met Gawain and to his right is his wife, Ghislaine."

"Thank you for having us," Jet replied. He noticed Ghislaine looking at Passion in a way that wasn't complimentary. Ghislaine wore elegant robes of soft gold, which seemed to enhance her paleness. She had dark hair and cold brown eyes. If Passion saw the look, she didn't comment.

"I understand you are interested in renewing an alliance," Ifan continued.

"Yes, I am sure your diplomats told you about the Grenich Corporation and what they're doing to my people," Jet began. "Grenich is run by Set, who used to go by the name Chaos."

"From what we understand, in renewing the old alliance, you are asking us to take part in an Earth conflict," Ifan commented, unbothered by the revelation. "Which goes against the laws of the Magic Orders."

"I fully understand that and I do not ask for the alliance lightly. My wife and co-leader, Lilly, and I believe if we ignore this threat, Grenich will spread to the other realms. We have evidence that Set can cause damage in different worlds."

"How is that possible?" Meirionwen asked. She wore a gauzy purple dress with gold inlay. Like her husband, a gold circlet sat on her brow, but hers had a pearl that rested in the middle of her forehead.

"Again, we are not certain. But he managed to decimate the vampire race and wiped out the goblins in the Seelie Court," Jet answered. "All we ask is that you come to the summit at the end of the month. Then we can discuss the level of involvement the Magic Orders would be comfortable with."

"Where will this summit take place?"

"It is scheduled to take place at the mansion on Earth," Jet responded. Ifan and Meirionwen exchanged a quick look, which made Jet a little uneasy. *Uh oh,* he thought, wondering if he should have scheduled the summit in the Meadows.

"The guardians shall also take part in this summit," Passion added. "Adonia and Aneurin are both going to be there. We believe this fight belongs to all of us, not just Earth-dwelling peoples."

The heads of the Magic Orders looked a little more reassured at Passion's statement. Jet glanced at Gawain, who hadn't moved since taking his seat. He sat rigidly, watching the proceedings. The nagas remained silent spectators in the background.

"May we have some time to discuss your proposal?" Ifan requested.

"Of course."

Ifan offered his thanks as he stood from his chair, offering his hand to his wife. She laid her hand atop his offered fist and rose. Jet noticed she was taller than Ifan. Gawain and Ghislaine mirrored the two leaders as they rose from their seats. The four proceeded out the door opposite the one Passion and Jet had entered through. They were followed by their nagas and the last one shut the large door behind them. Jet turned to Passion.

"I assume we're meant to wait here," Jet mentioned, looking around the small room. Their chairs were lower than the rulers of the Magic Orders on the other side of the table. The walls were bare and the same cold shades of gray and white surrounded them.

"It would appear so," Passion replied, searching his face. "How have you been, my friend? You look weary and Lilly told me you have been having trouble sleeping."

Jet looked down to his shoes. "One day at a time, it has become my new mantra. Just one day at a time."

"The loss of Brindy and Devlin weighs heavy on my heart as well. I would give anything to hear their voices, their laughter, just one more time," Passion replied, offering him a sympathetic smile. "I wish I could do more for you and Lilly. Grief is a profound experience, one none of us can avoid."

Jet swallowed. "The thought of their final moments haunts my sleep, what little I get. Were they scared? Were they in pain? I should have been stricter about going out. Guardians, we knew Grenich was going to retaliate. Why did I let them go out, Passion?"

"You could not have prevented them from living their lives, even if you'd have wanted to," Passion responded, reaching over and giving his hand a gentle squeeze. "Protectors lead dangerous lives, ones filled with tragedy.

I'm thankful I was not born the guardian of grief."

Jet looked up to the ceiling, letting out a soft laugh. "There's an Artemis joke in there somewhere, but I just can't quite think of it."

Passion playfully punched his shoulder, looking over to the door. "I wonder how long they'll deliberate your request. I know they have to put on a show, but I only have so much patience and this place is dull. And this circlet is cold and it tugs on my hair."

"I never thought members of the Magic Orders would be so aloof toward shape shifters," Jet mentioned. Passion played with the hem of one of her red bell sleeves.

"I don't know that much about them, but if they're descended from guardians, their aloofness doesn't surprise me in the slightest."

Jet glanced back at her again. "I've never been mistaken for a servant by the guardians, not even the more old fashioned ones."

Passion shrugged and rested her head on the back of her hand. "This is the first time I've met sorcerers and sorceresses. I'm not impressed."

"If I'm not mistaken, Ghislaine is still an enchantress," Jet pointed out. "The insignia on her sleeves were different from Ifan's, Meirionwen's, and Gawain's. Also, the stone in her ring was blue whereas the others had green stones."

"Look at you, detective Monroe," Passion teased with a smile. Jet chuckled, remembering his childhood when he was able to wow the guardians with his perceptiveness. He had always been able to pick up on small details others disregarded.

Jet lost track of time as he and Passion continued talking. The sound of the doorknob turning made them both stand up. Ghislaine stepped through the door, smiling at them. *Well, that is one of the most unconvincing smiles I've ever seen,* Jet thought, recognizing the mock civility in the gesture. Ghislaine wasn't even attempting to look in his direction.

"I'm afraid we are going to have to decline your request," Ghislaine told Passion. Jet felt his heart sink. The coldness of their surroundings seemed to seep into his skin and settle in his bones.

"Are you kidding?" Passion said, obviously not believing the response. "Do you mind explaining *why*?"

"Our laws are very clear. We are to put the Orders first. Interfering in any Earth matters or conflicts is a violation of that code. There is no gateway to our realm on Earth and for good reason."

"There would be no Magic Orders if there weren't a Meadows," Passion countered, unable to keep the anger out of her voice. "Your peaceful way of life is thanks to the guardians. If we fall, so does your world."

"We are well aware of that and should the necromancers threaten the Meadows, we are willing to lend our aid," Ghislaine replied. "But we cannot help the shape shifters."

Passion's mouth opened and closed a few times, like a fish trapped on dry land. Jet stepped forward, standing next to Passion. He didn't miss the exasperated look that flashed across Ghislaine's face. She couldn't believe the gall of a protector standing next to a guardian, his superior. Jet remembered when he had wed Lilly, the same day they had accepted the role of the leaders of the protectors. The Magic Orders had been the only group to not send an ambassador to the ceremony.

"May I please have a word with Ifan and Meirionwen in private?" he requested. Ghislaine turned toward him, crossing her arms over her chest.

"No, you may not. If I might be so bold, perhaps it is not right to ask others to sacrifice their lives for *your*," she looked back to Passion, who stared at her, "past indiscretions."

Jet felt his jaw drop open and was sure Passion was wearing a similar expression.

"*Excuse me*? What do my past indiscretions," Passion

said, making quote marks around the phrasing the enchantress used, "have to do with anything?"

"From what we understand about the situation and its cause, Set and Pyra are consumed with a desire to find a key spoken of in necromancer prophecy. Your daughter might be this key and is living under the Monroes' roof, along with another shape shifter who also might be the key. Yet you do nothing." Ghislaine turned up her nose. "Allowing sentimentality to cloud your judgment is not the mark of a good ruler."

Anger was radiating off of Passion. Jet blinked a couple times, not believing his ears. He was struggling to find the words.

"And what would you have us do? Kill two shape shifters, who have sought sanctuary with us?" Jet asked, shaking his head. "I am not an executioner."

"There are plenty of other shape shifters in the world. Ones who haven't been modified to be cold-blooded killers," Ghislaine replied. Jet thought he would be ill at the woman's nonchalant callousness. He turned his eyes to Passion, whose fists were clenching and unclenching at her sides.

"Pardon my language, but you have some damn nerve," Passion commented. Ghislaine smiled and brushed a lock of hair behind her ear.

"It was merely an observation, my lady. I meant no offense," Ghislaine mentioned, turning her attention to Jet. "Out of curiosity, how many lives have those two *innocent* shape shifters taken?"

Jet tried to remain neutral, but the young enchantress was really testing his patience. Still, her inquiry was one he would hear again. Truth be told, Jet had no idea how much damage the experiments had done during their time in the Grenich Corporation. Part of him didn't want to know. The enchantress smiled again, a strange almost feral look.

"We do hope you emerge victorious from this battle and regret we could not do more to help you," she said before she turned and went back to the door. When the door shut again, Jet dropped back down in the chair and ran his hands over his face.

"I've failed," he whispered, a sense of despondency overcoming him. Jet glanced over his shoulder, noticing Passion was clenching her fists so tightly they were white and shaking. She stormed across the room and the only thing that stopped her from charging through the door was Jet putting his body between it and her.

"Get out of my way, Jet," she warned. Jet looked at her for a moment. He was certain if given the chance, Passion would kick the door down. Her eyes weren't red yet, but he could see glints of scarlet starting to appear in her irises.

"Passion, no. She's not worth it," Jet said. "The last thing we need is another war on our hands. Just let it go, please. For Lilly and me."

Passion stared at him for a moment, letting out a breath, her shoulders slumping.

"I'm really sick and tired of taking the high road," Passion grumbled, adjusting the circlet on her head. *Can't say I particularly disagree,* Jet thought as he gestured to the door across the way. Their footsteps echoed on the smooth ground.

"I know," he agreed, sympathetically.

"When I become queen of the guardian women, guess what door is getting bricked over," Passion said as she opened the door and followed Jet out. He chuckled, knowing it was an empty threat. Jet glanced over to the bench where they left Steve and Raven. It was empty. Turning his attention to the balcony overlooking the main part of the enormous castle, he noticed the two protectors leaning down on the railing.

"What's got your attention?" Jet asked as he approached them. Steve's brow was furrowed and he tipped his chin up, gesturing to the crowd below them.

"I've been here since you went in to meet with the leaders, a little more than an hour ago," Steve started. "In that entire time, I haven't seen one person smile, not even a child. In a crowd this large and in that span of time, there is usually an assortment of facial expressions. I should have seen a few smiles."

Jet looked down to the sea of rich colors below, scanning the crowd. Sure enough, none of them were smiling. Not even the nagas, dressed more plainly than their charges. The protector leader squinted as he continued studying the crowd. Steve was right — not even the children smiled. That was ... odd.

"The Magic Orders are a very wise and ancient race. They value knowledge above all else and are known to be quite studious," Jet said. "Perhaps they're just not inclined to smile."

"They are not so different from the guardians and yet the guardians display a multitude of emotions," Steve countered. Jet looked back to the crowd milling about below them. Most of the richly dressed individuals were focused on whatever scroll or parchment they held. Some carried books in front of them.

"He's right, Jet," Raven stated from where she stood, a few feet away. "Something about this entire place just doesn't feel right."

They stood at the balcony for a few minutes, watching the crowd.

"Come, we need to return home," Jet finally said. Steve glanced at him and Jet could tell he wanted to stay. Steve was a great detective, partly because he never gave up. If something felt off, he was driven to figure out what was wrong. Jet's twin sister was similar, which made her an excellent field operative. Jet patted Steve's shoulder and turned to make his way back down the hall. Passion fell into step next to him.

Raven quickened her pace so she was walking on Jet's other side. "How did it go?"

"They won't help us. I couldn't even convince them to attend the summit."

"What?" Raven couldn't hide the shock in her voice.

"Because Jet won't execute Isis and Jack, he is somehow the villain in their warped little minds," Passion explained, not bothering to conceal her bitterness. Raven looked over at her brother. Behind them, Jet could hear Steve's quick footsteps.

"I think there was more to it than that," Jet commented as they turned down another hall. "They don't take part in Earth conflicts."

"So the summit is going to be the protectors, the rebels, the guardians, the lycanthropes, and the Seelie Court? Will they be enough?" Raven asked.

"They'll have to be," Jet replied as they reached the gate. He was wondering how to convince the two supernatural races who had agreed to attend the meeting to help them in their fight. It wouldn't be easy and Jet questioned whether or not he and Lilly could do it.

~~*~*~*

Night fell in the Meadows and most of the guardians turned in for the evening, except for the guardians who watched over the elements of night. Artemis sat across from Adonia's desk, her royal blue gown sparkling in the dusky light. She watched her mother page through an ancient book on the War of the Meadows, her long red hair loosely tied back from her face. They were awaiting a visitor and both looked over to the door when they heard knocking.

"Come in," Adonia called. The door opened and Hecate walked in. The gold inlay of her gown caught the light and shimmered. She sat next to Artemis, smiling in greeting to both guardians.

"Hecate, welcome," Adonia greeted, closing the old book in front of her. "You sent word requesting a meeting."

"I did," Hecate said, interlacing her fingers. "I'm sure you've heard that the Magic Orders rejected Jet's request about the summit."

"We did," Adonia replied, folding her hands in front of her. "That is very disappointing. I had hoped they would show more compassion and at least hear the protectors out."

"That's the thing. The Magic Orders have always been isolated and preferred that way of life, but they have never turned down a request for aid from the guardians and by extension, the protectors," Hecate explained.

"According to our legends, there were a few sorcerers and sorceresses in the War of the Meadows who fought valiantly," Artemis mentioned. "Part of our victory was thanks to their bravery and skill."

"Yes, I was just reading about that," Adonia agreed. "So why do you think they became more isolated to the point of turning away those in need?"

Hecate leaned forward a little. "A few years before Electra and Isis were born, there was a bit of upheaval in the Magic Orders. We don't know what happened, but the eldest daughter and heir of Ifan and Meirionwen suddenly and inexplicably left the Orders in the middle of her training. She hasn't been spoken of since and her name has almost become taboo in their world. I know about as much as you do about the incident — which is to say, nothing for certain. However, there were some rather ... unsettling rumors."

"There always are," Artemis said and Hecate nodded in agreement.

"Still, Olwen remains the only enchantress to ever leave the Magic Orders before achieving the rank of sorceress without a word of explanation."

"Do you think she was killed?" Adonia asked.

"No, no, nothing like that," Hecate said with a shake of her head. "Credible reports from protectors indicate she is now living on Earth with her naga. But ... it is interesting to note that her younger brother, Gawain, was once betrothed to another woman named Carys. She died about a year before Olwen left. Apparently, she and Olwen were rather close. Olwen even chose the young woman's naga as her own so he could stay in the Magic Orders. Before she left, Olwen was making quite a lot of noise about Carys having been poisoned."

"Was there any truth to the rumors?" Artemis asked, leaning over the arm of her chair, intrigued. She didn't know much about the Magic Orders, but had heard about the upheaval. Almost all guardians had. Olwen, though she could be standoffish, was a highly respected woman who was well-known to many guardians. She had the makings of a great sorceress and a great leader.

"I don't know. Investigators in the Magic Orders insist there wasn't and Carys died of a mysterious illness, which had begun to crop up around the same time," Hecate replied. "However, this has made me think about the deaths in the Seelie Court and in the realm of vampires. Something is going on and I should have seen it earlier."

"What is your conclusion?" Adonia asked.

"I believe the protectors are right in thinking Set has found a way into the other realms," Hecate explained. "It's impossible and I have no idea how he is doing it, but he has found a way in somehow."

Artemis exchanged a look of concern with Adonia. She could tell her mother felt the same uneasiness Artemis was feeling. If Set and Pyra had found a way into other worlds, they could potentially gain access to the Meadows.

"You are certain?" Adonia asked and Hecate shrugged.

"I can't think of any other explanation. There are just too many inexplicable factors, including at least two mysterious illnesses," Hecate stated.

Adonia was quiet for a moment. "There is the question of why they would choose to act so slowly. More than thirty years have passed since that incident in the Magic Orders. There's also the question of why they would wipe out vampires, but not the entirety of the Seelie Court. If they're just trying to rob Jet and Lilly of allies, they are doing it in a very peculiar way."

"Perhaps their goal is fear and intimidation," Artemis suggested. "Or perhaps Set just wants to create chaos."

Adonia folded her hands in front of her. "I fear it is more than that. The Magic Orders refusal to help means one less ally for Jet and Lilly. A powerful one."

A thoughtful look crossed Hecate's face. "It is not just the protectors who lost a powerful ally. I believe we have lost one as well."

Artemis leaned back in her chair, running her fingers over the arm. Passion had been so angry when she returned. Artemis was unable to understand what had happened and even Electra had difficulty deciphering the bits and pieces Passion was able to growl about. What they had both heard was the enchantress had suggested killing Isis and Jack to solve the Grenich problem. It had disturbed Artemis that the suggestion had been made so flippantly by a high-ranking member of the Magic Orders.

"Perhaps I'm leaping to conclusions, but is it possible Set has a plant in the Magic Orders?" Artemis asked. The question had been on her mind all day and she wasn't sure how to ask it. A non-guardian crossing into different worlds was impossible, yet there were just too many coincidences to ignore.

Hecate was quiet for a moment, thinking over the question. "At one time, I would have said absolutely not. As I mentioned earlier, now I'm not so sure."

Adonia leaned back in her chair. "If that is the case, then I fear we are losing this war before we even begin fighting."

~~*~*~*

Jet sat at his desk, looking at the empty couch in the center of his study. It had been Brindy's favorite place to read. When her parents were working late, she often stretched out on the couch with her nose buried in a classic novel. Looking down at the papers in front of him, his eyes once again slid over to the couch. It remained empty.

Jet closed his eyes and leaned back, turning his face up to the ceiling. The Four had been in a couple hours earlier to hear about his meeting with the leaders of the Magic Orders. *I wonder if it would have helped had Lilly been there,* Jet thought as he rested his hands on top of his head. He knew it wouldn't have mattered. The Magic Orders seemed rather cold toward protectors and probably shape shifters in general. Jet's brow furrowed as his mind drifted back to Steve's observation. The more he thought about it, the more it bothered him. He knew his twin sister felt the same way. Raven had been in more than enough dicey situations to know when something was off.

Jet opened his eyes and looked toward the door when he heard a soft creak. Hunter stood in the entrance to the study, her backpack still slung over one shoulder. She looked less burdened than she had when she left, but Jet could still see the grief in her eyes and in the way she held herself. She was wearing a green shirt and black pants, which seemed even darker in the soft lighting of the study. Hunter glanced at the couch briefly before looking at Jet.

"The lighting in here still sucks, I see," she commented. Jet stood up and made his way across the study, embracing his youngest. Hunter returned the embrace.

"I missed you," Jet whispered and felt her nod against him.

"You'll feel differently after a few days," she replied as they stepped out of the embrace and Jet laughed. "Where's Mom?"

"In the kitchen, making some tea. It's looking like it will be a late night," he answered, leaning against the arm of the couch. "How was the Sanctuary?"

Hunter shrugged, looking about the room. "Nice, I guess. Have you ever been there?"

"No, I haven't, though your mother has been, ages ago," Jet responded. "She told me it is a little like the Meadows."

"Yeah, I'd say it has more in common with Earth. But I

didn't really have a chance to wander around much," Hunter said, swallowing and shifting her weight. "Look, Dad—"

"Orion already told us about Milo," Jet interrupted, smiling at the look Hunter gave him. "Nobody gets in the mansion without our express permission, though we might want to keep our guest a secret for the time being."

"That shouldn't be a problem," Hunter replied, rubbing the side of her neck. Jet watched her for a moment. Just then, the door to the study opened and Lilly entered with two mugs of tea. Her eyes lit up when she saw Hunter and their youngest beamed at her mother. Jet took mugs Lilly held so she could embrace her daughter.

"When did you get back?" Lilly asked, running her fingers through Hunter's short hair.

"Just now," Hunter replied. "Dad and I were just talking about Milo."

"Ah," Lilly said with a knowing smile.

"What is your opinion of him?" Jet asked.

Hunter shrugged. "He can be rather grim at times, but he seems legit. I'm not exactly an expert on profiling, but I do believe Grenich wants Milo dead and he seems to genuinely want that place dismantled."

"He was the one who got Jack and Isis out of the laboratory, right?" Lilly asked as Jet sipped the hot tea.

"Yeah," Hunter answered. "Apparently at great risk to himself. He was at death's door the first time we met."

"How is he now?" Jet asked, wondering if he'd need to call on any of their doctors. He wasn't sure any of them would know the first thing about treating a necromancer.

"Mostly recovered," Hunter said, shifting her weight. "Mom, Dad, there's something else you should know. That night the Lair was attacked, I was bitten."

Jet remembered how bloodied Hunter had been. Her shoulder had been so torn up; he worried about how long it would take to heal her. Hunter pulled the sleeve of her shirt down and gestured at the shoulder. Both Jet and Lilly moved closer to get a better look at what she was indicating. Jet's eyes widened when he saw the faint line circling her shoulder.

"Since that night, I've been having these flashes," Hunter explained as Lilly gently ran her fingers over the scar. "I can see things, places, which aren't there. Milo says it's because I'm connected to Nick Chance. He can explain it better than I can, but he's going to teach me how to control it. He says I can help and I want to do it. If I can help in any way, I want to."

Jet looked at her, hesitant to let her get involved. Grenich had already stolen two children from him and he was uneasy at the idea of losing another one. Glancing over at Lilly, he could see a similar hesitance in her dark blue eyes. He turned his attention back to his daughter.

The determination in Hunter's blue-green eyes, so similar to his, made Jet realize he could not stop her. If Hunter wanted to help, she would. *She inherited the Monroe stubbornness,* Velvet had often pointed out when Hunter was growing up. Her twin brother, Cassidy, was the exact same way.

"Okay," Jet finally consented. "But you mustn't take any unnecessary risks. We can't lose you, Hunter."

Hunter was quiet for a moment. "I miss them."

"Me too."

~~*~*~*

In the basement of the mansion, Isis was working out. She had blindfolded herself and was practicing her kicks and punches. Flipping forward, she retrieved a knife from where she had laid it earlier and thrust forward as if there was an opponent in front of her. Leaning forward, she struck out with a powerful back kick. Leaping up into the air, Isis executed a flawless spin kick. Thrusting her elbow back and following through with a roundhouse kick, she remained focused on her exercise. Isis often worked out late at night, so she didn't have to hold back. She remained hyper-aware of the entire room and the stairway, in case someone came down.

Isis became aware of activity in the main hallway. There were a lot of voices, but no indication of distress. Someone had returned or perhaps Passion was visiting Jet and Lilly, which she frequently did. Isis leaned back as though away from a punch, dropped down into a crouch, and spun around once. She held the knife out as though warning her invisible opponent.

Isis thought about Jet's report of the Magic Orders refusal to attend the summit. It was an understandable survival strategy, but a flawed one. Quarantine was a temporary solution to a problem like Grenich — one that would ultimately fail. Isis dismissed the Magic Orders isolation as unimportant. If they wanted to remain in what they assumed to be a safe haven, she could do nothing to convince them otherwise nor would she go out of her way to prevent their inevitable slaughter. It would be difficult enough to get the shape shifters, guardians, and their allies through dismantling the necromancers' empire. Concerning herself with even more normals would just overcomplicate the problem.

Isis heard familiar footfalls on the steps, followed by a less familiar gait. The less familiar one was interesting to her. It was quiet, almost as quiet as a guardian. Her nostrils twitched as she took in the scents, trying to place them. Her muscles tensed up when she placed the unfamiliar scent. Changing the grip on her knife, Isis waited.

"Isis—"

Isis twisted and hurled the knife. She heard a yelp and tore the blindfold off her eyes, turning her attention to the stairs. Orion was crouched down, his hands held protectively over his head. His blue eyes were wide as he looked up to where the knife was embedded in the wall and then to her. Behind him, a man Isis didn't recognize was standing on the first step and leaning against the railing. He had black hair and expressive brown eyes. Clothed in midnight blue garb with black boots and gloves, he looked over to the wall where the knife was jutting out, close to his face. He looked back to her and smiled, impressed. Isis didn't like his nonchalance. At the very least, his eyes should have widened and his heart rate or respiration should have increased a little. The man was accustomed to violence, which made him dangerous and a potential threat.

"What have I told you about throwing weapons indoors or at people?" Orion chastised as he straightened up again. Isis' gaze didn't move from the stranger.

"What have I told you about approaching me without warning?" Isis countered. "I do not know that creature behind you. The scent is similar to necromancers. Who and what is that?"

Orion stared at her. "I missed you too, Isis."

"I am relieved you are alive. My question is still unanswered: what is that and why is it here?" she demanded, watching the stranger suspiciously.

The stranger, who had been admiring the craftsmanship of the knife, looked over at her. Orion scratched the back of his head, glancing back at the stranger.

"Isis, this is the man who extracted you and Jack from the laboratory," Orion said. The stranger ran a finger over the top of the knife, nodding in appreciation, and then turned his expressive brown eyes to her. She still regarded him with suspicion.

"I go by many names, but my given name is Milo," he stated as he stepped forward. "I'd offer my hand, but I know you aren't comfortable with physical contact."

Isis took a step forward and hesitated, carefully holding out her hand. Milo looked at it and then at Orion, obviously caught off guard. He looked back to her and cautiously accepted it. Isis tightened her grip and yanked him off his feet, throwing him to the ground. She placed her foot on his throat, pressing down to obstruct his oxygen intake. Ignoring Orion's shouted protests, she pulled his arm so it was uncomfortably extended. He gagged a little, but oddly, didn't panic or thrash about. Isis didn't like how unruffled the strange man was.

"Why have you brought a necromancer into the mansion?" Isis demanded without taking her attention off the man she held on the ground.

"Isis, he's not a necromancer! Would you just listen to me!?"

"He smells like a necromancer," she repeated, wondering how many times she would have to make that observation before Orion explained what the enemy was doing in their base of operations. Milo kicked up and hit her in the back, knocking her off balance. It was enough time for him to scurry out from under her heel. She spun around, immediately on the defensive. Isis could smell a little blood, but couldn't remember drawing any from him. She looked him over for any weak spots and she spotted the padding around his abdomen. Focusing back on his face, Isis noticed his complexion was pale. The stranger was hurt, likely recovering from a wound.

"I'm part necromancer, but I was disowned after I refused to participate in Grenich business," Milo explained, holding his fists up as he got in a defensive position but did not advance on her. "I've been working with Perrin, Orion, and Roan ever since. I've been fighting Grenich since before you were born. Believe it or not, Set and Pyra probably want me dead more than they want the Key."

"Necromancers lie."

"Seriously?" Milo looked over at Orion, frustrated. "You protectors have *really* got to take a look at yourselves and your prejudices."

Isis lunged forward and Milo nimbly danced back. Orion tried to place himself between them, but Isis kept darting around him.

"Isis, dammit, will you please stop? Can you just trust me?"

Isis shoved him away as she fixed on the man who smelled of necromancer. He had a scent similar to a shape shifter as well, but she disregarded it. Normals were too trusting. The risk of trusting anyone with ties to necromancers was too great. The stranger could be a double-agent; a Grenich spy. It was a risk she was unwilling to take.

Isis moved forward again when suddenly, Jack was standing between her and the stranger. He held his hand out, halting her attack. She stopped and looked up into his glowing brown eyes.

"Isis, we owe this man our lives and you will not harm him. Think back to when we were taken out of the laboratory and try to remember that night. Do you remember the masked man in midnight blue? Remember his scent?" Jack asked. Isis hesitated, thinking back to that night and the tension slowly left her body. When she was able to pull up what little memory she had of it, Isis did remember the different scents. The clearest memory she had of that particular night was the gentle hands that carefully removed the bindings from her wrists and the ID collar from her neck. At first, she thought she was remembering Orion's hands, but now that she matched the scent, Isis identified it as Milo's.

Isis glanced at him and then looked back to Jack. "It could still be a set up."

"To what end? I remember his file from the corporation. He frequently goes under the alias Anubis," Jack explained. Isis stared at Jack, leaned to the side and studied Milo, a little curious. Milo appeared more on edge, ready to go back on the defensive, but met her gaze.

"You're Anubis?" she asked skeptically.

"I am." He spread his hands and bowed, grimacing. "At your service."

"You're at the top of the kill on sight lists. How are you still alive?"

"I'm sure Set and Pyra are wondering the same thing,"

Milo replied. Jack glanced over at him and Orion moved to Milo's side. Isis heard him asking the man about his stitches and Milo waved him away, but held one arm over his abdomen.

"Why is he here now?" Isis asked, looking over at Milo. "You've torn at least two stitches, but the wound has healed enough that blood loss isn't too much of a concern. You should allow Orion to examine your wound. The guardians won't help you due to your being a descendant of their mortal enemy."

Milo gave her a thumbs up as he moved over to the boxing ring, sitting on the edge. Isis looked back to Jack, keeping Milo in her peripheral vision. She didn't trust him enough to let her guard down.

"Hunter's been linked to Nick Chance," Jack explained. "She was bitten by one of Set's followers the night of the massacre."

"We killed all of them. The chances of one escaping are minimal."

She paused, frowning when she thought back to the shape shifters' excursions to other worlds. The strange events required a reassessment of her facts and estimates.

"You also go by Blitz, right?" Milo asked as Orion examined his wound. Isis turned her glowing green eyes toward him, nodding once. He looked over to where the knife was still sticking out of the wall.

"I'm curious, have you attempted to use your guardian abilities since getting out of Grenich?" he asked, turning his eyes back to her.

"I can Appear," Isis replied, turning her attention back to Jack.

"You can do more than that," Milo stated, drawing her attention back to him. "You have telekinetic ability. I'm betting you know it too, but you hid it from the handlers."

Isis turned so she was facing him, crossing her arms over her chest. "Why would I do that?"

"Because like Orion, you feared Nick Chance. And if

there's one thing all experiments know, it's that any sign of difference could warrant a visit from the Butcher of Grenich," Milo answered, squinting as he studied her for a moment. "No, that's not right. You never feared anyone, not even Chance. He made you uneasy, but you weren't afraid of him. No, you hid your guardian abilities because it gave you an advantage. And whether you realized it or not, you always wanted to find some way to escape that place."

Isis didn't move, but continued watching him. The lights buzzed high above them and the training room had a slight chill as it usually did. Isis noticed Jack step up so he stood next to her. She could see his gray t-shirt in her peripheral vision. Milo smiled, but there was something rather sad about the expression.

"So, Blitz, may I see what you can do?" he asked and Orion looked back over his shoulder. Isis could read the curiosity in his expression. After a moment, she held her hand out flat with the palm turned up to the ceiling. The knife flew out of the wall and into her waiting grasp. She closed her fingers around the smooth grip, spun the knife around and stuck it into the sheath on her belt.

Orion straightened up. "You've never used your guardian abilities before."

"Using them in public risks drawing attention and when I was suffering from the Omni virus, they used up too much energy," Isis responded. "I've only recently begun practicing using them again, but I don't spend much time doing so. Such abilities offer limited advantages, nowhere near enough to warrant using them regularly. Relying too heavily on them would result in a severe hindrance."

Isis looked over to her left at Jack and then back at Milo.

"If you wish to be useful, the Magic Orders are the only supernatural race who have declined the protectors' request to attend the summit. The protectors and guardians suspect Set had some hand in this decision, which I believe is possible. I was never aware of any other worlds, but it appears as though he is. It would be helpful to know how much Set knows about them as well as his plans concerning them," Isis stated, not sparing him a glance.

"I'll see what my sources can dig up," Milo agreed as he sat back. "It is good to see you free, Blitz. Shape shifters were not meant to be caged."

Isis looked at him, still suspicious of his intentions and motivations. She turned back to Jack. It was odd, but she was pleased he was back. It had been strange being the only seven series in the mansion. She had never been separated from others of her series for so long and found herself wondering if that was what it was like for Shocker and Coop.

"It is good that you are back," Isis said to Jack. Then she turned and made her way over to the stairs, jogging up and leaving the training area.

CHAPTER THIRTEEN

In the meeting room of the mansion, Jet leaned against the table with his back to the door. It was just after dawn, so the mansion was still quiet. The summit was scheduled for the afternoon. Jet was looking out the window, his arms crossed over his chest. It was a beautiful spring morning. The green outside seemed all the more vibrant in the sunlight and the leaves shimmered when the wind swept through them. Jet didn't notice any of it, lost in his own thoughts. He and Lilly had spoken at length with Orion and Remington when they had returned from Perrin's Sanctuary. Regardless of how the summit went, they had to strike the Grenich laboratory by next week at the latest. By now, Set was probably preparing for an attack and the longer they waited, the more difficult it would be. The only thing working in their favor was the laboratory's location in the middle of nowhere.

Jet dropped his head, closing his eyes as he massaged the back of his neck. He hadn't questioned his ability as leader of the protectors for quite some time, but the past month had been trying. It seemed like no matter what he and Lilly did, the result was more loss of life. Thoughts of Brindy and Devlin haunted him and Jet knew the grief was distracting. He had been hiding in the mansion too much lately.

"You were awake before me. That is truly rare."

Jet smiled as he looked over his shoulder to the door where Lilly stood. She looked radiant in a green dress, which shimmered in the sunlight. She moved inside the room, sitting on the table beside him.

"Are you nervous about the summit?" Lilly asked, a subtle smile playing on her lips.

"If I screw this up, we're down even more allies," Jet answered, resting his brow against hers, taking comfort in her nearness. "I can get maybe seventy-five protectors to help with the raid, but it won't be enough. If what Orion and Isis describe is accurate — and we have no reason to doubt it's not — we're going to need an army."

"You are a good leader, Jet," Lilly stated. "I have known it from the moment we first met, all those years ago. We will be able to renew our alliances with the other supernatural races and we will defeat Set. We have faced seemingly impossible odds in the past and have always emerged triumphant. This will be no different."

"I wish I had your confidence."

Lilly smiled and kissed him. "You know I will always be by your side, no matter what."

"Actually, I wanted to discuss something with you." Jet pulled a seat out from the long table and sat down. "When this raid takes place, I am going to fight alongside the protectors. It is something the Monroes have always done. I spoke with Adonia yesterday and I would like you and our children to remain in the Meadows while we attack the laboratory. If this goes sideways, Set and Pyra will have all three Key possibilities and nothing will be able to stop them. The guardians will be forced to sever the link to Earth in order to prevent anyone from Appearing and Hecate will have to seal the doors to the other worlds. I don't want our family to be trapped here if that happens."

Lilly stared at him for a moment. "If that is what

happens, here is where I must be. The protectors are my people too. I will not desert them in their time of need and neither will any of our children."

"Lilly—"

"No, Jet. When we married, I swore to stand by you in good times and bad, to rule alongside you. I am more than capable of defending myself. I will not run."

Jet looked at his feet and then back out the window. Lilly had always been brave and resolute, never one to shy away from tough situations. He loved that about her. Even as a guardian, she had been completely unafraid to speak her mind. She had saved his skin more than a few times in the past. If he were to fall, she would be more than capable to continue leading the fight against Grenich. Still, the thought of her being targeted sent a spike of fear through Jet's heart.

"There is no way I'm going to talk you out of this, am I?"

Lilly shook her head. Jet laid his hands across his stomach and rested his head back against the headrest. His wife was strong, fearless, and wise and Jet knew he was lucky she was with him. Lilly stood from the table and sat in the seat next to him.

"Do you think the experiments should sit in?"

Jet stared at her. "God, no! No, the last thing we need is to spook the fey or remind Aneurin of their presence. He's just itching for an excuse to toss them in the dungeons."

"True, but it might be worthwhile to show our allies what Set is doing," Lilly suggested. "They might be more open to fighting if they saw what he was planning."

"I've considered that, but I would hate to use the experiments as props. I considered asking Coop or Jack—"

"What about Isis?" Lilly interrupted and Jet stared at her.

"Lilly, she went on a killing spree not that long ago.

While I admit she is a very skilled warrior and strategist, her social skills leave much to be desired."

"You don't need her to act as a diplomat. If anyone knows what Grenich is capable of, it's Isis," Lilly pointed out. Jet opened his mouth to respond but was interrupted by a knock on the door. He stood from his chair and made his way to the door, opening it. Remington stood out in the hall. He didn't look the slightest bit tired and Jet wondered what time he had gone to sleep.

"Alpha has arrived with two rebels," Remington reported.

Jet stared at him. "She's rather early."

"I got the impression she didn't come solely for the summit," Remington said, unbothered. Jet almost laughed at his cluelessness. *Of course, Jade and Sly are here,* he thought with a shake of his head.

"Would you mind letting her know the time and location of the summit? She and her companions can have full run of the mansion, of course. If they need anything, we will be happy to oblige."

"I will tell them right away," Remington said, nodding his head and turning to leave. He stopped only when Jet called his name.

"Lilly and I were speaking about possibly inviting the experiments to sit in on the summit. She thinks it's a good idea, but I have reservations. What's your opinion?"

Remington shrugged. "From what I've seen, if the experiments are interested in the summit, they will find some way to get the information they desire. As for the wisdom of such an idea, I have no opinion. There are drawbacks and benefits to both options."

"Thank you, Remington."

Remington bowed his head once and went on his way. Jet turned back to the meeting room, looking to where Lilly still sat at the table.

"Let's see how things go," Jet suggested. "If they seem unwilling, I'll call for one of the experiments. Perhaps they will be better able to articulate the threat Grenich poses."

Lilly spread her hands out on the table, studying her fingers. It was a bright and beautiful day. *At least the weather seems to be agreeable,* Jet thought as he returned to the chair next to Lilly and sat again.

Time seemed to stretch on for an eternity. Jet managed to eat a little breakfast, but skipped lunch. He moved through the halls of the mansion in a daze, going through every possible argument in his mind. He passed numerous shape shifters in the hall and managed polite civility, though his mind was miles away. He retrieved a tennis ball from the study he shared with Lilly and tossed it up and down as he wandered through the halls. In the early afternoon, he thought he caught a glimpse of Isis, but it was so brief he wondered if it was just a trick of the light.

An hour before the summit, Jet made his way to the main stairway and jogged up them to the second floor. Sunlight was streaming through the windows high above. When he reached the second floor, Jet glanced over to the side and noticed Isis standing at the railing. She was looking down to the floor below. Jet approached her and smiled in greeting. She didn't respond or acknowledge him, her eyes remaining on the first floor.

"It's a big day today," he stated as he leaned against the wall opposite the railing.

"It is a day like any other. The summit is what's important," Isis replied, crossing her arms over her chest. "They will bring guards with them. Do you wish for me to remain out of sight?"

"Isis, no. You are allowed to move about freely," Jet said. Isis looked over at him before turning her attention down the hall.

"Will the guards wait outside the meeting room?"

"I imagine they will. Why?"

"Experiments like to know of changes in their environments. It's why we do a lot of reconnaissance work on missions," Isis explained. "I overheard your conversation with Lilly earlier. You are concerned about the summit."

Jet dropped his head back against the wall. "I don't know how to convince two races who are relatively safe in their own worlds to fight, and likely die, on Earth."

"If you were negotiating with experiments in similar circumstances, you would stand no chance. However you are dealing with other normals," Isis said. Jet looked over to her, curious.

"Meaning?"

"Experiments are driven by logic, strategy, and self-preservation. Normals have a number of motivations and drives. Last night, I was doing research in the library on the supernatural races. Your grandparents and great-aunts wrote extensively on the topic."

"I believe they had to deal with them more. That was probably back when the Seelie Court was still trafficking lycanthrope, shape shifter, and vampire youth," Jet mentioned. "By the time I was born, the supernatural races had withdrawn to their own worlds and rarely used the crossroads. Even my parents didn't encounter them often."

"Only the fey trafficked in the young. The elves, mer-people, goblins, dwarves, and the other members of the Seelie Court didn't partake in it," Isis corrected. "In fact, many believe the elves were the ones who leaked the information about the trafficking. However, all the races in the Seelie Court face the same stigma due to their belonging to it, which is why they still harbor some resentment toward the fey. Not as much as the lycanthropes, but enough to concern the leaders. The fey are always worried about rebellion, despite what they might say or project."

Jet watched her for a moment, wondering what she was getting at. "Did you find anything that might help in the summit? Anything I might have missed?"

"Members of the Seelie Court are known to be proud,

which may help you when it comes to negotiations. Pride is often connected to a species' desire for a legacy. Members of the Seelie Court want to be remembered in legend and they want to be remembered favorably. The trafficking is a scandal the Court is still trying to overcome — the fey in particular. Destroying Grenich would help restore their tarnished reputation," Isis explained. "However, do not remind them of their past crimes. It will make them less open to fighting beside you."

Jet was impressed by her astuteness. Isis would probably credit it to her being an experiment, but she had always been bright — even before the experimentation. She turned her gaze up to the windows above them, studying the beams of sunlight. Jet could smell freshly baked bread and other dishes being prepared in the kitchen. The mansion was alive with noise and Jet could hear footsteps rushing about on the first floor. Looking back to Isis, he noticed how much she blended in with the darkness. Even the burgundy-colored carpet seemed to conceal her.

"The lycanthropes would be easy if it weren't for the Seelie Court. Lycanthropes have always been closely linked with shape shifters, especially the protectors, and willing to fight beside them. I do not know if their hatred of the fey will inhibit their loyalty to you. If it does, you have to make sure they understand Grenich is the bigger threat," Isis continued, wrapping her fingers around her wrist. Her silver charm glistened in the sunlight. She was wearing her pants and tank top, made of the same material as her catsuit. Jet knew she was concealing a few weapons on her, likely blades. She seemed to favor them.

Jet looked up at the nearest portrait. It was of a stern-looking woman with a gray wolf sitting next to her. She was dressed in a pearl-colored gown and looked to be from the Elizabethan era. He glanced at his watch, wondering if anyone would be early. The fey and the lycanthropes would be arriving in Hecate's castle and then escorted by her messengers to the mansion.

"Isis, what do you think of Milo?" Jet asked, curious. He had heard of their rocky introduction and wondered if her opinion of him had changed at all. Hunter seemed to be wary of him, but still trusted him enough to train her how to control her new ability.

"Orion trusts him and he did extract us from the laboratory. Grenich has placed a high bounty on his head, much higher than the one on Jensen. It's second only to the one on Jack and me," Isis answered, her gaze on the first floor.

"But you don't trust him?"

"Whether or not I trust him is inconsequential. Whether or not I can use him is of more importance," Isis replied. "Right now, he's proving to be useful."

Jet looked to the side when he heard a door open. The meeting room door opened and two tall elves stepped out, dressed in full armor. They took up their position just outside the door, one on either side, with their eyes glued on the wall opposite them. Lilly stepped out of the room.

"Jet, the guardians and fey have arrived," she reported with a small smile.

"I'll be right there," Jet said and turned his attention back to Isis, who had taken a step back the opposite way. He almost didn't see her as she concealed herself in the shade. Her glowing eyes, a shade of ocean blue, turned to him.

"Remember what I told you," she said. Jet nodded, squared his shoulders, and turned around, making his way down the hall. He paused just in front of the meeting room door and exhaled. Glancing up at the motionless elves, Jet pushed the door open.

"Good afternoon everyone," he greeted cordially as he stepped around the table and took his seat next to Lilly. Adonia smiled at him in greeting. Aneurin looked less than thrilled, but still smiled politely. He was wearing a white robe with gold trim and a golden circlet sat atop his head.

Next to them sat Titania and Oberon. The fey leaders wore similar styles of clothing, but their robes were purple and green in color with gold inlay. Titania wore ribbons with small gemstones in her hair, which sparkled when they caught the light. A crown of golden leaves sat atop Oberon's head. They had tan complexions and piercing eyes. Their wings were folded flat against their backs, glistening like gossamer in the sun.

"I'm sure the lycanthropes will be here shortly," Jet mentioned, looking down at the dossier on Grenich he and Lilly had spent a week compiling. They had one made up for each attendee and placed in front of every chair.

"I'm amazed you were able to lure them out of their fields," Oberon commented in a tone that suggested it was not a compliment. Aneurin smirked and looked over at the Monroes, waiting for their response. He had voiced his doubts about the summit when Jet and Lilly had first proposed it. *If you bring all the supernatural races together, you are asking for all hell to break loose. There's a reason they live in different worlds,* he warned the protectors.

"They have some time yet," Jet said, sorting through his papers. He looked up when the door opened again. Alpha walked in, dressed in her usual plain clothes, and threw a look over her shoulder.

"Whoever brought the pointy-eared statues, I don't care for their attitudes," she said as she dropped into an empty chair beside Jet. "Hello, Lilly. It is good to see you again."

Lilly smiled in greeting to the rebel leader.

"Is this your concubine?" Titania asked and Aneurin looked over to the shape shifters, smothering a chuckle. Alpha leaned forward, her gaze narrowing.

"Alpha is the leader of another group of shape shifters, the rebels," Lilly answered quickly.

"I'm nobody's *concubine*," Alpha added, jerking her thumb over to Jet. "And I'd like to think I could do better than him if I slept with men."

Jet could feel his face turn bright red as the fey whispered to each other. *Well this has gotten off to a spectacular start,* he thought as he massaged his forehead. Looking up, he noticed a bright light forming behind the fey. In a few seconds, messengers from the Pearl Castle stood where the light had been. Their hands rested on the shoulders of the lycanthropes.

Diego and Ella stood tall and thanked the messengers. All the lycanthropes had long hair, but Ella stood out with her dark red hair. Their two bodyguards stiffened when they saw Titania and Oberon. There was a quiet rumbling sound and Jet realized one had growled. The room seemed to shrink and Jet adjusted the collar of his shirt, clearing his throat. He felt Lilly interlace her fingers with his, reassuring him with a gentle squeeze. The room remained pleasantly cool, which was a relief.

"Here it comes," Aneurin muttered under his breath. Oberon glanced over his shoulder at the new arrivals. Their clothing was plain, made for long hours harvesting crops and other everyday work. Ella didn't wear a dress and her clothing was very similar to Diego's. There were wolves sewn into their lapels, identifying them from the wolf clan.

"I suppose we should be thankful they're clothed," Oberon commented.

"Let's try to keep things civil," Jet warned before smiling up at the lycanthropes. "Diego, Ella, welcome to the protectors' mansion."

"Jet, Lilly, thank you for having us. Despite some of the company, it is a pleasure," Ella said as she and Diego took their seats on the other side of the guardians. Alpha began twisting her chair to the left and right. Jet noticed she was smiling, entertained by the tension in the room. Knowing Alpha, she probably wanted to bring popcorn.

"You know Adonia and Aneurin of course," Jet mentioned. "To my right is Alpha, leader of the rebels."

Alpha gave a small wave of her hand when he

mentioned her name and the lycanthropes smiled, nodding politely in greeting. Jet folded his hands in front of him on the smooth table.

"I'm sure everyone here is aware of the very real threat we are facing," he began. "Grenich grows stronger every day and as it grows in influence, Set grows in power."

"We already know the threat Chaos and his consort pose to you," Titania began, interlacing her long thin fingers. "You have yet to explain the threat he poses to our lands and people."

"Well, we do have some evidence that Set can cross into different worlds. The vampires were supposed to attend the summit, but we found them slaughtered," Jet explained.

"One of the experiments who resides here recognized some Grenich technology and said the scene looked like a strategy the Corporation would use," Lilly added, her attention fixed on the fey. "Queen Titania and King Oberon, I understand the Seelie Court recently experienced a loss."

Titania and Oberon exchanged a look. Oberon looked back to the Monroes and leaned back in his chair, sizing them up for a moment.

"The goblins died out, a plague of some kind," he answered. "I don't see what that has to do with anything."

Lilly reached under the table and picked up a box resting at her feet. She slid it across the table to Oberon. The fey leader caught it and lifted it, turning it in his grasp. After a moment, he handed it to Titania so she could also examine it. She ran her fingers over the carved wood, frowning.

"A healer gave that to one of the shape shifters who accompanied me to your world," Lilly explained. "She wanted Sly to show it to the experiments, in the hopes one of them could identify it."

"This is from the Seelie Court," Titania confirmed, sliding the top wooden slot aside to look inside. "A miner's light? I don't understand."

"If you look closely, you'll be able to make out a strange symbol just under the light," Jet continued. "Both Coop and Isis, two of the experiments who live here, identified it as something used to transport viruses, one designed and used exclusively by Grenich."

Oberon still looked skeptical, but Titania seemed concerned. She handed the box to Aneurin, who examined the object.

"Perhaps it is just someone seeking retribution," Diego spoke up, drawing a very irritated look from Oberon.

"We don't believe that to be the case," Lilly said before the fey could respond. "The necromancers pose a danger to all of us. Your lands still have scars from the War of the Meadows. Chaos and Pyra walked across all lands when launching their attacks and where he stepped, nothing ever grows. If he manages to take control of the Earth, he will find a way into the Meadows and when that happens, none of you will be safe."

"What are you asking from us?" Ella asked.

"We are planning to strike at the laboratory in this state in the next few days. We don't have the numbers to succeed, even with the support of the protectors and the rebels. We need more allies with differing abilities to help us fight Set. He has an army and outnumbers us in resources and manpower," Jet explained. "If you both agreed to help us, it could tip the scales in our favor. Together, we could topple Grenich."

Diego glanced over at Ella, who watched Jet and Lilly. Titania and Oberon were also quiet.

"We still have to go to the High Council, but the laws of the guardians don't allow us to take an active part in Earth conflicts," Adonia spoke up. "Which is why we are looking to help the Monroes in other ways. Should you agree to this alliance, you will have the eternal gratitude of the guardians."

There was quiet for a moment as the leaders conferred

with each other. Jet looked over at Lilly. Her expression reflected the hope she felt and she offered him a grin. He often wished he had his wife's optimism, but Jet was more a pessimist by nature.

"Normally in the Seelie Court, we strengthen bonds and alliances with marriage," Oberon mentioned, looking over at the guardians. Lilly's smile fell a little and Jet dragged his hand down his face. He had expected the fey might bring up such a price, but he couldn't believe they would be so bold as to ask it of the guardians.

"The fey asking for more children, that's surprising," Diego commented, sarcasm dripping from every word.

"Excuse me, exactly how did children enter into this discussion?" Oberon asked.

"He's right, Diego," Ella mentioned, a coolness creeping into her voice. "The fey never ask for anything. They simply take what they want."

"I think we're getting a little off-track," Jet attempted to interrupt what was fast becoming a contentious disagreement.

"The hours working in the fields has addled your simple brains," Oberon replied with a dismissive wave of his hand. "Probably sun stroke or whatever it is that afflicts your kind."

"Wow, this guy's a dick," Alpha muttered under her breath to Jet.

"Our kind? Could you be any more speciest?"

Jet closed his eyes and ran his hands over his face as the fey and lycanthropes began to yell at each other. He could feel the heat from the sun on his back and heard Lilly trying to stop the argument. *Well at least they're not breaking out into a fistfight,* Jet thought as he inhaled and opened his mouth to help his wife break up the two shouting parties.

A loud bang out in the hall made everyone go quiet. There was a clattering sound, something shattering, and another thump. Jet looked over at Lilly, who looked just as puzzled as he felt. The door burst open as one of the elves flew through it and landed in a heap on the floor. *Uh oh*, Jet thought when he saw Isis standing in the now open door. He could just make out the shapes of the fallen bodyguards out in the hall. Jet glanced over at the messengers, who looked unsure about what to do.

Isis strode into the room to where the elf was trying to shake himself out of a daze and punched him in the face, knocking him out cold. She straightened up again, the sunlight gleaming on her shimmering clothes and the silver charm at her throat. Isis turned her glowing blue eyes to the people sitting around the table. The fey recoiled in horror when they saw her eyes and Jet could see the genuine fear in their faces. The lycanthropes also looked nervous and leaned back as though to distance themselves from the intimidating woman.

Isis moved over to the table, her eyes fixed on the lycanthropes and fey. "Those were your personal guards, so I assume they were your best fighters. It took me less than a minute to deal with them. You could have brought ten guards with you and it wouldn't have taken me more than five minutes to incapacitate them."

"What is she?" Oberon asked Jet and Lilly.

"I'm what Set is going to throw at you," Isis answered before the protectors could respond. "I'm from a line of experiments called the seven series and my series is made to be smart, strong, quick, and lethal. Set uses us to quell rebellions and overthrow leaders, among other things. He has his sights set on the Meadows and when he conquers the guardians, he will release things like me into your lands. Not only modified shape shifters — he has been experimenting with wereanimals as well. His army will be used to devastate the Earth, then the Meadows, and then your worlds. He will burn you, your people, everything you love to ashes. And yet you sit here, arguing with each other, rather than facing the very real threat before you."

Titania cleared her throat. "Who are you?"

"Some know me as Blitz, others as Isis. Right now, I'm one of the only ones standing between you and annihilation. If the protectors fall, that safeguard will go with them. If you don't help the protectors, I will make no effort to stop Set from conquering your worlds."

Isis turned and walked out of the meeting room. Jet watched as she stepped over the unconscious body of one of the lycanthrope guards, who appeared to be waking up. Out in the hall, the soft sounds of groaning could be heard from the fallen guards. Jet noticed shards of some broken vase or other decorative object on the ground.

"Girl knows how to make a point," Alpha stated with a smile.

~~*~*~*

Early the next morning, Orion was hunched over a roughly drawn outline of the Grenich laboratory. He was alone in a small room connected to the library. Across from him was a table on which he had put the small model of the Grenich laboratory Milo had built. Orion had to hand it to him: the man was good with his hands. Milo had constructed the model the previous night while most of the mansion's inhabitants slept. *We're finally coming for you, you bastards*, Orion thought as he ran the cap of his pen over the outline, tracing a route through the lines like a rat navigating a maze.

Orion rolled the outline up and tucked it in the back of his pants. He grabbed the base of the model and picked it up, making his way out of the small room. Orion headed to the training room door, which was propped open. The sounds of combat drifted up from the basement. The Four were undoubtedly practicing with the experiments and Orion was sure Milo and Hunter were also awake. Remington's deep voice called out something the eldest Deverell didn't catch. As he made his way down the stairs, the sounds and voices grew louder.

Orion reached the bottom of the stairs and made his way over to the table, where Milo was sitting cross-legged. He held a flash drive in one hand and was turning it around in a methodical motion. When Orion approached, Milo glanced over at him but returned his focus to the flash drive.

"Where have you been hiding?" Milo asked before turning his attention to where Hunter was attempting to navigate a maze while blindfolded. "I heard you step on that stick. Start making use of your other senses; try and use the mind's eye."

"What is she doing?" Orion asked, noticing how Hunter clenched her fists and gritted her teeth in obvious frustration.

"Unless we kill the demon that bit her or Nick Chance, Hunter's going to keep having flashes of what he sees. The visions compromise her ability to see for varying amounts of time, so she has to learn how to rely on her other senses at a moment's notice," Milo replied as he continued examining the flash drive.

"Is that what Isis retrieved from the personnel box in the bank?" Orion asked.

"It is," Milo answered. "A very brash move and not one I would have recommended, but it may prove to be useful if I can figure out what the hell it is. There's something about this thing I'm not seeing."

"Perhaps because it's not in a computer," Orion suggested. Milo gave him a dry look. Orion watched as Isis dodged low under a punch and followed through with a kick, knocking Jensen flat on his back. Flipping forward, she retrieved a wooden sword and leveled it at Jade's throat. She spun and threw the weapon to Jack, who caught it.

"Well, at least she has learned to slow down a little for the normals," Orion mentioned before whistling. The shape shifters all turned to look at him and he motioned them over. Hunter took off her blindfold and turned to where Orion was.

"Milo was kind enough—"

"Try *very* bored."

"To make a model of the Grenich laboratory," Orion continued. The experiments all leaned forward.

"This is just a basic idea," Milo explained. "There are some places in there I know exist but don't have an exact location for."

Hunter examined the small model, curiosity reflected in her expression. She closed her eyes tightly and shook her head, backing away again. The small reaction didn't escape Orion's notice.

"How do we plan to get inside?" Isis asked, leaning back a little. Orion shrugged.

"I was hoping you would have some ideas," he replied. Jack moved closer and motioned to the stairway.

"If Shocker knocks out the power, this will be easier to navigate," he observed.

"If we can get one or two guards to open the door, it would give us a small opportunity," Isis observed as she walked around to the other side of the table. "We would need some kind of diversion. Perhaps Jack or I could offer to turn ourselves in."

"That would not be a good strategy," Jack stated. "Capturing a possible Key would send the whole laboratory into complete lockdown. Coop, do you think you could do it?"

"Coop is an outdated product. They would just shoot him in the head," Isis said. "We need someone whom they would take inside but not kill immediately or engage lockdown protocol. Someone they would want to interrogate."

"Do we know anyone who fits that description?" Shae asked. Isis crossed her arms over her chest. Jack and Coop both looked at her.

"What about Anubis?" Hunter suggested, taking a swig from her water bottle. Everyone looked over at her, except for Milo.

"They definitely want to torture me to death," Milo said in his usual nonchalant way, not looking up. "Very, *very* slowly."

"It would divide up their guards," Isis mentioned with a small shrug. "Spread their forces out a bit, but you would be on your own for a while, long enough for them to do some serious damage to you. Are you willing to take that risk?"

Milo shrugged, unbothered. "Yeah, sure."

He hopped off the table and held the drive in his mouth, pulling a knife from his belt. Without warning, Milo dragged the blade across his palm and sliced it open, causing most of the shape shifters to cringe and stare at him as if he had lost his mind.

"What in name of the guardians are you doing?" Orion yelled in disbelief, quickly moving over to the shelf where the first aid kit was kept. Milo ignored him as he put the flash drive in his bloody palm and clenched his fist around it. Blood dripped from his hand and splattered on the dull green ground. He laid the bloody drive on the floor, which started to glow. A white screen was projected from the glowing drive, then another, each looking like a computer screen. Milo grabbed one screen and pulled it to the side. Another screen popped up and he smiled.

"This is a blood device," Milo explained, as he brought the next screen forward and scrolled with his other hand. "Activated by the blood of a necromancer, or half-necromancer in this case. You put it in a computer and you get a lot of gibberish. It's rather impressive."

Isis approached, staring at the floating screens. Some of the screens had symbols neither recognized. The other shape shifters were staring in amazement at the multiple screens projected from the small drive. Orion was distracted as he quickly cleaned Milo's palm. He glanced around at the multiple screens as he wrapped gauze around the cut.

"Milo, could you bring up this screen over here," Orion asked, gesturing to the screen he was referencing. Milo grabbed it with his uninjured hand and pulled it up, enlarging it. There were numbers and letters. Orion stepped closer to it, squinting as he tried to decipher a pattern.

"Any idea what these are?" Orion asked.

"Can't say for certain. They might be passcodes," Milo replied with a shrug.

"Could you bring this blank screen down and lay it flat?" Isis requested. Milo glanced at her, puzzled, but did as she asked. When he did, the screen changed color and became blue. It started to morph and stretch, forming a digital blueprint.

"Oh you clever woman. It's this state's main laboratory. I'll be damned," Milo said with a half-smile.

"Whoa," Jade breathed as she walked around the display, amazed at the detail. Jensen moved around the opposite direction and crouched down so he could look up through the bottom. The other shape shifters drew closer, forming a circle around the large map.

"How did you know it would do that?" Alex asked as she moved over to Isis.

"I remember seeing a similar hologram when I was in the laboratory. Carding would sometimes have them made for more complicated assignments and difficult missions," Isis explained, her gaze remaining on the detailed 3D map. "I never knew or cared where they came from. I just assumed it was made the usual way holograms are."

Milo snorted. "Grenich loves combining magic and technology. When it comes to that, they are always light years ahead of us."

Isis watched as the different levels of the laboratory separated. "This is meant for Set to rebuild the facility if needed."

She began to walk around the large hologram, her eyes fixed at a point near the top.

"Is that stairway the only entrance?" Jade asked, gesturing to the long stairway.

"The only way that anyone knows of," Jack answered.

"What about all these doors?" Shae asked, gesturing to the multiple doorways.

"They only open outward from the inside," Isis answered. "They're emergency exits, so there are alarms rigged to go off. The stairway is the only way to enter the laboratory."

"It's a death box," Jade observed. "I'm assuming these small glowing circles are guards."

"They are," Coop said. "These are old. After Jack and Isis were extracted, they would have at least doubled the amount of guards in the facility. Maybe even tripled them, and they would have spread out their positions."

Milo pulled up another screen, studying it for a minute. He pushed it away and turned his attention back to the large laboratory map. Zeroing in on the dome room, he focused on the positions of the guards. Orion glanced over at Hunter, who was standing back a bit. She didn't look as interested in the display as the other shape shifters. *Probably seen it more than enough times,* Orion thought as he tapped Milo's shoulder, gesturing for him to come closer.

"How much information about the Grenich laboratory has Hunter been able to absorb?" Orion asked. Milo turned his attention to Hunter briefly.

"A fair amount. Why?"

"Do you think she could direct us through the facility?"

Milo gave him a skeptical look. "Possibly, but do you really want to send Jet and Lilly's daughter inside the laboratory? There's going to be an awful lot of bullets flying and knives stabbing. I'm not sure putting her in the epicenter of a firefight is the wisest course of action."

"I was thinking more of having her in the van, directing via earpiece," Orion responded, watching as Hunter crouched down near where Isis was standing. The experiment looked at her and Hunter glanced up at her.

"She's still going to be in the center of a war zone," Milo pointed out. Orion looked over at him, surprised by the hesitance in his voice. For as long as he had known Milo, he had always been rather distant and unconcerned with things outside of the Grenich Corporation. Orion didn't even think he had friends, outside of Perrin. Roan had met him once and seemed impressed, or as impressed as Roan was capable of being.

Milo looked over at Orion, scrunching his brow. "What?"

"Nothing, it's just odd to hear you worried about someone," Orion answered.

"I'm worried about you pissing away opportunities and fighters," Milo responded. "No offense, doc, but you're not exactly a four star general. If you put Hunter that close to the laboratory, chances are one of the higher ups will take notice and they'll figure out what she can do. I don't have to remind you how the necromancers deal with perceived threats."

"They want to wipe out all protectors and they have already started targeting Jet and Lilly in particular. Hunter's already in danger being the daughter of the protectors' leaders. Besides, you'll be there to watch her back."

"Not if I get trapped in the facility, which is a likely scenario," Milo countered.

"If you can think of a better idea, I'm all ears," Orion said before moving over to where Isis was standing. She looked at him and followed when he gestured for her to do so. Orion gestured to Jack, who also followed him. He led them off to the side, near the weapons wall, glancing over Isis' shoulder to where the shape shifters were still talking about the map. Milo returned to them and moved a couple of the floor plans with his hands. Jack looked back briefly before turning his attention to Orion again.

"I am glad you are back," Isis spoke first and they both looked over at her. She shifted her weight a little as though unsure of what to do.

"Pardon?" Orion asked.

"I didn't have a chance to say it when you and Jack returned. It's good that none of you died," Isis clarified. Orion smiled a little, happy that she was at least attempting to understand why normals showed emotions. He knew both she and Jack were trying to find emotions in themselves, which was a more difficult task.

"You two both understand the objective of this mission, right?" Orion asked.

"Liberate the experiments and normals, take care of the guards," Isis answered.

"Avoid collateral damage and shut down the laboratory permanently," Jack added. Orion massaged the back of his neck. He lifted his face to the windows, enjoying the feeling of sun on his face. It had been a long and dreary winter. He had missed the sun.

"We don't know if the fey or lycanthropes will assist us," Orion began. "Jet and Lilly have called upon some protectors and Alpha has sent word out to rebels all over the country. I don't know if it will be enough."

The eldest Deverell looked at Isis and Jack, smiling tiredly. They had grown so much since they had first come to his cabin. Though they were different from regular shape shifters, they were learning how to be free again. Isis was reading book after book, most of which had nothing to do with war or battle strategies. Jack was interacting with normals on a regular basis to the point where he almost seemed comfortable in their presence. They were starting to grasp the concept of what it meant to be individuals. *I just hope I'm not about to lead them right back into imprisonment,* Orion thought, his shoulders dropping a bit.

"I'll be going with you when we launch our attack on the laboratory, but I won't be inside. You'll both be careful, won't you?"

Jack and Isis exchanged a puzzled look.

"I don't understand your question," Isis responded. "Where will you be, if not taking part in the raid?"

"I have some unfinished business I need to attend to outside the laboratory," Orion said, purposely being vague. He didn't know whether or not he would be back and he didn't want them to attempt to talk him out of what he had to do. Roan had already tried multiple times, but Orion didn't concern himself with what his brother thought. *They'll figure it out,* a small voice in the back of his mind chimed in. *It's what they do.*

Isis and Jack just stared at him, not knowing whether or not he wanted them to leave or say something more. Isis twisted and looked back to where the shape shifters were still studying the maps.

"You should go back and help the normals navigate that labyrinth Grenich calls a laboratory," Orion suggested. Jack glanced over at Isis and then at Orion again before walking back to the map. Orion watched as he moved over to where Shae was standing, smiling a little. The protector was leaning forward, studying one of the lower levels. Orion started to walk back to talk with Remington.

"I can predict what you're planning to do."

Orion turned to Isis, who was staring at the map and the normals studying it. She turned her glowing green eyes to him, which were no less luminous in the bright sunlight.

"You plan on killing Carding. Chance scares you too much, you would never even try to approach him, and it is unlikely he will be at the laboratory when we attack it. He moves around too often to predict his exact location at any given time," she continued, her voice still soft. "You have always wanted to kill Carding, even though you claim you do not."

"I'm not going to kill anyone, Isis. I'm a doctor, not a soldier," Orion replied. He had been around experiments long enough to know how easily they could read him. She was quite for a moment, her brow creasing as she studied his face.

"I would not stop you. It is a wise strategy, one with many benefits. But," Isis paused, looking down at her feet and swallowing. "I don't want you to. I have no good reason why. Normals change after they take a life and I don't like the idea of you changing in that way."

Orion stared at her for a moment. "Isis, you continually surprise me."

She met his gaze again. "I believe I was modified to do so."

Orion laughed at the response and looked down. Isis turned and made her way back to the map. Orion watched her go, still smiling. Despite her frequent slips, Isis gave him hope. Hell, she even gave Milo hope. There was a future and Grenich would not be part of it. Casualties were inevitable, but eventually, the necromancers would lose.

~~*~*~*

Electra paced outside her mother's room, her mind racing as she mentally rehearsed what she had come to say. It was just after dawn so Passion would be sleeping. *Or otherwise indisposed,* Electra thought. She looked down the hallway, studying the vaulting. The sunlight streamed in from the arched windows and illuminated the clean marble walls and floor. The young guardian was nervous and wanted to speak with her mother as soon as possible.

Electra turned when her mother's door opened. Passion yawned as she stepped outside, running a hand through her sleep-mussed hair. Despite having just woken up, she still looked radiant. Her eyes, which were blue on that day, fell on Electra.

"Why are you up so early?" Passion asked with a smile, stretching her arms over her head. Her short dress rose a little more above her knees.

"I need to talk with you," Electra answered. "Can we speak in your room?"

"Of course," Passion said and gestured to the open door. Electra moved inside and waited until Passion closed the door. Passion shook her hair out of her face, watching her daughter and waiting for her to speak.

"You look tense," she observed. "Let me guess: I'm not going to like whatever you're about to tell me."

Electra licked her lips and shook her head. "No, probably not. As you know, the protectors and whatever allies they managed to get are going to attack a Grenich laboratory tomorrow night. Isis is going to be there, on the front lines."

Passion moved over to the desk, where there was a decanter and a glass. She poured herself some water.

"Go on," she said, taking a sip of the water as she watched her daughter. Electra began fidgeting with her fingers, considering her next words.

"I've been training with Nemesis," Electra began and Passion chuckled, her expression lighting up with amusement as she looked back to her daughter.

"How on earth did you manage to do that? I rarely see Nemesis around the Pearl Castle," Passion said, setting her glass down as she moved over to the windows. They were opened, allowing in the fresh clean air. Electra crossed the room to stand opposite her mother by the windows.

"She uses the training room in the Pearl Castle every other day in the late afternoon," Electra replied with a small shrug. "I just waited and asked her. It took a little convincing, but she agreed."

Passion crossed her arms over her chest, patiently waiting for her daughter to continue. Electra glanced out the window, watching some messengers rush around in the courtyard. A few younger guardians were reading on benches in the gardens. The day was starting to get underway. Electra turned her eyes back to her mother.

"I'm going to help the protectors with the siege," she stated. "I won't let Isis fight alone. We lost her once and I refuse to let that happen again."

Passion pursed her lips a little and drummed her fingers on her arm, but she did not protest. Electra swallowed and rested her leg on the windowsill. She picked at her black pants, considering her next words.

"I won't go inside the laboratory, but I plan to help the shape shifters and their allies hold the perimeter. I don't want you to worry—"

Passion stared at her in disbelief. "Electra, I'm your mother. You're talking about going off to war and you think I'm *not* going to worry?"

"I have to do this, Mom," Electra protested. Passion smiled a little as she looked at her daughter, admiration shining in her eyes.

"I know you do. I won't try to stop you," Passion replied, brushing some hair behind her ear. Electra stared at her mother, who glistened in the sunlight. Passion was being unusually calm and not objecting at all. Electra had expected her mother to put up more of a protest.

"Guardians have mercy, you're planning on going to the laboratory," Electra said as realization dawned on her. Passion shrugged.

"The High Council isn't going to take an active part, but I'm not part of the Council nor am I ever likely to be," Passion responded. "I won't let my friends and family get slaughtered, not if I can do something to help them."

Electra stared at her. "Do you even know how to fight?"

"Yes, Electra. I'm not helpless," Passion said, somewhat offended. "The protectors will be there, so I won't be breaking any of our laws. Bending a few, perhaps."

"What about the law stating no interference in Earth matters?" Electra pointed out.

Passion waved a hand dismissively. "As I said, merely bending a few."

"Aneurin's going to be angry."

"Let him, he usually is," Passion replied with a shrug. "Electra, I know you're more than capable of fighting, but I want you to stay off the front lines. We can help defend the perimeter, but that's it. And you're to remain in my or Jet's sight at all times."

"Do you want to tell Jet or should I?"

Passion lifted her shoulders. "We'll surprise him. I have a feeling Lilly already knows."

Electra shook her head, smiling, and looked out across the land of the Meadows. She couldn't think of a time in her life when she was more worried or nervous. *I hope I can do some good. At least show my sister she's not alone.*

CHAPTER FOURTEEN

Set sat in a brown leather chair, squeezing a gripper in his right hand. The sound of the device was soothing and he squeezed the handles together at regular intervals. His feet were up on the windowsill and his gaze was outside, far out over his land. There was desert as far as the eye could see. The sand gleamed in the scorching sun, but Set was too angry to appreciate it as he normally did. Pyra sat nearby, paging through a magazine.

"Whose head should I collect for this recent slip-up, darling?" Set asked, calmly.

"I don't know, dear. If it were me, I would just burn down the bank with everyone inside," Pyra replied. Set squeezed the gripper again, his knuckles turning white with the intensity of his grip. He wanted to kill something, preferably slowly. He heard Pyra turn another page and struggled to maintain his indifferent demeanor. Rage was seething just under his flesh, yearning to be released.

"Explain to me again how a small group of shape shifters, most of them normals, managed to get into *my* bank, steal *my* drive, and escape with barely a scratch?" Set asked, keeping his composure as he cracked his neck. "What kind of staggering incompetence allowed that to happen?"

Pyra shrugged. "Send Chance out to remind them you are to be feared."

Set squeezed the grip again, letting out an angry little laugh. "Ah yes, Chance. Yet another problem I must deal with on a regular basis. Thanks to your son not having a modicum of self-control or foresight."

Pyra looked up, noticing Set's rigid posture. "You are getting worked up over nothing. The sensitive information on that drive can only be accessed with the living blood of a necromancer. The shape shifters won't be able to get that. The protectors are too moral to even consider torture, so we don't have to worry about them capturing a necromancer to drain them. If they even knew how to identify necromancers, which I made sure they never will."

Set rubbed his eyes with his free hand and then ran a finger over the arm of his chair. "Sweetheart, sometimes I *really* wonder how one as wise as you can be so utterly dense at times."

"Careful, dear," Pyra warned. "I'm not a minion you can push around or bully. Need I remind you what happened to the last person who tried?"

"I'm not in the mood to remind you of your place, but I will remind you that not all necromancers are loyal to us," Set said tersely, squeezing the grip again and releasing it. "Remember our other son's inability to control his own offspring."

Set looked over his shoulder, noticing his wife lean back against the leather couch. She spread her arms out over the back. Though Pyra looked unconcerned, Set could see the uncertainty flash across her face. He turned his attention back out the window to the emptiness beyond the pane of glass. The heat of the endless desert crept in through the walls, warming the large dwelling. Set didn't invest in air conditioning, preferring the arid heat.

"If you're referring to Anubis or whatever the hell he calls himself, he hasn't been seen since the two seven series were stolen. We put a high enough bounty on his head. If he's not already dead, he will be soon," Pyra stated. "He's not at the mansion or with the protectors. He would find no welcome among them."

Set gritted his teeth, his ire rising. "I cannot see into the mansion, lest you forgot. It would be the perfect place for him to hide and since he has sworn to destroy us, I'm fairly certain he would be able to find at least a few allies there."

Pyra placed her bare feet up on the table in front of the couch, rings glittering on her toes. "Are you actually *scared* of a half-breed necromancer? He's a normal. You have an army of living weapons at your disposal. One man isn't going to make a difference in this war. Besides, the guardians will never trust a necromancer, not even a half-breed. They'll throw him in the dungeons before he can get two words out. We'll retrieve him when we take the Meadows, make him suffer for his betrayal."

Set stood from his chair, laying the gripper on the window sill. The door to the main room opened, drawing both Pyra and Set's attention. Bram, their grandson, entered. He held a tablet in his large hands and had a confident smirk on his face. Out of all his family, Set found Bram to be one of the most arrogant. His parents had spoiled him and Set found him to be mostly useless.

"My lord Set, I have something that might interest you," Bram said, bowing.

"Oh good, I can't wait to see this," Set said as he crossed the room and took the tablet from Bram. Pyra ran her long fingers through her curly hair, watching the two.

"I have been reviewing the little information we retrieved from the bank that was robbed. As you know, most of the security footage was lost and we think the E-series might have shorted out the security cameras."

"Mm, yet another nuisance in my life," Set muttered, looking at the clean flat screen. His finger hovered over the screen.

"Well, we were able to retrieve a short amount of

footage from one of the cameras within the security box room."

Set glanced over at him, still unimpressed, and pressed the button on the screen. The video was grainy and he could barely make out a picture. Set watched as an eight series entered the room, then disappeared from the picture. Shortly afterward, some muzzle flashes appeared on the screen. The eight series stumbled back into frame and 7-299 — Blitz as she was better known — followed. The two experiments struggled and Set brought the tablet closer to his face.

"She's awfully good for a seven series," he observed. "An eight series should have brought her down by now."

"If you look in the background, you'll see the eight series managed to hit one of the other shape shifters," Bram pointed out. Set looked toward the corner of the screen and could just make out the blurry form on the ground. He turned his attention back to the fight, watching as the experiments disappeared out of frame again. The footage skipped and went fuzzy.

"If you keep watching to the end, it gets *a lot* more interesting," Bram said. Set watched as the seven series returned to the safe deposit room and ran to the fallen man and the Lock series.

"Is that the last Aldridge?" Set asked as he brought the tablet close to his face again.

"It is," Bram answered. Set continued watching the grainy footage. A thrill of excitement went up his spine as he watched the seven series retrieve a knife the eight series had dropped. He furrowed his brow when she sliced open her own palm and knelt beside the fallen man.

"What is she doing?" he asked himself, watching as she put her hand on the fallen man. He stared as her hands started to glow and a smile spread across his face. The footage skipped again and then showed the seven series helping the last Aldridge to his feet. The footage ended and Set handed the tablet back to Bram, waving him away.

Bram bowed low and left the room.

"Pyra, darling, on the women's side, the royal line is descended from Betha, is it not?" Set asked, rubbing his hands together with excitement.

"It is," Pyra responded, leaning forward and plucking a few grapes from the bowl on the table. Set chuckled as he continued rubbing his hands together.

"There are no healers in Betha's line; her abilities never passed down to her descendants, correct?" Set continued. Pyra shook her head.

"The royal line learns how to use herbs in medicinal ways, but they have never had the abilities of healers," she replied. "Why?"

"7-299 healed the last Aldridge," Set answered, drawing a line across his palm with the finger of his other hand. "Cut open her palm and laid it over his wound. Her hands were glowing, like the healers."

Pyra beamed. "She shouldn't be able to do that. Even if she did have healing abilities, she would have to be trained how to use them."

"And guardian healers have never had to spill blood to heal," Set added. "Who knows what other power is hidden in her."

"Not enough to tell whether or not she's the Key," Pyra pointed out.

"No, but she *is* special and therefore valuable."

Set made his way across the room, heading for the door.

"Where are you going now?"

"I didn't get this far by being blasé to the point of laziness," Set replied. "I'm going to make sure the laboratory is ready and waiting."

"You've already heightened security," Pyra reminded him, grabbing another magazine off the table.

"Yes, but now I want to transport the more promising products to another facility. If she somehow manages to get past the guards, I'd prefer she not get her hands on anything else of worth," Set responded. Pyra shrugged and started paging through her magazine. Set changed his direction and moved over to the couch. She looked at him when he leaned over the arm.

"Darling, you know how you can help me?" Set began, smiling. She closed the magazine and set it off to the side, looking at him with a small smirk.

"Go on," she said.

"Think you could make some fire traps for the laboratory? Ones that would melt the flesh off their bones?" Set requested. Pyra ran her fingers over the couch arm, pretending to think it over.

"Well, I suppose I could. If it would make you happy," she relented. He took her hand and kissed it, beaming from ear-to-ear.

~~*~*~*

The day of the raid, the mansion was alive with activity. A number of protectors had responded to Jet and Lilly's call for aid. Most of the shape shifters were quelling their nerves by spending time with their lovers and partners. There was no knowing how many would be coming back, so they were making the most of the time they had.

In her room, Isis was sitting at the small table. Her firearms were disassembled in front of her and she was cleaning the barrel of one. Jensen sat on the foot of her bed, sharpening one of his knives. They had been with each other since dawn. He seemed to enjoy her company and didn't distract her, so Isis allowed him to remain. Every now and again, she would catch him looking over at her. Isis reassembled one gun in a few seconds, as if she had been doing it since the day she was born.

Isis looked out the window she was sitting near. "There are at least seventy-five protectors by my count. We need more."

"Alpha is bringing a bunch of rebels," Jensen

mentioned, putting the knife in its sheath.

"We'll still need the Seelie Court and lycanthropes," Isis said, snapping a magazine into place without looking away from the window. She sat back, stretching her long legs out in front of her. A knock at her door drew their attention.

"The door is open," Isis called out when no one came in, resting a hand on one of the loaded handguns. The handle was pushed down and the door opened, revealing Orion and a tall stranger Isis didn't recognize. He had dark hair and aquiline features. The stranger held himself and moved in a very similar way to the guardians, but his flesh didn't glisten in the natural light. Isis glanced over at Jensen, noticing the recognition in his expression. She turned her attention back to Orion, waiting.

"Isis, I'd like to introduce you to Copper. He makes your weapons," Orion said. "Copper, this is—"

"The infamous Blitz, also known as Isis, happy to finally make your acquaintance," Copper interrupted, his gaze travelling over to the table. "Glad to see you respect those."

"The weapons you make are without equal," Isis complimented. "The finest I've ever wielded. You are quite talented."

Copper chuckled and stepped inside the room, laying a bag on the ground. He unzipped it to reveal more cartridges and some cylindrical objects.

"I have brought weapons for all the shape shifters and their allies, but I also made you a couple more things," Copper said with a grin. "More bullets for one thing. I know your guns have higher capacities, but it never hurts to have some backup."

Isis stood and approached, peering into the bag. Copper pulled out one of the small cylindrical objects and held it out for her to examine. She took the object in one hand, studying it. It was cool to the touch and had an unexpected weight to it.

"There is guardian silver in these," he explained, tapping the object with one finger. "It's similar to a grenade, but nowhere near as messy. There is a small explosion, but the dangerous part to wereanimals is the liquid silver inside. It disperses as a mist and will blind any wereanimal within fifty feet. It will also damage their lungs when they breathe it in and will cause a significant amount of irritation to their flesh."

"What about shape shifters or lycanthropes?" Orion asked. Copper waved him off.

"You won't be affected by it, unless you drink it. Orion, were you thinking of drinking guardian silver?" Copper asked with mock seriousness. Orion looked back out in the hall, muttering something under his breath. Copper snickered and looked back to Isis.

"I wish I could be there to see the look on the arrogant bastard's face when his empire crumbles," he said. Isis looked at him and he met her gaze, studying her for a moment.

"You are quite remarkable, you know," Copper observed. Isis tilted her head a little, confused. There was nothing remarkable about her, save being an experiment. She wasn't even a newer model. Normals found the strangest things impressive. Copper turned his blue eyes over to Jensen and reached in the bag.

"Jensen, I was hoping our paths would cross one day. I owe your family a great debt. They were always good to me, even after my exile. The Aldridges were the first to offer me a place to stay, after my family died. They never expected anything from me, never asked for anything, and were kind enough to keep me abreast of things in the world. Rarely a day goes by that I don't miss them," Copper explained, withdrawing a sheathed sword and a dagger from inside the bag. "A small gift. I was not there in their hour of need, but perhaps these will help protect you from those who would do you harm."

He handed over the blades, which Jensen accepted with

reverence. Jensen took the sword and pulled it from its sheath, marveling at the beauty of it. Isis stepped next to him, studying the engraving at the bottom. It was the Aldridge family crest, a unicorn and a wolf with the coat of arms between them and a star on top. Jensen tested the balance, whistling as he sheathed the weapon again.

"As an added trick, both blades will glow brighter if a necromancer is nearby," Copper added as he got to his feet again, nodding over toward Isis. "In case she's not around."

"These are the finest blades I've ever held," Jensen said as he examined the dagger, awestruck as he looked back to the former guardian. "Thank you."

Copper smiled and nodded once. "I've done what I can. The rest is up to the shape shifters and their allies."

He made his way out of the room. Orion started to follow, pausing at the door.

"I wanted to let you know, the Seelie Court and lycanthropes have agreed to send out troops to aid in our attack on the Grenich laboratory. They should be here just before sunset."

Orion left the room and closed the door behind him. Isis turned her attention over to where Jensen had sheathed his new dagger. She pulled the zipper down on the back of her catsuit and he looked over at her, smiling.

"Don't you need your adrenaline tonight?" he asked as she peeled the suit off and dropped it on the ground. Isis shrugged, about to respond to the strange question when Jensen moved over to her and captured her lips with his own as they backed up to the bed.

~~*~*~*

Shortly before sunset, Hunter drove down an empty road. Milo sat in the passenger seat, his eyes closed. He was clad in his midnight blue garb, topped off with black boots and gloves. Though his eyes were shut, Hunter knew he wasn't asleep. She couldn't remember being more on edge than she currently was.

"Hunter, I want you to listen to me," Milo began as he looked over at her. "Under no circumstances are you to leave the surveillance van. Do you understand?"

Hunter glanced over at him. "You think I'm just going to let shape shifters die? I'm more than capable of fighting and my father is going to need every able shape shifter on the field."

"I'm not questioning your ability or bravery. There are some pretty horrific things in that laboratory, things no shape shifter should have to see. And I'm not sure if we have the element of surprise. If we don't, Set is going to have some nasty things waiting for us inside," Milo explained, gesturing. "Pull over here."

Hunter did as instructed and put the car in park. She looked around at the towering trees surrounding them, following Milo as he moved through the forest, caution coloring his every step. Something was off about the forest. It didn't have the usual woodland scent and there was an unnatural chill in the air. Hunter pulled her light jacket tighter about herself.

"You think I don't know what goes on in the laboratory? I've got a window into that psycho's twisted imagination," Hunter whispered as Milo led her up a hill, which overlooked most of the forest.

"Chance is only the tip of a very large iceberg. What goes on in his mind and what he does, twisted as it is, is nothing compared to Set's or Pyra's."

As they neared the top, Milo got on his stomach and crawled under some tangled branches. Hunter stared after him before mirroring his movements. She paused when she was next to him, noticing he had pulled a small pair of binoculars out from his pocket. He lowered the binoculars and ran a thumb over his lower lip.

"It's a bit worse than I anticipated," he muttered,

handing the binoculars over to her. "We don't have the element of surprise. The woods surrounding the clearing are crawling with followers and wereanimals. Set also called in some other demons."

Hunter looked through the binoculars, staring into the clearing. There was an old shed that looked like it was on its last legs. It was surrounded by men in white uniforms, complete with helmets atop their heads. The nearest trees were brown and bare. The area in front of the shed was crawling with creatures that looked as though they had jumped out of a nightmare. Hunter felt a tremor go down her back when she saw the enormous gray beasts prowling about the woods. She had a flashback to the enormous werelion from the rebel Lair and her breathing quickened. Her vision started to go wavy, but she closed her eyes and counted to ten, willing the vision out of her mind the way Milo had taught her. Hunter opened her eyes again and her vision had gone back to normal. It wasn't the first time she was grateful to Milo for teaching her that trick. She turned her attention over to him, noticing he was still looking out over the land. He looked as scared as she had ever seen him look, but there was also a certain amount of anger in his expression.

"How are you going to get through that?" she whispered. Milo turned on his back and shrugged.

"I have the scent of a necromancer, so the wereanimals won't bother me. Their hatred of shape shifters is second only to their fear of necromancers," he explained. "This could work for us. Set might have his forces spread a little thinner than usual."

Hunter rested her chin on the back of her hands, looking out over the strange forest. It had an ominous feeling to it. There were numerous dead trees throughout the area. The whole place felt like some kind of underworld.

"I should head down," Milo whispered. "Remember, no Appearing when in the boundaries of the laboratory.

There's some kind of necromancer spell protecting the place and I'm not sure how far its reach is."

Milo scooted out again. Hunter turned to watch him disappear in some trees. She looked back out over the forest, pressing a button in her earpiece.

"Milo's going down now. Be warned — the woods are crawling with hostiles," she reported, looking back through the binoculars. After a moment, Hunter scooted back out and stood up, making her way back to the car. She had left a couple firearms in there and something told her she would need them before the night was over.

~~*~*~*

Once the sun set and the sky began to darken, the shape shifters and their allies arrived at the outskirts of the forest where the Grenich laboratory was located. A few had Appeared earlier and were waiting for the others. The Four, the Deverells, and Jet walked down the lines of lycanthropes, shape shifters, and the elves and fey from the Seelie Court. Isis noticed the Seelie Court warriors were wearing armor and the shape shifters were clad in Kevlar. The elves, fey, and lycanthropes had brought weapons more designed for close-proximity combat: swords, knives, staffs, bows and arrows. The shape shifters had opted for more modern weapons.

"The Seelie Court warriors and lycanthropes need to hold the forest, make sure no demons or wereanimals get out and send word for reinforcements," Isis told Jet. "Also, we want to keep the hostiles out of the laboratory. The creatures outside will not have guns, except for the guards protecting the entrance."

"We'll take care of those," Coop stated as he approached. Shocker followed close on his heels. His silver blond hair stood out in the night and his glowing eyes were wide. Isis could tell neither Coop nor Shocker was happy to be in such close proximity to the Corporation. Being so close to the facility was bringing up unpleasant memories for her too and Isis wanted to complete the raid as soon as possible.

"Where's Jack?" Shae asked, drawing Isis' attention to her. Shae and Jack had been in her room since the sun rose and only came down when it was time to leave.

"I'm here," Jack said as he approached. "I was helping Orion with some last minute set-up. They will have Milo in the interrogation room and Dane's in the skinning room, according to Hunter. He doesn't look in good shape."

"That's the last Key possibility?" Jet asked and Jack nodded. "Is Hunter with Orion?"

"She is," Jack answered and Jet massaged his forehead. Isis glanced at him, knowing he didn't like the idea of his youngest being in the midst of a battle.

"Are we late?"

The shape shifters all turned at the sound of Alpha's voice. She stood with Sly and a host of rebels. Isis stared, attempting to estimate how many rebels were there. It had to be at least fifty, probably more. She looked back to Jet, who looked beyond relieved. Sly sauntered over to where the Four were, wrapping an arm around Jade's waist.

"No, you are right on time," Jet said, gratitude clear in his voice. "Thank you, Alpha."

The rebel leader lifted her chin up and stood confidently. Shae and Alex both ran over to where Ace was standing among the rebels, greeting her enthusiastically. It was an exciting reunion for the three, judging by the amount of affection they showed. Isis looked back over her shoulder when Jensen approached.

"Okay, we move out in five minutes," Jet reported. The Deverells separated the protectors into groups while the elves and lycanthropes did the same.

Jensen took Isis' hand and led her a few steps away. She looked at him curiously as he held her palm out flat.

"I've been meaning to return this to you," he said as he

dropped a necklace into her hand. "It belongs to you. Coop gave it to me back when you first taken. I have kept it close ever since, but I think you should have it now."

Isis studied the emerald shamrock. It was made from guardian materials and engraved with a date, likely her birthdate, and the word "luck." She ran her thumb over the smooth stone then looked up at Jensen. Reaching up, she unclasped the cat charm around her throat. She took his hand and placed it in his palm.

"I know normals believe in luck and good fortune. If there is such a thing, this charm has given it to me," she explained. "No lasting harm has come to me while I wore it. Keep it safe for me."

Isis could see sadness in his expression. He was worried about her, about never seeing her again. *Very similar to what you're feeling right now,* the familiar voice of the ghost whispered in her ear. Jensen leaned forward and rested his forehead against hers and she closed her eyes, enjoying the simple contact. After a moment, Jensen straightened up.

"We need to go," he whispered. Isis stiffened when she heard a rustling sound behind her. Running toward it, she threw herself at the giant monstrosity, tackling the werewolf to the ground. The creature snarled and snapped, slashing at her with large talons. Removing a sai from her belt, Isis buried it deep in its skull. The werewolf shuddered and went still, melting back into its human form. Isis straightened up, looking around. The wereanimals had caught the scent of shape shifters and would start advancing.

"Bloody hell," Jensen breathed as he skidded to a stop beside her. She looked over at him and then back out into the woods.

"We need to move out now," she stated, turning back to him and gesturing for him to go back. "The elves and lycanthropes move first, drawing most of the attention toward them. Then Shocker knows what to do."

Jensen ran to relay her instructions to the waiting troops. Isis noticed a glint on the ground a few feet away and approached it, crouching down and retrieving the emerald necklace. Straightening up again, she placed it around her neck and tucked the charm in her catsuit. It felt pleasantly cool against her flesh.

~~*~*~*

Orion and Hunter both glanced to the side when something large slammed into the van, rocking it a little. Neither one was very concerned about the battle that was beginning outside. Orion didn't even look up when there was a heavy thump on top of the van. Hunter's hand drifted over the gun she was wearing at her hip while Orion sat back.

"So it begins," he said to himself. He reached forward and pressed a button on the small microphone on the table in front of them.

"Ajax, can you hear me?"

There was some crackling before Ajax's faint response. "Not very well."

"Remind Shocker there is a signal jammer installed in the facility, so we won't be able to direct you until he can short it out," Orion instructed him. There was a sound like thunder outside the van. Hunter could hear screams and yells alongside howling and snarling. The battle was increasing in intensity.

"Copy that."

Orion sat back and looked over at Hunter, who was staring at the back doors. She wanted to be outside, helping fight off whatever nightmares Set had released.

"Hardest job is sitting on the sidelines," Orion mentioned, looking over at the plain computer screens. The shape shifters wouldn't be able to see inside and were relying on maps programmed into handheld devices by

Milo and Shocker. Hunter began bouncing her leg, neurotically.

"Aren't you worried about your brothers?" she asked.

"Worried doesn't even begin to describe it. I imagine your mother is feeling something similar," Orion responded, folding one hand over the other. He knew that if she didn't have a duty as a ruler, Lilly would have been fighting alongside her husband and their people, as she had done in the past. But she had to remain at the mansion, in case Jet was killed in battle.

Hunter's eyes suddenly went wide and she looked toward the doors, rising from her chair.

"I have to go," she said as she grabbed the handle.

"Hunter, no. You have to stay here," Orion protested, rising and putting his hand on the door. "It's a war zone out there. Your parents would have my head."

"Listen, I can't explain it, but I'm needed in there," Hunter responded, desperation clear in her voice. Her hand remained on the door handle, gripping it tightly. "Chance is in there and he knows we're here, but he's not scared. If anything, he's excited."

Orion hesitated, a familiar tremor going through his left hand. He could feel his heart rate jump up. Knowing he couldn't stop her, Orion drew his hand away from the doors. Hunter threw one door open and jumped out into the chaos. Orion closed the door behind her and sat back, reaching under the table for the handgun he had brought. He checked to make sure it was loaded then tucked it in the back of his pants. Opening the door to the van, the eldest Deverell jumped out and hurried away into the night.

~~*~*~*

Isis watched as Shocker adjusted the small pack on his back and then laid his hand on the ground, looking ahead of them toward the shack in the clearing. There was a soft humming sound and a few small sparks began to shoot off the ends of his hair. Isis looked up to the small camera on the roof of the shack covering the entrance to the laboratory. The Seelie Court troops, lycanthropes, and shape shifters were doing a good job keeping the demons and wereanimals attention off of them. They had minimal trouble getting so close.

Isis saw the red light of the camera wink out and looked over to Coop and Jack, nodding once. Coop tapped Shocker's shoulder and the E-series stood up. The experiments ran forward, each attacking a guard. The guard Isis charged opened fire, drawing the attention of the other guards. Isis avoided the bullets and leapt at him, tackling him to the ground. The neck was the most vulnerable part of the uniform and Isis took advantage as she drew her knife, stabbing it deep into the jugular. Air hissed out of the wound and warm blood sprayed up in her face.

Isis looked over to where the other experiments were. They finished off their guards and Isis drew her guns, kicking open the shed door. There was an enormous, circular metal door in the center of the small area. The Grenich symbol was burned into it. Isis turned the metal wheel and pulled the heavy door open, her arms trembling under the weight. Once the round door was opened, she paused to listen for more guards. Normally there were fourteen, but now it sounded like seven. Isis glanced over her shoulder when Jack stepped inside. Their glowing eyes met and he pointed toward the entrance, indicating he would cover her. Isis turned back and jumped up on the ledge of the entrance. She dropped down past the first set of stairs into the shadows. The guards fired at the landing when they saw her shadow. She remained in a crouched position, just under the line of fire. Firing back, she took out five of the guards. Throwing herself over the railing, she twisted and fired behind her at the remaining two.

Landing in a crouching position, Isis looked around for any sign of movement.

Isis straightened up again, grabbed a small flashlight out of her belt and pointed it toward the stairway, flashing it twice. Soon, the other three experiments began leading the protectors down into the dome room. It was lit only with the yellow back-up lights, indicating Shocker had been able to knock out the main power. They didn't dare knock out the back-up power for fear of activating a self-destruct sequence.

"Jack, you and Sly take your team and evacuate the humans who work here," Isis instructed quietly, gesturing toward the door leading to the humans' quarters. "Shocker, take the Deverells and their team to the server room and download whatever information you can."

Shocker nodded and moved toward a door on the far side of the room, gesturing for his group to follow. Jensen winked at Isis and she pointed to her eyes, then to the door. He smiled and gave her a small salute.

"Last one out buys the drinks," Nero declared. Shocker pulled out a blank keycard with a magnetic strip and slid it through the door's lock. After typing in random numbers, he pulled open the heavy door and led the small group of shape shifters inside. Isis turned back to the remaining group. Jade, Alex, and Shae waited at the door to the barracks, waiting for Isis. Coop was also waiting, off to the side.

"The guards are revenants and heavily armed," Isis told them as she approached. "The experiments are not going to want to follow, which is why Shocker is going to turn on the evacuation signal. Try to stay out of their personal space and don't make physical contact."

Isis moved over to the door and slid the keycard through, punching in numbers. The light went from red to green and a loud click sounded. Isis hesitated, looking up at the door. That click was *not* a familiar noise.

"What's wrong?" Jade asked.

"I may have tripped something, a trap of some kind. Stand back," Isis warned as she grabbed the handle. Jade motioned for the other protectors to stand back, which they quickly did. Isis pulled open the heavy door and leapt to the side when she heard the roar of fire. She could feel the intense heat against the side of her face. After a moment, the fire died down and smoke hung thick in the air.

"What the hell was that?" Alex whispered as she straightened up again.

"A fire trap, made by Pyra," Isis replied, looking around for any other traps. "The flames are hotter than any found on Earth. Be extra careful where you step. There could be tripwires."

Isis turned out from the wall, crouching down so she could peer into the hall. She spotted the guards prowling around and shot one in the knee. A barrage of bullets caused Isis to spin back behind the cover of the wall. She pressed the button on her earpiece, waiting for Orion's response. When she received none, Isis turned back to where the protectors were getting in position. The jammer was still up. They were on their own.

Isis looked up when Jade spun out from behind the wall and fired a few rounds back. She returned to cover, glancing over to Alex, who was holding their device with the map of Grenich. Shae stood next to Isis, looking around the round room of doors.

"I could think of a couple hundred other places I would prefer to be right now," she mentioned as she spun out and fired at a guard. Isis gestured to one of the protectors who held some flash bombs, motioning for her to toss a couple in. She moved forward and pulled the pins, tossing the canisters inside. The shape shifters stood back, shielding their eyes and ears. After a moment, there was a bright flash of light and Jade motioned for the protectors to advance. Isis ran in, spotting two guards. She ran to one, grabbed his gun and fired at the second. Isis followed through by slamming her elbow into the throat of the first guard and then drew a throwing knife, hurling it at another approaching guard. She tossed the first guard over her hip, drew her handgun and fired into the helmet. Isis didn't stop moving as she ran to the door leading to the stairway down to the barracks.

"All right, I need ten protectors to stay here and hold this area," Jade instructed. "The rest come with us."

Jade, Alex, and Shae moved over to where Isis was typing in numbers. She paused, waiting for a noise. Letting out a breath, she pulled open the door and dove out of the way when the guards hiding inside began shooting. A couple protectors were hit and fell back. Isis threw herself to the side, firing up at the two revenants. They fell backward and one fell over the railing. Isis cautiously stepped into the stairwell, recognizing it almost instantly from her time at the corporation. She blinked, banishing whatever memories she had of her experiences at Grenich, and turned back to the protectors. Shae was helping one of the wounded ones, who was grimacing in pain.

"Barracks are down that way," Isis said, looking over to Coop. "Once the evacuation signal goes off, the experiments will start running out. Be careful when the doors open. There might be guards down there watching over the products and they will be patrolling the halls."

"What happens when they get outside?" Alex asked from where she was helping the second wounded protector to her feet. "Won't they start attacking us?"

"Unless we have specific orders otherwise, we tend to react more than instigate," Isis answered. "Get the wounded outside, if you can."

"Good luck," Shae said, offering Isis a small smile. Isis nodded once before following Coop out of the stairwell and back into the office area. There were revenant bodies everywhere and chances were there would soon be a couple protectors. The experiments were silent as they moved across the area, moving around the bodies, and back out into the dome room. Coop moved over to one of the neighboring doors, slid the keycard through the slot and punched in the numbers. The door beeped and Coop pulled it open, revealing a pitch black void. Isis peered down into the darkness, but saw nothing. She turned her eyes back to Coop, who met her gaze. She drew her gun and pointed it into the passageway, cautiously proceeding down and heading for the disciplinary rooms.

~~*~*~*

"You know what this reminds me of?"

Jensen grinned as he leaned out, firing at a couple guards in the hall. "Sicily, ninety-seven?"

Nero laughed. "Good times."

"That's because we were training, not fighting for our lives," Jensen responded, firing at a guard. The guards could take more punishment than anything he had ever been up against before. What was even more concerning was the lack of sweat. The head-to-toe uniform and the heat in the hallways would have made anyone perspire. The shape shifters were all sweating already, but the guards were not. *Revenants,* Jensen realized with a shake of his head as he fired again. He was wearing Kevlar over his suit, which was making him sweat more than usual.

Shocker put a hand on the ground, sparks beginning to shoot off the ends of his hair. Bright silver blue lines spread out from his fingers and raced across the floor. When they came into contact with the guards' feet, they started shaking violently and then collapsed. Shocker stood up again.

"That takes care of that," he said, brushing his hands off theatrically. "Server room is this way, gents."

Ajax walked up to Nero and Jensen, glancing over at the smoking heaps of the guards. "Malone and Devin will cover our backs along with the other protectors. How are things up here?"

He looked over when Shocker kicked open a door that blended in perfectly with the wall. Nero double-checked his gun to make sure he had enough rounds, nodding.

"The guards are revenants," Jensen reported, replacing the magazine in his gun. "They don't fall unless shot in the head."

Ajax moved over to the doorway where Shocker had disappeared, checking for any guards. A few pops were heard and then Shocker poked his head back out.

"The faster the better," he said, disappearing back inside the room. Nero and Jensen cautiously moved in first, followed closely by Ajax. Jensen looked around the space, noticing a series of blue, red, and green lights on the enormous machines. Some of the lights blinked while others remained constant. There was a soft humming noise throughout the room and it was a lot warmer than it had been in the hall.

"Welcome to the guts of the building," Shocker said wearily. "Guy with the laptop and funny-sounding name, you can plug in over here. Not sure how much useful information we'll be able to get, but it's worth a try."

Jensen could barely make out the forms of the other shape shifters in the dim light. Uneasiness was creeping into his mind. He didn't like being in such dark surroundings. It was too easy to be ambushed in such a situation.

"Nero, do me a favor," Jensen whispered to his friend. "Check to see if our earpieces are working yet."

"Orion, respond if you can hear me," Nero said, waiting for a reply. "Isis, Jade, Shae, anyone else? Please respond if you can hear me."

Jensen could just see Nero shrug. He bit the inside of his cheek and stiffened when he heard the familiar popping of gunfire outside. Turning back when he heard a loud pounding somewhere off to the side, Jensen squinted as he tried to see through the shadows.

"Evacuation signal has been switched on," Shocker reported, followed shortly by a loud crashing sound. "Now it won't be turned off."

"What about the signal jammer?" Jensen asked when Shocker approached them. The experiment's glowing silver eyes were all Jensen could see and it freaked him out. Shocker continued walking.

"I knocked that thing out when we first came in, right after I kicked the door in," Shocker replied as he continued back to where Ajax was. "Your earpieces should be working."

Jensen looked over at Nero, who was standing by the entrance. Noticing a shape stop by the doorway, Jensen hid behind one of the large machines. Bullets slammed into the bulky machine he was behind, and Jensen turned his face away. He looked back to Nero, who quickly returned fire and then sought cover. Turning back, Jensen heard gunfire toward the back of the room.

"Nero, you good?" Jensen called out.

"Yeah," Nero shouted back, leaning out from behind his cover to return fire. "Go check on my brother. I'll keep these guys off your back."

Jensen started making his way back to where the shots originated. A large bright bolt of what looked like lightning shot out from the right, forcing Jensen to close his eyes briefly. When the light died down, Jensen stared at where the electric bolt had been.

"Arseholes," Shocker's voice was barely audible over the racket. Jensen ran toward the back, ignoring the smell of cooking flesh. He reached the end of the row of machines and heard a groan of pain. He looked to the left and spotted Ajax's form slumped against the wall. Jensen could smell blood and noticed the older shape shifter clutching his upper arm. Shocker stood in front of him, one hand held out toward a smoking heap. He slowly dropped his arm, his gaze never moving from the man he'd just killed.

"That one's been shot," he reported. "Shoulder, bullet went straight through, nothing major was hit. Blood loss might be a concern. You normals are so fragile."

Jensen moved over to where Ajax was still on the ground. Ajax waved him off, indicating he would be fine.

"The laptop, get the laptop," Ajax managed to grunt out as he used the wall to push himself up. Jensen slid over to where the laptop was still opened, gritting his teeth when he saw it had taken a few rounds.

"Shocker, can you copy any useful files and other information you can find?" Jensen asked as the experiment looked back to him. "This laptop's finished."

"It won't be much, but I'll see what I can do," Shocker said as he approached them, taking the small pack off his back. He flipped open the top flap and removed a smaller laptop. "I'll meet you outside when I'm through. Shouldn't be more than a few minutes."

"Thank you." Jensen turned his attention back to Ajax. "We need to get outside, help fight off whatever's left of the hostiles."

Ajax gestured for Jensen to lead the way. Nero was waiting for them, covering the entryway.

"Ajax, what the hell? Did you get shot or something?" Nero asked when they approached. Ajax gave him a very dry look as they made their way back out into the hall, the yellow lights now blinking regularly. He remained between his younger brother and Jensen, trusting them to lead the way out. Jensen fired when a couple more revenants rounded the corner. They promptly returned fire and Jensen was knocked down by what felt like a battering ram.

"Jensen! No!" he heard Nero yell. "Don't die!"

"I'm not going to die," Jensen grumbled, returning fire as he staggered behind cover. "Kevlar, remember?"

Nero bolted across the hall, standing behind Jensen. "Aldridge, you have more lives than a damn cat."

"We need to figure out why our earpieces aren't working," Jensen called over his shoulder. Nero led them back toward the dome room, passing by the bodies of a few protectors and some revenants. Jensen looked around the hallway, suppressing a shudder. The entire place had the unnerving feeling of lifelessness to it and Jensen couldn't wait to be outside. He would take wereanimals over revenants any day.

The revenants continued advancing when a blindingly bright bolt of electricity shot out from the entryway. The two revenants shook violently as it pierced through them, dropping to the ground in smoking heaps.

"You're welcome," Shocker's faint voice called out.

"He may be a pain in the ass, but you gotta admit, he does come in handy," Nero mentioned from behind Jensen. Jensen kept his gun pointed in front of him as they started to make their way out.

~~*~*~*

Hunter made her way through the halls, her gun drawn and pointed in front of her. She felt as though she had been through the halls before. Chance had once roamed these corridors like a king, striking fear in anyone he came across. His memories proved to be a very useful tool. She knew where to duck and hide whenever a guard came by. Already several revenants had run right past her. *Being connected to a murdering psychopath has a few uses,* Hunter thought as she continued on. She could hear constant gunfire behind her, growing fainter as she got further inside the laboratory.

Turning another corner, Hunter quickly turned back. There were two guards standing in the hall, their backs to her. Her breathing quickened as she tried to figure out what to do. Though she was a capable fighter, Hunter had never been up against an opponent with a firearm. Taking a deep breath, she turned out from the corner and fired at the guards. She hit the first and he fell, but the second returned fire. Hunter ducked back behind the wall again, listening to the footsteps approaching. Throwing herself to the ground, she fired up at the approaching guard. Her shot found its mark and the guard toppled.

Hunter scrambled to her feet and crept through the hall, trying to ignore the discolored blood leaking out of the revenants. Everything was painted a strange shade of powder blue with the doors painted a shade or two darker. Somewhere ahead of her, she could hear the faint sound of flesh against flesh, followed by indistinct conversation. First there was a man's growl, followed by Milo's taunting retort. Hunter couldn't help but shake her head and roll her eyes. Of course he would be taunting them. Everyone connected to Grenich seemed to have a death wish.

Hunter approached the door, reaching out for the knob. An arm wrapped around her throat and Hunter felt her feet leave the floor as she was lifted clear off the ground. Gagging for air, she reached into her belt with her free hand and pulled her knife, thrusting it behind her. She buried the blade into the attacker up to the hilt but it didn't seem to affect him as much as it should have. Hunter was thrown across the hall where she collided with the wall and lost her grip on her gun. Dazed, Hunter shook her head a couple times to clear her vision.

Looking up into the face of an unnaturally tall, broad-shouldered man, Hunter swallowed her nervousness. He slowly pulled the knife out of his gut and hurled it at her with a snarl. Thinking fast, Hunter rolled out of the knife's trajectory and it embedded in the wall with a dull thud. She reached for her gun and fired at the enormous man, hitting him in the shoulder. It seemed to make him angrier as he roared and reached down for her head. Leaping up, she shot past his ear, causing him to reel away from the noise. Hunter ran for the door and kicked it open. Two guns were instantly turned on her and she pointed her own gun at the two guards in the room. Adrenaline was coursing through her system and she struggled to control her breathing.

Milo was being held as a shield by a petite blonde woman, who looked familiar to Hunter. He was sporting a black eye and she was certain his clothes hid more wounds.

"You can't even follow one relatively simple instruction? Really?" Milo asked with a shake of his head, closing his eyes in exasperation. "Fucking bullheaded protectors."

"A little gratitude wouldn't kill you, you know," Hunter responded, turning her attention to the woman who was using Milo as a shield. "Let him go and maybe I'll let you live."

"Hunter, listen to me. Shoot her," Milo called out to her. "In the face if you can."

The woman's lips curled up in a smile as she looked over Milo's shoulder to Hunter. "Aren't you just an adorable little thing? Acting all tough like a grown-up, Jet and Lilly must be so proud. Unfortunately, it's not survival of the nicest or bravest or even the most worthy. If that were the case, perhaps your brother and sister would still be alive. Sorry, love."

Without warning, the blonde woman buried her knife deep into Milo's stomach, causing him to yell out in pain. Once he dropped, Hunter fired at the blonde woman. The bullet pierced her chest, but didn't seem to faze her. She looked down at the blood blossoming on her shirt, amused.

"You cheeky little bitch. I just bought this," she smiled. "Normally, I'd make you lick it clean, but that will have to wait."

The woman waved her hand as if she were shooing a fly and Hunter went sailing backward, crashing into the opposite wall. She couldn't smother the cry of pain that escaped her. Pushing herself up on her hands, Hunter looked over to the strange woman.

"I've got a flight to catch and you probably want to make some futile attempt to save your friend. Silly little protector child," the woman finished in her condescending tone.

"Don't let her go," Milo choked out. The woman kicked him in the side, causing him to curl up in pain. The strange woman backed up into the shadows of the room, followed by her two armed guards. Hunter grimaced as she pushed herself to her feet, stumbling over to where Milo was laying, writhing in pain.

"Shit, fuck, dammit, Milo!" Hunter swore as she tore off her jacket and pressed it against the gaping wound in his gut. The wounded man was trembling and the color was draining from his face.

"Yeah, swearing will fix me," Milo groaned. "I'm done for anyway. You just let a top Grenich asset waltz out the door. You should have shot her in the head."

"We need to get you to a guardian healer," Hunter said, ignoring him. "Hold this against the wound and lean on me."

"Guardian magic won't work. Half-necromancer, remember?" Milo replied, allowing her to help him up. "Dammit, this really hurts."

"The earpieces still aren't working," Hunter told him, taking most of his weight onto her shoulders. He staggered as she started to lead him out of the room, keeping her eyes peeled for any sign of the giant she had encountered earlier. The lights in the hall were flashing yellow and then white.

"What the hell is that?"

"Evacuation signal," Milo replied, stumbling and almost bringing her down with him. "At least one part of the plan seems to have gone right."

~~*~*~*

Jet threw a strange reptilian-looking man over his hip,

stabbing him with the fighting dagger he had brought. Around him, the forest was alive with the sound of metal clashing against metal. It was still crawling with demons, Set's followers, and wereanimals. The protector leader was painfully aware of how long it had been since he had fought in a real battle. Every strike felt like it rattled his bones and he was sweating profusely. Jet had already taken a few nicks and he could feel the warm blood dripping down his arm.

"Jet, look out!"

Jet instinctively ducked and heard the twang of an arrow followed by a roar. He looked over to where the noise had been and saw a demon lying dangerously close to him. There was a guardian arrow sticking out of its eye socket.

"Passion!?" Jet asked, not believing his eyes when the guardian ran toward him. She leapt out of the way of an axe and deflected another blow with her battle knives. Kicking out, she knocked a large follower away from her. As she continued running for Jet, an arrow pierced the back of the demon's skull. Passion reached Jet and helped him to his feet. Her hair was tied tightly back and she was wearing guardian leather armor.

"What in the name of all the guardians are you doing here?" Jet demanded as she put her back against his.

"Saving your ass, like usual. Your wife would have my head if I let you get killed," Passion responded, blocking a blade and stabbing at a demon who attacked them. Jet looked around and noticed Electra standing a few feet away, with some elves. She had a bow and an arrow nocked, which she let fly. It killed a werelion that was stalking up to her mother and Jet.

"The High Council is going to have both your heads," Jet warned as he stabbed a follower who was running toward him. There was a hiss of air as the creature fell. He could feel Passion trading blows with another hostile. The stench of blood hung in the air and Jet could see both dead allies and enemies. The Seelie Court and lycanthropes were great fighters, but so were the forces of Grenich.

"How are things going in the laboratory?" Passion yelled over the melee. She deflected a sword and punched a large demon in the face. She kicked him in the chest and swung her knives down, burying one in the creature's throat. Gray blood sprayed up as the creature fell forward.

"I don't know," Jet replied. Passion turned to look at him when a werewolf lunged at her. A large battle knife pierced the air near her ear, slicing through the creature's skull. Both Passion and Jet turned and saw Donovan standing next to Electra, shaking his head in disappointment.

"You two are crap fighters," he observed. Electra drew another arrow and stabbed a demon that had been sneaking up on the night guardian. The demon fell backward, causing a few nearby elves to swing their bows around.

"You were saying?" she asked dryly.

CHAPTER FIFTEEN

Isis and Coop moved through the halls like sharks through water. The low lighting didn't hinder their ability to see at all. Antiseptic and bleach stung their sensitive noses, growing more pronounced the deeper they went into the lab. As they turned down another hall, they encountered four guards who opened fire. Both Isis and Coop dove out of the way, quickly holstering their firearms. Pausing for a moment, they pressed their heels into the ground and sprinted forward, positioning themselves in the center of the four guards. Pushing the rifle of one guard up, Isis spun into him and elbowed him in the throat. Forcing the rifle down, she smacked the side of the helmet with the butt of the firearm and then kicked him in the stomach. Yanking the gun out of his grip, she turned and fired at the guard behind her. Turning back, Isis shot the guard she had taken the rifle from. Looking back over her shoulder, she watched Coop take out the final guard. Isis removed the rounds from the rifle and then tossed the empty firearm away. Coop did the same and they continued forward toward the silver door at the end of the hall. Reaching out, Isis turned the knob and pushed the door open while keeping her back to the wall.

Both experiments peered inside the room, remaining hidden behind the relative safety of the wall. The room was pitch black except for the floodlights illuminating the nude man on the rack. His head was slumped forward and blood was dripping from dozens of wounds. He had been skinned fairly recently and the skin was slowly healing over the exposed muscles.

"That's Dane," Coop whispered, moving forward into the room.

"No, wait," Isis hissed, reaching out to grab him. Coop stepped into the room and was sent flying by a large hammer. Isis sprinted inside, ducking under another swing and spinning to face her opponent. She had to look up to see the sneering mask atop the giant. The man towered over her and was wearing what looked like an iron suit. Isis swallowed as she looked for any weaknesses. She back flipped when he swung at her with the enormous hammer again. As she came up, she pulled out her sais. The sound of someone clicking their tongue made her hesitate. She recognized his scent shortly before Coop had impulsively entered the room. In her peripheral vision, she could see the eggshell-colored suit emerge from the shadows. Isis kept her attention fixed on the giant with the hammer, which he now spun in his hand. The face molded into the iron helmet was one of anger, a snarling mouth baring its numerous teeth. Looking up, Isis could just make out the whites of the towering man's eyes. Everything about him was meant to intimidate, but she had found a few potential weak points in his armor. She attempted to position herself so she could keep her focus on both threats.

"The prodigal lab rat returns," Nick Chance said as he approached her. "Couldn't stay away could you?"

He swung the weighted end of his cane at her. Isis blocked with her sais. She stabbed forward and he moved away from her, smiling widely, as though entertained. The male symbols painted around his eyes made the bright blue of his irises stand out even in the shadows. Isis swallowed, steeling herself. Chance pressed a button just under the weighted end of the cane and the wood began to morph into steel. Soon, he was holding a serrated sword.

Isis dodged when he swept the blade down at her head. She parried another blow with her sais. Lunging backward, she narrowly avoided being disemboweled. Isis continued to dance just out of reach of the serrated sword. She heard a rush of air and arched back, avoiding getting her skull caved in by the enormous hammer. Turning back to Chance, she managed to escape getting run through, but the serrated edge sliced her side open and she gasped. Chance lunged forward and grabbed her throat, lifting her off the ground. She stabbed his wrist, but his vice-like grip didn't waver. He pressed the sword against her wounded side, preventing it from healing. Her vision went spotty as she struggled not to cry out. Isis swallowed and held his gaze, even as her vision swam.

"Did you really think a fucking lab rat could win against necromancers? We were working on genetic research when humans were still shitting in their drinking water," he growled at her, pressing the sword deeper into the wound. Isis kicked out, her foot striking him in the groin. Chance howled and dropped her to the ground. Isis scrambled to her feet, her wound rapidly beginning to heal. A giant hand latched onto the back of her neck and tossed her across the room as if she were a ragdoll. Isis hit the ground and rolled across the floor, colliding with the opposite wall. She started to get to her feet when Chance appeared over her and kicked her in the face, knocking her back against the wall again. He kicked her in the ribs a couple more times before stepping back, swinging his sword. Isis swallowed as she twisted around, watching him and preparing for his next attack. Adrenaline was coursing through her body and it needed an outlet. Her wounds had already healed and she was ready to attack again, but Isis was patient as she waited for the opportune moment.

"You're a monster, seven series. More than me, more

than Set," Chance stated, wiping the back of his hand over his mouth. "It's why you came back. You need this place because the only time you feel pleasure is when you're fighting and killing. The amount of blood on your hands? You can scrub all you like, it's *never* coming off. Sooner or later, the normals will understand that."

Isis just watched him, saying nothing. Chance lifted his sword, swinging it once, laughing gleefully as he advanced to finish her. He thrust down as if to spear her through. Isis spun away from the sword, rising to her feet in one fluid motion, and stabbed her sai deep into Chance's back. She felt his body stiffen and a high-pitched yelp came out of him. Yanking her sai free, Isis kicked him against the wall and he smashed into it face first. Leaping up into a spinning kick, Isis knocked him flat on the ground. She lunged forward, her sais drawn, but paused. Chance glared up at her, seething.

"What are you waiting for?"

Isis was quiet for a moment. "Grenich doesn't own me, neither do the necromancers. I make my own decisions and I won't ever kill for them again."

She ducked down and spun out of the way of another hammer strike. The enormous man came at her again and Isis backed up, trying not to lose sight of Chance. As she avoided the enormous hammer, she saw Chance pull a bejeweled knife out from behind his back. He waggled it at her before stabbing it into the air. She stared as he pulled the knife down, cutting open what looked like a curtain in thin air. Within a matter of seconds, Chance had pulled himself through the strange curtain and disappeared.

Isis grabbed hold of the arm of the enormous armored man, wrapped her legs around his neck, and used her momentum to swing around, throwing him to the ground. Grabbing the hammer out of his grasp, Isis lifted it up and smashed it into the back of the enormous man's head. Smashing it again, blood sprayed across the floor and pooled beneath the helmet as the body shuddered and twitched. Isis dropped the hammer and looked around the room. She could hear a man groaning but wasn't sure whether it was Dane or Coop. Coop stumbled to his feet and staggered over to where Dane was still hanging on the rack. He started working on his bindings, taking most of the wounded man's weight onto himself. Isis approached them, her senses sharp for any other threats.

"Coop?" Dane whispered weakly.

"I'm here," Coop responded, continuing to work on the bindings. "We're going to get you out of here. Just hang on."

Dane's head dropped forward and he rested his brow on Coop's shoulder, nodding a little. Isis studied Coop and he glanced at her briefly.

"I'm fine," Coop coughed as he finished with the bindings and carefully lowered Dane down from the rack. "My ribs were broken, but they're mostly healed."

They both looked over to the door when they heard it slam followed by a soft click. Isis dashed to the now shut door and tried the knob, finding it was locked. The yellow light turned red and she looked back to Coop. Red lights were not a good sign.

~~*~*~*

Orion continued through the forest, the sound of the helicopter blades getting louder. The Seelie Court warriors, lycanthropes, and shape shifters were doing a brilliant job keeping the Grenich allies at bay, but it was a double-edged sword. By keeping them busy, more important quarry could escape. The nightmarish creatures were cannon fodder, a distraction. Orion could see a light up ahead and the whirring of the blades was much closer. As Orion emerged into another clearing, he saw the man in the long gray coat moving toward the waiting helicopter. A petite blond woman was walking alongside him.

"Carding!" Orion shouted, aiming his gun at the man's head. Carding stopped as did the woman, who Orion recognized as Tracy. Tracy moved to Carding's other side, aiming her own gun at Orion. He didn't care though. Orion had been waiting for this moment for years and he wasn't about to let it slip through his fingers. He had questioned whether he would be able to pull the trigger, but there was no question any longer. Carding was going to die, even if it cost Orion his own life.

Carding turned around, his form massive in the night. The lights around the helicopter framed him, making him appear larger than he was. Even from where he was standing, Orion could see the jovial smile on his face. Tracy remained standing beside him, her gun trained on Orion. Her face betrayed no emotion. The strong winds from the chopper barely moved her hair.

"Dr. Deverell," Carding greeted in his typical booming boisterous way. "It is good to see you again. Tracy, look, it's our old friend, Dr. Deverell. How are you, doctor?"

"You ordered my family's murder and the murders of countless other shape shifters. I'm here to return the favor," Orion shouted back. Carding held up a hand, reaching into his pocket.

"Don't!" Orion snapped.

"I just want to show you something, Dr. Deverell," Carding reassured him, pulling a small blue and gray device out of one pocket. "Do you know what this is?"

Orion stared at the gadget, but couldn't identify it. He looked back to Carding, who waggled it. He glanced over to Tracy, nodding once. With her free hand, she pulled out a thin silver cylindrical device with a red button on top. The button was glowing.

"You see, Dr. Deverell, we had a feeling you would cause some trouble, so precautions were taken. What Tracy holds is a kill switch, which we activated about a minute or so ago. In a little more than five minutes, a fire created by Pyra will spread through the entire facility, destroying everything and everyone inside. After that, it will collapse in on itself. Not even an experiment will be able to survive that," Carding explained. "Now what I'm holding is a portable signal jammer. It has a limited range but it can't be deactivated. Once I'm up in that chopper, your communicative devices will go back online. You can evacuate whomever may be left in the facility. *Or* you can kill me, Tracy will kill you, and whoever is left in the facility will meet a fiery painful end. Your call, doctor."

Orion gritted his teeth, his eyes narrowing. He could feel winds from the chopper beating against him. Carding smirked, pocketing the jammer again.

"How many lives are you willing to sacrifice, doctor?" Tracy called out.

"Fuck!" Orion yelled in frustration, lowering his gun. Carding smirked and made his way to the helicopter.

"You know, I would shoot you, but watching you tear yourself apart is just too entertaining," Tracy called over to him before running for the waiting chopper. Orion watched as the helicopter took off, disappearing into the night sky. His earpiece crackled once and Orion pressed the button on it.

"Everyone, you have maybe four minutes to get out of the facility. Get out of there now!" Orion shouted as he ran back toward the facility. The air was alive with the sounds of battle and death.

~~*~*~*

"Man, I can't even remember the last time I fought with a sword."

Jensen couldn't help but chuckle at Nero's excitement. The youngest Deverell stabbed at a demon that looked like a cross between a bat and a human. The creature snarled and lashed out at Nero with his long tail, slicing open his cheek.

"Ow! Fuck you! That's not fair!" Nero groused, letting out a yip when an arrow pierced the demon's throat. Jensen stabbed a wereleopard and looked over at the fallen demon.

"That's not a Seelie Court arrow," he observed. "That's from the Meadows!"

Both Nero and Jensen turned to look where the arrow had come from. They soon spotted Electra as she nocked another arrow, letting it fly. They exchanged a lock of surprise, wondering if Passion knew her daughter was out in the pandemonium. Jensen shrugged and they turned their focus back to the fight.

"Jensen, Nero, fall back!" Jade yelled as she and Alex ran past them. "The facility is going to collapse!"

"Wait, is everyone out?" Nero asked as he and Jensen followed the two women, cutting down whatever enemies remained. The Grenich allies seemed to be retreating into the night in the opposite direction. All that remained were the bodies of the fallen. There were a number of protectors, Seelie Court warriors, and lycanthropes dead alongside wereanimals, demons, and Set's followers.

"We evacuated all the experiments and humans, but not everyone has checked in yet," Alex replied as they continued running. The ground started shaking and there was a soft roaring, similar to fire. They reached the surveillance van where the surviving allies had gathered. Nobody had escaped unscathed and everyone looked exhausted. Jensen noticed Passion wrapping gauze around Jet's shoulder. The protector leader was grimacing in pain, blood flowing from a number of wounds. Ajax sat nearby, still clutching his wounded arm.

"Dad!"

Both Jet and Jensen turned at Hunter's voice. Devin and Malone stood next to her, helping to hold up Milo, who didn't look good. His head lolled around, his face was colorless, and there was blood flowing from a deep wound in his abdomen.

"Found them out in the field," Devin reported as Hunter ran to her wounded father.

"What were you doing out of the surveillance van?" Jet asked, trying to sound angry.

"Jet, stay still," Passion ordered crossly. "You're worse than a child."

Jensen glanced over to Electra, who put her bow over her back and moved to help with Milo. He noticed Donovan standing nearby, talking with some warriors from the Seelie Court. *How many guardians are here?* Jensen wondered, looking around. He saw Ace standing near a tall woman, whom he recognized as Sabina.

"Devin, could you and your brothers take a count? See how many we lost," Jet requested. Devin and Malone started moving toward the field. They paused when they heard Electra.

"Where's Isis?"

Things went quiet and everyone looked around. Jensen felt his heart sink as he searched the night, running his thumb over the cat charm in his pocket. He could see nothing but shadows. It was pleasantly cool, but there was a distinct smell of fire and blood in the air.

"Isis, please report," Alex said into her earpiece, pausing and waiting for a response. Everyone with earpieces waited for a reply, but it remained silent. Alex repeated the call and waited again. Again there was no answer. Jensen looked up when Orion came around the corner of the van, taking in the sight before him. Sweat glistened on his brow and his short hair looked windswept.

"Did everyone get out?" the eldest Deverell asked, out of breath. He looked over to Ace and then at Jack, relief apparent in his expression.

"We can't find Isis," Jet told him as Passion continued binding his wounds, staring at Orion suspiciously. "Where were you?"

"Coop's missing too, by the way. In case you lot forgot about him," Shocker grumbled as he approached from the front of the van. Orion looked around, almost frantically. He rested a hand on his head, stroking his hair.

"Orion, where were you?"

"I went after Carding," Orion answered, still looking out into the night. "He had a jammer, which is why the earpieces were down even after Shocker shorted out the one in the facility."

"Jensen, Nero, you want to help us?" Malone asked. Both men nodded and moved to follow the two Deverell brothers back out into the field. Electra jogged over to them, standing next to Jensen.

"I'm coming with you," she said, pausing as she looked over in the distance. "Wow, look at that."

Jensen and Nero followed her gaze to the field beyond the Seelie Court warriors and lycanthropes, where the liberated experiments were. They couldn't see anything besides their glowing eyes. All the colors of the rainbow were seen in the large group. Most had no expression but there were a few who looked fearful or uncertain. As Jensen watched them, he tried to count how many there were but found he could not.

"Do we know how many there are?" he asked quietly to no one in particular.

"Orion estimates more than two-hundred," Malone answered, shaking his head. "Guardians have mercy, who knows what they've been going through."

They watched as Jack approached the large group of experiments, who seemed to lean toward him. They obviously didn't know what to do and were looking for some kind of instructions or orders.

The small group all stiffened when they heard a familiar metallic whisper, followed by a soft thud. Jensen spun around, noticing the body of a follower lying a few feet away from him. It was holding a gigantic scythe. Looking up, Jensen saw two pairs of glowing eyes, one green and the other blue. Isis and Coop stood a few feet away from the follower, a barely conscious man with glowing brown eyes held between them.

"You shoot like a human girl," the stranger laughed, which turned into a cough. His body shuddered in pain and he dropped his head to his chest.

"I am a woman, not a girl, and there is no discernible gendered difference in shooting," Isis responded as she ducked out from under the man's arm. Electra ran over to her sister and wrapped her arms around her. Isis looked a bit confused and went slightly rigid, but returned the hug with one arm. Passion straightened up and her eyes welled up when she saw her two daughters. Jensen waited patiently until Electra stepped out of the embrace. Isis approached him.

"You're not dead," she observed. Jensen chuckled at her forthrightness. She frowned and reached out, touching the hole in his suit from where the guard had shot him.

"Disappointed?"

She stared at him. "Your humor is confusing."

Jensen grinned and kissed her, which she returned. After a moment, she pulled back and rested her forehead against his. For the first time since returning to the mansion, Jensen thought he saw a hint of a smile. It was gone as soon as he thought he saw it and she took a step back, her gaze turning to the large group of experiments.

"Did we take any prisoners?" Isis asked the Deverells. Malone looked over at his brothers in the thinning night. He looked back to Isis and shook his head. She seemed mildly disappointed at the answer. Jensen followed Isis as she moved over to where Passion was helping Jet to his feet.

"You are wounded," she observed.

"I've had worse," Jet said, smiling at her. "You look a bit singed."

"We narrowly made it out before the fire, but Set wouldn't have let two possible Keys burn," Isis stated, turning her attention over to where Coop was helping the experiment sit on the bumper of the van. "There was an emergency exit door hidden in the room. We managed to force it open and get out."

"Is he okay?" Passion asked, nodding over to the stranger, who fell off the bumper. Isis looked back to where she was indicating.

"He's called Dane, another seven series, earlier than Jack or I, the last Key possibility. He's been tortured for the past couple weeks, probably for information on Jack or myself," she explained. "His body is healing and he'll soon go into a sleeping state. Depending on the amount of damage we sustain, our bodies go into a recuperative rest that resembles sleep."

"We need to gather the wounded and the dead," Jet mentioned. "Have the Deverells secure the scene so the healers can do their job."

"The experiments might be better equipped for such a task," Isis suggested. "Jack and I can speak with them."

Jet looked a little unsure, but relented. Jensen watched as Isis approached Jack, who had been speaking with Shae. The two experiments moved over to the large mass of glowing eyes.

"Man, those are the creepiest shape shifters," Jensen overheard a protector comment.

"Are they shape shifters?" another responded. "One of them broke Harris' arm, like it was nothing more than a twig. All he did was try to direct her the right way."

"Seems like we just created a bigger problem than we started with."

"Let's hope the guardians at least confine some of the less stable ones."

Jensen turned, trying to find the two protectors but couldn't. Looking over at Nero, he could see the youngest Deverell had heard the exchange. Jensen swallowed, scanning the living shape shifters for the rebels. He noticed Alpha speaking with Sabina and made his way over to them. The rebels were standing in a large group, trading flasks and talking amongst themselves. A few of the older rebels were helping the wounded, wrapping busted limbs and bandaging gashes.

"Alpha, may I have a word?" Jensen requested, smiling politely at Sabina. The two women looked at him and he kicked himself for forgetting rebel traditions. There wasn't a discernable hierarchy and they tended to be more transparent than protectors.

"I was just wondering what the rebels' opinion was on experiments," he continued, sticking his hands in his pockets. Sabina looked over at Alpha with a half-smile. The rebel leader had leaves and twigs in her hair and splashes of mud and blood on her face. Both rebels looked to the side when the experiments started to move out, canvassing the battleground for any lurking enemies.

"Unlike protectors, we have some individuality," Alpha stated, unable to pass up an opportunity to jab at the protectors.

"Are you scared of them?"

"I think I would be a fool not to be," Alpha replied. "Still, they're shape shifters, albeit with no allegiance to any group. They've been through a horrendous ordeal and likely are traumatized to some extent, but shape shifters nonetheless. Why?"

"I overheard some protectors talking just now about how they think the experiments are a problem and I worry," Jensen admitted. "What if we've liberated one prison and created another?"

Alpha let out a soft huff of laughter as she looked at him. "Jensen, did you think experiments were ever going to have it easy? Think back to when Jack and Isis first came to the mansion. They're not exactly normal, are they? With beings like experiments, there's bound to be some bumps in the road and some prejudice. Give it time. The shape shifters will grow to accept the experiments once they get used to them."

Jensen smiled, wishing he felt reassured. He turned and made his way back to the Deverells, looking off to the side. Every now and again, he would catch a glimpse of glowing eyes in the dissipating shadows.

~~*~*~*

Isis stood in the well-lit healing wing of the Pearl Castle, watching her teammates and allies get tended to by the guardians. The apprentices were looking after the less serious wounds. The wounded who needed the most attention were cared for by the experienced healers. It had taken close to three hours to get all the wounded off the field. The messengers were still transporting the dead to the Meadows where the supernatural races would take them back to their lands. Isis had watched the allies work together to sort the wounded and the dead, intrigued by their ability to disregard their differences and feuds temporarily in order to help each other.

Orion stood near her. He hadn't said a word since they had arrived in the Meadows. Something was bothering him, but Isis wasn't sure what. She knew he would tell her eventually. Judging by the rigid way he stood, he was angry.

When she heard the doors opening, Isis turned her gaze to the left. Lilly ran into the healing rooms. When her sapphire blue eyes fell on Jet, she beamed and ran over to his bed. Once she reached it, she kissed his face repeatedly. He ran his fingers through her long golden hair, smiling happily for the first time in weeks. Isis could see the tears in Lilly's eyes and wondered what had brought on sadness. Lilly ran her fingers down Jet's face and kissed him again before embracing him. Amethyst straightened up from the bed she had been hunched over, wiping some sweat from her brow with the back of her hand. She looked over to where Lilly and Jet were, smiling faintly.

Looking back to the doors, Isis saw Steve and Remington enter. Steve smiled when he saw her and gave a little wave. She dropped her head in a nod, acknowledging him.

"You let Chance get away," Orion stated, a peculiar flatness to his voice. It wasn't the monotone of experiments. It was more like he was repressing something.

"You let Carding get away," Isis countered, not looking at him. "I needed to let Chance get away. I knew he would have an escape route somewhere in that room. He's arrogant, but he's not stupid or suicidal. I had a hunch finding it would answer some questions I had."

"You have an excuse for everything. I really hope this one was worth the cost," Orion replied, clasping his hands behind his back. Isis furrowed her brow and looked over at him.

"Are you angry with me for not killing a man?"

"I'm angry that animal is still alive and out there, free to torture and kill who knows how many more shape shifters."

"You normals are so contradictory. First you don't want me to kill, then you do. Next you'll not want me to kill again, and then you'll come up with another reason for me to kill. Do you expect me to play the role of executioner or not?"

"It's very simple, Isis. Don't kill the innocent."

"You had a problem with me killing the Grenich recruitment team," Isis pointed out. "They did not qualify as innocent by any definition."

Orion was about to respond when Sly approached them. She looked radiant as ever. Isis had been impressed with her fighting ability. She had been one of the few shape shifters to not be injured during the raid and yet she had fought as fiercely as the protectors and rebels.

"I have something to run by you," she began. "There weren't that many humans there, only twenty or so like you said. But there is something wrong with them. They're lifeless, like the people in that bank. It's like they're just going through the motions. None of them are speaking or responding. They're like blank slates."

"Necromancers keep their humans in a stupor," Orion explained. "They have no family and no lives outside the Corporation. It will take a couple months before they wake up and function normally. They'll need to be kept under protector watch, just to make sure they acclimate back into regular day-to-day life."

"I know Jet and Lilly have a couple allies who own apartment buildings. They can probably set them up there," Sly mentioned.

"Grenich might make attempts on their lives," Isis said. "In all likelihood, their work was sensitive. The protectors will have to be extra vigilant for the first few years, if you wish for them to survive."

Sly half-smiled. "I'll make sure Jet and Lilly know that."

Isis turned to Orion when Sly sauntered away. "We need to liberate the other facilities. A great part of Set's power resides in his army."

Orion's shoulders dropped and his expression became tired. "We will, Isis. For now, let's just be grateful for this small victory. That laboratory is finished. No shape shifters will suffer there ever again."

Isis turned and looked at the numerous wounded shape shifters, Seelie Court warriors, and lycanthropes. She thought about the experiments still under Grenich control and it bothered her. Set's army was still vast and strong and growing. They had taken his possible Keys, which meant he would be angry. When Set was angry, things got bad.

~~*~*~*

Hunter sat with her feet up on Milo's bed, flipping through a Vonnegut novel. She looked up at the enormous window, watching a blue bird chirp in the tree just outside. Milo groaned softly, his face scrunching up in pain. Hunter poked him with her foot.

"Milo?" she called out, continuing to prod him with her foot. "Are we going to wake up today?"

"Maybe if you stop jabbing me," he grumbled, not opening his eyes. "Where am I?"

"The mansion, in a guest room," Hunter replied. "You've been out for a couple days. The guardians wouldn't allow you in the Meadows, so the healers had to care for you here. There were times when we thought you would die for sure. But seems you're full of surprises."

Milo's eyes opened and he stared up at the ceiling. "Just lucky. How many did we lose?"

Hunter opened her book again. "The Seelie Court lost twenty-one, the lycanthropes lost seventeen, and the protectors lost thirty-seven. The rebels only lost about five, so they're apparently better at fighting than any of us."

"How many experiments?" Milo asked.

Hunter looked up from her book, surprised by the question. "There were two hundred and fifty-two experiments in the facility. They all got out."

Milo grimaced. "No, that's too few. There should have been more. Dammit, Set must have moved them."

He let out his breath and ran his hands over his face, looking over at Hunter. "Where are they now?"

"We decided the safest thing was for them to stay at Perrin's Sanctuary for the time being. Many were confused and some seemed a little disoriented," Hunter continued. "A few decided they would rather stay with Shocker. They want to fight."

"It's all they know," Milo responded, grimacing as he pushed himself up into a sitting position. He flopped back against the wall behind him, his gaze traveling out the window. Hunter turned her attention back to her book, turning a page.

"My father got hit with a bolt in the shoulder, but he's okay. Guardian healing and all," she continued. "Almost everyone was healed within a day. The Seelie Court and lycanthropes already went back to their worlds, but have said we can call on them whenever we have need."

Milo's attention didn't move from the window. "Both of them? Never thought I'd see the day the Seelie Court and lycanthropes fought side-by-side. Your parents must be a very persuasive."

"My parents are good leaders. The Seelie Court and lycanthropes have their issues, but they recognize Grenich is a bigger threat," Hunter said. Milo looked over at her and Hunter pretended not to notice.

"Have any more visions?" he asked. She bit her bottom lip.

"Not since we infiltrated the facility, when I used it to find you," she answered, turning another page. A wind swept through the open window, rustling the curtains. Hunter could feel Milo watching her, which was annoying.

"I suppose you'll be heading back to Perrin's Sanctuary," she mentioned. "She'll probably need your help with all the new residents."

Milo was quiet for a while and Hunter wondered if he would say anything at all. She looked up again, noticing Milo was looking back out the window. He was still quite pale and his expression was contemplative. Hunter dropped the book in her lap and leaned back in the chair, her feet still resting on his bed.

"The Sanctuary has been the closest thing to a home I've ever had," Milo said, looking back to Hunter. "But when I'm there, I sometimes forget how much damage Grenich is doing to the outside world. Set and Pyra grow in power every day and they control so much already. I never thought we'd manage to get the Key possibilities."

Milo went quiet again for a little while. "I think I have spent too much time there lately. I'm no good while in hiding and you never know when you're going to need some necromancer blood. Besides, someone needs to watch your back."

Hunter interlaced her fingers. "If I recall, *I'm* the one

who saved *your* ass."

"Why do I get the distinct impression you'll never let me forget that?"

"Wow, you learned something about me. Color me surprised."

Milo chuckled and Hunter couldn't help but smile.

~~*~*~*

Isis had a number of books spread out in front of her in the guardian library. The other members of the Four each had a book in front of them and a copy of something Isis had sketched. Electra and Phoenix approached with more heavy books.

"This is the last batch," Electra reported, pushing a strand of hair out of her face. "Everything referencing any weapons made in the Meadows. I don't understand why you didn't just ask Copper or Silver."

"I did ask them," Isis said, not looking up from the book in front of her. "Neither recognized the weapon."

The musty smell invaded her senses and she could feel every last fiber in the paper. She had seen Athena glancing over at her, but disregarded it as unimportant information. Turning a page back and then forward again, Isis' glowing eyes skimmed the large print. There was nothing in the book and Isis shut it, pushing it away. A week had passed since the raid and life was very gradually getting back to normal. Jet, Lilly, and Orion were trying to figure out what their next move was. The Monroes had contacted their allies in other countries and informed them about what to be on the lookout for. None of the Grenich higher-ups had made threats of retaliation, which Isis had expected. They would be consolidating their power and Set never struck out in anger. To do so would be sloppy and do more harm than good. He would bide his time, waiting for the perfect moment.

Isis couldn't get the last encounter with Chance out of

her head. Something about that knife was important. The craftsmanship reminded her of weapons made by guardian smiths. She had sketched the knife and showed it to Copper and then Silver. Copper thought it looked somewhat familiar, but couldn't say for certain where he had seen it before.

Isis had to divide her time between her search and the abandoned power plant, where the experiments were still getting used to their new surroundings. Coop had gone to Perrin's Sanctuary to help her with the experiments staying there. Dane was staying at the mansion due to his possible importance. He was almost fully recovered from the months-long torture session he had been subjected to. Nick Chance had gotten particularly creative and sadistic over the years.

Isis drummed her fingers on the table, pushing her chair out. "I want to check something. Do you mind looking through the rest of these books?"

Shae looked up at her. "Where are you going?"

"There are a couple guardians I want to ask about this knife. I will meet you back at the mansion later this afternoon."

"I'll go with you," Electra said. Isis stared at her, wondering why her twin wanted to follow her around. Then she remembered the rule stating she needed to be watched for at least ten years after her release from the dungeons. She shrugged and looked back to the other three shape shifters still sitting around the table. The warm sunlight beamed down in the library, casting different shades from the stained glass.

"Go on," Jade said, waving her away. "Stay out of trouble."

Isis frowned and looked at her, puzzled. "What kind of trouble could I get in here? Or are you concerned about me starting trouble? It is not my intention."

The way Jade stared at her made Isis realize she had missed something. She turned away from the table and led

Electra out of the library.

The hours passed and Isis returned to the mansion much later than she anticipated. The sun was already setting, but she didn't pay it any mind. What she had learned over the afternoon weighed heavily on her mind. She knew Set was a dangerous foe, but she was beginning to get an idea of just how dangerous he was.

The mansion was quiet, as it had been the past couple days. Jet and Lilly had been to ceremonies in the Seelie Court realm and the lycanthrope realm, honoring the fallen. As she Appeared in the hall, Isis looked around for any occupants but saw none. She heard pages turning in the library and moved for that room. Jade, Alex, and Shae were sitting under the windows, surrounded by books. She approached and crouched down near them.

"It's worse than we thought," she stated, clasping her hands in front of her. "Set has the dagger of Oriana."

"Oriana, the architect of the Argentine Path in the Meadows?" Alex asked. Isis nodded as she tapped her finger tips together, her brow furrowing. She sorted all the information in her mind, quickly deciding where to start.

"Wouldn't that be in the Meadows?" Shae asked.

"It should have been, but the one I saw was a fake. They didn't know it because it hasn't been used or needed in millennia," Isis explained. "The guardians didn't recognize the sketch because the dagger has been altered and covered in necromancer stones. The original wasn't decorated at all. Guardians tend not to decorate their tools and weapons so garishly."

"I don't understand — how could Set steal it and why?" Jade asked. Isis looked over at her.

"Oriana used the dagger to create the openings between worlds," Isis explained. "She gifted it to the guardians of magic so they could open the realms for the other supernatural races. The worlds were always there, but they were never connected. Circe, one of the early guardians of magic, was the one who decided to make

Earth a crossroads for all the supernatural races. Except for the Magic Orders, who were allowed to opt out because of their closeness with the guardians."

All the protectors were watching her except for Alex, who was flipping through a book in front of her.

"Were these gateways created before or after the War of the Meadows?" Alex asked.

"Before," Isis answered. "But the supernatural races didn't live in their worlds until after the war. There are a few uninhabited and unexplored realms. Most of those gateways are lost or forgotten. I think Set is living in one of those worlds, probably with quite a few other necromancers."

"But how did he get the dagger in the first place?" Jade asked.

"The most likely possibility is sometime during the War of the Meadows," Isis said. "It is likely Set and Pyra have been able to cross planes for some time now, but have had no reason to do so. I think this dagger has somehow been repurposed to open doorways on Earth. When Coop and I were in the disciplinary room, it looked like Chance cut a tent flap out of the air."

"Do you think they can get into the Meadows?" Alex asked.

Isis pressed her hands together. "I don't believe so. It is possible that they can and don't in order to stay hidden, but I don't believe that's the case. It would be too tempting to launch a surprise assault on the guardians. However, I think they might have allies in other worlds."

"But if they have access to these worlds, why not just wipe all our allies out?" Shae asked and Isis shook her head.

"I don't know. His strategies do not make sense to me and perhaps that's the point," Isis explained. "Experiments are merely tools to achieve a bigger goal."

"So what can we do?" Jade asked.

"Nick Chance made a mistake using that dagger

because now I know about it. He must have taken it from Set as insurance, in case he got trapped in the laboratory. So that's one thing in our favor," Isis said. "We need to focus on a couple things. We need to liberate more facilities in order to chip away at Set's power even more. Right now, he's angry so he'll bide his time for a bit, just long enough to calm down. We should take the time to pool together all the information we have and what we know about Grenich. When Set does strike again, we need to be prepared. Now that we have all the Key possibilities, he's going to be even more brutal and ruthless than he was before."

The four women sat in silence for a moment, each lost in their own thoughts. After a moment, Jade leaned back on her elbows.

"So this is what the Book of Oracle was talking about when it referenced a coming darkness," she said, smiling at her teammates. "Guess it's up to the women to save the world."

"It always is," Shae replied as she rested her head on Jade's shoulder, smiling at her teammate. Alex grinned and shook her head, closing the book in front of her. Isis sat back, looking up at the setting sun. The sky was painted different shades of red, orange, and purple. She looked back to the women in the room, observing them for a bit. Normals were a funny group, one with a surprising strength and resilience. Isis didn't know how they would do against an organization like Grenich. They hadn't lost as many as she had predicted they would during the raid. She looked up to the second floor, glimpsing the form as it slunk away behind the bookshelves.

~~*~*~*

Orion stood in the forest where the doorway to

Perrin's sanctuary was located. He set his pack down and pulled out a jar of chalk dust. Unscrewing the top, he moved around in a circle and sprinkled the dust on the ground. Once he had made the circle, he reached into the jar and grabbed a handful of the powdery substance.

"I have need of counsel," he whispered under his breath as he threw the chalk into the circle. As it fell from his hand, it morphed into a sparkling silver substance. It glistened on the grass like the stars in the night sky. A breeze swept through the forest, rustling the leaves in the trees. Orion put the jar down and brushed the dust off his hands. He pulled his jacket tighter, protecting himself against the cold night.

"It has been many years since we last spoke, son of Dayton," a sultry feminine voice came from behind him. "Not since the night I helped you save your brother."

She came up beside him, her pale face ghostly in the night. Her piercing blue eyes stared out into the forest. Orion turned to look at her. She still wore black, the same material that Isis wore, but hers was more elegant. She had a corset protecting her chest and gauntlets on her arms, which had designs of the stars sewn into the material. Twin knives, both made of guardian silver, sat in sheaths at her hips and a bow sat over her shoulder along with a quiver full of arrows. She was wearing a cloak with the hood up, which covered most of her face. Her arms were crossed over her chest and her skin still had a faint guardian glisten to it, which stood out especially at night.

"We managed to destroy the laboratory Isis and Jack had been held in. Not without casualties though," Orion began evenly. She stepped forward and raised her hand, circling it once. The chalk and sparkling silver disappeared from the grass.

"Did you get the third Key possibility?" the woman asked.

"Yes, we did."

"Then it wasn't a completely pointless endeavor," she

stated with a shrug. Orion felt his mouth drop open in shock. A cool wind blew through the trees and she lifted her face up toward the sky.

"Completely pointless?" he managed to stammer out.

"The laboratory wasn't a worthwhile target. Set had already transported most of the valuable experiments to another location," she explained, unbothered by his disbelief. "That laboratory was one of many, you know this."

"We saved hundreds of shape shifters," Orion protested, trying to quell his anger. He could not believe how callous his ally could be.

"Set has close to a thousand more. Destroying one laboratory isn't going to stop him," she replied. "It won't even cause him much damage. If anything, it probably entertained him or it would have, had he not lost his last possible Key."

Orion looked away and she studied him. Her full red lips curved up slightly in a small smile, which had a menacing edge.

"Have I offended you, son of Dayton?"

Orion turned his gaze up to the towering trees above them. The woman next to him frightened him with her indifference and calculating demeanor. In legend, she was portrayed as the most compassionate woman to ever walk the Meadows. The long years since the War of the Meadows had hardened her, turning her heart to stone. Though she was still wise and clever, she no longer resembled the beloved night guardian of legend so revered by shape shifters and guardians.

"Answer me one question, Selene," Orion began after a moment. "Did you let Set take Isis? Could you have prevented the experimentation?"

Selene was quiet for a moment, looking back to where the chalk circle had once been. She looked almost amused by the question. "What an odd thing to ask."

Orion watched her, trying to figure out what she was

thinking. He had never been able to. Orion knew next to nothing about the guardian. She always sent messages through Perrin and he had rarely ever seen her. Selene was as much a mystery to him as she was to everyone. Orion still had no idea how she had found him or why she had contacted him to begin with. He was also clueless about what her ultimate plan was. *I'm just a chess piece. One of many she moves when it suits her,* he thought.

"Are we nothing but cannon fodder to you?" Orion asked. The faint smile faded from Selene's face and her gaze remained in the distance. Her fingers brushed against the small silver charm she wore at her throat. It was the shape of a sun.

"This is war, Orion. There will be casualties and death and pain," she said, her soft voice weary. "Set and Pyra started this and if you do not fight back, they will win. They seek to destroy everything that's good and they will not stop until they achieve that goal."

Selene looked up at him, her face flashing with ferocity. "I will not allow that to happen, not while I still draw breath. They took everything from me and I plan to respond in kind. I love my people and yours too much to stand by and do nothing."

Orion looked off into the night. "You didn't answer my earlier question about Isis."

Selene was quiet for a moment. "I know you do not like my tactics and you do not trust me completely. You want me to take a more active part in this fight. I cannot, not yet. The shape shifters are the protectors of Earth and it is only them who can win this war."

"Perhaps you might explain how because right now, I don't know what our next move is," Orion said. "We are still outnumbered and Set's influence over the world continues to grow."

Selene looked contemplative for a moment. "Look to the experiments to guide you. This is their fight more than anyone else's. I imagine they will be the ones who can remove Set's plants from their positions of power. With the experiments and Milo, you stand a chance against Set and Pyra's empire, for they know the inner workings of Grenich more than any other."

"Isis wants to continue targeting the laboratories," Orion mentioned, looking up to the sky when the winds picked up. "She also thinks we should focus on getting the dagger of Oriana away from him."

"That is important, but unlikely to happen. First, you need to find the entrance to his world," Selene said. "I will have my sources focus on that and send word to you if they come up with anything. As for the laboratories, let the experiments focus on them. Perhaps they will be able to make a dent in the necromancers' army."

Selene stepped in front of him and looked up at Orion, drawing his attention to her. "Above all, you keep those three experiments out of his grasp. Do whatever you must but make sure he doesn't get his hands on them again. They are more important than any of us."

Orion nodded in understanding. He didn't always like Selene's tactics or the way she disregarded things she believed unimportant, but she did seem to know what she was doing. The night guardian never did anything without purpose.

"Before I leave, I must pass on a warning. Set is setting up more surveillance around the world. Soon he will have eyes everywhere and when that happens, nowhere will be safe for shape shifters. Be on your guard, for Set will retaliate in time."

Selene adjusted her hood so her face was concealed even more and began to walk off into the trees. "Do not call on me again, son of Dayton. It is important that I remain nothing more than a legend. Look to the Four. They will be an important part of ending this conflict."

Orion was quiet for a moment, turning to watch her. "Will you ever come out from the shadows?"

She hesitated, turning her head. Then she continued

forward, the night swallowing her up. Orion was once again left alone.

~~*~*~*

"We interrupt our regularly scheduled programming to bring you a special report. A little more than a week ago, a laboratory specializing in viral research was broken into by vandals. This laboratory was home to patients suffering from an extremely rare virus and, fearing for their safety, some ran away. They have been off their medication regimen ever since and are now extremely contagious. Sufferers of this virus display a number of symptoms including aggression, listlessness, aloofness, paranoia, and bizarre behavior. Dr. Seth Carver, head of research, has said the most obvious symptom is the eyes of the afflicted, which appear to glow. The afflicted may attempt to conceal this by hiding their eyes behind tinted glasses or contact lenses. Dr. Carver warns people not to approach the afflicted under any circumstances and do not hesitate to contact your local law enforcement agency if you observe any suspicious behavior.

We go now to our own Mary Roteland with an exclusive interview with Dr. Carver."

To Be Continued

ACKNOWLEDGMENTS

Thank you so much to my friends and family, who are continually supportive of me. Thank you to my parents for their endless patience, love, and support. Thank you to my brother, Michael, and Mom for being great proofreaders. Thank you to my amazing godmother, Leandra Torres (Aunt Punkey), a woman who I very much admire and who is always there with an encouraging word.

Thank you to my amazing editor, Rose Anne Roper. Thank you to my cover artist, Najla Qamber. Thank you to my always awesome beta reader, Taia Hartman.

Thank you so much to Crimson Fox/Snowy Wings Publishing for helping me achieve a dream and providing support, as well as helping immensely with marketing. I must give a very special thank you to my good friend, Lyssa Chiavari, who invited me to join Snowy Wings and for being one of the absolute best people in the world. It is truly an honor to know you and call you a friend.

Thank you so much to all the wonderful professors in my life, who have taught me and continue to teach me to this day. Thank you so much, Alex and Jess Hall for your continued knowledge of all things concerning mythology. It is an honor to know you both. Thank you, Marco Benassi and Alexander Bolyanatz, for never giving up on me and providing advice when needed. Thank you Ángela Rebellón (the best ASL teacher there is). Thank you to all the professors and teachers who I've thanked in previous novels. If you enjoyed this novel, it is thanks to them. Any success I've experienced is thanks in large part to the dedicated professors and teachers I've had the privilege to learn from.

Thank you so much to all the incredible asexual artists who I have met through Asexual Artists. Thank you to my dear friends, Joel Cornah, Darcie Little Badger, and T. Hueston. You put such beautiful art into the world and it inspires me so very much. I love you all.

Thank you so much to my family and friends for providing me with the support I need to continue on the rocky path that is writing. Thank you, Billy Payne, for coming to my first reading and making the experience a lot less terrifying. Thank you Robyn Byrd, Emily Kittell-Queller (extra special thanks to you and your housemates for being a safe haven on the holidays), Julie Denninger-Greensly, Ryan Prior, Leigh Hellman, and anyone else who I'm forgetting (and will undoubtedly feel just awful about later). Your love, kind words, encouragement, and support make a world of difference in my life.

A special thank you to Becca (who gave me the most wonderful compliment a writer can ever hope to hear) and Susan Sandahl, who continue to be active on my author page and are some of the most awesome people I've ever had the pleasure of meeting. You're both my favorite readers and I apologize for the ridiculously long wait.

Again, I must thank all my readers. Thank you for your kind words and gestures. Thank you for getting lost in the crazy world I created. Thank you for continuing to be so generous with your time. I cannot begin to express my gratitude to you all. You continue to humble me and I hope this book lived up to your expectations. Thank you all, so very, very much.

ABOUT THE AUTHOR

Lauren Jankowski, an openly aromantic asexual feminist activist and author from Illinois, has been an avid reader and a genre feminist for most of her life. She holds a degree in Women and Genders Studies from Beloit College. In 2015, she founded "Asexual Artists," a Tumblr and WordPress site dedicated to highlighting the contributions of asexual identifying individuals to the arts.

She has been writing fiction since high school, when she noticed a lack of strong women in the popular genre books. When she's not writing or researching, she enjoys reading (particularly anything relating to ancient myths) or playing with her pets. She participates in activism for asexual visibility and feminist causes. She hopes to bring more strong heroines to literature, including badass asexual women.

Her ongoing fantasy series is *The Shape Shifter Chronicles*, which is published through Crimson Fox Publishing.